Reportage Press

About the Author

Charlotte Eagar was educated at Oxford University. She took time out in 1989 to cover the Romanian Revolution, but came back to finish her degree. She headed straight to Bosnia in 1992 as a freelancer, as soon as she had taken her finals, getting her degree results in Split. She is an award-winning foreign correspondent, investigative journalist and travel writer, and has reported from places as diverse as Bosnia, Afghanistan, Baghdad, Moscow and Rome. Based in Sarajevo during the height of the siege as the *Observer*'s Balkans correspondent, she has also worked for the *Sunday Telegraph*, *The Spectator*, *Harpers & Queen*, *Mail on Sunday* and the *Times Magazine*, as well as most other British papers. She is now a contributing editor on the *Evening Standard*'s *ES Magazine* and lives in west London.

The Girl in the Film

The Girl in the Film

CHARLOTTE EAGAR

REPORTAGE PRESS FICTION

Published by Reportage Press
26 Richmond Way, London W12 8LY United Kingdom
Tel: 0044 (0)7971 461 935
e-mail: info@reportagepress.com
www.reportagepress.com

British Library Cataloguing in Publication Data.
A catalogue record for this book is available from the British Library.
Hardback ISBN-13: 978-0-9555729-2-0
Paperback ISBN: 978-0-9558302-7-3
Cover design by Wall Creative at www.wallcreative.com
Cover photograph: Paul Lowe Back cover: TomStoddart, Paul Lowe
Typeset by Alex Ingr at www.lettersandlight.com
Printed and bound in Great Britain by Antony Rowe Ltd,
Chippenham, Wiltshire, UK
www.antonyrowe.co.uk

To the pigeon family,
who would never have had
a son like Amir.

And for my mother,
who also wrote books.

Acknowledgements

There are obviously many people who I have to thank for their help in writing this book. Firstly, the people of Sarajevo, without whose suffering this book could not exist and who made me so welcome, both during my time in the war and when I returned; particularly Bobo, his mother and his late father. I would also like to thank my editor, Rosie Whitehouse; my agent, Lucinda Prain at William Morris; Emma Mahmood, Tertia Bailey, Francesca Riario, and the numerous other friends who have read my book and held my hand along the way; in particular, Paul Lowe who inspired me to start the book and gave me a few good quotes to use, and his wife, Amra Abadzic and Allan Little. I would also like to thank Malcolm Brabant, Dina Hamzic, Cathy Jenkins and the late Bob Simpson of the BBC, for their wartime advice and hospitality; Misha Glenny for teaching me about the Balkans; Lara Nettelfield for guiding me through post-war Sarajevo; the late Elizabeth Neuffner for her unfailing good humour and niceness as a colleague; my former foreign editor at the *Observer*, Ann Treneman, for taking a punt on me and sending me chocolate; Alija Hodzic for his help in Sarajevo's mortuary; Dr Dobraca for his kind information on autopsies; Inspector Dragan Mijokovic for his advice on Sarajevo police and criminal procedure; Jamie, Nick and Mark for telling me about guns and other useful things; Patrick Bishop and Janine di Giovanni for being good friends and the Frankopans, without whose encouragement I would never have left for the Balkans in the first place.

Bosnia-Herzegovina
Frontlines 1993-4

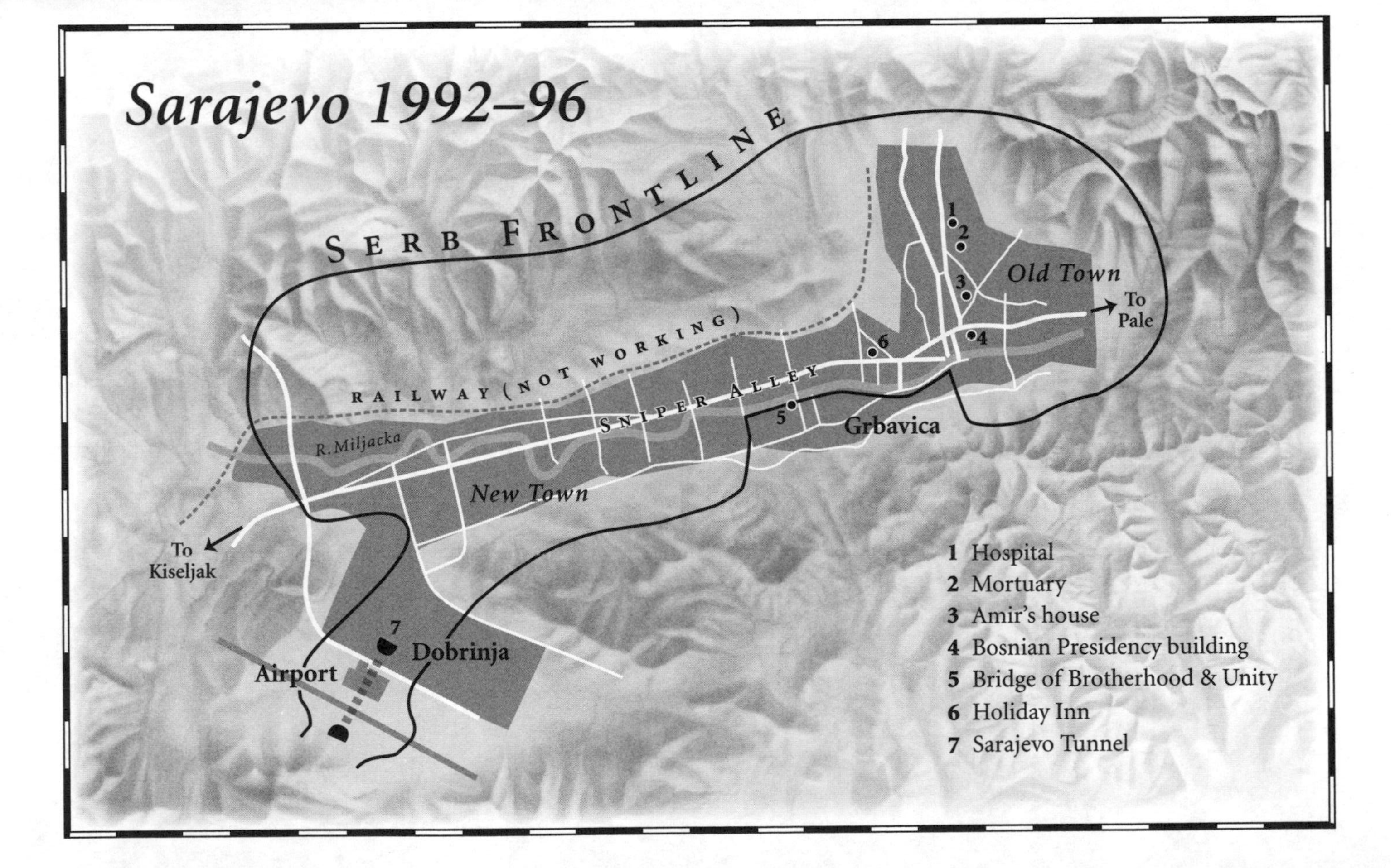
Sarajevo 1992–96
Serb Frontline
Railway (not working)
Sniper Alley
Old Town
To Pale
Grbavica
R. Miljacka
New Town
To Kiseljak
Dobrinja
Airport
1 Hospital
2 Mortuary
3 Amir's house
4 Bosnian Presidency building
5 Bridge of Brotherhood & Unity
6 Holiday Inn
7 Sarajevo Tunnel
1
2
3
4
5
6
7

Note on pronunciation for Serbo-Croat or whatever you want to call it

The letters *ic* at the end of names are commonly pronounced *itch*
– as in *Milosevic*

The letters *dz* are commonly pronounced liked *dge* in fudge
– as in *Karadzic*

The letters *ica* together are commonly pronounced *itsa*
– as in *Srebrenica*

The UN is an umbrella that comes down when it rains.

—Remark doing the rounds when the UN withdrew troops from Sinai in 1967

Sarajevo 1994

The man sat in his car on Sniper Alley. He was young but the war had made him old and now the war had killed him before he reached the age he looked. Against the grey plastic upholstery and the grey dawn, the front of his shirt was thick and clotted red.

A white armoured Land Rover drove past, stopped, reversed back to the car then parked on its southern side, the side facing the frontlines. Three soldiers climbed gingerly out. The man, what had been a man and now was just a corpse, waited in his car, the inescapable wait inflicted by death on one who, brought up in the queue-ridden, wait-weighted culture of communism, had never waited before if he could find a way out.

"Well, he's not looking at all well, is he, Sarge," said one; Sarge swore and lifted up his radio to his blue-helmeted head.

Slowly the well-practised Sarajevo body retrieval mechanism, slickened by the blood of so many thousands dead, cranked into action, and the man, who always tried to be different, to stand out from the common herd, became yet another body killed on Sniper Alley, arriving at Sarajevo mortuary on yet another morning, to join the thousands who'd been levered onto those marble slabs before; where Osman Muhovic, the mortuary's director, would enter the name in his thickening Book of the Dead, whose pages, laid out with the name, date, time of arrival and place of death, he would sadly show to anyone who asked.

In a way, of course, the man in the car had been dead for some time, the lingering death that started in April 1992, when the Serbs first cauterised the arteries into Sarajevo and its population began to wither. Some of the bodies, most of the bodies, the ones not fretted full of holes by the shrapnel's sculpture nor punctured by the ping of a sniper's bullet, might continue to live, to breathe, eat (when they could), pee, shit, have sex, but what was slowly starved of its vital flow was their feeling of who they themselves had been or might be. They existed at the whim of the men who sat with the guns in the hills. They ate at the charity of the International Community. They moved only in the pen their city had become.

Prije rata, before the war, and what they had been or done then, was the measure by which the Sarajevans kept their identities; the war had fired them all into some sort of limbo. Many turned up to their offices for most of the war, unpaid, to do no work, just to keep some sense of who they thought they were. After the war, of course, they would realise that at some point during the four long years they had stopped being foresters or lawyers, architects or truck drivers and become simply professional dwellers under siege.

But now, at last, after so long trying, the man in the car had stopped living under siege. Here he was, setting off on his penultimate trip, where Osman Muhovic waited for him as a father might wait for a runaway son, with sorrow but in the sure knowledge that one day he would come. For the mortuary's Austro-Hungarian splendour had seen not just the dead of this war, but two previous world wars before, not forgetting the thousand or so dead who arrived each year, even in peace. For the mortuary, even more than for the Sarajevo medics, the man's death was just routine.

First the UN armoured ambulance drew up, his transport for his second-last journey and probably the most expensive vehicle he'd ever travelled in, planes apart – something which, alive, would have given him enormous pleasure. The armoured ambulance parked in the shadow of the right-hand old apartment buildings so the sniper who'd shot the man from the Serb side of the river couldn't get a shot at the medics as they scrambled out.

Then the French Foreign Legion arrived, because Sniper Alley was in their patch, with their bulging forearms, their secret pasts, their tape measures and notebooks, to plot the bullet's trajectory, parking their armoured car to the south again between the man's corpse and the unseen, ever-watching Serbs across the frontline, to give them the shelter they needed for their work. Then the local police, with their Sarajevo grey complexions, appeared; they milled gingerly in shelter of the buildings, occasionally nipping across to the shelter of the cars for a closer look, taking their notes, to reinforce the point that a sniping was a murder, not just a random casualty of war.

One of the UN medics, a jolly Swede who was worried that the man's death might signal a return to the overwork of which his predecessor had complained, picked the man up under the shoulders and another Swede smashed at his knee caps to break the rigor in his legs so they could more easily get him out of the car. Pulling at his shins, they yanked him out and onto the stretcher. The body bag was zipped and he vanished, shutting off the sightless eyes whose next wasted view would be the white rafters of the Sarajevo mortuary. And in that cool marble block, built in the days before refrigeration, in the shade of a tree, its high ceilings slashed with vents to let out the foul air and deep hooded windows to keep off the heavy Balkan sun, sat Osman, now huddled in the cold of the deep Balkan winter, who had seen most of Sarajevo pass his way in the last two years, since everyone in the town had lost someone they loved.

Part One

LONDON 1999

When I found the diary, I cried. It wasn't just for Amir – although of course he was part of it. But it wasn't only for him, or even Valida or Aida or all those other bewildered relics in that little Turkish town, stranded, squirming in their rock pool when the tides of empire and ideology had ebbed. I cried for me.

I can't remember who it was who said if the gods want to destroy you, they give you what you ask for. But I expect it was the Greeks. It usually is. I love clichés; they are so bloody true.

Of course, it wasn't really a diary; to call it that would give it an importance – or at least substance – that it didn't have. It was too short, to start with. Just a few days. And that final entry was an aberration: like a plonking discord by a disillusioned composer tacked on to an early melody.

It was a blue exercise book, like the ones I always used. I found it when I was moving house. The builders had left in a flurry of "see you around, loves" and left me on my own, unpacking the accumulation of my life as the evening sun pooled on my brand new floor.

I never meant to open that box. It had got muddled up with everything else. But I recognised the notebooks, of course, from the moment I saw them. Even if I hadn't touched them for nearly five years. Their shiny covers gave no hint of the accumulated misery they held; all those starving women, ragged soldiers, those fat-faced evil men. Phil used to tease me about my books; more fifth-form French than foreign correspondent, he said. But they worked; you could lean on the hard cover, they fitted in my handbag and you could buy them everywhere, from Belgrade to Mostar. I liked that. It proved that the maps were right: it had all been one country once. And I loved the way you could dent their shiny cover with your nail.

When I first saw them, in their box, strewn with their pall of builders' dust, I couldn't look away. There was an old Croatian 100... *thingie*... note on the top. I stared at it, and then, as you do with money, I picked it up, even though I knew the currency had long since changed – so long ago, I couldn't remember its name. It left a banknote-sized hole in the dust. I smiled as I felt the thick linen paper – typically Croat, to print their notes on the *best* paper – and tried to remember the name of the man in the wig looking up at me, like one of those dead fish the waiters in Split would bring out to your table for you to choose. Suddenly the harsh winter light was bouncing round the Venetian piazza. I was drinking cappuccino by the sea, in my woolly hat, with Phil, and the scent of lemon and cyprus in my nose, the way it was, the moment you stood at the aeroplane doors in Split. I breathed in sharp, and drew my war deep into my lungs.

A whole war of books, lying in a box. And when the war was over I put them all away. I must have poured in the dregs of my long-unpacked bag, like some kind of libation, because under the dust the books were covered with my stuff I'd carried for so long: more useless currencies, abandoned by world events, a first aid kit, a Swiss army knife, the Serbo-Croat phrase book which never had any useful phrases like "can you tell me the way to the mass funeral" and "is the road safe ahead", and four years' worth of tobacco shreds.

I saw my hand move to take one out. I didn't stop it: I remember thinking that I'd be relatively safe – that the lid would be hard to open on this Pandora's box. It was a long time ago and my notes had been difficult enough to read that week when the air was still thick with the smell and the misery of those who had spoken the words now scrawled on the page.

But I was wrong. I picked the wrong book; the first one. The only one that was about me. "Zagreb, Monday 13th July 1992." I should have guessed just by seeing the page, because it was written in the exam-neat whorls of the recent graduate; not scrawled, in gloved hands, as I perched on the corner of a bed, in a room, perhaps in a school, or an old police station, in some lost mountain town; a tiny room, thick with the sweet smell of old sweat and fake coffee, strangely empty despite the eight desperate faces staring at me, since they had brought only what they could carry as they ran. And the grown-ups mainly would have carried the children.

I couldn't stop myself reading on. It was like picking a scab.

It was a dull little tale. I'd spent the day on the train; my love of clichés showed even then: Vienna railway station was a temple of transport, its trains grinding off to long-lost imperial outposts. I invoked Agatha Christie, the Orient Express; the chocolate-box scenery I'd seen from the train – the pointy little alps, the haystacks "the shape they are in fairy tales" (those were the haystacks Phil used to think followed us around at night – but back on that train Phil was just a voice on the radio to me). There is no feeling that I'm on a one-way ticket; that there is no way back; that I am going through the looking glass into another life. It's just the optimistic drivel of the traveller.

The tears welled up as I read about my day. There was a Muslim woman on the train; her two children huddled into her flanks – my first refugees, but the sanitised end: well dressed, well educated, just with their whole lives lost. She was blonde. I seem to have been surprised by that.

I could hardly believe that girl who wrote this guff was me. But then I cannot remember what I was like before the war. A young girl, 25, straight out of her MA, the Ph.D. dumped for reasons I can hardly remember now, but think were partly financial and partly due to an already shortening attention span, heading off to war to make her fortune, on an inter-rail ticket her father had bought her (his last words were "promise me you won't go anywhere dangerous").

At least she was honest. It was all there: the hope, the ambition, the zeal of the idealist, the lack of money; as she gets closer to the war, on the Croatian coast, you get the seventies decor of the tourist-free package holiday hotels; their lobbies milling with zombied refugees wondering what on earth to do with the rest of their lives, now that their world had been reduced to a balcony full of laundry, a twin bedroom (bathroom ensuite) packed with seven of their closest relations, with the bill being picked up by a resentful Croat government. No free shampoo, and the telephones had been removed from the sockets, but most of them did at least have a sea view. She is horrified that she can feel disgust.

Hanging out in the lobby of the Hotel Split, white concrete, and blue plastic to go with the sea, she hooks up with another journalist who knows the war. The next day they are to drive into Bosnia itself – not Sarajevo, she knows she's not ready for that yet, but somewhere, anywhere, where the war is going on.

Then it stops. She does try, a few days later, to write down what she's seen the last few days. But it straggles off. She says she'll write more later, but she never does. But I already know what happened next.

I'd achieved everything that girl had wanted, beyond her wildest dreams. But what do you do with a head of memories like that?

It never mentions Amir at all. Why would it? I hadn't even met him then.

Amir. I can hardly remember not knowing you. Just thinking like that feels like peeling flesh from a wound.

You're in this box. You're in those books. I wrote you down, when I first met you. Then nearly every word I wrote came through you – at least when I wasn't out of Sarajevo, somewhere else. You hated that so much, when I'd go away.

The photograph's not here. The one that Henri took. I put that away long before the books.

I was crying by the time I found the photograph; I had to push my way through a whole stack of boxes, before I found the one marked Hall Cupboard. Under the bank statements and the single socks, I finally touched its frame.

You're laughing, trying out my helmet, holding it high above my head. I'm jumping up to try and pull it down. Down at the bottom of the picture, your other hand is holding tight to mine. It looks like love but I remember your fingers hurt as you gripped my hand; you didn't loosen it, however much I tried to pull away.

It's in black and white. Henri always shot war in black and white. He said it suited war. It suited you too: the shadows of your cheekbones, the slash of your grin, your eyes hooded into darkness, your lovely thick hair, that I used to run through my fingers; love the smell on my fingers, of hair grease, a little oil, your sweat. The scent of you.

We were saying goodbye. Phil was taking me to the airport: being local, they wouldn't let you through the checkpoints to see me off on the plane.

I can't see my face, because I'm facing you; maybe that's why I loved this photograph so much. I'm too vain to like myself in photographs. There's the back of my head, my blonde hair bouncing on my flak-jacketed shoulders as I jump up. It's early winter, then, because I used to cut my hair with the seasons – warm and long for winter, bobbed short for the sun. I am in my anorak and clumpy boots but there's no snow. By my feet is one of those big soft suitcases with tiny little wheels for easy dragging, and in the background, the sloping letters "BBC" on the side of a Land Rover. Beyond the Land Rover, there's some twisted metal that was once, I think, a bus stop. It never seemed sensible to look close enough. Behind the bus stop stretches an open grass and concrete space, up to the little row of white flats, whose boxy windows are all boarded up. Huge holes, like ink blots, splodge their façades and the planks on the windows are gouged with scars. Between the flats, in the narrow street, run four or five interlocking rows of grey metal gym lockers, jutting out from either side, making a kind of chicane. Above them, strung on ropes stretched across the street from first floor to first floor, like washing lines in a Neapolitan slum, are blankets, grey and ragged from the wind. It's too far away in this photograph to see that the blankets and the lockers are riddled with bullet holes. In front of the flats are three twisted, blackened cars, what's left of their windows, stars of clouded glass.

You can't see the charred skeletons of the two tower blocks, to the right – the UNIS towers, named for some company long fled from the war, but presciently, as though they knew that their whole country would soon be stickered with the initials UN. Their shards of shattered glass would flare up again every sunset, as though they were nightly consumed by flame. But I know they are there – even if I still don't know what vanished business UNIS did.

I know that view by heart. You can't smell a photograph, but suddenly the smell is with me in the room. I know that smell like I know the view; I can feel it collect, like saliva, at the back of my nose. It smells of smoke and pine trees. The sweet rasp of rubbish burning in the crisp mountain air. And a faint whiff of cordite on the breeze.

You had a thing about my helmet. You said I only wore it when I was going to leave; I never normally put it on. None of us did. How could we look Sarajevans in the eye when their brains could be splattered out at a madman's whim and ours were snug and safe inside their Kevlar shell? Unless it was *really* dangerous of course... But the United Nations, who ran the airlift into Sarajevo, wouldn't let me get on the plane without it. That day, you'd said, if you kept the helmet, I'd have to stay. But we both knew Phil had a spare in the back of the car.

I had been with you for nine months by then and it was still the bad days of the war.

I can't stop the tears now. I'm swamped by huge, sucking gulps. I don't know how to stop this madness that engulfs my brain like marmalade. If I looked out of my west London window, I could see hundreds of refugees – the Kurds, the Albanians, the Lebanese, God knows, probably Bosnian; if you had never met me, maybe you'd be here too, living in those council blocks opposite my stucco corner of Ladbroke Grove, scraping a living from doing up kitchens.

But now I am far away. I am with you. And the blocks of flats are fretted with gunfire and shell blast. I swallow as I see minarets poking up into the still, cold air, the white houses crawling up the mountainside, through the straggle of the frontline, and from the tens of thousands of those tin wood-burning stoves, given by the world to Sarajevo to make your war less deadly because we couldn't stop it, seeps the sweet smell of burning rubbish, sealed into the city by the snowbound clouds.

MUJO IS FISHING in the Miljacka River and he catches a golden fish. The fish says to him: "Don't eat me, put me back. I am a magic fish, and if you set me free, I shall give you a wish."

Mujo says, "I'm fed up of being a peasant. I want to be a prince. I want to be married to a beautiful princess who I am in love with and who loves me. And I want to live in a palace, and sleep in a bed with velvet curtains and I want servants to wait on me hand and foot."

The fish says: "Go home tonight. Go to sleep in your little bed next to your wife Fata as usual, and tomorrow you will be a prince."

So Mujo puts the fish back and goes home. The next morning, when he wakes, the room seems strangely dark. He realises he is in a bed hung with heavy red curtains and lying in his arms is a beautiful woman, who opens her eyes and smiles up at him. There is a knock at the door, the curtains are drawn, and a manservant puts down his tray of steaming hot chocolate and says:

"Wake up, Your Imperial Highness. It is time for your trip to Sarajevo."

SARAJEVO 1993

I

It was my first day in Sarajevo, when I met you. It was an awful day, or what passed for an awful day by April 1993. You could think it ironic that I found you by mistake when, in the end, you were all the war to me. When I think of you, as I last saw you, your eyes pleading at me through the smoke and I think, if I'd stopped you then, at that party, if I'd believed you – or at least if I had wanted you to know I believed you – because I did believe you, I always had – then maybe you'd be with me now. But I didn't. I just behaved like a girl at a party, not a woman in a war.

The shells were crashing to and fro, high above the streets, amongst the pine-forested crags. The clouds lay heavy over the mountains, sealing the siege like a kettle drum, pushing the boom of the artillery down, past the minarets, into the rubbish-strewn streets; so that every time the explosion came, the sound felt like it began inside your head and came out through your ears, not coming in from outside, the other way round. In vicious wafts, the cordite, kept in by the clouds, mixed in your nostrils with the bite of snow and the sweetness of decay; and then the snipers, the crack of their bullets the staccato beat of Sarajevo life.

Of course, the old hands said this was nothing. You should have been here last year, they said; and shuddered as they described the bloody anarchy of the first few months, when the Sarajevans really did not know whether they could hold their town, whether the Serbs would crash through the makeshift army of defenders, and rampage the streets with fire and rape as they had down the Drina valley, or in Vukovar, a year before. That was before the United Nations moved in to Sarajevo – to referee; to watch, to mark the lines, and wave their pointless blue flags every time there was a foul.

But I was a new hand and this was my first time in the city and it was quite scary enough for me. Those endless trips, on and off, for the best part of nine months, had finally paid off; trailing round the cheaper parts of the war (Sarajevo, like all sieges, was expensive to cover: somebody has to pay all the smugglers who bring the food in for the hacks); filing my stories to almost anywhere with a scatter-gun approach, slowly building up a relationship with unseen voices on the telephone on foreign desks back in England, from the first wheedling of them to accept my words, via a reverse charge call – "Hello, this is Molly Taylor, um, (fill in name of high-powered journalist on the relevant paper who I'd have met over dinner in some ravaged town) suggested I rang. I'm in (fill in the place of the moment) and XXX has just happened (maybe the Serbs opened up a concentration camp or the Croats have retaken a bridge) and I wondered if you'd be interested…" – to the blissful point where they began to depend on me; endless rounds of bumming lifts, sleeping on floors, returning home, cobbling together some dough, lobbying papers and then dragging myself back out here again. I'd given up for a bit, and got a job in London, but I chucked it in. The pull of the Balkans was too great. I don't know why. So it wasn't just you, because I didn't know you then. Then finally, I got my break.

Back in London, for a quick recoup, I had rung up the news editor on the *Evening News*, the most prestigious of the papers I had been freelancing for.

"It's the first anniversary of the siege," I said, "in two weeks' time. I've never been to Sarajevo before. I'd love to go. Please let me. Please. I can just do a quick trip. In and out. There's a plane from Split."

He took me to lunch at Kensington Place, the restaurant the executives from his paper used as a staff canteen. All around us his pinky and perky colleagues, bloated with years of office politics, were having the full Fleet Street bottle-and-two-courses. I pushed forkfuls of chicken and goat's cheese mousse into my mouth with the natural appetite of one who had not eaten anything pleasant for some time, while the news editor told me about all his friends who had been war correspondents and now did PR for ski firms. I didn't have a clue what he was talking about.

"Do you really want to do this?" he asked. But I couldn't imagine why he needed to ask.

"Of course. It's a fantastic story." I probably looked at him as if he were an idiot; in hindsight, I think he looked back with something like pity. Then he shrugged and smiled and offered me my air fare and a £300 cash advance. I was almost incoherent with joy. That was £300 more than anyone had ever given me in advance before. A war economy is cash only and, in Bosnia, Deutschmarks for preference to boot. Up to now I'd had to fund myself and, when

I came back to London, fearfully spread the debt between the various papers I had written for, spending hours forging signatures and crinkling receipts on the table in my flat.

"I want 2,000 words. And they had better be bloody good. Do you have a flak jacket? Better take one of ours."

This was what I had been waiting for: 2,000 words was a spread, in an influential paper, read by commuters, but more importantly, grabbed by all editors the moment it appeared in their office before lunch. I was being allowed to do a major story, which everyone would *see* – even if they didn't read it. However well I did for the *News*, I knew they would never keep someone permanently in the Balkans. But the broadsheets all had resident correspondents: stringers, on monthly retainers and then paid by the word, as well as the big hitters, the firemen, who flew in and out. And if my byline was seen often enough in the *News*, then one day, when someone – maybe *The Times*, or the *Telegraph* or one of the Sundays – moved on, maybe I'd be in with a chance to get their job.

"Don't file from Sarajevo unless you have to," he added. "They've only got satellite phones there and they're incredibly expensive. About £20 a minute. So, whatever you do, please don't dictate. Unless you absolutely have to, of course. Under the circumstances, I think you should have pudding."

It's hard to describe the pull Sarajevo had for me, months before I'd ever met you. To begin with, my first summer, 1992, I really did not want to go there. Not only did I think it too expensive (although I know now that freelance journalists always make money in that kind of place when the story is hot) but also too dangerous. I had talked to colleagues and seen the pictures on the TV (the dead lying in their blood, their shopping rolling through their splattered brains on the pavement, no-one daring to stop and help). But in the last few months, something had changed. It had become for me a siren singing at the centre of the vortex. All this time, I had felt I was skirting the edge, and the longer I spent in Bosnia, the more I found myself being drawn to that battered little town, by a lure so strong that it was almost visceral. And I suppose, too, logically, that after nine months of war, my definition of dangerous had slipped a gear or two.

That trip, I'd given myself ten days to get to Sarajevo just in case something did go wrong – I knew enough by then to know you can never trust travel arrangements in a war – but I honestly didn't think it would. I had this idea that, like the firemen who came and went with the regularity of commuters, I would fly into Sarajevo, do my stuff and leave. Instead, I ended up having to go there by bus.

It wasn't my idea, of course, but Robert's – the guy from the *Herald*, an impoverished Sunday paper of ancient lineage and liberal views. You remember him – you met him with me, although by definition you didn't meet him much since I became Robert, so to speak. Robert had come out to the Balkan backwater of Belgrade as a stringer in 1988, when the Berlin Wall was permanent and communism had a future; he still wore an air of bewildered resentment at how big the story had got. Poor Robert: you hated his book *God's Own People*. You thought it was pro-Serb. Everyone thought it was pro-Serb, except for the Serbs.

I bumped into him when we landed at the airport in Split. We must have come on the same plane from Zagreb together – later he admitted he'd seen me in the departure lounge but hadn't wanted to say hello. I was quite offended, but he said he'd wanted to be alone. Like me, he was going to Sarajevo to do an anniversary piece. He'd come down from Belgrade to Zagreb by train (now a day-long, three-country logistical nightmare, rather than the pre-war two-and-a-half-hour run in the tracks of the old Orient Express); it was easier, he said, to get to Sarajevo from Split. In hindsight I think he just liked eating fish.

I didn't know him well, but I'd met him once before, travelling in a Serb press bus on the concentration camp story in 1992. We both knew each other, of course. His work was quite famous in the Balkans then. After a bit, he suggested we hook up. He said it made things less lonely and helped cut the cost.

Normally, at least that year, although it changed with the war, if an international like me – a foreigner, not a Bosnian – wanted to get to Sarajevo, we flew, unless we had an armoured car we wanted to take into town. Sarajevo was encircled by what was called an "active frontline", i.e. people shot people on it. Crossing in a soft-skinned – normal – car wasn't to be recommended. You, my love, couldn't get in or out of Sarajevo at all, because it was completely surrounded by Serbs, and they were your enemies, waging war on you.

The United Nations High Commissioner for Refugees, the UNHCR, ran an airlift from Split, staffed by UN soldiers – part of their "sorry we can't stop your war but have some wheat flour" approach that the western world took. It became the longest airlift in history – do you remember the party one of the aid agencies gave, when it overtook the eleven-month record set by the Berlin airlift in 1949?

You were so envious of me getting on those planes; you'd stand and stare up at them (if we were in a safe place) as they soared through the mountains, with an expression almost like pain on your face. The airlift went pretty much daily, unless it was cancelled, which it quite often was; a relay of RAF Hercules – those big military cargo planes, all camouflage and propellers, with seats running along the sides, and the walls festooned with webbing to grab if the plane did a sudden move, trying to avoid a missile lock-on say, or just a particularly purposeful piece of anti-aircraft fire. They were stuffed with nappies, or tins of tuna, or white armoured Land Rovers emblazoned with important-sounding initials, all the paraphernalia of international relief, and flown by the RAF. We, the people, would be crammed in round the edges.

The UN soldiers, Dutch, they were, who ran the airlift called it Maybe Airlines – "maybe you get there, maybe you don't" – and gave us a stamp for our passports. I still have it in mine. When I had to renew the passport the other day, I sellotaped it in the new one, just for nostalgia.

In those days, I'd set off with my computer and my flak jacket and my helmet and my luggage and go and wait at the airport where the ghosts of all those package tours haunted the departures lounge. Through the rows of cyprus trees, ranged with all the beauteous order of a Merchant Ivory film, I could see the Adriatic sparkling a mile away and the air would be sharp with that lemony pine smell that commercial air fresheners so futilely attempt to replicate. It was the sharp scent of the coast and it reached deep into my throat and even now, just to remember it makes me sigh with pleasure. It is the smell of happiness, of excitement or relief. For when I smelled it, I was either on my way back into Sarajevo, back to you, high on anticipation, on love, on the story; or I had got out, back to the real world, of electric light and black risotto, where wine tasted good and water came out of the taps.

The Dutch would check my UN press pass, white with blue stripe, and my happy grinning face, photographed against the UN flag, a white globe on blue festooned with wreaths of… olive leaves for peace? I never knew. Maybe I should ring up the press office and ask. Then they'd check I had a flak jacket and a helmet, because I wasn't allowed on without them; they didn't care if I had any clothes, or a computer or enough money to leave, or if I might get hurt, or somebody might mind if I died. Anyone with the right UN pass, helmet and flak jacket could get on the plane – although we journalists were bottom of the list. First came UN officials; after them, people who worked for the international aid agencies: Médecins Sans Frontières, Save the Children, and all those funny little ones no-one had ever heard of, because they were either religious or made up by the CIA. And finally came the press. Well actually, not finally. There was a lower level: local press. Their UN cards wouldn't let them on the plane at all. Otherwise you and all your friends could have set up newspapers and flown out to freedom.

The Dutch UN soldiers would give me a boarding pass, just a pink cardboard rectangle with a number, and then I'd sit down to wait, drinking cappuccinos in the observation restaurant; chatting to my colleagues if there were any similarly stranded, or just reading. I got through the whole of Trollope during one year of that war. I also learned a lot of Serbo-Croat irregular verbs.

Then I'd hear the pregnant growl of the Hercules coming down out of the sky, laden with hope for me – and its passengers about to achieve their goal of leaving Sarajevo. I'd see it start its descent from the top of the cliffs, looping down from the honey crags that soared the length of the coast and separated the slim strip of Riviera from the mountainous killing grounds behind. Then the plane would taxi to a halt, the shafts of the propellers slowly emerge from their blur of speed (at Sarajevo airport, they kept them running so they could take off at will). I'd see the people spilling out of the ramp at the back onto the tarmac: hassled aid workers, grimy journalists, the odd immaculate-looking Bosnian (the Sarajevans were always well dressed and coiffed, however awful the siege). All of them, flak jackets and bags in hand, huge grins on their faces, eyes bemused, staring around the runway, overwhelmed by the sense of space created by the knowledge that this airport was not surrounded by men constantly popping off their guns, pulling the cyprus scent deep into their lungs as though normality, the real world, would flood into their blood like oxygen, and circulate and flush out the last vestiges of siege.

Then I'd get all excited and ready to go, and sometimes I'd even get right down to the tarmac, and then the Dutch guy would come and tell me I'd been bumped by someone with a more important pass, and I'd have to sit down and wait an hour or so for the next flight to come in.

Robert took control of the trip from the start. In those days, as you knew, I hardly spoke the language, but Robert was fluent – those first few years before the war began, he'd had a lot of time to learn his vocab lists. He chose the hotel, taking me away from where the hack pack normally stayed. ("Let's stay at the Bellevue. I loathe the commie staff at the Hotel Split. The Bellevue's much prettier and half the price. And it's in the centre of town.")

He wasn't the ideal travelling companion, being either very mean or very broke; I wasn't sure which. I was used, when I travelled with *proper* correspondents, to them taking me under their wing and picking up part of my tab. But, considering my budget was extremely limited, it was probably a good thing not to be with someone too extravagant. And I'd never been to Sarajevo before, so I felt safer with him. I was less likely to do something silly with someone who knew the ropes.

It was too late to go to Sarajevo, by the time we landed in Split, so we took the airport bus, like the tourists used to do – there was no question of Robert paying for a taxi. But when I wanted to chat, he took a thick book from his bag. I could have got out my *War and Peace* to his *Suitable Boy*, but I didn't need to read. I stared out of the window and dreamt of glory. I was living my own story now.

Robert was right about the bus: it was cheaper and more convenient and I was travelling so light, flak jacket apart, that lugging everything the last 200 yards was no hardship. He was right about the prettiness of the hotel too. Inside, the Bellevue was just the standard decorating hell of all Yugoslav hotels – coffee-coloured glass and chocolate-painted wood and mustard swirly carpets. It was a shame their tourist trade renaissance was in the seventies. But from the outside, it was a mini-Uffizi, end on to the sea, the sort of hotel where Hercule Poirot might once have tapped out onto the terrace to exercise his little grey cells, and it lined a balconied square that would have set Romeo and Juliet alight. The Hotel Split, in contrast, where I had stayed before, was a white concrete package-tourist dormitory, in the cement-stacked outskirts of town, half its characterless rooms now packed with refugees who sat sadly sunning themselves on their balconies (the hotel staff wouldn't let them use the pool). But it was one of those war hotels that become, by osmosis, the *only* place to stay, in whose blue-tiled lobby journalists would congregate on their way in and out of Bosnia. It was expensive and ugly but if you went there – I mean, when we went there, because of course you could never go there during the war

– you'd be guaranteed someone to talk to, or a lift into Bosnia, and you'd know, if you were missing the story as you sipped your glass of wine and watched the sun set over the Adriatic, that whichever of your competitors you were drinking with was missing it too. But when I opened my shutters in the hotel Bellevue and the sea tossed back the marbled twilight at the end of the piazza, I vowed never to stay at the Hotel Split again. It was a promise I would never keep until years after the war, when the Hotel Split's swimming-pool bar was empty save for ghosts.

At Reception, Robert suggested sharing a room, on the grounds of economy. I shot him a look. I didn't know him very well and I certainly didn't fancy him; he wasn't much taller than me, and about ten years older, with wispy blond hair, and a face already reddening with war and too much cheap wine. I'd shared rooms with journalists before on stories, and purely platonically, but only ones I knew well. And, if you were somewhere scary, it was often much nicer to have someone with you. But I didn't know how Robert would behave and also, for the first time, I could afford my own space.

"It's OK," I said. "I'm on expenses."

He went slightly redder. "I'll see you for dinner," he said. "I'll meet you on the terrace at eight. Our last decent meal." And quickly took his key.

It was a warm night, for late March. Robert was drinking wine and staring out to sea, when I came down, framed against the moonlit Adriatic.

To begin with, the atmosphere was slightly constrained, by the pass Robert had probably not made and I had turned down. He took me to a supermarket and practicality broke the ice. We laid in for the siege, with chocolate and biscuits, because there was no nice food in Sarajevo; *prsut* (smoked ham – pronounced *prsht*, like prosciutto, its name a relic of Venetian days), cheese and bread for emergencies, whisky, whatever else sprang to mind. And of course, the cheap Croatian cigarettes to hand out as bribes, which all had names that were quite, but not exactly, like famous brands, such as

Ronhill and Benston. I gave some to you the first time we met.

It's beautiful, Split, at least the centre is. But of course you knew that. You'd been living here, you said, just before the war broke out. The outskirts are the usual run of commie factories and tower blocks, but the centre is a wonder of age-smooth marble and stone. The Roman emperor Diocletian came from here and retired home when he was fed up of ruling the known world. He built a vast palace by the sea, and it still stands today, not a ruin, but the teeming hub of the city, running along the whole of the Esplanade, ending in the piazza that flanked the Bellevue. For years, hundreds of years, after the Roman Empire ended, his palace was a slum. But lately, I found out, the palace had become fashionable, and Split's chic and the *jeunesse dorée* of Yugoslavia had moved into the little apartments which had spread, like a web of fungus, throughout the centuries, their Venetian double windows cluttered randomly beneath the roofline. So I guess the syringes we saw, down a stygian alley, rolling to and fro on the uneven paving stones, could well have belong to the war-bored children of the bourgeoisie rather than the dregs of society, unless you count them the same.

You couldn't believe, when we met, that three days ago I'd been in Split. Your stuff was still in your friend's flat there, you said, in one of the narrow streets winding through Diocletian's palace, with glimpses of the Adriatic flashing up, like a slide-show, in alley-end slots of sunlight and glittery sea. Above one of those café-filled squares dotted with niches of medieval saints, you said. Obviously, you hadn't been able to pay the rent for the last year. It was your favourite town, in all of Yugoslavia, you said. You sent me there to pick your stuff up, one time, and I was dying to meet this friend who'd known your life outside of the siege, but one of his aunts opened the door, middle-aged, slightly round, blonde-coiffed and sad, a refugee from Vukovar, she said. She gave me two bags, dusty piled in a cupboard, and told me, over a tiny cup of coffee in her orange kitchen, that your friend was off fighting somewhere in Bosnia; which frankly made it worth the trip, because President

Tudjman of Croatia was always denying that his Croatian soldiers were sent to help their fellow Croats in Bosnia.

Robert and I wandered the narrow alleys, popping out into squares bright with the click of high heels on marble and the crack of laughter bouncing off the walls. All around us milled the youth and beauty of Dalmatia, girls with four-foot legs and twenty-inch waists, just emerged from their winter cocoons, their faces and figures a fantastic felicity between the local Slavs and the Venetian colonists; the men six foot or more, with the kind of looks Mills and Boon writers conjure up from their villas in the Isle of Man: smouldering eyes, high cheekbones, dark stubble, broad shoulders, devil-may-care attitude, and all the rest. They were probably your friends, or at least your friends before the war.

War seemed a million miles away, with the sea, and the parade, until I noticed the graffiti sprayed on the wall; something about Serbs or *Chetniks*, the name Serb nationalist soldiers called themselves, after the royalist Serb resistance in World War II. Sometimes we'd even see the word *Ustase*, the Croat version of the Fascist party when the Croats sided with the Nazis in the same war.

Sometimes we'd see soldiers, slightly drunker than the rest, a few still proudly wearing their pistols as a badge of rank. Their uniform was the swirly greens and browns that the Croats either bought or copied from the Americans. You used to think the Croats hoped that if they dressed like Yanks, then the Americans would help them win the war. And actually, America did, so perhaps the strategy worked.

I, too, was in my war uniform: clumpy boots, old jeans, fleece. I felt like a complete frump in comparison to the promenading beauties and their beaux.

"Just remember what they look like when they're middle-aged," Robert said.

But I couldn't bear to. Perhaps I was too young. There is nothing comforting in your twenties about imagining those beautiful bodies bloating round the middle until the six-packs bulged into the vast bellies that adorned so many of the men I'd seen lolling round checkpoints. Although in Sarajevo, like you, everyone was thin – everyone except the black-marketers of course.

We chose a restaurant Robert knew, in a wide, open square, with tables outside; he knew a lot of restaurants in Split, which was a good thing, as it turned out.

"Right," said Robert, as the waiters hovered with flapping napkins. "Let's go to town. This is our last decent meal. The food in the Holiday Inn is vile." Which I already knew.

We drank Posip, the crisp dry white of the coast that made me think of long evenings and cicadas.

"Our last decent drink," Robert mourned, "the wine in the Holiday Inn is as vile as the food."

"This is like Pinot Grigio," I said.

"But not as nice," said Robert. "A lot of the stuff here is like Italy but not as nice. Mediterranean food produced by Slavs. Forget having *prsut* – it's just prosciutto but not as nice. Anyway you'll be living off it for days in Sarajevo. You should always have fish here." He ordered squid.

Later, as we wandered home, Robert leant on a white marble balustrade overlooking Odysseus' wine-dark sea.

"Oh God, why do we ever have to leave Split? It's so beautiful and Bosnia's so grim!"

I was shocked. "But it is interesting, Bosnia?"

"Too bloody interesting," he said. "We'd better get an early night. I think we should get there as early as possible. The first bus leaves for the airport at 7.35 and there's always a risk we'll get bumped off the plane."

When we got back to the hotel, I sat on my bed, fiddling with the alarm on my little Sony shortwave. It was 10.59 now and I ought to hear the news. I pulled out the aerial and went over to the balcony. Three rooms down, Robert was leaning out, aerial poked out towards the sea. I could hear the blur of static. We smiled at each other as we listened: Sarajevo was quiet.

"There's something happening up near Tuzla," he said, when it was over. Which I knew too, as we'd both been listening to the same bulletin.

"Why didn't you go to Sarajevo directly from Belgrade?" I'd asked him, as we walked home. "It must be shorter." It didn't look far on the map.

"Are you mad?" he'd almost shouted. "If I went from Belgrade, I'd have to get permission from the bloody Bosnian Serbs to go into their stupid country and their glorious capital Pale, then get on a nightmare bus full of fat old Serb ladies and go bump, bump, bump, and the Muslims would probably ambush us near Srebrenica. And then I'd have to deal with the nightmare Bosnian Serbs again in bloody Pale for some more bloody permissions; and then, then, which would be even worse, I'd have to hang out in Pale, which is the ultimate one-horse town, until I managed to hitch a lift from some nice passing hack who was crossing the frontlines. I loathe Pale," he said. "Pale is *vuko jebine*." He gave me a look to see if I knew what that meant, which I did of course, as it was about the first joke any hack learnt here. It was Serbo-Croat for the middle of nowhere, and it meant, "where the wolves fuck". And I knew what he meant about Pale too; it was the former royal Yugoslav ski resort, and probably one of the few capital cities with the same number of politicians as goats.

"This way's much better. I get to eat fish and we just hop on a plane. We should be there by lunch."

But he was wrong. We waited three days, and the last decent meals lost their sense of celebration, but no planes left at all; the airlift had been cancelled indefinitely.

"This is a nightmare," said Robert, surlier and surlier by the end of our second day. "All that Dutch guy will say is: 'Don't ask me, ask the Serbs. They are the ones stopping us to fly.' And this place is starting to look like a refugee camp." The airport was slowly filling up with earnest men with beards, disconsolate by their piles of luggage, flak jackets propped against their chairs, reading enormous books.

"For displaced aid workers," I said.

"They've all got higher priority than us," said Robert. "Even if the flights start, there's no guarantee we'll get on for days."

"The anniversary's not till next Tuesday," I said. "We've got a week." It was Tuesday now.

"You've got a week," he said. "I work for a Sunday. Mine's got to run on the Sunday before, so I've got to file by Saturday morning, which means, realistically, if I don't get there by Friday, the whole thing's been a complete waste of time."

He walked over to the window, staring up over the crags as if he could will a plane to appear out of the sky. "It's ridiculous. It's only an hour away."

Stuck inside Sarajevo, it must have seemed all the more ridiculous to you.

By the third day, Robert was almost unbearable; silent and snappy, increasingly hung over, and our table littered with picnic crumbs – Robert, of course, had baulked at the cost of the airport canteen.

"Sod this. Let's take the bus," he said.

"There's a *bus* to Sarajevo?" I asked.

"There's always a bus," he said. "Well, not exactly to Sarajevo, but we can get quite close anyway: Kiseljak." I didn't have to ask where Kiseljak was – I knew it was technically the last Bosnian government-held town before the Serb lines circling Sarajevo, if full of Croats. "We're bound to get a lift in Kiseljak. There's a BBC office there. Millions of people go through Kiseljak every day."

The hotel, used to reporters and their strange requests, told us that the buses for Bosnia left from the coach station in Split, just by the ferry terminal where the boats come in from the islands; a place deep in mourning for Croatia's lost tourist gold.

The man in the little booth on the white marble quay did not even blink when Robert asked when the bus left. He stared out across the oily water, to the pine-covered island basking on the horizon, out to the memory of good times past. And then he said, "23.00 hours, or, about 23.00 hours," depending, he added, on how many people turned up.

"It's safer at night," he said. He wouldn't sell us a ticket, but told us we should pay the driver. His shrug implied our journey was nothing to do with him.

"But what if the bus is full?" asked Robert.

"It won't be," said the ticket man, looking at him as if he were mad; so off we went out for our final last decent meal, and stocked up again at the supermarket – three days of airport picnics having depleted our supplies.

That was almost the last conversation Robert had for hours. He settled into the grimness of his silence. We chewed olives in silence in a fishing-net-bedecked restaurant, like those married couples I used to see when my father was based in Rome, holidaying to fill the vast vacuum in their long-dead conversation. I trawled the menu for something I hadn't eaten during the last three days and wished I could find some way to leave him; but I couldn't. Like the married couples, I needed him, or someone like him: I had never been to Sarajevo before. But he didn't need me.

Then suddenly, his po-face cracked with laughing. He pointed to the menu: "Well, don't have that. Look, 'Warm gypsy spit.'"

I started to laugh too, the pair of us giggling uncontrollably – I guess the Posip had taken effect – that and the excitement of finally being on our way.

"What *is* warm gypsy spit?" I asked.

"God knows… maybe a kebab? I think I'll give it a miss."

I laughed again, partly just with relief that Robert was being nice.

"God, I tell you, I'm glad you're here," he said, when he was comfortably through his piece of grilled fish.

"You *are*?" I nearly dropped my fork.

"Yeah! Of course. You don't think I fancy taking a bus into Bosnia on my own do you? Shall we get another bottle?"

THE BUSH administration's pronouncements on the Yugoslav crisis between February and August exhibited the worst sort of hypocrisy. I know. I wrote them... The trick was to ignore facts – whether they pertained to atrocities, rumours of concentration camps, or starvation – that would just complicate the policy goal of not getting involved...every day it was lies. One time I even proposed the department spokesman said: "US officials lied yesterday."

—GEORGE KENNEY,
FORMER US PRESS OFFICER FOR BOSNIA

II

I tried to tell you, the day we met, about our journey. I tried to tell you, because I was trying to explain about Mrs Selimovic. I wanted to tell you about the man who had come up to us in the little café, in Tarcin, just where our bus had to leave the old main road to Sarajevo and judder off into the mountains. But you didn't seem that interested when I tried to tell you, and, I suppose, in your shoes, I would have felt the same. You didn't care how hard it had been for me to get into Sarajevo. You, and all your friends, just wanted to get out.

The bus was waiting by the quay; one of those ancient Bosnian buses that the war had resurrected, dragged out of some motor retirement home by coach companies who had lagged their newer stock until the dawn of peace but understood that, war or not, people were prepared to pay to travel. I'd taken a lot of those buses round the Serb side. The seats were ripped, the windows and windscreen spider-webbed with bullet holes, and little blue curtains hung from their frames, which the driver told us he would ask us to draw if he thought there was a risk of attracting fire.

It was long past midnight before we left. The bus slowly filled up with worried-looking people, with vast amounts of luggage; those red-and-white checked bags you always see with refugees, stuffed with whatever it took to make their return to Bosnia worthwhile: food maybe, or cigarettes, or liquor. Finally, with a grunt and a crashing of gears, the driver judged it enough and off we swirled, along the coast for two or three hours, and then turned sharp left into the hills, up the Neretva valley and the old main road to Sarajevo. At the border between Bosnia and Croatia, amongst the parquet of filthy, becalmed lorries, the Croat border guards spent a good hour or so, carefully unpacking all those red and white bags,

"They're checking for guns," Robert explained.

"But I thought the Croats and Muslims were allies."

He rolled his eyes: "They *were*… but it's never going to last."

We stopped in Mostar in the middle of the night, Bosnia's second city. Down a side road, the old Turkish bridge gleamed in the moonlight, spanning the gorge with its single arc, as it had since Suleiman the Magnificent had ordered its construction four hundred years before. I might have bothered to get out and take a proper look, if I'd known that within a few months – weeks even – Mostar would be divided, as dangerous as Sarajevo, the Muslims driven at gunpoint across the bridge, and that delicate arc would soon lie broken beneath the torrent, shattered by a Croat rocket; that the journey we were taking would become impossible for the next two years, that the villages we drove through would be totally cut off, more isolated from the outside world even than Sarajevo, which at least had a hundred TV crews chronicling each day.

Our bus drew itself together as the mountains crowded in. Higher and higher, we wound, Walter Scott crags silhouetted against the moonlight, the Neretva churning creamy green to our left, past the dam Antony Quinn and Barbara Bach blew up in *Force 10 from Navarone*, the vast lake bulging behind it, glittering in the moonlight.

As first light crept into the bus, and I woke, I saw the gorge had widened again, into a broad and fertile valley, laid out like a carpet between the mountains, dotted with wooden houses with steep red roofs, each in their own little patch of field. It was dawn but we seemed to have gone back in time. There was snow on the ground, now, albeit the greyish-white of spring, with the crystalline crunchiness of refrozen icecream. The country around also looked as if time had slipped.

In a little village, we finally shuddered to a halt, where a forestry track led high up into the peaks to our left. The little houses were strung to either side and, at the *pension*, the driver turfed us all out to eat. By the side of the road was a bullet-riddled sign saying "Sarajevo, 40 kilometres". "Not any more…" Robert laughed.

"Our last decent breakfast," he said, as he tucked into Turkish coffee, cheese omelette, rolls and honey. "Better eat a lot. God knows when we'll see this kind of stuff again."

"Where are we?"

"This is Tarcin," he said, in tones of great gloom. "This is where we have to leave the main road and head for the hills. The first thing the Serbs did was take all the main roads."

The valley was awakening now, the peasants starting the eternal tasks of rural life, with such a look of bovine routine that one might have thought the war had totally passed them by. I said this to Robert and a passing peasant, chatting to the owner of the bar, leant over and interrupted me. He turned out to be a computer programmer, a Muslim who'd been working in Belgrade, exiled by the war to his ancestral village in the middle of Bosnia. He asked us to take a food parcel and a letter to his mother-in-law in Sarajevo – and dashed off, running back ten minutes later with a hastily wrapped bulky lump of brown paper. They hadn't seen her for a year, he said; even though she was only thirty miles away as the crow flew, but the Serbs held the road and no-one could cross the lines. But when I told you about the computer programmer, who'd lost his job, his flat, his life, I told you that he'd shown us the key of his Belgrade flat – he carried it all the time, on his key ring, just in case, he'd said, you just shrugged; that was normal to you. He was lucky to be stuck outside Sarajevo, you said. The only thing that surprised you was when I told you that Robert had asked the man if he could read the letter he'd written. What business was it of Robert's? you asked. I was surprised to feel embarrassed when I replied: "He wanted it for his story." Why wouldn't he? A year of siege, a year of sundered lives, and he knew he was running out of time.

We couldn't cross the lines up the main road either; above us, to either side, the mountain rose.

"Do you see that bridge? At the top of the waterfall?" said Robert, pointing north.

I stared up, cricking my neck, making out a tiny wooden span, with a white ribbon spouting beneath it, hundreds of feet high.

"We're going to cross that," said Robert. "There are only about two ways into Bosnia now the Serbs have cut the main road and this is one of them. It takes bloody ages. And I'm going back to sleep. But we should be in Sarajevo by dark. The BBC has people going in all the time."

For three or four hours we laced up and down those mountains, slithering along a snowy traffic jam of aid trucks and military vehicles and lorries full of whatever goods people find lucrative to sell in a war – the same lorries, maybe, we had seen queued up by the border; ancient VW Golfs, battered old Yugos and UN white armoured vehicles, all of us inching back and forth through a hobbit world of mountains and ravines and ragged woodland creatures – manning checkpoints or begging for cigarettes, or just chopping wood – who could hardly believe their remote villages were suddenly on the main motorway to central Bosnia.

"Now this is *vuko jebine*," I said. "It makes Pale look like Paris. At least it has paved roads." But Robert was asleep. I should have slept too, but Bosnia was flooding through my veins.

You know the history of your country off by heart, or at least the version Tito wanted you to learn, but for me, the last year had been a crash course in geo-politics. Think of Bosnia as an arrow shape, Robert had told me, when we'd met in Serb-held Banja Luka a year before: "The arrow of the Turks, pressing into the soft underbelly of Europe" as paranoid local (non-Muslim) historians would have it, pointing north, into Croatia. In the old days, Bosnia and Serbia were all part of the Ottoman Empire, but the Croats were ruled by Austria-Hungary, Christian and Catholic to boot. When the empires collapsed, Bosnia was left forty per cent Muslim, thirty-five per cent Serbs, who were Christians but Orthodox, and ninteeen per cent Catholic Croats – the rest was a mishmash of gypsies and other even smaller minorities. The Serbs ended up running Yugoslavia, because they sided with the victorious Britain and France in World War I (Archduke Franz Ferdinand of Austria-Hungary, whose death was the catalyst for World War I, was assassinated in Sarajevo by a Bosnian Serb, as any schoolboy knows). After World War II, the Serbs ended up on top again because the Croats played on the German side. When Croatia and Bosnia wanted out half a century later, the Serbs objected. And that's how the war began. Unfortunately the Serbs controlled most of Yugoslavia's army, so that's why they are winning everything, Robert had explained, mesmerised by my ignorance. When the war began, the Serbs surrounded Sarajevo and captured a great stretch of land, sixty per cent of the country, which ran down from the north, along Bosnia's western and eastern flanks. They also took control of most of the roads, which is why we were bumping through the middle of nowhere on this icy track.

As for Sarajevo, the old capital, it sits in the centre of Bosnia, in a cleft in the mountains in which the 1984 Winter Olympics were held. It was you who told me on quiet days the Serbs would stop their shelling and ski.

The only big town in the north the Bosnian government managed to keep was Tuzla, connected by yet more mountains to the rest of their territory. So the Republika Srpska, as the Serbs called their Passport-to-Pimlico statelet, looked like a boomerang with a chunk bitten out. All that was left to the Bosnian government was a wobbly triangle, with Sarajevo at its apex, leading down to the Croat-held coast, and a funny bit sticking out to the north. Oh, except for a few funny blobs full of Muslims in the east which we used to call enclaves.

We slithered down into Kiseljak at about 11 a.m. Robert was happy again, scurrying around, finding us a taxi driver in the market place, a bustling square stuffed with fat head-scarfed women and dodgy leather-jacketed men, selling everything from sour cream and hub caps to CDs. As we set off towards the BBC, I said: "Maybe we'll be in Sarajevo for lunch?"

"Might as well lunch here," he said.

It turned out to be rather more than lunch. You laughed when you heard I'd spent three days in Kiseljak; you'd never even stopped there before the war. It was nearly *vuko jebine* as well. A typical celebrity of its times: tiny, utterly unimportant, the sort of place even Bosnians didn't know, until the war shot it to fame. Like Srebrenica, most notorious, now, of those Muslim enclaves in the east, whose name, later in the war, became a byword for atrocity, after that hot July day in 1995 when the Serbs finally overran the town. Gloating and heady after four years of siege, the Serbs herded the 7,000 remaining Muslim men, bound and unarmed, into trucks, and drove them off, to be butchered in the football stadium in Nova Kasaba, fourteen miles away. And all the while Dutch UN troops, stationed to make sure the Safe Haven was safe, cowered in their battery factory-base in Potocari, on the outskirts of town, where the men of Srebrenica all lie now, in the Memorial graveyard, as an eternal rebuke. Kiseljak's population was luckier – its notoriety came not from death, but as the last non-Serb stronghold to the north of Sarajevo, a border town where everything could be bought and sold.

Robert and I got to know it very well. We took a taxi to the BBC office, Robert joking with the driver, asking him questions about what was going on. The main street was flanked by little white houses, their modern starkness softened by the snow on their red roofs. Fairy-tale haystacks stood by each house. The hobbit mountains we'd crawled over on the bus fenced us in from the south, and Red Riding Hood fir trees came right up to the road. There was even an ancient Hansel and Gretel house: wattle and daub, shutters, upper storey bulging under its square-pitched layer of snow, a bridge with a little stream trailing icicles on the twigs on its bank as it gurgled by. Just past the bridge were the remains of the mosque, its pine panelling stained, its roof gutted and charred, and the felled minaret like a burnt-out rocket, under its dusting of snow; around its corpse, the blackened houses gaped by the side of the road. This was a Croat town now, they didn't like Muslims here.

Unfortunately, when we arrived at the BBC office – two rooms above a bar – the interpreter, a Croat beauty with iridescent blonde hair and a personality to match the mountains outside, told us with every degree of satisfaction that the correspondent and crew had left for Tuzla the previous day. "Everyone's gone to Tuzla. I don't know when they'll be back," she said.

We spent two days walking up and down the main street, but no-one we knew came by. It was quite cold, but we didn't dare wait inside, just in case we missed someone passing. We sat with our luggage by the side of the road and played pooh-sticks in the half-frozen stream, Robert alternating between heaving stress and hysteria; the town in its fairyland drugged and timeless sleep. Except that, Hansel and Gretel house apart, the buildings, like the bridge, seemed surprisingly modern.

"Why do you never normally see a traditional Bosnian house?" I asked Robert.

He just snorted – "Why do you think?"

Every hour we'd turn our short-waves on, and hear the absent correspondent filing from Tuzla – the Serbs were pushing in on Srebrenica even then. And Robert would say, "Maybe I should go to Tuzla instead." And then, he'd wait a bit, and say, "Maybe not."

At night, we got drunk, and smoked too much and sang Abba songs. If it were a film, we would have fallen in love and had lots of adventures and fantastic sex – singing "Do you hear the guns, Fernando?" to a backing track of distant artillery and occasional recreational bursts of automatic fire is a heady mix. But it wasn't a film. Perhaps I was waiting to fall in love with you.

After two days of taking walks up and down the main road, I suggested we try hitching our lift from the military base the UN had set up in an old school, two miles away, in the centre of town. The UN liked old schools, they were full of rooms you could stuff with soldiers and cover with maps saying where the latest attack you couldn't stop had happened, and at which checkpoints the convoys of humanitarian aid you were there to escort had been held up.

Robert flipped. Anyone but a total amateur, he said, would know that the UN didn't give people lifts. I said I thought it would be worth a try; it was better than missing our deadlines and going for more walks in Kiseljak. I didn't say I was young and blonde, and Robert was red-faced, bald and middle-aged (or at least what I thought was middle-aged then, but he was only 35, I guess), and soldiers tended to be more helpful to young blondes. We had a row then, a screaming match. I said I'd walk to the UN on my own, and he said I couldn't. "You're young and blonde," he said. "War zones are full of nuts," and I don't think either of us saw the joke.

Our landlord ended up taking us crammed in his car, and charging some astronomical amount that made Robert go even redder with rage. But it worked. I left Robert in the car park, guarding our stuff, and, being young and blonde, and putting on my most Sandhurst-friendly accent, found two British officers who said they would take us in. They were both about the same age as me and, hair colour apart, they were weirdly identical: same height, same shape, same British fatigues; same age, probably, a bit older than me. When I'd proudly walked them towards Robert in the Kiseljak car park, he'd hardly grunted his thanks, but as we were putting our stuff in the car, he'd whispered to me: "They're clones. Combat clones. Identical twins. What did you do? Walk in and ask for one in each colour?" Which I suppose was the nearest Robert got to saying sorry, but I had a funny feeling that both of them heard.

It seemed weird, after so many days of trying, that the trip from Kiseljak to Sarajevo should be so short, now we were in an UNPROFOR car – just twenty minutes or so, tootling along between pretty green hills, the houses we passed increasingly burnt-out. But Robert said, almost like you did: "It must be even weirder if you are stuck inside." And then, as we left the Croat chequerboard flag behind, snaking warily between the huge lumps of cement dumped in the road, and out into the deserted street, towards the double-headed Serb eagle and the next row of mines, 200 yards and several ruins away, Robert said: "A whole week on the road, and now I suppose I'm back in Greater Serbia again."

At the last checkpoint, before we left Serbia for the frontline and Sarajevo, that bearded lady of Sierra One, the fat Serb policewoman, tried to flirt with Robert – the one with a beer gut, and the fag stuck to her fuchsia-pink lips. She'd been chatting to two Chetniks inside her police station and they came out to watch her dealing with us; I couldn't help feeling slightly sick as I looked at those two heroes of Greater Serbia, their fur hats, emblazoned, of course, with the double-headed eagle, neatly balancing their bushy black beards, their truly appalling teeth. I couldn't forget all the things the Serb irregulars had done in that first blood-soaked summer of war – the lost villages of the Drina valley, the charred Lego houses of Prijedor, the rotting corpses, the school gyms full of bewildered refugees. They were grinning as the bearded lady went through her Rosa Klebb routine. I felt rather sorry for her in those days – she was so ugly, and her make-up was so bad, with her Aeroflot-blonde two-inch dark roots, and the bristles poking through the orange foundation on her chin. I got used to her in the end. At least, that first trip, she didn't try and steal our money; perhaps it was because we were with the UN. She certainly tried her best to flirt with our drivers, who heroically flirted back. And the mines – they looked so innocuous, like green plastic cowpats – but I knew, as she nonchalantly rolled them away with her foot, that if we'd driven over one, they'd have had to hose us off the road. But you'd never have met her either. You could never go to that checkpoint. That's so odd. She is such an absolute part of my war. I wonder what she's doing now?

Then we left Greater Serbia behind, the broken houses to either side, decaying as the war dragged on, beams poking into the sky, windows gouged, winter foliage trampled underfoot by the soldiers peering through their wrecked walls at their enemy a few hundred yards away. As for me, at that frontline; then, at least, I'd never been so scared. You see it on TV, but a twenty-four inch screen can't do justice to a blasted, open concrete space, ringed round with house after roofless house; walls half blown away; bald winter branches sprouting from their windows. The snow lay fresh on the mine-fields to either side.

You don't know what that frontline was like. How could you have known? It was keeping you inside and before the war, you would have used the normal road. Although you might have seen it on TV. Like I did, before I came. Although maybe not, as you had no electricity.

It was Robert who had to show us all the way. There were no signs. No other cars around; a creepily empty urban space. As funny as it is to me now, on that trip, Robert, who hardly knew Sarajevo in the war, was to me as omniscient as a god. There was a flyover, at the end of that space, curling round a graveyard, whose stones poked up through the mine-rich virgin snow. In its shadow, a tattered flag, the Bosnian fleur de lys on a shield, hung from a wire above a makeshift chicane of oil drums.

A hand appeared from behind a concrete pillar and, like a fairy tale again, a ragged soldier beckoned us round. He was much thinner than the bearded lady we had just left behind; dark-haired, like you, and probably, once, as handsome. He showed our passes to his friend, a tow-haired goblin huddled by a fire.

"Welcome to Sarajevo," the ragged soldier said. They both laughed and the goblin showed a mouth full of goblin teeth; he showed them again when the clone in the passenger seat threw him a pack of Marlboro Red. It was hard to believe that both men had the same job; this whey-faced goblin, shooting out his claw to catch the largesse thrown his way, his fatigues shiny with grime and use, shrinking behind his brazier in the shadow of the bridge; and the dark-haired boy – man, really – in our car, all bursting and luminous with testosterone.

"Good day to come," said the ragged soldier. "Still ceasefire. Is nearly record. Drive fast, you maybe reach Holiday Inn before Chetniks change their minds…" And he and goblin roared with laughter again.

Suddenly we were on a great dual carriageway, built for traffic jams, with tank tracks in the snow; except we were alone. A jumble of trolley bus cables lay along the central reservation, and the shadow of some tramlines showed faintly through.

Robert said: "Well this is it. Whatever you do, don't turn right. That's where the Serbs are."

The two UN soldiers and I all looked to the right. The flats on our flank were toy-town red, mauve and blue; through their dustings of snow, the great grey splash marks of shrapnel looked the more obscene, as though someone had burnt a child. One building towered over the rest, or half of it did; the other half had been peeled off and lay dangling above the remains of a warehouse below. Behind them, the mountains reared up to the clouds.

It was as if some aesthete, with a grudge against modern architecture, had set about achieving his fantasy with a tank. To either side was a row of greyish flats, some warehouses, office blocks, and garages; the stuff you see in any modern town. Except the roofs gaped, girders poked up to the grey clouds, walls ended in craters of broken concrete, festooned with the black trails of downed power cables. And the grey spring snow leeched the colour from it all.

"Is this Sniper Alley?" I asked. But Robert said, "No, it's the airport road. The frontline's gone behind that little hill. But I'd still drive fast."

"You know this place?" said the other clone, the driver.

"A bit," Robert said.

"Could you give us the tour?"

But Robert didn't speak, he just sat and stared out of the window, till I said: "What's that?" And waved towards the toy-town flats to our right.

"That's Dobrinje," he muttered. We waited, then he added, "It was completely cut off for the first part of the war." As he spoke, it was as though his engine had warmed up. "The phones still worked then, so every day I used to ring this woman up who lived there. Now, it's linked up by that little road, but it's still basically a peninsula, pointing into the Serbs' territory. You can get shot on every side. Half of it is actually held by the Serbs. The woman I used to speak to said that she could hear the Serb soldiers talking through the wall of her apartment." He stopped. Then he said: "I was going to try and see how she was for my piece this week, but I suppose we don't have time."

"How long have you spent here?" asked the blond twin again.

When Robert spoke again his voice had lost its colour: "Before the war, this was my favourite town in Yugoslavia."

Friends who covered Grozny or "shock and awe" in Baghdad said that in comparison Sarajevo was nothing – and it's true, I suppose. The UN no-fly zone was imposed quite early on in the war, so the Serbs did very little aerial bombardment. Shelling makes a much smaller mess. But it still looked pretty bad. I'd seen it on the news before, but it's not the same. What makes it so macabre is the intent. Earthquakes look worse, but the thing about an earthquake is that nobody did it on purpose to someone else.

I tried to keep it out of my face but Robert suddenly said: "Of course, you've never seen this before."

I said: "No." I was about to say that I'd seen other things. But then I stopped. The other things didn't seem the same.

Robert didn't say much for the rest of the trip. Just, at one point, when we passed some graffiti that said: "Welcome to Hell." He said, "This is where Sniper Alley starts. The frontline runs right beside us here." And we all turned to look to the right again.

I never asked you what Sniper Alley was really called. It must have had some self-important name – "Boulevard of the Victory of Socialism" – something like that; big and leading to a better future. It was always just Sniper Alley to me.

The buildings to either side had changed. Against the backdrop of the mountains rose cement stacks of flats; every now and then, the stucco grace of Austria-Hungary. All of them, ripped by the war: a pistachio plaster column, its capital smashed into a deep grey scar; blackened roof beams poking up through the snow like spider's legs; and all with their windows boarded with planks.

"That's Grbavica," Robert suddenly said, pointing to our right. "Over the river. That's where the Serbs are. Those white blocks of flats. Just across the bridge."

Only Robert could tell there was a river in the way, because he was seeing where it was before the war. There must have been a bridge, but a huge lorry, slewed across the gap between the buildings, blocked the view. Its tyres were as flat as tyres in a cartoon. Snow had drifted on the earth piled up round its wheels and on the mines lying fatly to either side. Between the lorry and the buildings to right and left, mattresses were stacked, a row of gym lockers stood, punched through with holes and, strung across from either side, blankets were draped over ropes. They were riddled with bullet holes, and their edges trailed down into the razor wire and mines. "That's the Bridge of Brotherhood and Unity," said Robert. I was too scared then to laugh at the inappropriateness of the name.

The flats beyond looked just like the flats here: the same concrete layers of people, the same blackened shell-holes. They were so close, we'd have seen someone staring out of a window smile, except that all the windows, like the ones on our side, were boarded up.

The next junction was exactly the same: the makeshift barricades, the tattered blankets blocking out the line of sight. It was all very different from the war I had seen so far: the blackened villages, burnt-out farms and half-mad skeletons in camps; refugees in their hundreds lying head to toe in school gyms, places people fled from and to. Not places where people were trapped and had to live.

Then I heard Robert say: "We're here."

I gawped. I couldn't believe I was finally here. It was like my first day at Oxford, when it seemed utterly unreal that I finally belonged in this honey-coloured quad. Just like Oxford, it was all new to me, but familiar, as I had seen every view in the papers or on TV, except in real life it was worse. The road had opened up into one of those seventies municipal spaces. There was a piazza, with a lifeless fountain whose parapet was traced with strange score marks in the snow. Behind it, to our left, tower blocks, their windows boarded up, and the same pale-ringed blackened holes smashed into their sides; opposite them, over Sniper Alley, the wreck of the Bosnian Parliament, fifteen storeys or so of charred cement. On the near side of the fountain square was a long green building, or at least its shell, all blackened stucco and burnt-out roof. It was a while before I discovered that the Serbs couldn't be blamed for that – it had been used as an ammunition factory, and suffered an industrial accident early in the war.

Bang in the middle was an egg-yolk-yellow lump, like a multi-storey child's toy. It looked as if it had been dropped by a spaceship into the centre of town, but no-one who'd watched the news for the last year would have needed to read the words "Holiday Inn" looped along one side.

The top half was just a black mass of holes: the hole to hotel ratio weighted heavily towards holes. Apart from the shrapnel scars and the bullet holes, the lower storeys were relatively unscathed, except the restaurant at the front looked as if it had been attacked by a tank.

Beyond the hotel stretched away several hundred yards of

empty snow, ending at a pair of the tower blocks on the other side; the UNIS towers, I later learned, the twin glass skyscrapers just beyond the hotel, which were burnt out so spectacularly in the early days of the war that I think the photograph made the cover of *Time*. From their windows, the remains of slatted vertical blinds flailed in the wind, like the fingers of the blind reaching out for help; and from everywhere the dirty snow leeched the last remnants of life.

The combat twins were staring at the hotel too. "I'm glad I'm not sleeping in that," said the dark one.

"How do you get in and out?" asked the blond. "There's no cover."

I said: "It's where everybody stays."

At the same time Robert said: "There isn't anywhere else any more."

The snipers' bullets cracked across the grass, as we screeched round to the back of the hotel. We'd hardly had time to thank the soldiers, before an armoured Land Rover appeared and a man got out who, like the buildings, looked a bit worse than he did on the television. Like the buildings, too, his face bore the marks of war – not scars, just brown eyes sunken from lack of sleep, and scuffed blond hair. He bounced at Robert with a hug and a "Robert! How are you, mate!"

The far door opened, and a girl got out; a beauty, with thick white skin, the sort novelists call alabaster, and black, springy hair, cut into a modern version of an Ava Gardner bob. She looked like Snow White, but much more chic. She wore bright red lipstick, a dark hat on her head, and her flak jacket was worn over a smart tweed coat; the flak jacket and her clumpy boots were the only similarities between her clothes and mine.

"*Robert!*" Big smile; she brushed her lips over his cheek, hardly halting her sweep to the door. "You came back. Sarajevo is not fashionable at the moment, everyone has gone to Tuzla." Her voice was Bond Girl Slav. I didn't even warrant a hello.

Robert stared at the door after she had gone through. "The beautiful Valida."

"She's still taken though," said the man.

Robert blushed: "Shut up, let a man have his dreams." Then he turned to me and said: "Have you met Molly? And," he turned to introduce the combat clones, except of course, we didn't know either of their names.

Instead of filling in the gap left by Robert saying: "This is Phil Kennedy," and Phil sticking out his hand, the blond twin just shook it and said, "Phil Kennedy, you were in the Gulf?" Then he said to Robert, "What's the best way into town from here?" Robert pointed on down the grey road, but Phil broke in with: "I'd go the back way, up, behind the hotel. It's safer." He pointed up behind the hotel, where a road led up a little hill between some blocks of flats. Laced across it were rows of grey metal gym lockers, interspersed with blankets draped from ropes.

"I thought there was a ceasefire," said the dark twin.

"Quaint Sarajevo rules," said Phil. "Snipers don't count in ceasefires..."

"It doesn't make any difference to them, their car is armoured," said Robert, in a querulous voice.

"No it's not," chorused Phil and the clones at once. Phil hit the Land Rover – it rang tinnily back. Robert went white. The dark twin looked at me: "Are you sure you want to stay?"

"Oh yes," I said.

"Maybe see you around," he said, and left. I stood in the yard watching until their car swerved behind the first row of lockers, envying them being a pair. It was only later I realised they'd never said their names.

Phil was perfectly polite, but went straight back to Robert. I hung behind them, feeling shy. I thought Robert wouldn't need me any more. I followed them over the rutted ice to a small door, into a cold dark room, smelling of cigarettes and, slightly, pee. Later I would discover that most of Sarajevo smelt slightly of pee. I was here to cover the first anniversary of the plumbing failing, as well as everything else. The windows were boarded up, and thick grains of dust danced in the rays of light sneaking through at the corners. The rotting carpet stuck to my feet; it reminded me of temping at the *Independent*. In the far corner, by another door, three Bosnian soldiers and a dark-eyed girl sat smoking beside a metal detector.

"Is that thing working?" asked Robert.

"Dream on. There's no power," said Phil. "It's just for show." The tallest of the soldiers, with sad, gaunt eyes, made a great play of shining his torch onto our passes. Even Phil's, though he must only have left the hotel an hour ago.

We passed through a door. A vast atrium, seven or eight storeys high, opened up; four bulging pillars soared into the shadows of the roof. The architect had obviously had ambition to rise above his medium; or maybe to him, the hotel was socio-realist sculpture: the walls were raw concrete and naked brick, and the predominant lines were curved. Down the centre hung an enormous chandelier, bulbous and modern, the type that communists always seemed to install, as if it would light up their new world. It was dead, of course, and, as I saw when I went upstairs, covered with chunks of plaster dust. A rocket had crashed through fifth floor a few months ago, Phil explained: "I think the manager must have been late with his bribe."

The grey walls were striped and, as my eyes grew accustomed to the gloom, the stripes materialised into galleries. To my left, some sad-eyed men sat drinking small cups of coffee at a horseshoe-shaped bar, where a sad-eyed waiter was polishing glasses dressed, despite the war, in immaculate black tie.

The light came from the right, pouring in over an Astroturf carpet dotted with purple toadstool seats. The whole length of the hotel must once have been glass, two storeys high. Instead now plastic sheeting hung in huge folds, like the curtains on a stage, and glued in position by the ubiquitous white sticky tape with its cheery blue UN logos that was stuck everywhere. It seems odd that the UN needed to advertise their failure, by running their logo through nearly every former window in Sarajevo. It made the whole country look as if it was just being kept together by them; I suppose it was. Beyond the blur of the plastic hung huge shards of glass, like the ruins of an ice queen's palace; they also glittered on what must once have been the turning circle of the hotel; and beyond that slept the fountain we had seen from the road. Since the windows had been broken – a shell? A lucky shot? God knows how long ago – it had obviously not been safe enough to get out front and clean up.

Robert and Phil were standing at Reception, where the plastic met up with the naked brick walls. Robert handed his passport to a middle-aged woman who took it in her gloved hands, her orange lips, above her scarf, screwed into a sour smile of recognition, woolly hat nodding up and down. Her desk, so close to where the glass walls had been, looked both cold and dangerous. I wondered why they hadn't moved it; perhaps the key slots behind were too convenient? Or perhaps she'd decided to sit it out until forced to leave, like people who stay in their village until they hear the tanks up the road.

"Is it good to be home?" asked Phil.

"This is not my home," said Robert. "I'm not as sad as you." Then he turned round and looked for me.

I was hovering two yards behind. He walked me over to one of the mushrooms.

"Molly," he said, very quietly. "I don't want to be rude or to make this difficult." And I remember thinking, oh shit, this is like being chucked, but with Phil here, why would he need to hang out with me any more? So I wasn't expecting Robert to say: "How much money have you got left? Do you want to share a room?" My face froze and I blushed, but he quickly said: "Don't worry. I've a girlfriend in Belgrade." I blushed even more, but he went on: "This place costs a bomb and the *Herald* is always whining about money. Besides," he added, before I could speak, "I hate being here. It's much less miserable if you're with someone else. And I owe you for picking up the combat clones."

Phil made a face when we checked in but surprisingly, it wasn't the eyebrow-raising kind I'd thought he'd make. Instead, he said: "Sharing a room in Sarajevo can be kind of gross." I nodded, but actually I had no idea of what he meant, but I know that you'd agree with him. But, of course, you had no choice but to put up with that kind of gross. It was just as gross when you were at home.

It was later that afternoon that I met you.

I suppose it was a stupid decision to get out of the car, but if I hadn't, I wouldn't have met you at all. I'd been out with Phil and Robert, clanking from interview to interview in Phil's BBC armoured car. Phil didn't even react when we heard a bullet crack.

Robert was outraged: "I thought you said there was a ceasefire!" he said again. But Robert was always being outraged by things. To be fair, in the last few years, he'd seen a lot of outrageous stuff go on.

"I told you. Sarajevo tradition," said Phil. "Ceasefires don't include snipers. You should know that: you've just spent too long in Belgrade."

Robert said: "Oh God. I think I've blanked it all out."

"The ceasefire's bound to end soon anyway. It's lasted four days. That's nearly a record."

"That's what those Bosnian soldiers said when we came in," I said.

"Really?" said Phil.

But Robert snorted and said, "What on earth do they know?"

I was trotting down the street when the ceasefire broke, trying to look as if I knew what I was about. But the street was completely empty except for me, and strung between the walls on either side of the Presidency, the ragged blankets of the sniper barricades fluttered on their washing lines. I ran downhill towards it, keeping to the side of the road, to try and keep out of the sight of the snipers on the snow-covered peaks rising beyond the river behind. I'd insisted that I get out and go back: we'd delivered Mrs Selimovic her parcel earlier that day, before setting off on our round of interviews with politicians and generals, the Muslim manager of the brewery, and the man who ran the mortuary, who of course, then, I didn't know at all, little thought I would get to know so well. She lived in one of those Austro-Hungarian blocks, up the hill to the right, looking down towards the Presidency. After Mrs Selimovic had unpacked the oil, and the eggs, and the strange orange spice, and cried over the photographs of grandchildren she said she hadn't seen for a year, and could hardly see now in the gloom of her flat, she'd asked us, a little shyly, if we could take a letter back. At least, she asked Robert, as he had to do all the translating – Phil had given Valida the afternoon off, and he hardly spoke a word of the language himself which surprised me, although I didn't then either, so I don't know why it should have done. We'd said yes to the letter. Phil had even given her a pen, but later on, at the end of our day, Robert said he just didn't have time to pick it up; he had too much to do: "I've got enough material now anyway." But I thought we shouldn't leave anyone waiting, if we'd said we'd come back, particularly not an old woman on her own.

It was dusk by the time I managed to get away; I had to spend half an hour looking at photographs of Mrs Selimovic's fat happy life before the war. I didn't know enough Serbo-Croat to leave politely. It didn't matter so much. Phil and Robert were waiting at the Presidency – they were interviewing some politician and I could get the stuff off them. I knew where it was – Phil had pointed it out earlier on: raspberry and custard stripes.

"Don't you think it looks just like a Victorian blancmange," he'd said. I said, one of those synthetic cakes you get in Zagreb coffee shops, pink and yellow layers, with snow as the icing.

The Presidency was set back, the other side of the broad, grey boulevard of Marshal Tito Street; to one side, a grey office block, where Austrian civil servants had run the last decades of their Reich; to the other, a honey-coloured mosque, tumbled tombstones sticking up in the grimy snow. Opposite was a little park, but there were no trees there now. They'd all been cut down for firewood last year, at night, when the gunmen on the hills were drunk or asleep; I'd seen Phil's documentary about that just before I came out.

Not far now. Phil had said I needed to sprint the last bit. "You see the hills," he said, from the car. "That's where the Serbs are. If you can see the hills, they can see you. Run straight across, then the Presidency will give you cover. We'll be inside."

Like every building whose windows faced onto this main boulevard, the Presidency had no glass – every window was filled in by planks held in by white UN sticky tape. There were sandbags piled on the windowsills, and at the massive double doors which topped the steps Archduke Franz Ferdinand would have been heralded up, if only he had lived to the end of his procession. The splintered planks, the great gashes on the stucco, all showed the sandbags weren't just there to make a point.

I couldn't see the BBC Land Rover, but Phil said they made him park it round the side – "Not still!" said Robert. "*They* can see you there." Rob's *they* were obviously different to the people who made up the parking rules in town.

Phil shrugged: "The Mossies like to keep the front Presidential. At least the accountants would approve: the Serbs are always trying to shell the front, so if I left it there, the car might get a direct hit."

"Would they prefer you died rather than the car?" I asked.

"I'm easy to replace. Armoured cars cost a fortune."

"What if she gets hit?" Robert asked, as I hopped out of the car.

I said nothing.

"I always say you have to be bloody unlucky to be hit by a shell. This place is full of locals, and most of them are still alive," said Phil.

"Apart from the ones who are dead, of course," said Robert.

Then I said, because I believed it: "Don't worry, I'll be fine."

Phil turned to me: "If anything happens, just get inside."

I was nearly on Marshal Tito Street when the first shell fell. I stopped dead for a moment. I did not know what to do. Get inside, Phil had said, if anything happens. But I froze. In where? Then a shell made up my mind because I heard it coming and I threw myself into the nearest doorway as it crashed into the street. Another one came. The Presidency was only 200 yards away, but the shells were falling in between. The snipers' bullets speeded up their tempo, as though today's ceasefire had just been the slow movement. Another shell. I tried the door I was leaning against; it was locked. I thumped at it, but nothing moved inside. The windows were boarded up, but that meant nothing. Every window I'd seen so far was boarded up. I didn't know much but I knew enough that if a shell fell nearby – and they were not that far – then my little doorway was not really going to help. I looked up and down the street, and the buildings stared blankly back. Then I thought, Mrs Selimovic; she was just a street away.

I turned and ran back up the hill, and turned right up her street. I must have looked ridiculous, my flak jacket bumping on my shoulders, skittering across the ice, trying not to slip. I was too scared to look too closely at the block of flats, but it looked the same, three or four storeys of swagged and figured stucco, although the war had made an amputees' *fête champêtre* of the façade. I got to the double wooden doors just as a shell crashed again. I hurled myself in.

The stairs *felt* like Mrs Selimovic's stairs – it was too dark inside to see that much. They were the same wide, shallow, Austrian steps, the same wrought-iron balustrade. The wooden banisters were coated in the same thick layer of concrete grit, and the same grit crunched underfoot on the tiled floor; like builders' dust, but this came from destruction; they also had the same faint smell of dirt and pee.

My heart was still pounding as I tried to work out what to say – particularly as Mrs Selimovic and I didn't really have a common language – but then I thought the crash of the bombardment would say it all. Sarajevans must be used to people being stranded in places by now. She could show me the rest of the photographs. I pressed the bell, set to the side of the panelled double doors, out of habit even though I knew it hadn't worked before. Then I pounded on the frosted glass instead.

So if I hadn't been so scared that I got the wrong house, or if the Serbs had started shelling five minutes later and I'd had time to cross the road, or if I hadn't felt so guilty about poor Mrs Selimovic, waiting on her own, in her freezing, dark flat, for us to return for the letter Robert had promised to deliver to her daughter, that I'd told Phil and Robert I'd nip back, and meet them at the Presidency; if I hadn't let her spend half an hour showing me photographs of her grandchildren in a language I couldn't understand, I'd have missed the bombardment, met up with the others at the Presidency, and bumped back in Phil's armoured Land Rover to the Holiday Inn. And I might never have met you at all.

YOU HAVE MY permission to shell, but do not touch the industrial infrastructure because we need the machinery. Shoot only at human flesh. Shell only human flesh. Only human flesh.

—RADIO INTERCEPT OF GENERAL RATKO MLADIC, SERB COMMANDER, ORDERING HIS TROOPS TO ATTACK THE TOWN OF ZELENI JADAR, NEAR SREBRENICA, 1993

III

I can't imagine never having met you. I know that most people who know me, I suppose, say that I would be much better off if I hadn't. But not as much better off as you would have been, if you'd been out that afternoon, queuing for water, or stealing firewood, or getting cold and bored on your old frontline; if I'd had to wait in your stairwell till the shelling stopped and had then left without us ever having met.

I got a shock when you opened the door. Although it was dark on the landing, it wasn't hard to see that you weren't Mrs Selimovic. You were about a foot taller, and instead of old lady mustiness, you smelled of boy; I could taste the taint of sweat at the back of my nose. And I swallowed. Only the background of piss and wood smoke was the same.

I must have looked surprised, but you could hardly have seen my face, or maybe you were better used to the dark. When I said, "I'm sorry. Is Mrs Selimovic here?" you shook your head.

"My English not good."

I tried again. "*Gde je Gospodja Selimovic, molim?*"

"Mrs Selimovic not live here," you said, which proved your English was better than my Serbo-Croat.

"Oh. I'm sorry." I turned to go, bewildered, I wasn't sure where. Another huge bang echoed down the street. You solved that problem by grabbing at my hand.

"Don't go. Not safe. Even with *pancir*, not safe," and you moved the hand up to touch my bulletproof vest. "*Granata*. Wait here. *Granata* will stop, maybe one hour, maybe two. Stay. Please." You moved your hand down again to clasp my wrist; I couldn't stop myself looking down at your hand on mine.

I actually hesitated. It was something to do with some ingrained habit about not talking to strange men – but it was more than that. I think I was scared of you. I think I was scared of your scent in my throat, your touch on my arm. Then we heard a shell whiz down a street away. I let you pull me in. We were in a long, high-ceilinged hall, with doors to either side. In the gloom I could see coats hung by the door, and the gleam of parquet underfoot.

"Go in kitchen," you said. "Is…" there was a silence as you tried to find the word.

"Safer?" I said into the gap.

"Safer." I saw your head nod. "No *granata*. Other side." I think you smiled, but I still couldn't see your face.

It was warmer in the kitchen, and much less dark, with the moonlight reflecting off the snow outside, thrown back by a shiny metal range in the corner. I could see you now. You were about my age, and your face, in the moonbeams, seemed beautiful to me, with great hollowed cheekbones and huge dark eyes, made darker and huger by the night outside. You said nothing, just looked back at me. I suddenly wished I was wearing something more flattering than my boots, a fleece, jeans and a lumpy great flak jacket, hat, my thick padded coat. Something elegant, and pretty, where I could flick my hair. I felt a frump, but in your silver ski jacket, you just looked like an advert on the side of a bus. I suddenly felt rather shy. I looked away from your face, and that was when I saw the sling.

"Your arm!" I think I was grateful for something to say. "What happened?"

"Is nothing."

"But you're hurt!"

"I got it on frontline." Your eyes gleamed.

"You were shot!"

"Not shot." A shrug. "Little piece of *granata*. But is nothing."

"How awful!" I know it was trite, but I couldn't bear to think of anything hurting you, even then.

"Don't worry." Maybe you didn't want me to be upset. You undid your sling, and pulled back the bandage. "It is not bad. See." A puckered line snaked five inches up the dark hairs on your forearm. The frozen moonlight leeched the light from your skin, but I could see it was still swollen.

"It must have been agony." I sounded pathetic, even to my own ears.

"What? No. Look, not so bad..." You smiled at me. "You want coffee?"

Before I could say yes or no, you opened a door on the other side of the kitchen. It had a homemade sign on it, saying *Ratna Zona* – war zone – with a death's head, a spoof of the ones you see on checkpoints right near the frontline.

"Is it dangerous in there?" I said, as you came back with a jar of brown powder.

"Not for you." You grinned. I smiled back.

"Sit down," you said. And I looked around, through the gloom: a stripped wood table, wooden chairs, wooden units, all finished off with orange and brown formica. In the middle of the room was a metal stove, with a Heath Robinson pipe snaking towards the window and something warming in a saucepan on its hob. The electric stove, covered in jars and plates, was obviously being used as just an extra bit of surface. "You like coffee?"

"Oh..." I didn't want you to waste your coffee on me. "I..."

"Not real coffee. Only war coffee." When I still hesitated, you said: "I want coffee." And went over to the stove.

I thought the coffee might be in the little pan, but it couldn't have been, because you dipped a metal jug into a huge blue bin, drew it dripping out and put it on the hob, moving the saucepan to one side. You turned and caught me looking at you. Neither of us spoke, until I looked away. Outside, a shell crumped down. You said: "Please, sit." I was grateful for that. It gave me something to do.

I was just pulling out a chair when I heard a living sound.

"What's *that*?" I stopped.

"My prisoner."

"Your prisoner!" You grabbed at me with your good arm, and pulled me towards the door. I hung back, as much as I could still being polite. I could hear Robert's voice in Kiseljak this morning: "War zones are full of nuts!"

You must have noticed me pulling, but all you said was: "Don't worry. No problem." And opened the door.

It was a larder, tall and square, but the shelves up the walls were largely empty; just a couple of bags of rice, cans of oil, and the labelled tins of meat and fish that I later realised were always given out in wars by the UNHCR. On one shelf, from a cage, a pigeon eyed us warily; it didn't flap round its cage, it just looked depressed. One of its wings hung limply at its side.

"What's that for?" I said.

"*Golub*. I not know your word."

"Pigeon. We call it a pigeon. But what's it for?"

"To eat." You said it, half proudly, half as if I were an idiot.

"How did you get it?"

"We shoot." You walked to the window. I hadn't noticed the gun leant up against the wall. You picked up the gun and Robert's voice came back again: "Full of nuts!" I was terrified for a moment; then you pointed it at the window, where the moonlight fought in through the plastic sheets. Then I thought you were mad: I thought somebody would see you and shoot straight back. I said: "Be careful!" just as you said: "Bang!"

Neither of us spoke for a few seconds, then from outside, from the hills, came an answering bang; the huge, round, generalised crash of a shell. You laughed, I laughed too. I was too nervous not to. It was then I saw it was just an air rifle. And we were laughing together.

"Your arm," I said, when we stopped. Because I had to say something.

"Is not so bad. Is one month now." You put down the gun and with your other hand, you took mine and guided my fingers along the scar. I caught my breath. For a moment neither of us spoke. Then you let my hand go and put your arm back in its sling. "For *Armija*, is still *very* bad."

"Oh..." You must have heard my slight disapproval that you were dodging the draft, because you quickly said, "Was very bad."

"Oh. OK." But then I supposed, to be fair, I wouldn't have wanted to sit on the lines this winter either. It was still about minus five, and we were into April now.

"Doctor thinks maybe have to cut arm off."

"Oh, my God!"

"But now is nearly OK." You lit the candle on the table, using both hands, then smiled at me, shrugged and slipped it back into its sling.

"Isn't it dangerous to point a gun out of the window?"

"Why?" You sounded amazed.

"Wouldn't someone see...the Serbs..." I trailed off... they might shoot back, I thought.

"Oh no. Serbs can't see here." You waved at the hill with the hospital. "They are on other side. How you not know that?"

"It's my first day in Sarajevo. I got here this morning."

"First day...you came in today?" You looked bewildered.

"It's been a nightmare," I said. "We'd been trying to get in for a week."

"I have not been outside Sarajevo for a year."

Perhaps it was a good thing the water boiled then. I watched you tip the coffee into the jug, stir it, and pour out two cups, keeping the grounds back with the long metal spoon. Your bad arm seemed quite good enough for that. You handed me a cup and watched as I took a sip.

"It's delicious," I said. "Thank you." But actually, it was horrid: bitter, grainy and sort of blank.

"Not delicious," you said, bitter as the coffee. "War coffee. Before war, in Sarajevo, we had best coffee in the world."

"Can you buy real coffee here now?" I hadn't seen any open shops.

You snorted. "Buy. You can *buy*. If you find. But costs eighty Deutschmark for kilo. Is only for mafia." I couldn't think of what to say: I'd drunk two cups of coffee in the Holiday Inn.

There was another loud crash. I jumped.

"Is OK," you said. "No shell ever in our garden." You gave me a reassuring smile.

"Thank you." I smiled back. And the silence stretched. I couldn't think of anything to say. It was as though I had to wait for something else to crack: another shell, or maybe another pigeon, or… then there was a plopping sound from the stove.

"Is ready." You leapt up.

"What are you cooking?"

You raised your eyebrows and grinned at me. "Death."

"*What!*"

"Death for pigeons. Look." You took my arm again and led me to the stove. In the pan was a thick, silver liquid. A bubble glooped up to the surface and popped.

"What is it?" You still had your hand on my elbow.

"I don't know how to say. Is metal. You make bullets."

"Lead?"

"I don't know." You hesitated. "I can write its name. I need pen." Mrs Selimovic hadn't had a pen either.

"I've got a pen. And paper. I'm a journalist."

"Journalist," you said. "That is why you are here."

I didn't really listen to your tone of voice. I was too busy rummaging around in my bag, amongst the torch, and the cigarettes, the Deutschmarks and the batteries. It was rather a relief to get my notebook out; it was a relief to have a good excuse. I always found it embarrassing, when you're talking to someone, and they think you are making conversation, but you start taking notes. And it breaks the connection.

But this connection – I wanted to break it. You kept staring at me. I kept staring back. The book would help. And also, all the interviews we'd done this afternoon would appear on the BBC, in Robert's piece in the *Herald* on Sunday. My piece wasn't coming out until the real anniversary on Tuesday. But this interview was all for me; it wasn't going to appear anywhere first. Besides, mild embarrassment is a constant state in journalism and I was getting used to it by now.

You took the pen from my hand.

"In chemistry, this," and wrote Pb.

"Lead," I said. I took the pen back and wrote it down.

'L...E...A...D *led*?" You read it from my page.

I nodded. "What is it for?"

"For rifle. I make bullets, then I shoot the pigeons."

"You make bullets?"

"How else I get them?"

"*How* do you make them? Where do you get the lead?" I looked up at you. "May I write this down? For my newspaper. Do you mind?"

"Why not?" But then you looked sad, and you said: "In Sarajevo, we are all stories now." I thought of Phil, saying as we'd spent lunch, in the icy dining room of the Holiday Inn, working out who we should see this afternoon: "The thing about Sarajevo is you can go up to anyone in the street and they're a great story."

You were a great story. The *News* loved your story. And later the *Herald* learnt to love you too. You told me about going out at night to the wrecks of shelled houses; taking lead from the pipes to melt, stair-treads and beams to burn; sun-dried bricks from the old Turkish houses, which you watered back into mud to make the bullet moulds, into which you poured the molten lead. I wrote it all down. And as we talked, you dredged your English up from the back of your brain where you'd kept it for the last year or so of war.

"It's like *Blue Peter*," I said: I wrote that down.

"What is *Blue Peter*?"

"Oh, it's nothing. I was just talking to myself."

"Talk to me. I am here." You sounded almost angry.

"It was just a stupid joke."

"I like jokes. Tell me."

"I can't explain..."

"Yes, you can." I looked up at you. Your face was set, and I felt butterflies of something leap in my stomach.

"It's a children's television programme in England..." there was another loud crash outside. I swallowed. I even gave a little laugh.

"Why you laugh?" You didn't sound funny.

"Because it's so ridiculous; to talk about an English children's television programme in the middle of a war."

"Tell me," you said. "Like there was no war."

So I told you about pencil holders made out of loo paper rolls, coat-hanger advent calendars and shoe boxes turned into dollies' beds. You said, rather sadly: "That is what all our life is now." You were silent, but this time you weren't looking at me. You were looking at some kind of past in your head. You said: "When we eat the pigeon, we pick out the pellets. Then we melt them down and use the lead again." I didn't say anything to that. I couldn't think of what to say.

It might have been nearly a minute before you took my hand.

"Come," you said, and pulled me to my feet. With your bad hand, you picked up the candle on the table.

"Don't worry, I've got a torch," I said. I was glad I had to disentangle my hand from yours to get the torch from my bag. You took it from me, and we crossed the hall and through the double doors you opened on the other side.

You flashed the beam round the room: it was the classic Austro-Hungarian cube, high ceilinged, a cornice and a picture rail, three tall windows wide, a shrouded chandelier hanging over it all. In the corner, on an old-fashioned tiled stove, shepherdesses danced through fields of ceramic flowers. The moonlight was blurred through the plastic sheeting taped where the glass ought to have been. The walls were pale, some colour it was too dark to see, but I could see they were almost completely covered with pictures. I squinted through the gloom: landscapes, abstracts, portraits, anything.

"Who's that?" A Victorian lady glowered down above a door in the right-hand wall.

"Grandmother of my mother," you said.

"She doesn't look like a Muslim," I blurted out.

For a few seconds, you didn't speak. And then you said: "She was *Hrvat*. She came from Austria a hundred years ago."

"Your mother's Croat?"

Another silence. Then you laughed. "My mother's mother was *Hrvat*. Her father *Srb*."

"You're a *Serb*!" I think I pulled back. I knew there had been Serbs in Sarajevo – before the war, the city had been thirty per cent Serb. But I didn't think you just bumped into them. I didn't think there were that many left.

You laughed again. "No," you said. "My father is Muslim."

"You're *mixed*?" I couldn't write it down as my book was in one hand and you had the other. But I didn't think I was going to forget.

"I am everything. Like Sarajevo." You turned away. The moonbeams danced over a grand piano; behind it, a huge hole gaped into the street. Like the windows, it was taped up with plastic sheeting.

You opened the doors beneath your great-great-grandmother. The room beyond was lined with books, but you could hardly get in for the detritus of war: dresses, a flowery bikini, a stiletto shoe, an ironing board, rigor-stiff, serpentine tangles of flexes, all bundled into cardboard boxes. A kettle, a toaster, a Magimix. It looked like a downmarket fence's lair. Or the *Generation Game* conveyor belt, but after *Blue Peter* I couldn't face explaining Bruce Forsyth too. Shrouding everything was a thick layer of dust, the gritty chunks thrown up by the artillery smashing the street outside.

"My computer," you said, and you kicked a box. A TV stood in one corner, as pointless as an idol in the British Museum. At its feet lay an electric guitar. You knelt and put your arm round its neck.

"My guitar," you said, about the same time as I said: "It's an electric mass grave."

"Grave." You nodded. "War killed them all. Like us." Then you looked up at me anxiously: "No, not grave...They are not dead. They will work again, after war? Won't they? Won't they?" It nearly hurt, the way you gripped onto my hand.

"Of course...The moment the electricity comes back. You'll just plug them in."

"Maybe war lasts too long?"

"They will work," I said again, because you looked so sad. "They will."

"Maybe..." Then you glanced across the room and smiled. "This, this works in war."

On a desk, in the corner, stood a tangle of glass, at one end of which a tube drained into a huge plastic bin.

"What is it?"

"Is slivovic. Spirit. Alcohol."

"Are you making it?" You nodded. I went and touched the still.

"Where did you get it from?"

"From university. My father is professor. *Granata* hit his laboratory."

I leant on the desk to write, my flak jacket heavy and in the way. "What do you make it from?" I said, without looking up.

"Fruit. We pick on frontline." I carried on writing.

"What does your mother do?"

"Architect. She jokes how she have lot of work after the war."

I could hear you smiling but I didn't look up as I asked: "What's your name?"

"Amir. Hadzibegovic, Amir."

I looked up then, and showed it to you: "Is that the right spelling?" You nodded.

"And how old are you?"

"Twenty-eight... How old are you?"

It was like I'd tripped on a stair. I raised my head.

"What?"

"How old are you?"

"Why?"

"You ask me. I ask you." You almost glared.

"I'm twenty-six," I said. But it felt strange telling him, as though he was seeing something private.

"So, I am older. What's *your* name?"

"I'm sorry, I should have said," this was more normal stuff. "My name's Molly Taylor. I'm writing for the *Evening News*. It's an English paper."

"I know *Evening News*," you said. I must have looked slightly surprised, because you explained: "We know all the papers here now. We are journalism experts in Sarajevo. CNN, BBC, Reuters. All here. You want drink?" You picked up one of the glasses sitting on the desk, wiped the dust off with your shirt and dipped it in the liquid and handed it to me.

"Slivovic." You got yourself a glass. "*Zivjeli,*" you said, and raised your glass to me.

I've always hated slivovic. Now I hate it more. Just the smell of it takes me straight back to you, to checkpoints in the snow. To drinking to false friendship with men in furry hats with cigarettes glued to their lips, so that they'll kick the anti-tank mines out of the way and let you pass. Then it just tasted like the worst drink you ever drank on holiday. It was always the same dilemma: too slowly, you could taste it. Too fast, they poured you more.

It would have been too rude not to drink your slivovic.

"*Zivjeli,*" I sipped.

"Is good, no?"

"Yes, it's good." Or as good as I could possibly expect. Another shell crashed down.

"Go back to kitchen. Is... safer. Yes?" You smiled as you produced the word. "Back of house safer."

"Much safer." I smiled back. There was a warm fizz in my blood and the slivovic no longer tasted so bad. "Would you like a cigarette?"

"Cigarette?" you gasped, as though I were offering gold.

I gave you the choice of the Ronstons I'd bought in Split, and a packet of my duty-free Silk Cut. You went for the Balkan lung exterminators. Later you used to say you could never see the point of Silk Cut; too weak to smoke. We must have smoked about twenty and both got slightly drunk. You told me what you had done before the war: you'd been a travel agent, you said, down in Split. Your parents had wanted you to be a lawyer but you wanted to make a fortune and see the world.

"Now all I ever see is the view on my frontline. Not even that now," you pointed to your arm. I wrote some of it down, but the longer I stayed, the less I wrote; it didn't seem to matter, I didn't think I'd ever forget.

You asked me why I was here, and I held my breath. Then I said, I just couldn't imagine not wanting to be here. You laughed and said, you couldn't imagine not wanting to get out. I said, what's happening here is just so *unfair*. And you looked very sad, as though you couldn't explain. You said, for some of you it was impossible to understand why it had happened. There had never been problems before.

"How long you been in Sarajevo?"

"I told you. This is my first day."

"First day! So... Am I your first Sarajevan?"

"Not quite." I told you about meeting the man in Tarcin three days ago, who'd asked us to take Mrs Selimovic her parcel. I didn't even notice your guilty look when I mentioned her name. Then I told you about the men I'd met with Phil that afternoon: the brewery manager, the Muslim still making beer, and the man in the mortuary, with the heavy eyebrows, and the sadness carved into his face, who showed us in his candlelit office what he called the book of the dead, while behind him on the sofa a man wept into a woman's breast, as she gently tried to stroke the grief from his hair. Phil called him the tallyman of the siege. He had given me the score for the week. You knew him too.

"Everyone in Sarajevo knows Osman now."

"That's what Osman said too."

"So, first day in Sarajevo..."

"But not first day in Bosnia..." I told him about my job. I'd got fed up, I said, of having to write pieces about inflatable bikinis in London for the *Daily Mail*. You said, "No bikinis here."

You asked me if I were married, and I said, no. You asked me if I had a boyfriend. I thought briefly of Johnny, back in his bank, half a continent away; and suddenly, for the first time in weeks, I minded much less that he fucked that other girl the last time I'd been away, and then told me I was mainlining on someone else's war. You asked about my parents, and I explained about Daddy being a diplomat, thousands of miles away, and my mother being dead.

"So you are alone," you smiled at me.

"Oh no. I've got a brother. But he's abroad too." I didn't explain he was currently mine-clearing in Afghanistan.

Then you asked me how long I would be in Sarajevo.

"I'm only here to write about the anniversary of the siege," I laughed. "It's my big break. But it's just a few days. Sarajevo costs a fortune, you know."

You laughed: "I know," you said. Neither of us mentioned the danger at all.

"What were you doing," I asked you, "when the war began?"

You didn't answer at first. I let the silence run. I knew by then that was the way to get someone to talk. I was disappointed when all you said was: "I wish we had music. I want to play you song." You waved at the darkness. "I have cassette player but there is no power."

"I have batteries," I said. "In my bag."

"*Batteries!*" You spoke as though I had said I carried something precious or exotic, like diamonds or pomegranates, or a model Ferrari.

You took my torch and went back across the hall. I heard the sound of rummaging in the other room, then you came back with a ghetto blaster, coated with dust, and a tape.

"This is my song," you said, and put it on.

"I came up from coast for few days, one year ago. War started and I could not get back." You shrugged, and the tape gave its starting whir.

"I did not want to leave, then, you understand." You stared straight into my eyes. "We all had to help. But nobody thought it would be a year..." You stopped. You were staring at something far away. You took a drag of your cigarette. Then I heard you say:

"First time I killed someone, I was so scared. He came towards me, he was across street. I was so *scared*," you said again. "I shot until gun was empty. Thirty-six bullets."

Out of the tape recorder, Freddie Mercury sang: "*Mama, just killed a man, put a gun against his head. Pulled my trigger now he's dead. Mama, life had just begun, but now I've gone and thrown it all away...*"

"He was same age as me," you said. "He could have been my friend."

In the silence after that I realised that the bombardment had stopped; it's only when you haven't heard a crash for a while that you know.

"I'd better go back," I said.

"Stay here," you put your hand on my arm. For a moment, I had this urge to stay with you. But I shook it off, as I shook off your arm. I couldn't quite understand what was going on. Today was all too new, too strange for me.

"I have to go."

"Do you have to really?"

"Yes. I really do." But I didn't really, except it was all too much.

"Where to? Where you stay?"

There would be no point going to the Presidency now; they'd have left ages ago. "The Holiday Inn," I said. I felt a thrill of pride as I said its name. Your face fell.

"Why you stay there?" I didn't know what to say. I mean, everyone stayed there, didn't they?

"Everyone stays there," I said.

"Is very dangerous," you said. But I couldn't see it would be more dangerous than here.

"I have to go back. My friends will be worried about me."

"OK." You seemed to accept that as an excuse. "My mother come back soon, now bombardment over...I hope she come back...she went to see friend..."

I stared at you in shock and it was you who took my hand as if to console me. "Don't worry. She come back. She not go far. Here..." You picked up the tape recorder and took the batteries out.

"I don't need them," I said, and took my hand away.

You stood there uncertain.

"Keep them," I said. "I've got lots of spares."

"Thank you," you said, and stared down at them in your palm, as if they had been diamonds indeed.

"So, goodbye..." I said.

You looked up at me: "I see you again?"

"I'm leaving on Tuesday." I wasn't sure, but I think I wanted to run away.

"Today is Friday," you said. We looked at each other. I didn't know what to say. I didn't know what I wanted to say. And then I remembered with relief I'd need a photograph; and as we agreed for a photographer to come the next day, all the tensions seeped out of our farewell.

It was as you shepherded me to the door, palm on my back, that you said, "How you go to Holiday?"

"Walk."

"No." You stopped. "Is not safe to walk to Holiday Inn."

"I'll run. I'll be fine," I said. "I've got this." I touched the front of the flak jacket with the arm I'd just picked up from under yours. I was still wearing it. I'd been wearing it all the time. "It's not far."

"Is dark."

"At least the snipers can't see me."

"Girls do not walk in dark. I come with you."

I felt terrified for you in a way I hadn't for me. "That's stupid. You'll just have to come back."

"Is OK."

"No," I said. "It's not OK. I'm fine on my own."

"Really?"

"Really."

You nodded. "OK. So. Tomorrow then."

"Tomorrow. With the photographer."

It was at the door you turned and said to me: "Tomorrow, you can stay. Stay for dinner. My mother is here. She cook pigeon."

I didn't even hesitate. "I'd love to," I said.

And then of course you asked if I knew the way.

"I came from the hotel," I said, "but I was in a car." I was suddenly afraid. What I did know is that it was novices like me who were always getting shot.

"I show you."

"It's fine…"

"Come, I just show you. Don't go down to Presidency – very bad. Hotel is over there," you pointed over the main road at the end of your street, where a slice of empty dual carriageway showed at the end of the alley beyond. "Go here. At street, run. Snipers can see you. Over big road run very fast. Then go along street, maybe two-hundred metres. Every time you cross roads, snipers can see you. Snipers are on mountain. Every time you see mountain, sniper can see you, so run. Go left, past hospital, down little hill. By white apartment buildings, down hill. You will see hotel. But run. Is very bad round hotel."

"I'll run."

You kissed me on the cheek, but as we drew back, you said: "I come with you to end of street."

I couldn't think of a reason to say no. Actually, I couldn't think of anything to say as you held my arm.

"Ice," you said. "Is…"

"Slippery."

"Slippery. Yes. But snipers can't see here."

"Just shells."

You laughed. There was a silence again; the moonlight had cleaned the filthy snow on the road. And above the roofs, we could see a slice of sky. Ahead of us, beyond the two streets I had to cross, a street rambled up between low blocks of flats.

"Look at the stars," I said. "They are incredible. You never see stars like that in London any more."

"No electricity."

We reached the road. You pulled us into the shadow of a house. A bullet cracked. The ragged blankets strung from the power lines above the road wafted in the breeze. There were the ubiquitous gym lockers, but they were too far down the road to be any use to me.

"Is very dangerous here. Run very fast."

Another crack. I was suddenly terrified. I think it was the first time I realised what I was about to do, but you didn't notice, you carried on explaining. "It's dark. Really they cannot see you. And maybe they are drunk. They always drink in evening. But run. Always, when you see the mountains. There is one very bad place. But you must just run."

You kissed me again, and this time it just missed my lips.

"I wait till you get to other side of road."

"Yes." My heart was pounding, the spit had gathered in my mouth, and my stomach felt watery and sick. "I'll see you tomorrow," I said.

"Run."

I ran. As fast as I could, as I dared, skidding over the ice. I didn't want to be a sprawling target in the slush. The moonbeams on the snow were lighting my way, but that meant anyone who wanted could see me too. I ran until I reached the shelter of the other side. When I turned, you were still there. You waved, I waved back. "Run!" you yelled. So I turned, and ran again.

I ran up the hill, keeping to the left, so I ran deep in the shadow of the flats. I didn't have to run, the hills couldn't see me, but I wasn't sure enough to stop running yet. I ran past a turning down to my left, I hardly looked, I didn't dare, but I still saw a glimpse of mountain between the bullet-riddled sheets strung across the alley. I ran on, and then suddenly the flats fell away to my left, and for maybe fifty yards, the view of the mountains opened up. Below some railings was a playground, at least I think it was that, but I didn't stop to look; a row of gym lockers, leant against the railings, tried to block off as much as it could of the view. It must have been beautiful, with the moon on the snow, and the fir trees black, hiding their secrets on the crags, but I just ran. I didn't give myself time to look, with the moonlight shining in jets through the holes in the gym lockers. I ran and ran, my flak jacket thumping up and down, till I reached the flats on the other side. And then I stopped. Even I could tell they couldn't see me here. If I could live that last fifty yards, I could live through anything.

I walked, but fast, until I reached the next gap. I poked my head round and pulled it back; there was the Holiday Inn, down below, maybe a hundred yards away. I hadn't even spent one night in it, and yet when I saw it I knew I was nearly home.

There was a slope, covered, as much as it could be, with the now-familiar gym locker and hanging sheet routine. The lockers were arranged in rows, like interlocking teeth, so you could slalom your way through the chicane, and stay out of sight as long as you could; the ones in the background of that photograph.

At the bottom, the slope opened up into a large open space of grass and cement. There were no gym lockers here, no hanging sheets. The space was too wide. There was nothing to hang the sheets from. At its centre was the Holiday Inn, set like a postcard, against the mountains beyond. I took a deep breath and I started to run.

MUJO AND SULJO are talking in their trench.

"Do you know Haso is dead?" Suljo said. "He was shot by a sniper."

"Where was he hit?"

"In the finger," said Suljo.

"Well, why's he dead?"

"He was picking his nose."

IV

It was dark by the time I crunched back up your stairs. I meant to come earlier, in the afternoon, but I couldn't. I had to work. You didn't understand that. You never really could.

I heard voices through the frosted glass as I knocked. I swallowed as your footsteps approached, to keep the butterflies from choking me.

I put my face up at an angle as you opened the door – I thought you'd kiss me hello, as you'd kissed me goodbye – not anything else, just a social kiss. But instead, you stood back and said: "I thought you not come."

"I'm sorry."

I didn't need your face to see how angry you were. Your voice sounded tight, and your shoulders were rigid against the faint glow of light.

"You said you come with photographer but you did not come."

"I'm sorry," I said again, but I was surprised, really, not sorry. "I had to work." But you turned away from me, and I followed you into the hall. That must have been the first time I felt angry with you – I thought, I've risked my life to see you tonight, and you are sulking because I couldn't come this afternoon. I was *working*... I didn't have a choice.

"I thought you decided to stay with your friends," you said, and

I caught your scent. It was different today. A cleaner smell. Not that you'd smelt bad yesterday – it was too cold to sweat – but your hair was featherier against the light. "I thought you not come."

"They're not my friends," I said; "I hardly know them at all."

I could see them all, breath vapour and smoke in the candlelight; sitting in Phil's office, high up on one of those galleries, room 309 of the Holiday Inn, after dinner last night. Huddled in their fleeces, their little woolly hats, drinking the whisky and wine Robert or someone had brought in from Split. "You don't want to drink the wine here if you can avoid it," said Phil. "You don't know where it's been." "But we do know," said an American girl with a ridiculous name. "We're in a *siege*. It can only have been in the cellar of the Holiday Inn. Unless you think – gasp – the management has been *smuggling*!" And she put up her hand to her mouth in mock-shock like one of the girls in *Scooby Doo*. She looked like one of the *Scooby Doo* girls too, the clever one, with the glasses and the bob. Everyone laughed; they always seemed to be laughing at things she said; they must have been in-jokes, because most of them went over my head, although I definitely found them funnier as the evening went on.

We'd sat chain-smoking, feet up on the glass coffee table in the candlelight, the room full of waving arms, as people took turns to hold forth – names like Karadzic and Mladic – the Bosnian Serb sports psychiatrist-turned-president and his bull-necked general – bandied around by people who'd actually met the guys. "*Met* them! I've had Karadzic read me his poetry!" said the American girl. "And Mladic has this huge boil on the back of his neck. Last time I was itching to just give it a squeeze…"

Robert, on what Slobo – as everyone called President Milosevic – was *really* up to in Belgrade these days; the American girl on whether we really all *ought* to be in Tuzla; Phil pointing Tuzla out, far in the corner of one of those maps of Bosnia stuck up on nearly every wall: ethnic maps and political maps and maps where the UN thought the frontlines were, marked "United Nations: not to be shown to members of the local population" as though, said the American girl, someone who'd lived there all their life might suddenly say "so now I know where Tuzla is". Every now and then, there'd be a knock, and someone would come in and ask Phil if they could use the phone; I already knew the phones in the rest of Sarajevo hadn't worked for a year, but Robert explained that the BBC had one of the only two satellite phones in the hotel, and charged £8 a minute for other journalists to use it, "Thank God," said Phil, "otherwise I wouldn't have any friends." He'd wave to it in the corner and say: "Just write it down – the Beeb will bill your paper direct." I'd noticed, last night, that he didn't offer everyone drinks, although most people seemed to want to hang around. Valida just sat there, on the grey draylon sofa with Henri, not that you could see it was grey in the candlelight reflecting off the smeary glass.

I'd felt a bit shy at first, but Phil had waved me in: "This is Molly," he said. "She's here for the *News*." And they nodded, and seemed to take me as one of them, although so far, most of them didn't really talk to me.

This evening had been exactly the same. I kept looking at my watch and I knew I ought to leave, but somehow it was very hard to make myself actually stand up. I'd been looking forward to coming: to see you again, to spend time with you, to spend time with Sarajevo. I'd crashed from interview to interview with Phil today, but I wanted to get to know Sarajevo, I wanted to know its soul. Doing interviews with Phil wouldn't be enough for that. But every time I thought I ought to leave, someone poured me another glass of wine. The American girl, Muffy, she seemed to be called, although that sounded rather unlikely but I'd met so many new people these last few days, said I was mad to go out tonight. I said I'd promised. But she said, it's too nasty today. Listen to the snipers. We all stared at where the plastic sheets hung in the window, as if we could see the noise amongst the mountains silhouetted against the moon. There was an answering run of cracks. In our silence, we could hear Phil signing off, in his bedroom next door: "This is Phil Kennedy, for the BBC, in Sarajevo."

Phil came back in as Henri – Valida's boyfriend, I'd realised by now, and the photographer I'd sent round to you this afternoon – was saying: "You see. You're mad. Eez a shooting gallery out zere," and Phil said in fake French, "shooting gallerrrrrrrEEEEEEEE…"

"You don't die, just because you said you'd go for dinner," said Muffy. And Valida suddenly spoke: "If you say you go for dinner, you should go."

I nodded, and smiled at her. "I think so too." For the first time, she gave me a little smile back. There was an embarrassed silence. Muffy just shrugged. Phil gave me a long hard look, I stared back. Finally he said: "Don't worry, I'll give you a lift." But part of me wished I could have stayed; we could hear their laughter echoing right down the atrium.

But I didn't. I came here. And all you did was sulk.

You were still sulking as you introduced me to your mother, but she was so pleased to see me it almost made up for the ill-will I could feel simmering at my back.

Like Phil's office, your kitchen was full of candlelight, the thick smell of cooking meat; I could feel my saliva beginning to collect. I was starving. I'd eaten nothing since lunch, apart from a Mars Bar at about five, and a few crisps at the BBC. It was warmer than the hall, but the woman standing by the window still needed her coat. She was slim (she later told me she had lost twenty kilos in the war – the Sarajevo diet, she said. Sarajevo is my gym) and her face must once have been lovely but beneath the same thick foundation and lipstick that Valida wore, you could see the darkness of this war furrowed deep in her skin. As she turned to me, I saw the glint of gold at her ears, and a pendant round her neck. Your mother had put on her best clothes for me.

You introduced me. We shook hands. And then nothing was said. You were too sulky to speak, and your mother and I had no way to talk. We gestured at each other – she glanced at you, but you were just glaring at me. So I handed her the plastic bag I was carrying instead. At least I knew the Serbo-Croat for that.

Her eyes widened when she opened the bag. "*Kafa, cokolada,* whisky, cigarettes," she said as she pulled them out onto the table. "Mollee!" she stared at me in amazement. And said something else. I glanced at you. You had changed now – you looked too confused to sulk.

"My mother says is too much. It is too much."

"It's not," I said. I knew it wasn't, because Phil had given it to me. Take these, he'd said, you can't go to dinner in Sarajevo empty-handed; he'd gone to a cupboard by the side of the door. In the twilight I could see rows of stuff like Marmite, boxes of PG Tips and blocks of cheese. He shrugged when I said I'd pay him back; he said I could buy him some stuff at the PX. I didn't ask what that was. I felt a bit thick, but I did tell him I could pay him back with the spare cigarettes up in my room.

"Too much," you looked angry again, but it was a different kind of anger; you didn't seem to be angry with me. When I looked at you, suddenly I could see that you'd shaved. "You did not have to do this."

"It's nothing," I said. "I was given it by a friend. I'll just get him some more." I didn't understand then why you looked so confused.

Your mother had lit herself one of the cigarettes, and was staring where the moonlight striped in through the shutters from the snows outside. You lit one too. I pulled out mine from my bag. Have one of these, you said, they're yours, waving the packet at me. But I said, no, thanks, they're too strong, as I lit myself a Silk Cut.

Then she spoke: you laughed, then you said: "She wants to know when you leave."

"Tuesday," I said, and I felt sad as I said it. Your mother's face fell.

"She says Tuesday is too soon. She says thank you very much."

"I know," I said. "I wish I could stay."

You laughed. You translated and your mother laughed too.

"She says everyone else here wishes to leave." She took another drag, and spoke sadly to me, before fixing her eyes back on the shutters again.

"She says before war she always try to give up. Now is no point to give up, but she never has cigarettes."

It was maybe a minute before your mother came back to life.

"Whisky!" she said, and picked up the glasses on the table.

"Or maybe you prefer our slivovic," you said, and your voice was heavy with irony. I didn't know what to say. I hated slivovic. But I didn't want your mother to waste her whisky on me. So I said slivovic; but that was obviously wrong. You looked astonished and your mother's face fell.

"You can't mean that," you said, as if you thought I was lying. Your mother laughed. She said something which sounded like, she likes our slivo. You didn't translate, but I could get that much.

"I don't mind." I just wanted to do the right thing. But she started pouring us all whisky anyway. She rolled it round her mouth, sighed and said something else, then lapsed back into silence again.

"She says she hasn't had whisky since the war began."

You and I didn't speak. It was one of those silences it became embarrassing to break, the tensions growing as the silence went on, to snap back on whoever broke it first. It hadn't been like this yesterday. I suppose it was your mother, but then she didn't seem to notice it. She seemed lost somewhere, drawing memories into her lungs.

Finally she stubbed out her cigarette, and checked her watch. She looked very sad as she moved over to the stove. I think my stomach rumbled in relief; I had been drooling from the smell ever since I walked in.

There was a heavy black pan on the side of the stove. She took the lid off it, prodded it, and put it onto the heat. You apologised, as you put some pickled carrots on the table.

"I love carrots," I said but actually I'd had pickled carrots for every meal for the last two days, and back in those days I hated pickles anyway.

You shot me a suspicious look.

"In England," I said, "we say carrots make you see in the dark."

"That is good for Sarajevo." Then, for the first time that evening, you smiled at me; your kooky teeth lit up your face, and you leant over and stroked my hand. I didn't pull it back; I let you hold it and smiled back into your eyes, and as I smiled, I felt nothing could ever go wrong again.

"I thought I never see you again," you said.

"I said I would come, so I came."

If your mother hadn't arrived with a plate, I don't know when we'd have moved. But before I ate, I knew there was something I wanted to do. I stood up, and said, "Can you give me a hand?" Then I uncrunched the Velcro at my waist and pulled my flak jacket over my head. You took it from me, brushing my hair, and propped it up against the wall. It slumped, as though it had been shot, and the white label on its chest suddenly seemed self-important and silly: Molly Taylor, *Evening News*, A+ (for my blood group, not my performance as a hack, but I was new enough out of university to like the mark).

"It's just in case…" the foreign editor had said, and neither of us had finished the sentence…

You smiled. "Much better. Before, you look like…I don't know, little animal," you mimed it, "with shell and little head."

"A tortoise…"

"Yes, tortoise. Now you look like girl." I blushed, but you had already turned to the stove.

The food on the plate you handed me was a brown mess of rice. You both were watching as I lifted my fork. I schooled my expression, just in case. But it lived up to its smell.

"This is the best thing I've eaten in Sarajevo." Your mother blushed. You didn't add that I'd only got here yesterday, and my only other food had been a watery soup, the pickled carrots, of course, with a strange flat meatball thing the Holiday Inn had served, both at dinner last night and at lunch today. I didn't know, of course, then, that it was all they ever served. Nor, then, did I know I'd be grateful for it.

"Mama is top chef at war cooking. It is pigeon from yesterday."

I thought of the sad-eyed bird staring at me with hope mixed with resignation from its cage.

Your mother laughed and spoke. "Poor pigeon. But," you shrugged as you translated, "she says, is war, what you can do?"

I got the recipe off her, before the evening was out. It was a good enough excuse to get out my book; I knew I had to. I knew I wouldn't remember it all. I was worried it would be like yesterday, when you hadn't seemed to like it when I started to write. But it wasn't, and your mother wanted to tell me how her life had become: the monthly rations doled out by the UNHCR, standing in line for her tins of tuna, oil, milk powder; the flour they gave, so full of maggots, she said, you called it protein powder.

"Before war," you explained, as she broke off, "my mother says you must know. We have communism here, but not like in Romania or Russia. We had *good* communism...we have everything we want... we have mountains, we have sea. We can travel, go to Italy on holiday. If Polish and Czech people come here, we are like kings to them, but now... now we are worse, much worse than people in Poland or Russia."

Your mother listed the endless chores of the war: queuing for bread, foraging for something to burn in the house, queuing for water down in the street – water to drink, water to wash, water to flush the loo. No wonder, I thought, you didn't shave much.

"The water's a nightmare," I said. Your mother looked utterly bewildered as I broke in, as if the war could have nothing to do with me. "We don't have any either. I had to carry loads up from the restaurant last night. Five flights of stairs."

Or I had been supposed to. It wasn't that I'd forgotten, I'd just drunk so much with Phil last night that somehow the water hadn't seemed to matter that much. Even though Robert's last words to me, as he went upstairs to finally write his piece, were: "Whatever you do, don't forget the water. Like Phil said, sharing a room in Sarajevo can be pretty gross." But, then, I didn't really understand what he meant; and anyway, I was too busy, like a new girl, drinking the whole thing in.

Even in twenty-four hours, I could see the Holiday Inn had its own hierarchy: based partly on the importance of your news organisation and partly on residence. Like the BBC, Reuters, CNN and the *New York Times* had kept a bureau here, with their correspondents rotating in and out. The British broadsheets mostly had stringers – retained correspondents. It was just that most of them had gone off to Tuzla. As a freelancer, on my first day, writing a one-off for a British tabloid, I was pretty low (although not as low as the ex-marine freelancing for the *Anchorage Bugle*, it became apparent from Muffy's sneer, who lived in an apartment in town and had never been known to file). Muffy, who worked for one of those East Coast American papers read by earnest people who care about world affairs, explained a lot of things, like whether to wear your flak jacket in bed ("I never do," she said, "but people have been known to. I never even wear mine inside").

Anyway, being the product of embassies and the English public school system, hierarchies make me feel at home and this was like being let in to the cool gang at school. I'd always been towards the nerd end of the cool-o-meter before: nudging the Chinese physicists. Johnny used to say if I hadn't been pretty, I would have been a total dork.

But these people were far too clever to have ever made the real cool gang either. Like me, they'd have been the swots; worked hard, passed exams, only smoked behind the bike sheds if they had a contingency plan. Got the work/drink ratio right at university, been conscientious and ambitious in their careers, and had now broken away to form their own autonomous cool gang in this freezing hotel, where snipers pinged bullets outside the windows and the night was bisected by the green slash of tracer fire. Chain-smoking, downing the whisky people brought in and always talking the story, in circles, the story, so it was just like being at university but we were all reading the same course.

"You're mad to leave Sarajevo once you've got here," said Phil. "Would you stay if you had a string?"

And I said: "Like a shot."

So it wasn't surprising that the water slipped my mind. Robert had said four or five bottles, but, by the time I left Phil, it seemed far too much. I only took two. It didn't seem to matter too much anyway. Cleaning my teeth or my face seemed totally pointless, and I couldn't have flushed the loo because it would wake Robert, so the fact that there was no water made no difference to me either. I really couldn't see what everyone complained about. I didn't even feel cold.

I probably wouldn't have woken Robert at all, in fact, if I hadn't tripped over my bag. I had decided not to use my torch as it would ruin my night vision. I said "sorry", and "it's only me", and then "go back to sleep". Although I took advantage of having woken him up to look for my pyjamas. I couldn't find them for a bit; they seemed to have changed shape and got much noisier. Then I drank straight off one of the bottles of water I had carried up. I put the other bottle by my bed, got into my pyjamas, which kept on crackling, and went to the loo, shutting myself into the pitch-dark box to minimise the incredible noise my pee seemed to make, found my bed and went to sleep, the moment my head touched the pillow, just like one of the Famous Five.

When I'd woken this morning, my eyeballs felt like they had been poached in vinegar and rolled in sand, and the fumes were slowly expanding and crushing my brain. I rushed to the loo, and sat, with my hangover crap, cooling my forehead on the tiles of this pitch-black box. And then there was nothing to wash it all away – all your hooch, that disgusting Holiday Inn wine, and the whisky Phil had weaned me onto by the end. And the only water was five whole floors down.

"Our water is two streets away," I heard you say. "And snipers shoot us as we run back."

Your mother smiled and looked proud, you blushed, she repeated it, nodding at me. "She says to tell you I have made cart," you said. But you looked embarrassed. "To pull water home," you explained.

I was still hungry. There was some risotto left in the pan; our servings had been only the size that rich women push round smart restaurant plates. I couldn't stop myself staring at it, but it obviously wasn't on offer, because your mother got up and put some coffee on. I remembered wistfully the cheese I still had stashed in my room from the supplies Robert and I had bought in Split. And I thought of Phil, asking me if I'd eaten before coming out; no, I said, they're giving me dinner. He'd made a face and said: "Better to always eat something before you go round to Sarajevans for dinner." But I hadn't bothered because, God help me, I was worried that, after all those last decent meals, I had put on weight.

You must have seen my glance. Because you said: "Is for father. He is on frontline. He come back soon." Your mother spoke some English, because she understood that; she closed her eyes quickly, then nodded at me, as if anything else would be too horrible to think.

I was glad it was dark, because you couldn't see me blush.

"Where is he?"

There was a silence, then you said: "Zuc."

We both knew there'd been a lot of fighting up there today. I'd watched it from the BBC office, with a mug of Nescafé in my hand, after Phil had driven me back from the daily UN briefing. He'd called it "the nine o'clock follies" but I thought it was more like a weather forecast, and the military spokesman had certainly said it was stormy on Zuc. Peering round the window frame, perched on Phil's desk, I could see the plumes of smoke, curling up through the snow-covered pines, to be lost in white wisps across the azure sky. Seconds later, we would hear the blast. So beautiful, so far away; it was hard to believe that real people were manning those guns, they should have been plastic soldiers, about an inch and a half high.

Your mother had gone quiet again. She sat smoking, and picked up her whisky. Finally she started to speak, and the good humour of earlier on had gone. "It's terrible," that's what you told me she said. "*Grozny.* Terrible. How can we live like this? Cabbage costs twenty Deutschmarks in the market. How can we live?" That was pre-euro of course, and it was all in Deutschmarks, and there were 2.5 of them to the pound. For some reason, the dollar was virtually worthless here.

The water boiled, and she picked up the shiny packet I'd given her and went to the stove. "Coffee… real coffee…" you translated as she spoke. "I have not had real coffee for months. Thank you for this." She spooned it into the water, and poured the coffee into tiny cups, keeping the grounds back with a spoon. She repeated, as you had yesterday, "Eighty Deutschmarks, one kilo for coffee. Sugar… thirty Deutschmarks. How can we live? We have no sugar now."

I thought of the sugar bowls sitting on the dining room tables of the Holiday Inn, the sugar I didn't take because I didn't want to get fat.

"I can get you sugar," I said. "We have it in the hotel."

You said something to your mother who shook her head.

"She says the Holiday Inn is another world."

There was a sound from the front door. You leapt to your feet but your mother pushed past you, out of the door. I could hear her crying "Murat, Murat, Murat!"

You said to me: "Is *Tata*. He is home."

The man who came into the kitchen was in camouflage fatigues, as so many men of his age were here. He had grey hair and the greyness of exhaustion showed in his skin. He had his arm round your mother, and as she looked into his eyes, his smile pushed its way through the weariness. They walked towards you, and he gathered you into his other arm. I didn't need to speak Serbo-Croat to understand what he said. It was just "my son," which is nearly the same.

Perhaps he was just too tired to have noticed me, but you took him by the arm and did the introductions. He was almost too tired to look surprised. Or perhaps the war had knocked all surprise out of him.

"*Dragomir je,*" he said, and nodded at me.

"*Dragomir je,*" I said in return. Then he turned away. He sat down at the table very carefully, as if he was worried he would not be able to control his descent. His wife said something about pigeons. He smiled, stroked her hand, and used his other to prop up his head. She put a plate in front of him and handed him a fork. It took a while before he lifted the first mouthful, as though getting the fork to his mouth was too much to do. Then he tasted it, looked up at her, smiled, "*Vrlo dobro,*" and had another mouthful. You could see it was a fight for him not to shovel it in. She watched him eat with such intensity; as if she were scared if she looked away, he might vanish, maybe into a puff of smoke, and curl up to the crags below which he had been fighting all day.

This was a thousand poems, I thought; the warrior returns. I had scanned it in Latin, struggled over it in Greek, admired its chiaroscuro in Italian galleries and wept as I watched it played out on screen. But I had never yet witnessed it in real life.

He had probably eaten half his plateful before he saw the bottle. "Visky! ahh." His wife poured him a glass. I heard her mention my name, because he turned to me and said "thank you" in heavily accented English.

"You speak English?" I said. He shook his head. "*Deutsch. I Russki? Gavarete pa-russki?*"

I shook my head back. He turned to you.

"He wants to tell you something," you said.

"OK."

But having said that, your father didn't seem to know what it was. He pushed his fork round the plate for a moment before he began. You translated as the sentences came.

"He says when he was boy, his father have one house in woods. We shoot pigeons in woods…" your father broke off; he looked almost angry… "Even pigeons are thin now with war, he says… He wants to know what you are doing here?"

"I'm a journalist," I said; I felt embarrassed again, it sounded so silly: "I'm writing a piece about the anniversary of the siege."

Your father snorted.

"A year ago he says he just finish one film for TV, with best director in Yugoslavia. About his trees… My father is professor of forestry. Now director of film is in Beograd, making propaganda… He says he is still with his trees, but now he is in trench in frontline in woods… He wants to show you film. He says has video but no electricity… He says before war we have one of best National Parks in the world, virgin forest. Now, all is mined. He wants to know, when it will change?"

You and he looked to me as if I might know the answer.

As I said, "I don't know," I felt failure dig its fingers into my heart. I glanced at your mother, but she was just staring into her glass.

"He says he will show you his film, when electricity is back."

"I would like that," I said. Then I couldn't think of anything else to say.

His eyes lit up when your mother offered coffee. "*I cokolada*," she said and Amir gestured at me. Your father smiled, leant across the table and shook my hand.

"He says you have made him a special welcome home feast. He says you can come again whenever you like."

The food seemed to have reinflated him. He looked at me, and raised his glass.

"*Zivjeli!*" He knocked some back. "Look, me *Mujahadeen*." He jabbed at his nose and rolled his eyes. He had your dark hair, dark eyes welling out of the same pale skin, although his skin had been weathered by war. In truth, with his profile sweeping from his high forehead to the bridge of his nose, he looked very much like the Turkish warriors his ancestors must have been, galloping north, ramming their scimitars deep into Europe. He drained the whisky and put his glass out for more.

"Fundamentalist. Crazy." He tapped the side of his head; in the next bit all I understood were "Islamic" and "Maria". You spoke.

"The *Chetniks* say we want to make Islamic state here. Is crazy. Why he want Islamic state, he says. He not want my mother to wear..." I met your eyes as you trailed your hand over your mouth.

"A yashmak?" I said, but I was looking at your lips.

"Yashmak. Is Turkish word?"

"I guess so," I said. Murat twitched his head in denial.

"He say my mother is Christian."

Maria gave a sad laugh and spoke.

"My mother says she is not Christian. She was good communist."

This time I let you walk me home. Your mother insisted anyway: the whisky bottle was over half gone and she had reached the expansive hospitality stage.

"Sarajevo is for walking," she said. "Was. It was beautiful to walk."

Your street was a ravine, deep in its shadow, just the stars sharp in the blackness above. We walked to the corner and the view opened up. It was another majestic night. I looked, as I found I was always looking, up to the hills: the houses, clinging to their lower slopes, the darkness of the pines rimming the cliffs, hiding God knows what kind of threat; the moon, and the snowfields stretching up until they cracked against the starlit sky. Down to the Presidency to the right, through the blankets limply straddling the street.

You grabbed my hand. "Here we must run."

So we ran. When we reached the other side, you didn't let go. We walked hand in hand for 200 yards. "Run here!" you said. "Big road. This is very bad..." You waved at the blankets, again, hanging from the power lines, and lumps of ice lying in our way; the twisted sign-posts, the shattered windows of the flats opposite, all like a black and white film, in the silvery light, and moonbeams again, gleaming off the dome of the Pasha's mosque, half hidden in shadow at the mountains' foot. We ran and ran, laughing like lunatics, the way you do when you're afraid and with a friend. Then we walked, still holding hands; walking until the next bit of open ground, with the railings, and the gym lockers beneath the mountains and the moon. "Run," you said, and we ran again, and this time when we stopped you put your arm round my shoulder. "It's cold," you said. And then you said, "This *pancir* feels very strange." You thumped it and laughed. I laughed too. And wanted to stroke my head across your chest. But I didn't. I just carried on walking.

We walked till we reached the end of the flats. There we stopped and peeped round, to where the moonlit mountains opened up; in the straight-sided gully between the blocks, beneath blanket shrouds, the road to the Holiday Inn zigzagged around its gym-locker chicanes. Beyond it, the vast open square, the twisted bus stop and the hotel itself, dwarfed in the blackened shadow of the parliament beyond.

"I'll go on my own from here," I said.

"No, I come with you."

"It's stupid," I said. "You've just got to go back." I had a stab of fear at the thought of you running this way. "It's bad enough to do this once."

"I said I take you home; so, I take you home. Anyway, all snipers are drunk or asleep. Listen, is quiet." It was true. Nothing stirred in the frozen night, then suddenly, the silence cracked. Somewhere, someone was playing jazz, and laughter drifted over the snow.

"That's music," you said.

"There's a piano in the dining room of the Holiday Inn," I said. I still thought that noise was pretty then. "One of the cameramen was playing it yesterday."

"Let's run to music," you said.

So we ran, hand in hand, through the chicanes and dashed across the open stretch to the back of the hotel. We were laughing again when we reached the back door. Then we stopped, and suddenly we weren't laughing at all. You took my other hand, and we stood there for a moment, saying nothing. Then, as I had known you were going to do, all night, since we first met, yesterday afternoon, you kissed me. I kissed you back, the pair of us, safe, in the shadow of the hotel. You pushed me away.

"I must go home. Go inside." But that wasn't what I found myself wanting at all. Then you said, "When can I see you again?"

"I have to go back to England soon. My newspaper won't pay to keep me here." I couldn't bear the thought of leaving this place – I couldn't bear the thought of leaving you.

You kissed me, again, for longer this time, breaking off to say my name, and then kissing me deeper, the tentative exploration changing to assumption of control. I felt my stomach twist, my core turn liquid, my mouth sing with the taste of your spit. I opened my eyes and stroked your cheek, and suddenly Johnny seemed a lifetime away.

"Are you here tomorrow? Can you come tomorrow?" You pulled away. I swallowed and said yes; I knew then that, whatever the paper said, I would never leave. I could have stood here kissing you, in the dark, all night.

You kissed me quickly again, then you turned and ran – I watched you through the moonlight, crunching over the ice, the taste of you still tingling in my mouth, long after you were lost to me behind the chicanes. Till tomorrow, I thought. I'll see you tomorrow.

But of course I didn't. I went to Tuzla instead. But I didn't know, when you left me, that Robert was about to give me his job.

Mujo was shot in his leg. The doctors said they would have to cut it off. Mujo said: "I Insist my friend Suljo does the operation."

When Suljo came, he cut off the leg, and both Mujo's arms.

The doctors were horrified: "What have you done?"

Suljo said: "You don't know my friend. He would just fiddle with the wound until it got infected."

1999

I can see a large tree from my window. It's very English in shape – England as a foreigner would think of it, but I don't know what it is. I've spent too much of my life abroad. It's set against an English sky – it's actually, even, quite a nice day – just not quite in the middle of an English lawn. You can hardly see the trench, at the end of the lawn, the ha ha, keeping out the sheep in what the woman downstairs calls the park. Actually, she calls the whole place "The Park". It looks like one of those places in films, where terrorists are holed up or spies are trained. It's railway-station Gothic. I quite like that. It reminds me of university. Life was so simple, when all you had to do was write two essays a week.

I wonder what they'd think, whoever planted those trees, a century ago, if they knew that their house would be full of fruitcakes paying £400 a night. Sometimes I sit at dinner, staring up at their plaster coats of arms, the cupids strewing flowers, the tipsy coronets, and think, this is just like the Holiday Inn. We're all trapped. Here voluntarily (most of us, anyway), and for the same reason. But trapped. Although the food's better. And it's much less fun.

The day I found the diary was the day I finally flipped, although Ireeeneeeeeee tells me that it was inevitable. That I shouldn't feel guilty for going bananas and being found rocking backwards and forwards on the floor of my flat; thank God Muffy was coming round – she's American and they know about these things. My father would probably just have given me a stiff drink. But then, he's in Kyrgyzstan, so it wouldn't have been him.

Irene says it's very common, this kind of delayed reaction. The woman downstairs agrees. She says they see that kind of thing the whole time. She says this summer's Kosovo war was probably the trigger – it had been building up for the last few months. But she's just the receptionist so what does she know. I asked Ireeeeeneeee and she asked me what I thought. I said I thought that the receptionist was probably right, because until the war – the new one – I was fine.

At least I think I was fine, although it's surprising now, now that I'm so obviously not, how many people have said that they knew all along. I wish they'd told me. Although, what the other people say here, the ones you can have a conversation with, is that one of the classic symptoms of being potty is that you think you're perfectly all right; I asked Ireeeeeneeeee if she thought that was true and she asked me what *I* thought. I said, I supposed so. She said, I mustn't feel guilty for not realising I was round the bend. The receptionist (Sarah, 32, who was brought up in Lewes, fifteen miles away) said she agreed. She said they see a lot of that here.

Until the new war, I'd kept it all under control. I left the *Herald*, three years ago – I'd worked for them, since Robert handed his string to me on that first trip to Sarajevo; I hadn't realised it was his valedictory tour – he'd been moving to London to work for the Beeb. But I left them in the end – shortly after the war in Bosnia ground to a halt. That was apparently inevitable too. I like all this inevitability. It lets me right off the hook. And I'm not the only war-barmy person here – there's some guy who was in the SAS who's gone round the bend from "slotting", as he says, too many terrorists. He didn't want to talk to me for a bit, once he discovered that I was a journalist, but now we get on like a house on fire. I said I wished he'd been allowed to slot some Serbs, but he said he was never sent to Bosnia.

Ireeeneee's spot on where the *Herald*'s concerned. They didn't know what to do with me when peace broke out; there aren't that many jobs in normal life for girls whose major qualifications are that they don't mind being very uncomfortable for quite a long time and can always get to a phone (or nearly always, except, of course, for the market massacre day, but Ireeneeeeeeeee tells me I'm not to feel guilty about that, although frankly I don't think you and Ireeneeeeeeee would see eye to eye). Particularly if the girl in question has got too grand to wear inflatable bikinis any more. She just sits around the office, reading the wires, a visible reproach for the triviality of life.

So I left them, left that whole world behind and went to work as a features editor on a glossy magazine, sending girls, just like I had been, to try out inflatable bikinis. But at least I got to stay in one place.

I could have found another war. If a war's what you want, there are lots around, even if newspapers don't care about most of them. Africa's good for that. But Africa doesn't do it for me: I'm scared of insects and I faint in heat.

But it wasn't just Africa. I couldn't face another war. I couldn't face wandering into people's lives and making them like me and trust me and tell me about themselves and watching them remember for a moment what they once had been; their homes, before the soldiers came. To revisit, for me, the stream tumbling down the steep-sided valley, the little mosque, before it was blackened with flames, the plum trees, the white house, red roof, orange blankets on the beds, and the goat tethered amongst the chickens outside; and then shutting my notebook and walking out, leaving them in their tiny room – in the school or the town hall or the hotel, or their summer tent, with the UNICEF donated nappies strung from wall to wall and their UNHCR tins of food stacked neatly above the UNHCR wood-burning stove, and their father-in-law and their granny in bed, looking at it all afresh with eyes newly wrenched from the past I'd made them conjure up. I couldn't bear leaving them. I couldn't bear leaving you. I couldn't bear the thought of minding that much ever again. At the time, I thought it was common sense. It's not, apparently, but it's understandable. Eye-reen-eeee says I mustn't feel guilty about that.

You would have hated me to find another war.

I never read the *Herald* after I left – just to see the typeface made me feel sick. Ireeeneeeeeee says that's normal too. Luckily they've redesigned it so much since I left – desperately trying to make more people buy it when being less smug and more interesting might work better instead – that I could read it again, if I wanted to. I never read anything about the Balkans, anyway, whatever paper it's in. And I didn't really bother to keep in touch with people, apart from Phil, obviously, because he was my friend. But he's in Moscow now, so I never see him. And I never saw Robert, because he was back in Sarajevo. Sometimes I used to cry, but not very often. Probably no more than any normal person would. Although maybe normal people don't cry in the credits of *Dad's Army*.

So in a way, the new war took me by surprise. I knew it was coming, obviously – anybody would – but I really thought that I wouldn't care. I thought I would be able to convince myself that this time it had nothing to do with me. After all, it was Kosovo – Albanians and Serbs – and I'd only been there once, on a really slow week somewhere in the summer of 1993, a kind of round-up trip of "and meanwhile let's see whether Yugoslavia's other war is ready yet – oops, not quite. Put it back in for a bit": the Albanians still had another six years to go before they gave up trying to win with passive resistance.

I thought that I had done with that part of my life, that I no longer wanted to wake up to the lazy rattle of a machine gun each day, to drive those endless winding roads through burnt-out villages, to get so used to the blackened corpses of buildings that an intact row of houses was a shock; to have the hit of adrenalin when you come up to a checkpoint, and the surge of elation when you get your story through. I thought that I had grown out of that, that it was under control. And in a way, it was – at least in the run-up to the thing. Then, I didn't even read the newspapers, I didn't watch the telly, I didn't go and buy the books my old colleagues had hurriedly rushed out so that all their other colleagues could buy them before they set off to war, and swap the same second-hand facts round the hotel bar.

I did none of those things. I thought I was immune, until it began, and then I couldn't stop watching it on TV: the same little white houses, the same sunset-shaped bars twisted in the remains of the same shell-shattered windows, the same tractors bristling with refugees, the same swirly blue uniforms on the same military police beating them on their way; the same people, my old friends, sweating into their flak jackets in the hard June sun. Phil squinting into the camera as he filed from the makeshift camps – because technology had changed a lot in the last four years and you could file now, really, even for TV, from wherever you liked.

I watched the war the way my father watched cricket – glued to the television, with the volume off, and my shortwave radio stuck in one ear; the commentary's much better on the radio.

I had this desperate urge to be there again, to smell the dust, the dry grass, the faint whiff of cordite, to be with people who were dealing with matters of life and death. I lost all concentration in the office – and it had to be pointed out that, on a glossy magazine, flicking through Reuters could not be described as work. It was on the second day of the war that I started to smoke again. At least they approved of that at work – it's a well-known weight control and it makes you look cool. But they did say, "Welcome back," when the war came to an end.

Then the diary – well, that was the final straw. And the last bit, the yellowing press cutting in the *Herald*'s old font, stuck in with sellotape. The bit about you.

I never fell in love after you. It was as though that part of me had been tidied away with the helmet (the *Herald* let me keep it as a souvenir) and the Serbo-Croat phrase books and the Swiss Army knife. As I said, I never wanted to mind that much again.

Ireeeeeeeeeeneeeeeeeeeee says that's normal too, I mustn't feel guilty about not falling in love. Ireeeeeneeeeee keeps telling me I shouldn't feel guilty about anything. But what kind of a monster would I be, if I didn't feel guilty about you?

MUJO WAS PULLING his sledge through the street on the way to get water, when he saw Suljo, standing at the top of a building, about to jump.

"Stop it! What are you doing?" he yelled.

"I was shot by a sniper," shouted Suljo. "The doctors had to cut off my dick and take out my guts. I just want to die."

"There's no point living without a dick," Mujo agreed, and went on. Two hours later, as he was pulling the jerry cans back, he saw Suljo was still there.

"Why didn't you jump?"

"No guts," said Suljo.

SARAJEVO 1993

V

I don't know what you did that month I wasn't there. I never really did know what you did when I wasn't there; although I suppose that was what I was interviewing you about the day we first met. Forage for wood, in the dark, so the snipers couldn't see; hide in the kitchen when the shelling was bad; fetch the water – at night again; queue for food. That took up a lot of your time, helping your mother, while your father commuted on foot to the front. Sometimes, in the sunlight, you could read a book. You didn't read by candlelight, you said; there were not enough candles to go round. Before you met me, you said, you'd sit there in the dark, waiting for the war to end. And after? Wondering when I'd come back.

You always said we started going out when I got back from Tuzla. But of course, we hardly ever went out, exactly, as outside was so dangerous. What we really did was stay inside together. But then that's what Johnny and I did too, back at Oxford, and nobody was waiting to shoot us at the corner of his street. You said that first month didn't count, because I was away, and I didn't say, because I thought it would just open a can of worms, that if you didn't count every time I was away, then we'd lose months from our lives.

I'm not saying I thought of you all the time I was in Tuzla. There were too many other people to feel pity for – not that it was pity I seemed to feel for you. The Serbs had been burning their way through the forests of eastern Bosnia for weeks, village after village, driving those Muslims, the ones who weren't killed on the way, until they were all – men, women, children – crushed into a little town, in a gorge, at the end of the mountains. It was called Srebrenica but Srebrenica wasn't famous then. There was a ceasefire: General Morrillon, the Frenchman who ran the UN in Bosnia, went to Srebrenica, and the women and children lay under the wheels of his Armoured Personnel Carrier, so he was trapped; the women refused to move until the UN arranged an evacuation of refugees – although the UN were loath to agree on a matter of principle: the UNHCR said it would be doing the Serbs' ethnic cleansing for them, and they had a point, but then, if they didn't, all the people were going to die. The lorries that finally reached Tuzla from Srebrenica, through the snowdrifts and the minefields, disgorged a load of old men, young women and their babies, the sick, the wounded, and the bodies of those who had failed to survive the trip. They told of a world lost deep in pine-forested ravines, where children, playing football, were shelled and bled to death in the snow, and the artillery kept battering into the streets, where everyone had fled from some other village the Serbs had burnt up in the Drina valley, of no food, no fuel, no future. And the UN did nothing – not that there was much they could do, they said, in the snow: their Armoured Personnel Carriers couldn't even make it over the mountains to Tuzla, the tracks kept skidding in the ice.

So I didn't think of you all the time, as we counted the wounded and heard their stories and taunted the world into trying to act. I did think of you but I didn't know what to think. And when the story finally faded away and Srebrenica, like Tuzla, like Sarajevo, Gorazde, Bihac and Zepa – wherever Muslims were packed together, still holding out against the Serbs – had been declared a Safe Area by the UN, Muffy and I got into the white armoured Land Rover driven by some American friend of Muffy's she'd known from her days in Central America and returned to Sarajevo. He called himself an aid worker but Muffy said, yeah right, funny how he saved the world in places like Salvador and the Afghan border. She called him John the Spy and had been very happy to bump into him in the bar. Although the hotel was so full she and I had to share a room, most of the nights she never made it back. Even the last night, after she'd wept as she told me about the girl John had married a few years ago, who bred babies in Virginia, while he went round saving the world. Then she talked about the jazz musician she lived with in New York, and then she washed her face, put her mascara on and said to me, "I'm going out. Don't wait up."

As we drove back to Sarajevo, I had two days to think about you in the car. I wasn't sure what to do. Maybe you kissed lots of girls like that. Maybe I would just be making a fool of myself, a stupid foreign journalist not getting the point. In London, I would have waited for you to ring, but your phone hadn't worked, along with everyone else's since the PTT building received a direct hit at the start of the war. You couldn't write to me because I didn't have an address, and anyway the post hadn't worked for a year either – postmen being very averse to being shot by a sniper when on their rounds. You couldn't email, because your computer didn't work because there was no electricity, and anyway, strange to think, this was the dawn of the internet, so most people weren't on email anyway. So I didn't know what to do. I'd never had to pursue a man before and I wasn't sure if Sarajevo was the right place to start.

Our car luged down a track that looked as if it had been carved into the mountain in walls of ice; an Olympic toboggan run, but in an armoured car. Snow-laden fir trees drooped over the road, and beyond, the cliffs dropped sheer to one side, where lost houses by lost rivers could be made out in the meadows far below. On the other, the peaks soared up. We skidded through villages that Suleiman the Magnificent's generals would have thought unchanged: pitched roofs, those strange pointy haystacks, muffled women chopping logs, like the villagers in the mountains on the way to Kiseljak, so blasé after a year of war that they barely stopped to stare as the caravans of aid lorries skated by. Except to beg for cigarettes. Before the war, those villages wouldn't have seen a stranger from one year to the next.

I didn't go and see you at first. I kept putting it off; it's easy to put off real life in Sarajevo. I had to find my feet, do my work, I had a lot to do, I had to get it right. With Robert's job, I'd started to panic the same way he had – a fever rising to crisis at the end of the week, with Sunday a sort of floppy convalescent fug; later a distinguished old journalist told me writing for a Sunday paper was like having a weekly disease.

Phil had gone, to be replaced by the man who was in Tuzla, but Muffy used to hire a driver for the day; his car wasn't armoured, but he drove very fast. I asked if it was safe; she said: "He was a dentist; it was his brand new Audi. He doesn't want any holes in it either." She took me to see the UNHCR, and a general, the one I had been to with Phil; General Divjak, a Bosnian Serb who'd stayed in Sarajevo; I was beginning to recognise people now. We went to the hospital and the orphanage and met some refugees who'd managed somehow to walk here from Srebrenica. Phil's replacement, Tim, dark haired and fifty, made me feel shy because I had seen his face on TV reporting from every war since I'd watched John Craven tell me about Mozambique on *Newsround* when I was six; but he let me hang out in his office, the way Phil had done. So I didn't really miss you, but I always looked wistfully up your street as we clanked by.

Late Monday afternoon, as I was wandering along the gallery to the BBC, I heard a voice floating out through the open door.

"Why do you let her hang out here so much?" I recognised that voice; so would most of America, and a million lonely businessmen worldwide. A woman, rather tough, very famous, about fifteen years older than me. I'd met her a couple of times last summer and then again in Tuzla, but she'd never been very nice. She didn't spend so much time at the BBC as a lot of other journalists; being TV, she had her own office and a crew, so she had her own little court, but she was here now, like a visiting queen, and for some reason, although there was nothing that I could put my finger on, I stayed put.

"She's sweet," I heard Tim, the BBC correspondent, say. "And she's funny."

"You mean she's young and pretty."

"Well, that always helps."

The woman snorted. I felt slightly sick as I heard her say: "I don't know what she's doing here."

A silence, then Muffy's voice: "Same as us, Marina. She's a journalist." I wanted to hug her.

"What does she do exactly? She's just one of those girls who hangs around the Holiday Inn for a few weeks. Fucks people and fucks off."

"That's not a nice thing to say," said Tim. "Besides, I don't think she's fucked anyone here yet."

"She didn't in Tuzla," said Muffy. "I was sharing her room." I thought, nice of her to say so, but how would she know? She hadn't been there very much.

Marina sounded a bit embarrassed, but she ploughed on. "I don't mean to sound – bitchy..." I thought, you're doing a pretty good job. "But does she do any *work*? She never seems to leave the hotel... She just seems to hang out with you two all the time."

"Oh Marina," said Muffy. "What do you know? She seemed to be working OK in Tuzla. You're down at the TV centre most of the day. It's really hard to work in Sarajevo without an armoured car."

"Well, that's my point. If she can't work here properly, then there's no point in being here at all. It's not a finishing school. She should leave."

"At least she's here. Robert never came here at all..." said Tim.

"Oh, *please*! Robert's *Robert*. At least, *he* knew what was going on."

I turned back along the gallery towards the stairs. I wanted to go to my room and cry. I had loved being here. I had thought, I had deluded myself, I suppose, they seemed to like me: I'd finally been asked to join the cool gang at school. And now there was this bitch, the undeniable queen of the hotel, being vile. Maybe she has a point. Then I thought, fuck her, I'm just trying to find my feet. It's all right for people with armoured cars and satellite engineers to be smug. Then I thought again, well maybe she's right. Maybe I should go, and stop wasting everyone's time. I mean, I was so *tired*. Maybe the *Herald* was mad to even think I could do this. How could I follow on from Robert, who spoke the language and had been here for years?

I walked downstairs, just for something to do, but there really wasn't much to do in Sarajevo. Where the plate-glass lobby wall should have been, the evening light streamed through the plastic sheets. Three old men were drinking coffee on the mushroom stools on the astro-turf, nestling behind one of the huge pillars that kept up the roof, in case a shell should suddenly land outside; sitting there, with their cars outside, hoping, one of us would come down and pay them 100 DM a day to risk their lives. Marina's driver's face lit up as he saw me come in, but I shook my head and he sank back onto his plastic stool. He wasn't that old anyway; it was just the war. It made everyone old.

It wasn't true that I didn't talk to Sarajevans, I did. When I interviewed them. But interviewing and meeting people isn't the same. How many Sarajevans did Marina meet anyway? With her entourage of TV crews and satellite dishes, every time she did a story, it was like the Queen opening a swimming pool.

I only *knew* one person in Sarajevo and that was you. Maybe I should go into town and try and meet someone else, but it was Monday, and there was lots of shooting outside. What was the point, if you worked for a Sunday paper, of going for a walk down Sniper Alley, when you were five days off your deadline, on the off chance you might make a friend?

It was the waiter, when I bought my second cup, who said, "Did your friend find you?"

"What friend?"

"Young guy. One of ours. He came to find you, maybe two weeks ago. He ask reception. He ask here. I saw him two times." I was already signing my bill. I swallowed, and my skin was tingling.

I asked: "Did he have his arm in a sling?" But I knew it had to be you. As I said, I didn't know anyone else in Sarajevo anyway. I went upstairs for my flak jacket, then I ran out of the door. I stopped in the doorway – what could I bring? I couldn't bring any coffee. I'd run out. I stood stock still, and then I thought I'd go anyway.

I had a pit in my stomach as I crunched up your stairs in the darkness. I was breathless, but that must have been the run. I thought, this is just journalism; journalists are always following up contacts they make. I thought you'd know that, even though I knew I was lying to myself; I thought, if you were cold and funny, it wouldn't matter anyway. I could just leave. But I still felt sick as I knocked on your door.

You were cold and funny. "Oh, it's you. I thought you gone."

"I came back," I said, but I thought, maybe I should just go now.

"I went to hotel. I tried to leave message."

"I know. They only told me today. You shouldn't have done that. You could have been killed."

There was maybe a five-second pause before he said: "And you would not like that, if I had been killed?"

"I wouldn't like that at all."

It was dark but I could feel you, like a forcefield, a foot away. You said nothing, and then you took hold of my arms and drew me towards you. I couldn't see you, but I smelt you, and I didn't need to see you as I kissed you. I could have kissed you for ever. Except the flak jacket kept getting in the way. I pulled back.

"I think I'll take this off," I said.

"Let me help."

You lifted it off my shoulders and propped it against the wall. Then you kissed me again, and we sank down on the top stairs. The steps were stone cold and smelled, like everything, of pee, but at least it was private. I could feel the gritty little cubes of rubble, biting into the backs of my legs, then I forgot them completely as you kissed me some more. We could have stayed there until the siege was lifted, I suppose, if your mother hadn't yelled through the door.

She was pleased to see me, at any rate; even if I didn't have any coffee this time. I gave her the Benstons in my bag instead; the ones I always kept, just in case, for making friends and bribes.

I looked up at you. You were looking at me. It was the first time I had seen you in daylight, I suppose. As I said, war makes people look old. I'd been here a month and I looked like shit. You looked tired, but you were smiling at me, so the huge bags beneath your eyes didn't matter to me. Your skin had the same greyish tinge as Muffy's driver in the Holiday Inn; greyer. And you were much thinner than him; thin like a model on a poster on the side of a bus. It was warmer, now, and you weren't wearing your coat. Your sweater had risen up, one side, from your jeans; I snatched a look, a slice of stomach, pale, scooped hollow, with thick dark hairs marching in a line towards your flies. You saw me looking, I blushed and looked away.

And then your mother made coffee for us. I told you about my new job. You said, "So, you will stay?" As I said, "Yes," your mother nodded happily through her nicotine haze.

When it was dark, you walked me back to the hotel – or ran me back. We were breathless, giggling from the rush, when we reached the back door. When you kissed me this time, you didn't say you had to go. So we went up to my room, up the six flights of marble stairs, my spindly torch beam luring us on. We didn't talk, and that may just have been the effort of the climb, but we didn't exchange a word until we got to the door. I couldn't find the key, for a moment, in my bag, which was strange because the key ring was the standard huge lump of plastic. I opened the door and the moonlight streamed towards us across the carpet – I had the room to myself now, since the *Herald* was footing the bill. I think I made some sort of banal remark like, "Well, here we are. I hope it's not too untidy," (which it shouldn't have been since the chambermaid still came in daily despite the war, but that's what we were paying the hotel for, I suppose).

I was trying to find the candles with my torch, when you started kissing me again. I think I was technically still going out with Johnny at the time, but I never thought of him at all. You were kissing me and kissing me and I was kissing you back, the way I never tired of kissing you. You took my flak jacket off again, and kissed me again, the back of my neck. Suddenly it was as if a film had been speeded up. You pushed me so I sat down on the bed, and then suddenly I was lying flat. And I wasn't sure… I didn't know whether to stop you or not; I froze for a moment. I think I said, "Stop," but you started kissing me again; kissing my lips, taking little nibbles from my neck, behind my ears, your cheekbones hard in my collar. I remember for a moment, trying to push you away and I remember, definitely remember, part of me asking you to stop but then my body started helping you, while my mind was still thinking, this is too fast, too soon, I don't know this man. I shouldn't be doing this now – and I thought of Johnny again, the only man I'd slept with for the last three years, and the stately procession of dates with which he paved his seduction, and here I was, having my knickers ripped down, on a hotel bed, by a man I hardly knew, and I even remember thinking, by a *foreigner* I hardly knew, as though that made it worse. And then also, thank God, I am still on the pill, since you were quite obviously not bothering to ask responsible questions about contraception. And I didn't think I could have stopped you, actually, even if I had wanted to. And I didn't want to, because your fingers on my skin were tracing lines of fire. And then I thought, maybe this is like hitchhiking, the rules are different here. But also, and this sounds pathetic but it's true, there really wasn't anything else to do. The courtship rituals of Sarajevo were very easily exhausted. And then I didn't think about anything at all.

Afterwards, we lay there, on my clean hotel sheets, and I looked across at the pale blur of your face in the dark, the vapour of your breath, floating up in the moonlight; I felt almost enveloped in your scent. You stroked my cheek and said things to me in Serbo-Croat I could not understand, because they were, in those days, still far removed from my working vocabulary of cups of coffee and refugees and whether the road was safe ahead. Then we made love again. And afterwards, I felt your cheek wet against my face. Then we dozed for a while. When we woke up I was hungry.

"Everybody in Sarajevo is hungry," you said.

"No, I mean, shall we go and have dinner. It's only half past nine."

"Where?" You were amazed.

"Here," I said. "In the hotel. I mean, the food's not nice, but it's food." Although it was dark, I could almost see the hesitation on your face. When you spoke, I could hear the embarrassment: "Molly, this hotel very expensive."

It was my turn to feel embarrassed. "Don't be stupid, Amir," I said. "We'll just put it on my room."

"No. You not pay."

"No. I not pay," I laughed. "My newspaper pay. You're a justifiable expense. I wrote about you."

The laughter from the dining room rose up through the icy darkness of the atrium. The dining room was packed when I opened the door – much fuller than it had been when I'd first got here; everyone else had come back from Tuzla now.

Some turned their heads as we came in through the door: rows of faces, shining yellow in the candlelight, disembodied, their dark-coated torsos blurring with the night, as though some Turkish warlord, one of your ancestors perhaps, had set a banquet before the spiked heads of his enemies. They were sitting, as they always did, like a medieval village – grouped by profession or national blocks – the French photographers' table, the Japanese reporters' corner, the row of laughing Australian cameramen.

I hadn't even thought about introducing you to this world. I had a moment of panic, I nearly suggested we left, but God knows where we could have got anything else to eat. Then you said, "They look like boiled eggs." I laughed and it was too late.

"Molly, we're over here. Where have you been?" I heard Muffy's voice. I felt a surge of gratitude as I remembered her earlier defence.

"Here!" A torch danced on the faces of Marina, Valida, Henri and Tim. Valida and Henri, dark and beautiful in the lamplight; Tim's bald jolliness making him look even more like a boiled egg. Marina's washed-out blonde, knackered and cross. I dropped your hand as we walked over, although I suppose in the darkness nobody could have seen.

"Where've you been?" said Muffy. "We were worried about you."

Marina said nothing.

"I went to see a friend," I said. "Marina, this is Amir. Amir, Marina, Tim." You nodded at them.

"Hello Amir. Grab a chair," said Tim.

"Well, Amir," said Marina, looking him up and down. "This is a surprise."

"Owz your pigeon?" said Henri. And you smiled at him, suddenly recognising him amongst the ranks of hacks. Then suddenly Valida gave a squawk and swooped on you, giving you double kisses, pecking at you in Serbo-Croat. I stared at you, but you had eyes just for her. I untangled my name from the snarl of consonants. Valida had her hand on your arm, but she looked, wide-eyed at me, then the astonishment on her face broke into a smile. She had never smiled at me before. She leant across.

"Amir and I were at university, together, before the war. We have not seen each other since war began. But he is here." You were grinning at each other; eyes gleaming liquid in the candlelight. "He is alive."

Some people – not Valida, she never said that – used to say you were just with me for what you could get. They said it later, of course, when they thought it would make me feel better, but I never believed them. I remember what you were like back then: you didn't even realise I could give you a square meal. You ate slowly, that night, with a degree of disbelief, and with an anorexic's lack of haste – you were accustomed to a world beyond food. All three courses, soup, the strange flat burger of no known flesh, the baklava that tasted of engine oil. When I didn't eat mine, you didn't say anything, but you stared at it.

"Have it. I don't like it."

"I think I take it home."

We went up to the BBC after dinner. I got most of the jokes by now. I knew the armoured car was called Miss Piggy ("Temperamental," Tim explained, "and she's ex-RUC; in Northern Ireland they're known as Pigs"). I knew that Valida's father was an important Bosnian general, and as a result, she could get almost anyone she wanted on the phone. I could even try the odd bit of political analysis. You flickered in and out of invisibility, next to me on the sofa, drinking the whisky which was handed to you without any of the ceremony it had in your flat. We didn't hold hands but I could feel the heat of you through my clothes. Sometimes Valida would talk to you. Muffy tried to make conversation, but then someone else would say something, and she'd leap into that with a speed which showed her mind had been half on it anyway. The ex-US marine, Ray, was there – God it was a long time ago – a bullet-head nutter with a thousand-yard stare, who said he worked for something like the *Anchorage Bugle*. "But you have to wonder how interested the *Anchorage Bugle* is," Muffy'd said, sotto voce, after our first introduction. "To my knowledge, he's never filed a story."

Ray made some remark about the "locals" that made me wince. Then you looked at your watch.

"I must go," you said. "Is late."

"Why?" I didn't want you to leave.

Valida said, "Curfew."

You repeated, "Curfew."

"Shit," said Ray. "I'll come along with you. Which way you heading?"

I thought, no, you bastard, don't get in the way of my goodbye, but he was already heaving himself out of the chair.

"Don't you stay here?" I asked.

"Hell, no. Gets me closer to the story. C'mon Samir. Let's face the guns."

"I'll come down with you," I said.

As we crashed down the stairs, Ray interrogated you on where you fought. "I spend most of my time on the frontline..." he said. You pointed at your sling and said that you hadn't been there for a bit. "You bin hit?" asked Ray, and you nodded your head, and in the dark I blushed as I remembered how much better your arm had seemed three hours ago.

When we reached the back door, we let Ray go through first.

"Can't you stay?"

"No." For a moment I thought, maybe you've had your fuck and your free meal and that's enough. Maybe you'd rather be with Ray. But then you said, "Mama... she will think snipers get me. I wish I could stay."

I wanted to yell, what about me? What if you're killed on the way home?

"Tomorrow I see you?"

"Yes." You kissed me, stroked my hair, and whispered my name. And when you stopped, you said, "When I see you tomorrow?" Tuesday, only Tuesday. I would have time to myself.

"Is the afternoon OK? I can get a lift into town," I said, but actually I could hardly speak. You started kissing me again. Maybe you wouldn't have gone, but we heard Ray's voice, through the door, saying, "C'mon you guys…"

Ray was waiting, staring out at the skeletons of the skyscrapers against the stars, the broken moonlight shining back from the fragments of their glass. "God, it's beautiful, this place."

"Better before."

"Shit, I love it like this. Let's go…"

I watched you run the gauntlet up to the chicanes, while the odd crack of a bullet echoed around the square. Ray, I supposed, must have been still pretty fit for his age. He ran in a way a man runs when he's been trained to run. But I wasn't thinking about Ray, just you. I could still feel your mouth on mine, I can still feel it now, and the musk of your saliva jangling on my tongue. I missed your smell, your touch, as though a part of me had been taken out. This must be love, I remember thinking, because it physically hurts and I'd forgotten that – human beings are programmed not to remember pain. Otherwise, who would ever fall in love twice?

I climbed back up in the darkness, with my little torch. I wanted to be alone, I wanted to go to my room to be on my own, with the cinema in my head, but as I passed the floor with the BBC office, I could hear the laughter. I stopped.

I knew I no longer had a choice about you. The thing was done. I must have known that from the start. Maybe it was that, the inverse of the magnet, that had nearly sent me back out into the shells that first afternoon. Oh God, I hoped you weren't lying with your brains pooling on the pavement, hit by the only sniper who wasn't pissed at this time of night. I shocked myself by hoping that the sniper would shoot Ray first.

Then, for the first time, I pitied Johnny. I understood now at least part of why he slept with that girl. It was all right for me, being out here – just as you were thinking now of nothing but running up that street – but it must have been awful for Johnny, sitting in his bank; not knowing that news footage, with its frantic shell bursts and blood, bears as much relation to war as cricket highlights do to a five-day test. No wonder Johnny said I left him for a country.

I turned to carry on back up the stairs, to be alone with you in my head, but I saw another pinpoint of light jiggling up the stairs.

"Who's that, Molly? I thought it was you. It's so difficult to see anything in this place. How are you? Jeez. It took me days to get here. At least Tuzla had electricity."

It was Ed. I should have been honoured by his friendliness – he was, after all, very distinguished; one of those big American writers who do big stories for big magazines, in between writing big thick books – but I wanted to keep the memory of you. He didn't seem to notice I didn't speak.

"I hear Tim's in town. Are you coming in?"

I said yes, and turned back towards the BBC.

BODY PARTS and human flesh clung to the schoolyard fence. The ground was literally soaked in blood. One child, about six years of age, had been decapitated. I saw two ox-carts covered with bodies. I did not look forward to closing my eyes at night for fear that I would relive the images. I will never be able to convey the horror.

—LOUIS GENTILE, UNHCR OFFICIAL, SREBENICA

1993

VI

You used to say you felt like you'd walked onto the set of a film, when the first checkpoints appeared on the bridge – the one I used to just think of as being halfway down Sniper Alley, the Bridge of Brotherhood and Unity, it was called, Tito's old slogan, which always made us hacks laugh and even you had begun to find funny after a while with us. One day there was a man, you said, with the Chetniks' instant patriotism kit – beard, fur hat and double-headed white eagle – who fixed you with his eye and ran his finger across his throat, as you walked by. You said you'd turned to the friend you were walking with and said, "This isn't real. This is just like a film." And I said, I know just how you feel.

If this *were* a film, the next few weeks would have been our falling-in-love montage. We'd have run hand in hand, the music fast, but in a minor key, across minefields, interviewing refugees, or huddling during a bombardment in a particularly striking ruin, making love by candlelight to machine gunfire. We never argued – not properly, back then. Just the teasing friction of people in love. Perhaps, now I think about it, you didn't dare start a fight. Not at the beginning. Not until you knew how much I needed you too.

Our first big row was the day I got back from Mostar. But it wasn't directly from Mostar, and that was what the row was about. I hadn't seen it coming. I suppose I should have done.

The Big Row was just a continuation, I suppose, of what would have been the first row, if I hadn't taken evasive action. In most relationships, rows tend to be about the same thing, I always think. We find our fault-lines and are drawn to the edge – teetering, arms flailing on the brink, sometimes just to admire the view, until we either tumble into the abyss, or build some kind of swaying Andean bridge. Maybe some people build concrete flyovers and think they are safe. But they are just deluded. It's easy to blow up a concrete flyover – I've seen the remains of a few – and they take much longer to rebuild than a few bits of plaited rope.

The first row happened a week or so after you'd started working for me. Everybody agreed it made sense for you to work for me; you spoke English; your father, on his forty-eight hours back from the front, lent you his car. It had been swaddled in blankets in a garage, waiting for the war to end, its battery cannibalised in your house, its tank with just enough petrol left to flee – you couldn't afford any more, at fifty Deutschmarks a litre, but – well, I had to pay *somebody* to translate and drive me around and I'd much rather give the money to you than one of those bitter men in the slave market in the atrium of the Holiday Inn. Muffy said most of them were working the black market anyway. They were a lot fatter than everyone else, but maybe that was because they were getting fed on the money they were charging to drive us around. I actually think it was Muffy's idea at first anyway. It wasn't yours, whatever people said afterwards. As I said, I don't think you had the slightest idea – and I didn't realise I could hire anyone I liked.

It was a quiet day and you said you wanted to come to the briefing. I would normally hitch a lift with Tim, or Phil now, as he had come back. You'd wait, in my room, or drinking coffee in the BBC, until we all got back. But you didn't like that. You wanted to come. You said Valida got to go to the briefing. You said you'd know what was going on if you came. You said it would help me, if you knew that too. It would help you come up with the stories for me, you said.

You'd come up with some pretty good stories already I couldn't have got on my own: the man who'd walked from Srebrenica to Sarajevo, through the mountains ("We always said the people in eastern Bosnia were thick. Why on earth would he want to end up here?" you said.) And the "comfort girls", girls who'd go to the frontline to sleep with the soldiers. Not prostitutes, you said, quickly, it was their war effort. You were a bit embarrassed about that one. Particularly when the girl with bobbed dark hair, maroon dye halfway grown out, when we knocked on her door, screamed your name and gave you an enormous kiss.

When I said the UN wouldn't let you in because you didn't have a UN pass, you said, you didn't care. You just wanted to get out.

The briefings were held at the PTT, an enormous cement fortress down Sniper Alley, where the UN had holed themselves up at the start of the war. It had been the telecom building before; Robert had explained to me that Tito liked to fortify everything just in case. "He was totally paranoid," Robert had said. "Maybe he had a point," I said.

We zoomed down the dual carriageway for a couple of miles, between tower blocks, with their pitted windows boarded up, and abandoned lorries stuffed in makeshift frontlines; the wrong side of the road, the left side, because it was safer – the houses gave you more cover from the snipers on the far side. We were probably the only unarmoured car on the road. But I was getting used to driving around with you by now.

We turned for the PTT where a stream came out. Some old women were hoeing the ground beside the road, between the blocks of flats, next to a wall of sandbags, by some white armoured personnel carriers corralled with razor wire. It looked like Bruegel, touched up by Dalí. "What are they doing?" I asked, and you explained, there'd been some new law, this summer, that all the untarmac-ed earth in the city had to be sown for food; all the bits that were relatively safe to work. I looked back at the women. They were hoeing in the shadow of a little hill, safe from snipers, as long as they weren't shelled. Maybe they weren't that old. They just looked like they were.

Tito would have approved of the PTT now. Every window was padded with sandbags, every wall iced with razor wire. I was just apologising again, as we bumped along the track, for the fact that the French Foreign Legionnaires on the gates weren't going to let you in, because you didn't have a UN pass like me, when you stopped the car. There was a chain across the road and a boy, scrawny, spiky dark hair, in swirly green camouflage, with the fleur de lys of the Bosnian Army on his shoulder flash, was flagging us down. He was grey-faced tired, the way you were when we first met; already your skin had a different bloom. He checked your papers, showed them to his friend, who was scuffing the chain wound round the oil drum. He shook his head. You pointed at me and I smiled at them, but it didn't matter what we did, he wasn't going to let you through. It wasn't a UN checkpoint – this was fifty yards before, but you didn't have a Bosnian press pass either. I hadn't even thought of getting you one. To me, then, you were just my boyfriend who was driving me around. The two boys seemed rather to enjoy making you stay.

You said you'd wait by the car; I left you with the boys, warming your hands. I walked on through. It was hot in the sun, but the air was still chill. Outside the armoured car and the hotel, Sarajevo smelt sweetly of spring and the rubbish smouldering beside the checkpoint. I turned to wave: you were offering them each a cigarette and I noticed you'd slipped your arm back into its sling. Somehow you looked bigger than them, taller, perhaps, or maybe just fuller. Phil said you should be OK, when I saw him inside. Like the old women, the snipers couldn't see you and the Serbs were unlikely to shell the UN HQ: "You'd have to be bloody unlucky to be hit there." And at least it wasn't raining.

You didn't seem to mind that much, when I left you there. It was when I came back with Edin that you did. Even then, you weren't angry; you were never angry with me then. Perhaps you weren't sure enough of me. You were just sad. It was I who was angry with myself.

Edin was teasing me as he stopped the armoured car, telling me I couldn't have another Jaffa Cake. He was the fixer for CTV, one of the big North American networks, although not as big as it used to be. When he saw you, he leapt out of the car. You hugged each other, and both started jabbering in Serbo-Croat.

Edin was the same height as you, the same sort of age, the same high cheekbones, the same dark hair flopping onto the same pale skin. But next to Edin, you looked almost ill again. He clapped you on the back and said to me – "He's still all here!" Then he grinned at you, said something again, said, "See you later," to me, offered the Jaffa Cakes to the guys on the checkpoint, who grabbed at them with a grin, then drove off.

Normally, when I got in the car, you would say, "where to, Madam?" and laugh at me. This time, you just stared at the wheel. It was only when we were turning out onto the road that you said: "Edin says he's at TV station. He wants me to come for coffee."

I had time to spare. It was Tuesday. There was nothing *urgent* I had to do. I liked the TV station; there was a phone that was a tenth of the price of the one in the BBC. Besides, it made a change from the hotel. It was then you asked me about the Jaffa Cakes. That was when I told you about the PX shop, the UN military shop, inside the PTT, where people with UN accreditation could buy chocolate and biscuits, cigarettes and booze.

"I've got some Jaffa Cakes, too," I said. "Don't worry. I've got some cigarettes as well, and some coffee."

Then you asked me: "How Edin get in there?"

"He's got an UNPROFOR pass."

"Like yours?"

"No, not like mine. His is local press. He can't get in and out of Sarajevo."

"But he can still use shop?"

"Yes," I said.

You didn't speak. You just drove up the road. I said: "The cigarettes are still rationed." As though it somehow made it better. And then I said: "I can get you anything you want."

The TV station was just like the PTT – huge and concrete and fortified with sandbags and planks, but instead of being covered with the logos of UNPROFOR, its windows had stickers with TV, NBC or CNN. You parked the car – like the PTT, the TV centre was sheltered behind a hill from the snipers: maybe Tito had a good idea where the firing was likely to come from. But, like the PTT, the Bosnian soldiers at the door wouldn't let you in. No pass. No UN pass. No Bosnian pass. I had to go upstairs for Edin, who talked them round, along with a packet of Marlboro Red. Edin took me aside, as the soldiers made you fill out a form, and said with reproach, "You should get him a pass." I blushed. "I know, he's only just... just started working for me."

I let you go off with Edin, and went to use the phone. The TV station was, I guess, like most TV stations in the world, large and labyrinthine and full of cameramen. They swarmed the halls, greeting each other with harsh Australian cries, leaning against the windows chatting up pale-skinned, red-lipped girls; the passages hummed with the generators installed from the same paranoia, so amply justified, that led the building to be clad in ferro-concrete. Like the Holiday Inn, the carpet was grey and stuck to your feet as you walked. Like the rest of Sarajevo, it smelled of pee. There was an office, the European Broadcasting Union, where Balkan beauties drank instant coffee, while TV producers sent stories from their satellite dishes, and writers like me would come in and use the phone. I rang the desk. I rang some friends. I had a cup of coffee with Muffy, who was ringing people too. Then I went to find you.

The air in CTV was squeaky with the sound of running tape and the throb of the generator. You were sitting on the edge of a desk, swinging your foot, eating cheese from one of those huge catering blocks the TV companies flew in, talking to a pale-skinned girl, who was giggling back. I stood in the doorway, suddenly left out, but the moment you saw me, you leapt up.

"Aida, this is Molly, I was telling you about."

She didn't smile. She didn't move from her chair. We must have been about the same age I suppose, but she was much better dressed than me. She was beautiful, but then, so many of these people were, and beautifully made up, with dark hair straight to her bra strap at the back. It even looked clean. Mine needed a wash and I'd been living in my jeans for the last month. Her trousers were some kind of well-cut flannel. I looked at her feet. She was in high heels. I had my 'school of Timberland' boots.

"Aida's Valida's sister. I have not seen her since before war," you said, keen to include me in this exciting reunion. The girl glared.

"BBC Valida?" Nod. "She's lovely." Still no smile. So I said to you, "Sorry, I think we ought to go. I said we'd give Muffy a lift." She said something to you in Serbo-Croat, something about tomorrow. You smiled at me, and said in English, "You have to ask the boss."

You didn't mention the pass. You didn't say anything at all. You just got back into the car when we got outside and I stood and looked up at the overcast skies, the clouds pushing down on us, like the guns pushed in; as Muffy got into the back, I turned to him: "I'm sorry. I didn't think. I'll get a pass for you, if you like. I'm sorry."

You turned on the ignition: "If you want me to work for you, I think is better." You were strangely unenthusiastic. I didn't know then that was how you dealt with anything you really wanted. "If you want me to be like real interpreter. Like Edin."

"You are a real interpreter," I said. "I couldn't work here without you."

Suddenly it was sunny again. You grinned at me. "Where to, Madam?" I laughed back and leant across and squeezed your hand. From the back, Muffy said: "C'mon guys, don't let's hang around out here."

It wasn't that I didn't think you were a real interpreter: I think I wasn't sure yet that I was a real journalist, so I didn't want to ask for too much. But the foreign editor, when I asked for a letter accrediting you, just said he'd get Melinda, the secretary, to fax it that afternoon.

Phil read the letter out loud when it arrived on his fax. "This is to confirm that Amir Hadzibegovic is working in Sarajevo as interpreter and driver for Molly Taylor, Balkans Correspondent of the London *Herald*. Any problems, please contact Roger Highsmith."

Somewhere I heard Phil say: "Christ, I used to know him. He's a complete arse." But I wasn't even listening; the last words I'd heard had been Balkans Correspondent – I didn't even know that's what I had become.

BRITISH squaddie joke:
"What's the difference between a Warrior and a Lada?"
"You can get to Tuzla in a Lada."

VII

You loved driving me to the briefing each day. You loved the UN having to tell you what was going on. You loved the way the press conference changed UNPROFOR from being the lord of Sarajevo to a fumbling press spokesman, shiftily trying to justify the daily inertia to us baying hordes. It was like a party, you said, seeing so many friends, people you'd known at university but hadn't seen during the war. The Edins, the Aidas, there must have been a hundred of them, Sarajevans, like you, all working for alphabet soup. CNN, BBC, WTN, UNHCR, MSF, UNICEF – every westerner in Bosnia worked for some kind of initials and each one had their own local staff. After being so trapped, you said, you loved driving your car.

But I thought it was too dangerous for you. People died on that road every day, I said. Your car wasn't armoured and however fast we drove, the snipers were shooting people who drove as fast as us. I could get a lift, I said, in Phil's armoured car.

You said I didn't want you there, you said I wanted to go off on my own, be with Phil, but that wasn't true. I did want to be with you. I could see you loved the briefings. I loved you for that; and it meant you could join in all our jokes. But I was worried about your mother, left on her own, your father at the front, alone all day, with no-one to help fetch water or wood.

You said that your mother did quite well out of you going to the briefings. You said, if people had jobs, they were out all day. Your mother understood that, you said. That was what the money was for; 100 DM a day, you said, even though it was a bit less than other driver/interpreters got (I felt awful about that, but I did pay you seven days a week, and I wouldn't have had anyone else for the whole week). Besides, you pointed out, we used the car to get her water in the afternoons. And she did well out of those chocolates I was always bringing her. She made money from that. And the coffee.

I didn't know, until then, you were selling the chocolate and stuff. I thought I was giving your mother a present. I was surprised how much I minded that, but Muffy said, presents are different in a war. I wanted to ask you where you sold them, but I didn't think I could. You might have thought I didn't approve; I didn't really but that didn't stop me being curious.

In the end, we settled into a routine, like all couples do. On Monday and Tuesday I'd go with Phil, and you'd go home and help your mother. I'd meet you after lunch, hitch a lift into town. Sometimes I'd even stay the night, but I didn't like being that far away from the Mother Ship; I used to take my shortwave with me and listen to it every hour. You said, can't you go an hour without listening to Phil. I said, "Shh, it's just in case something has happened."

From Wednesday, you worked all day for me; taking me to interviews, coming up with ideas of people we should see, telling me stories of Sarajevo before the war, when you'd drive to the coast for the weekend, or ski in the mountains from which the Serbs now shot into the town.

On Saturdays, you learnt to keep quiet, lying in bed while I wrote like hell, and then hung around filing down Phil's sat phone, waiting for the queries the desk might have. You'd wander down to the shiny horseshoe bar in the lobby, where you drank endless tiny cups of coffee which appeared on my bill. It was boring, I agreed, but you couldn't leave me, I said, because I needed the car; just in case something happened. On Sundays, we seemed to spend most of the day in bed, making love or just talking, listening to the sniper chipping away at the fountain outside, wondering if he never got bored with pinging bullets off those tiles. I would worry about whether the piece I had filed had been OK and what on earth I was going to write the next week. And most days we'd eat with the others downstairs, and drink too much of Holiday Inn's horrible Hepok wine and whisky in the BBC office with Phil.

You hated it when I went over to the Serb side with Phil, to Pale, but I had to go: to interview Karadzic, or Mladic, or just to see how the average Serb was enjoying their breakaway statelet's international notoriety. But you saw the point, when I returned with an entire Bosnian supermarket trolley for your mother, dozens of eggs and cheese, sugar and salt, coffee and bottles of oil, and jars of Ajvar, the orange pepper paste that everyone talked about so wistfully, and I learnt to love. Phil said he felt like Father Christmas afterwards, as he unpacked the bags with your mother, explaining how we'd smuggled the food through the Serb checkpoints hidden under a rug.

"I sent Molly out to distract the guards," he said. "She batted her eyelashes and showed some leg..." And you laughed and pulled at my filthy jeans. You only minded then, when we had to stay overnight. You pretended not to mind, but I knew you still did. But what could I do? I had to work.

You took me to a party with one of your friends. It wasn't like I didn't want to go; I begged to come. You'd told me of the parties you use to have. I'd sighed but, you'd said, there aren't any parties here now. But then, Edin told you that one of your friends, some guy who'd been in the same year as you at school, had said come round.

"Selim was on the frontline in Dobrinje with me," you said. "All my old friends from the frontline will be there."

"How late do Sarajevo parties go on?" I asked.

"Till dawn," you laughed. "They have to because of the curfew."

It was dark as we drove up outside the block of flats, parking on the far side, so the snipers couldn't hit the car. We could hear the party echoing down the stairwell. Selim lived on the fourteenth floor. We climbed for long minutes in the filthy dark, your torchlight trailing over lumps of stuff that frankly I'd rather not have. When we got there, the door stood ajar, the candlelight leaking onto the landing. We could hardly see the room for the smoke and candlelight, but people shouted out your name as we walked in. A man with a red bandana round his head, gold chains at his neck, still in camouflage fatigues, came up and gave you a high-five. You laughed back, and were swallowed into a throng of those maroon-lipped skinny girls, all white skin, and long dark hair. I felt, suddenly, incredibly shy. I looked around. The room stank of unwashed clothes, and smoke, neat alcohol, and heavily, like a student party, of dope. And of course, like everywhere, slightly of pee.

Music was coming from a stereo, wired up to a car battery in the corner. A young man sat beside it, passing a pile of records, one by one, to the boy smoking next to him. They saw me staring, smiled. I smiled back. They mimed cigarettes, so I passed them some. They grinned at each other. Then I noticed one of them didn't have any legs.

The noise was a noise like any party noise, except I couldn't understand a word they said. I looked for you, but you were nowhere to be seen. I didn't even have a drink, you'd gone off with the whisky we'd brought. I saw Aida from CTV, sipping orange stuff from a little cup, but when I smiled at her she turned away. The girls were all in tight little skirts and tight little tops. Their gold jewellery glittered in the flickering light. I was in my flak jacket and my jeans. I wanted to take the flak jacket off. I started to, when a voice said to me: "I wouldn't do that; you might never see it again."

I turned round. It was a man, a bit older than you. Maybe 35, with a pointy beard and absolutely exhausted-looking eyes.

"Pleez," he said, embarrassed, "may I have cigarette." He was in fatigues, like the man in the bandana. A lot of the men at this party were in fatigues – although there were some in jeans like you.

"Of course…" I took out one of the two packs I had brought to this party especially for this. He looked familiar, when I saw his face in my lighter flame. I knew I'd met him somewhere before. He got me a drink. "What is it?"

"Don't ask," he said. "Selim makes it himself." I thought of the still you'd shown me in your apartment.

"You work at the theatre," I said. "I met you with Phil Lennox. BBC."

"Sometimes," he said. "Sometimes I am on frontline with Selim." Then he grinned at me and said: "Is the same – just directing. Now I direct my men in war, but it's real." I wished I had my notebook to write it down. He started talking about special effects, about blood, about how you could never get it right on film. How the real thing was so much greater, but also, in many ways, banal. So if you did get it right, it would be all wrong.

"War is boring," he said, and took another cigarette. "So much of war is boring. We used to have the best parties in Yugoslavia here. Now look, something like this, we have so few. How can we have party? We have best parties on frontline. You come up there. Come up to my frontline. I show you then what I direct. I show you the parties. We hear the Chetniks when they are drinking. We shout at each other. They hear our parties. They say, 'Drink up you Mujahadeen pigs. Soon you will never drink again!'"

"I'd love to come," I was saying, when suddenly you came back. You said something to him, he looked surprised, but then said again to me, "Come. Come to my frontline. I must go and get another drink."

You asked me then, if I was OK. I said I was fine. You said good, then you asked me to dance. There was a room of people heaving away, it was all frantic, and then the music changed and it was *Brothers in Arms*, and everyone fell on each other as though they were about to starve. Two of your friends came up and asked if they could have a cigarette. I said of course.

Three girls sat, one crying, in the corner, the tears streaking mascara black down her face. The other two partly consoled her, partly waved cigarettes at each other, as if to reinforce the point of what each was trying to say. After a bit, the weeping one got up and pushed her way out of the flat. I didn't know why she was crying. Was somebody dead, or had her boyfriend just left her for somebody else? Maybe she was drunk – and then I looked at what they were drinking. It looked like squash: the humanitarian aid fruit juice powder drink. Maybe it was some kind of vodka and orange aid. Then I remembered I'd never seen Valida drink. She said it wasn't religion, she just didn't like the taste. I wanted to go over and check. None of the girls looked drunk, but their skin wasn't the kind of skin that flushed anyway. Another of the girls came over to you, you both screeched with joy, and the next thing I knew, she had dragged you off for a dance and I was alone again. I turned round and saw the amputee by the stereo smiling at me. I smiled back again. He patted the cushion, but I really didn't feel up to a conversation with a legless stranger in a language I couldn't speak. I couldn't find you. I went into another room, and then went out again fast, as a couple were having sex under a heaving pile of coats on a bed; he was a soldier, his legs were still in fatigues. I thought of the comfort girls I'd written about. I couldn't even go to the loo for something to do because the loo was indescribably dreadful, the way it would be, if you had 100 people pissing in a flat with no plumbing. One bloke had gone out onto the balcony to pee, but everyone start yelling, watch out for the sniper. I understood that at least; sniper was a word I knew. I just couldn't do party talk.

The theatre man came back. "Your friend has gone?"

I was so grateful for someone to talk to. It was like walking into a foreign film with no subtitles. He started asking me about Phil. Then I started asking him things, what he did all day. It was small talk, but it was just like I was interviewing him.

You came back. I think he must have been drunk, because he swayed slightly as he got up and he said something to you which I didn't understand. Whatever he said, you didn't like. I saw your face go dark and I felt your arms rigid beside me. I said your name. The man smiled at me.

"Come and visit me," he said. Then he looked back at you. "Bring your boyfriend too, if you can get him up on the line." You snarled something at him. I felt your fists clenched, and I dragged onto your arm. I didn't want to ask him what he had meant.

Then you said, "Come on, it's late, let's go." I looked at my watch. It was half past twelve. "You don't have to leave because of me," I said. But I was glad to go. I was knackered.

As we left, someone said, and I recognised the word, what about the curfew? But you pointed to me. And I smiled. Then we walked out of the door. We would have gone, if Edin hadn't been coming up the stairs, with a bag in his hand that, from the weight and the clinking sounds, must have had a lot more than one bottle of whisky in it.

So, we went back in. Are you sure you OK? you asked, and I smiled, I'm fine, I said. You said, I must talk to Edin, and vanished back into another room.

Muffy had said earlier, "God, a Sarajevo party. How fascinating. I wish I could come. I've got a deadline." I wished she was here now. At least there'd be somebody I could share it with.

I spoke enough of the language now to understand nothing. It was all a blur, a party noise blur. The director with the beard, Fuad, he was called, asked me to dance. I felt mean, after what he'd said to you, but I had another slug of the pale spirit he gave me and thought, what the hell, I don't know anyone else here. So I danced with him. I danced for maybe twenty minutes or so. I kept looking for you, but I couldn't see you anywhere. I felt ridiculous dancing in my flak jacket, so Fuad hid it for me, under one of the beds – the bonking couple had long gone. Then we went back and danced some more. You still weren't anywhere to be seen. Someone else cut in, then, another man, then the man with the beard again; then one of the earlier girls asked me for two cigarettes. I decided to look for you. But you weren't in any of the rooms I tried. Then I got worried that my flak jacket might be stolen, so I went back to try and find where it was under the bed, but Fuad followed me in and suggested we did something else in the bedroom other than just look for my flak jacket. He wasn't being creepy; he was just making me an offer. But I kindly explained that I didn't think so. He took one last cigarette off me, and went back and I last saw him dancing with somebody else, kissing the neck of one of the maroon-lipped beauties I'd given a cigarette to earlier on.

I went and sat with the amputee DJ. He was all alone now. I'd seen his friend dancing with one of the slate-faced girls. He didn't speak English but we did very well. He smiled at me, I smiled at him. He touched my flak jacket and I blushed. I offered him a cigarette, he beamed back. He said he was called Haris, I told him my name, limping along in basic Serbo-Croat. "*Ja novinarka engleska. Moy boyfriend Amir.*" Etc. etc. He told me in sign language about the shell that had taken his legs off; I tried a few words back, saying, what – I'm sorry your life's ruined… It was almost easier to talk about it without a common language… Suddenly, he started to speak, on and on, a river of things I couldn't understand. All I could do was sit there, and say I don't understand, while words I knew like war, or before the war, and life, and Serbs, and love flashed by. Then he gave up. We just sat there and smiled at each other. For a while. Until he said, sadly, in English, "I love Manchester United. Football," he said. And pointed to his empty jeans, where his legs had been. I gave him another cigarette. I'd run out now. I'd been giving people cigarettes for hours.

I went to look for you in the end. You were in a room, at the end of the flat, with Edin, who was holding court, like a pasha on a divan. All of you, with little glasses of whisky in your hand. Edin was just passing you a joint. Your hair was sticking up, all tufty to one side, and your eyes were nearly crossed, you were so pissed. I felt this great, welling wave of love and I smiled at you, and came over, perching on the sofa at your side. I was so glad to see you having a good time. You saw me, and leant out an arm, then you pulled me to you and kissed me long on the mouth. Then I heard you say to everyone, "This is Molly," in Serbo-Croat. I would have been embarrassed, if I hadn't loved you so much. As it was, I just ruffled your hair and felt proud. The red bandana man laughed at my flak jacket, so I took it off again, and stacked it by the sofa. He put it on and started prancing around, and we all laughed. We laughed a lot. Then Edin passed me the joint again.

I sat in the crook of your arm for twenty minutes or so, trying to understand what was being said. Edin, the guy with the red bandana, and you were all talking hard. I heard you say at one point, *"Don't worry, she doesn't understand."* As you stroked my hair. I smiled up at you and said, *"I understand little."* And they all laughed. I had some more of your joint and I laughed too. Everything seemed so funny then. Suddenly I felt very tired. I looked at my watch. It was 2.30 a.m.

It took half an hour to drag you away. In the end, I really had to say, "Amir, I *mean* it." I had to work tomorrow. I knew this was working now, but I had to be able to concentrate tomorrow. I didn't yet know what the week would throw up. If I didn't get out soon, I thought *I* would throw up.

You had a good time anyway. But I, I don't know; that night was torture for me – I couldn't talk to anyone, but I couldn't relax. I kept wanting to write everything down. Luckily they didn't have parties in Sarajevo very often in those days so we did spend most of our evenings in the Holiday Inn.

Red Bandana nearly didn't give the flak jacket up. I heard him say to you, hey, I'm on the frontline. Where's she? And you said something like, go on, give it back. It was Edin who managed to talk him round. He took it off, then he gave me a look and said in English. "You come. You come to my frontline."

"We will," I said and I smiled at you. But you just shook your head. And the man in the bandana, who turned out to be our host, Selim, laughed and went "Bang! Bang!"

But I didn't. The next day, I had to leave.

WHEN THE WAR started in Bosnia, Mujo was drafted to fight in the Chetnik army. Commander asked him: "Who are your enemies?"

Mujo replied: "The Ustase of course. They are fucking Chetniks."

VIII

There is a town called Mostar, in Herzegovina, where the mountains start to open out to the sea. It means the town of the bridge and it clings to either side of the Neretva gorge. There was more than one bridge when the war fighting began, now they are easy to build, but for four hundred years the ravine was spanned by a single arc of Ottoman stone, bleached white by the sun, smoothed by thousands of travellers' feet. I'd gone through Mostar, with Robert, on the bus, on our way to Sarajevo in April. It felt like a lifetime ago, but in fact it was only a couple of months.

The new bridges were blown up when the killing began. First the Serbs had attacked, and the Muslims and Croats repelled them together, back in spring 1992. Then, as the Serbs remained on the cliffs above, lobbing the occasional shell into town, Mostar split along its gorge, and the Croats – better armed, with more to gain – took the west bank. They rounded up the Muslim men and drove their women at gunpoint over the river into the old Turkish quarter, on the eastern bank of the town, at the foot of the Serb-held cliffs. Then they blew the bridges up, cut off the roads to either end of the town, and shot and starved the ghetto stuck between the gorge and the towering cliffs behind. Only the single arc of stone remained, sniped at, shelled, the Muslims' one link with the other side.

So I went. I had to go. It was scary, horrible. It was like living on Sniper Alley all the time but it was where the story was.

It's hard to describe being at the centre of a story, when it's pushing everything else off the front page, when you turn on the World Service and your story leads the news, when you know you're in absolutely the right place at the right time and it doesn't matter that you're writing by candlelight or you can't wash, or the roof of the house next door has been blown off by a shell, or you're living off sandwiches cobbled together from stale bread, Marmite and cheese triangles for days, or the only water you can find gives you diarrhoea, or you have to hitch across the lines to find a phone. And your heart leaps every time you hear a sniper fire as you run down the street, and every time you reach your destination your grin nearly splits your face. I guess it's like skiing, the momentum takes over; nothing else exists, except you and the mountain. Or maybe it's like falling in love.

I was away for nearly a month. I tried to send you messages while I was there. Tim was there too, and he let me ring Valida on the satellite phone. She said you seemed fine. You'd obviously got the messages, because when I came back, you were waiting for me, when I got out of the armoured shuttle from the airport, at the PTT. But you didn't kiss me when I ran to you. And you didn't ask me any questions about what it had been like. In fact, you hardly spoke to me at all, as we drove back to the Holiday Inn.

I tried to explain that it had been *worse* than Sarajevo; that I would much rather you had been with me as I huddled by the old bridge, watching people draw their water in buckets from the gorge beneath the snipers' sights; but the more I told of their sufferings, the angrier you got. And what I couldn't say was that I'd rather not have gone, because that wouldn't have been true.

It was when you saw my bikini marks you went mad. You were undressing me, back at the hotel. Suddenly, you stopped and stood back.

"Where you get that."

"Sunbathing," I said, but even then, I thought, Oh God.

"You did not sunbathe in Mostar."

I actually laughed, even though I knew you were furious. I knew why. But it was such a stupid image, me spreadeagled in a bikini, as the shells fell on the rooftops to either side.

"No, I didn't sunbathe in Mostar."

"You said you went to Mostar for work."

"I did go to Mostar for work."

"Then why you have this?" You almost slapped your hand against the white skin of my breast. I sat up and pulled up the sheet.

"I sunbathed in Split." I said, in the flat voice you use when you know there is nothing you can say.

"*Split!*" You spat it out as though I said I had been to Paris with another man. "You told me, you go to Mostar."

"I did go to Mostar. I was there for weeks."

"You said you come straight back."

Did I? I don't remember saying that but I probably did.

"I had to go to Split. I couldn't get back into Sarajevo any other way. The road's cut off. You know that. I had to get the plane. They fly from Split."

"You not sunbathe waiting for the plane."

Suddenly I lost my temper with you. It was better than feeling guilty all the time.

"Amir, for Christ's sake. I don't understand. Why are you so angry? All I did was spend a couple of days in Split."

Actually, it was four days, and it was bliss. Muffy and I went to one of the islands, and spent a couple of nights in an old Venetian palazzo on Hvar, drinking Posip in the sunset, swimming for hours in the sea. I'd still got only the clothes I'd come with in March; I'd sent my one pair of filthy jeans to the hotel laundry, bought some new underwear, flowery sundresses and some flip-flops in the market, bought some other summer clothes. I could hardly buy clothes in Sarajevo. All the shops were shut.

I wished you'd been there. It would have been better if you'd been there. But what shocked me, as I stocked up in the supermarket in Split with cheese and spices and oil for your mother, was how depressed I was at the thought of coming back.

But I couldn't explain that to you. You wouldn't understand, and anyway the depression lifted the moment I heard – as I felt, just as a vibration in my chest – the low roar of the Hercules coming down out of the mountains to Split and the sea; and adrenalin started surging and a smile opened across my face and I turned round to the man sitting next to me in the UN queue, some bloke I'd never met before, and said, "Here we go again!" And he grinned back.

"The paper gave me a couple of days off," I said.

"The paper. The paper. You just do what they say, all the time. It's the paper."

"But Amir," and I looked at you in genuine amazement, "the paper's why I am here." You didn't speak. You just got off the bed and started getting dressed.

"Where are you going?"

"Home. You not need me. You've got your paper."

I burst into tears. "I do need you," I said. "I do. I came back because of you. The paper wanted me to go to England. They wanted me to take two weeks off. But I came back for you. I wanted to see you. Please don't go. Please."

Nothing.

I went on: "I'm sorry. I'm sorry I didn't come back. I… I just needed to be somewhere nice for a few days. Please don't go."

"Somewhere nice… Split! When do I go somewhere nice?"

"Oh…………!" I must have looked ridiculous, sitting in bed on my own, in the afternoon sun, crying, with my white breasts luminous against my brown skin. "Please don't go," I wailed; I was so tired. I couldn't bear this too. "Don't leave me. I came back for you."

I didn't see you come back. I was crying too hard, but I felt the bed dent beneath your weight. Then you held me in your arms, and just said, "Molly." And then we made love, and I couldn't imagine how I could have put it off, what on earth I'd been thinking of going to Hvar with Muffy.

Afterwards, I said, "I missed you."

"I missed you too. I worried for you. Mostar is dangerous."

"I was worried about *you*." But actually, I hadn't worried that much. Mostar's swirling anarchy of war was so much more terrifying than Sarajevo's UN-held frontlines.

"I was worried you not come back."

"I will always come back," I said.

Later, when we were walking up to the Beeb after dinner, I said, "What did you do while I was away?"

You laughed, a little sadly.

"Not much," you said. "Like Sarajevo in old days. Before I met you. Stay at home. Sometimes I go to briefing, to TV station and see Edin, have beer. Go see Valida, see if she has a message from you. Maybe go and see some friends. Read... more light now in the evening. I don't know. Without you, not much to do."

I had a horrible vision of you driving round Sarajevo, risking your life out of loneliness, while Muffy and I were listening to cicadas, above an azure sea. Then I thought that, at 50 DM a litre, you probably hadn't even driven that far. Money, I thought. What had you done for money? You were used to me paying you by then. It's no good saying you'd had no money before, you could have no money again. People don't get used to going back. I asked you, and, in the candlelight, you looked suddenly ashamed. "It's OK," you said. "I do some stuff for Edin."

I stood stock still in the gallery, staring down into the darkness. The moonlight gleamed up from the marble floor below, and two figures sat, by a tiny yellow flame, drinking at the bar. I took your hand.

"I'm so sorry," I whispered; it was my turn to be ashamed. You must have thought me like a child who had got tired of a toy. "I'm so sorry."

Then you said to me, "So, tell me, how was the coast?"

I kissed your hair, I kissed your face, I wrapped you in my arms, as I said, "One day, I promise, we can go to the coast together." I'd get us out, even if it was just for a week. I'd somehow get you out for a break.

"One day," you said. "When the war is over." But I couldn't even think that far ahead.

Next time I went away, you worked for Ed, the American guy, who turned up again. The *Herald* had said I had to come back, even though I really didn't want to go, but the story was having one of its momentary lulls. Ed had returned for a couple of weeks to do a Big Piece for his Big Magazine on "wars I have known". I thought Ed was a bit of an arse – a self-important cynic – but Phil said he was a genius and to be fair, he'd always been very nice to me. He'd won the Pulitzer for some book he'd written on Vietnam or Korea called *I Hate My Brother's Guts,* when he was about ten. His young man's war. "It's a wonderful book," said Phil. "It made me cry. It's part of the reason I went to Beirut."

I'd have thought Ed would hire a beauty like Valida, but he was quite definite: "I want a man," he said. "I am a martyr to Interpreter Syndrome," Ed said.

"What's that?"

But he just looked at Phil and laughed and Phil said: "Not any more..."

It took me a long while to work it out, but I guess it's something you have to work out for yourself.

You and Ed drove me down to the PTT, that day, where the armoured shuttle was waiting to take me to the airport. It was a Heidi day, warm and blue, with white fluffy clouds sailing above the pine trees on the mountainside, where the men with beards sat with their mortars and rifles, drinking their little cups of coffee, and occasionally trying to kill someone.

The sun was gleaming off the APC's metal roof. It was a funny little thing, like a white throat lozenge, a little white tank, but with only a small gun. It was parked in the muddy car park, below the concrete ramparts, where the French Foreign Legionnaires hid behind their sandbags. It was filling up with the normal crew of hacks, and aid workers, people whose organisations were too small to have their own armoured cars, and the odd Bosnian. I couldn't understand quite how they were being allowed to leave. They looked scared. Ed said he didn't blame them, when you think what the fucking French had let the Serbs do to that foreign minister.

"Turajlic," you said.

"Yeah, last year. Those UN APCs aren't supposed to stop for checkpoints. But the fucking French let the Serbs shoot the poor bastard." I looked at the Foreign Legionnaires checking our papers but either they couldn't understand, or they chose not to hear. "The arseholes stopped at a checkpoint, opened the doors, and just stood there while the fucking Serbs pulled the poor sonofabitch out. He was on his way back from meeting some fucking foreign politician at the airport who didn't have the balls to come into Sarajevo himself. Fucking bastards." It wasn't clear if the last bastards were the Serbs, the French or even foreign politicians in general, and if the Legionnaires could understand Ed's rant, they made no sign. They just checked my passport and told me to get in.

I couldn't believe I was leaving you again. I was crying, saying I didn't want to go. It was Ed who had to disentangle me. "Come on, young lady, go home and sign those contracts while you're still covered in glory. Then you can come back. Sarajevo isn't going anywhere."

You said sadly, "I'm not going anywhere." And that made me cry even more. I thought, this is so unfair, why can't you come out with me as well. There was a bang, and Ed said, "We shouldn't hang around."

I clung to you, and you kissed me again, then you said to me, "Get into APC."

Ed turned to you and said, "Come on Amir, let's go commit journalism."

You looked at me, then back at him, then you said: "I love you. I want you to know. Please come back."

There was another loud bang, and then a third, and the whiff of cordite and rubbish drifted through the air. I said, "Amir, I love you too. I will always come back."

At about the same time as Ed said: "I think we should go."

Ed loved you as well. He said you were sharp. He said you were a real operator. He wrote me a letter saying: "Watch out, but he's worth hanging on to…" I burnt with pride. You learnt a lot, I think, working for Ed. And I learnt a lot from you afterwards. Ed had spent twenty-four hours in casualty, so we did that too. We went to the cigarette factory and the mortuary like him. And he'd spent the night in your friend Selim's trench, although you didn't want to do that this time, so I spent the night there with Phil instead, who said afterwards he would never complain about the Holiday Inn again. We were both freaked out that we'd bumped into Ray, the ex-US Marine who had said he was filing for the *Anchorage Bugle*. He seemed to have taken up residence in Selim's trench, and said plaintively he'd run out of film. "Although why that should matter," said Muffy when we told her, "since I don't think he's ever filed a story at all…"

I thanked Ed, when he came back in the autumn, and he laughed when I told him that I'd done all his stories again; he said – there's no such thing as a new story; they were Amir's stories anyway. He grilled me on everything that I had got, just to see if he'd missed something out. The only one I couldn't help him on were the black marketeers, because you never did that story with me. I meant to ask you why, but that was the day we saw the man get shot, so it put everything out of my mind.

Mujo goes fishing and he catches a golden fish. The golden fish says, I am a magic fish, and if you set me free, I shall give you a wish.

Mujo says, I want to get out of Sarajevo. I will die if I stay. But I don't want to crawl like a rat through the tunnel under the airport, and I don't want to run like a rabbit across the airport at night. I want to be driven to the plane in a UN armoured personnel carrier, like a government minister.

The fish says, go to sleep. You will have your wish.

The next day Mujo wakes up to find he's in a large apartment; he looks out of the window, he's in the centre of town. A dark maroon suit is laid over a chair. As he's getting dressed, fumbling with his unaccustomed tie, there is a discreet knock at the door, and a woman who looks like a secretary comes in. "Good morning Mr Turajlic," she says. "It's time for your trip to the airport."

IX

You knew, didn't you, that day, that I was ashamed? I tried to say sorry – I think I did, at the time – but then suddenly everything started happening so fast.

The man driving towards us was in a Golf, just like ours. The snows hadn't fallen yet and the clouds lay as grey as the tarmac and heavy over the town. We passed him as you were driving me back to the hotel from the PTT. The great dual carriageway was empty but for us. There was no movement from the pock-marked tower blocks to either side. On the right, over the frontline, in Grbavica, the Serbs' white, war-battered flats seemed as motionless as ours. I held my breath as we drove past the horribly dangerous bit, where the Bridge of Brotherhood and Unity reached out, unseen, towards the Serbs, behind its barricades of sandbags, gym lockers and parked ten-ton trucks, with the weeds growing thick on the earth piled round their sides, and the snipers picking off people through the gaps. At least, I suppose the bridge was still there, but we certainly couldn't see it: although I'd have known if it had been destroyed. The Bridge of Brotherhood and Unity being blown up would have been a great story. When I let out my breath, it came in a cloud, like the clouds pushing down on the mountains above. I always held my breath as we passed this bridge, except when we were in Phil's armoured car. In Phil's car, you'd make jokes about the absurdity of Tito's political slogans; now you didn't, maybe because you were worried about getting shot.

Like us, the other Golf was in the lane closest to the frontline, where the houses along where the river still must flow gave a little protection. It was our side of the road, as it happened, but that hadn't mattered since the war began eighteen months before.

I smiled at the driver as he passed. His face flashed from grim concentration into a quick smile back; it was a recognition, a brief, amused resignation, between those who still had to risk this road. He was middle-aged, dark-haired, with one of those high-cheek-boned faces and, beneath his grey anorak, he was wearing a tie. I wondered idly what he'd been doing that mattered enough to put a tie on today, to drive down this road.

We didn't hear the shot but I heard you swear, your eyes on the mirror, your face as though you had seen the devil over your shoulder at Halloween. I turned back, to see the other car crash into the wall. Anywhere else, he could have swerved to miss a child, or had a blow-out or something. But there were no children here.

"He's been shot," I said. "We should go back."

But you kept on driving.

"Amir! We ought to go back."

Nothing.

"Amir, stop!... We've got to help him. *Stop*."

Then you said: "No." You speeded up.

You'd never refused to do what I'd asked you before. But then, before this I don't think I'd ever questioned your judgement.

"Amir! He might need help." I think I thought you hadn't understood what I said.

You didn't look at me as you said: "Is too dangerous. Nothing we can do. He is dead." You looked at the road, whipping past us, a long grey blur of rotting weeds and boarded-up cement. I could see a muscle twitching in your leg; your face really did look as if all its blood had drained. Beads of sweat were springing up on your upper lip.

"Stop! You don't know he is dead."

"I am not going to stop."

You didn't. You kept driving faster and faster. It didn't matter what I said. I gave up after a bit anyway. There's a limit to how many times you can keep shouting stop! You didn't stop until we swerved round the egg-yolk-yellow and shell-black façade of the hotel, to its safe back door.

Miss Piggy stood waiting, opposite the twisted bus stop. I jumped out of the car, not looking at you.

"Molly, where you going?" you yelled.

"To get Phil."

"Wait!" I ran towards the door. You grabbed at my arm, but I pulled away.

"Let go of me!"

"What are you doing?"

"I'm going to get help."

"We can't help. It's too dangerous."

"Yes we can."

"It's what they want. You know that. They shoot someone and then they wait till people come to help and they shoot again."

"That's not the point!"

"Is point for me!" you screamed. "I don't want to die."

"Neither do I! But we have to go back!"

"I don't!"

"Well don't then," I said. "But let me go."

I shook off your arm and turned and ran into the hotel, nearly skidding on the slimy remains of last summer's weeds.

I rang Phil from reception.

"I'm coming down," he said. "Do we need Valida?"

"I don't think Amir's coming."

You were waiting in the shadows by the bar, putting an empty glass onto the burnished steel and your face was nearly as grey as the day we first met.

"Where are you going?" you said. I could smell the slivovic on your breath.

"You don't get it, do you?" My voice was quieter now. "He may still be alive."

The doors at the bottom of the stairs burst open and out ran Phil, his flak jacket flapping over the top of his fleece, like a little boy who hadn't got his ninja turtle fancy dress done up right. Bits of shaving foam clung to one of his cheeks, and the other still had stubble on it. His sandy hair, neat enough at the briefing, was damp in front and sticking up like Tintin. His tape recorder was slung over his shoulder and in his right hand, like an Olympic flame, he held his mike; from his left hung the helmet we never normally wore. "Phil!" I came out of the gloom.

"Great. Let's go."

I turned to follow but you grabbed my arm again. Whatever you were going to say never came, because the doors opened again, and out swung Valida. Like Phil, she was wearing her flak jacket. Between her scarlet nails, her helmet swung with the air of an evening bag.

"Where's Phil?"

"He's gone out to Miss Piggy. Amir, let me go."

But you didn't, you just said, "Molly, please..."

"If you want to come, Amir," said Valida, "we'd better get going. There's a helmet in the car."

"I don't think Amir is coming, Valida," I said.

"Yes I am." You let go of my arm. I looked amazed.

"You don't have to come, Amir," Valida said. "They've got me."

"I want to come."

Valida looked from you to me, standing a yard apart, hardly meeting each other's eyes. She shrugged. "Whatever we do, we must do now. Phil is waiting."

I followed her out of the door. I didn't look back, but I could hear you following me.

Phil didn't make any of his normal jokes as we piled into the car – the ones about school trips, or parents taking their children on picnics. He asked Valida: "Did you get through to the UN?"

"Yes. Barry said he'd try and get armoured ambulance."

It was cold in Miss Piggy – her armour plating was steel. She smelled of rust and oil and digestive biscuits. Two benches ran inside her down either side. In the middle, piled up against the back of the front seats, was a drift of the detritus of war reporting: a couple of flak jackets, a piece of rope, a first aid kit in a green plastic box, some jerry cans, an ancient copy of *The Times* that someone must have brought in one day, open at the TV listings, inexplicably given that we were two thousand miles from the nearest British TV, and didn't have any electricity anyway; a six-pack of mineral water, some sleeping bags, mini-Mars bars, a half-eaten packet of the biscuits that were giving her the smell. If the sniper pinned us down we could probably survive for days. Like an abandoned battle trophy, a helmet rolled backwards and forwards on the floor with the movement of the car.

You were opposite me, huddled in on yourself, and you wouldn't look me in the eye.

"Shit. I don't think I've got any spare batteries," said Phil. "Valida – you couldn't see if..."

"Spares are in glove compartment, Phil. I checked yesterday."

"Great."

Suddenly you sat up and gave a snort.

"You and Phil, you don't want to help that man. He is just story for you."

I didn't know what to say. You repeated it. "That is all. He is just a story for you."

"What do you mean?"

"You are going to write about him."

"Well, yes…" I wrote about everything here.

"So, he is just a story for you. You don't want to help. You just stop so you have your story."

"That's not fair!"

"Yes it is. This is all just story for you. All journalists are like that. You say you are doing good but is always just story."

"Well, it's better to do something, not just leave him to die."

"He is dead anyway."

"You don't know he's dead."

"Stop it, Amir," said Valida, leaning round over the back.

"Would you rather I wasn't here?" I asked Amir. "Is that what you are saying? Would you rather I left?"

"You won't leave. This is your job. You keep telling me that. That's why you are here."

"Well, it's true."

"You keep saying this is your job, then you say you love Sarajevo, but I bet if better war came along, you would leave and go to that. Well I can't leave. I did not choose to come here. This is my home. I had no choice. You did."

I gawped, but he carried on: "And I want to survive. You choose your job. You like your job. And you make good money out of all this death and shit. So don't make me feel like coward if I don't want to die to see a man who is already dead just for your story."

"It's not that I think you were a coward," (although I did, to be honest). "It's just that I thought we ought to have gone to help."

"No, you wanted him for your job."

We both ignored Phil saying: "Calm down you two."

"It is just standard human *decency*, but it is also my job."

"Well it is not mine."

"No, Amir, it *is* your job." I'd almost forgotten there was anyone else in the car. But it was Valida, leaning over the back of her seat. "You work for Molly. Of course she and Phil are going to do a story about him. That's why they are here. And she pays you, so you make good money out of this war too. You and me, we both do."

"They are like vultures. They like it when things get bad."

Valida broke into Serbo-Croat. I heard her say something about remembering what it was like before, when Amir had no money. And she said, look at other people, see how they live; you wouldn't be wearing that fancy coat without Molly – it was plaid, Giorgio Armani, and I'd bought it for him in London; he'd preened and put it on and said, "Do I look like the advert?" And he did.

Then I spoke, in Serbo-Croat: "*He wants paying me for coat but I not letting him.*" They both gawped.

"*Well, whose money was he using to pay you then, money you had given him?*" said Valida.

"*Amir's a good interpreter. He earns them. Maybe he's right about today. As he says, I make choice to come here. He no choice.*"

"*Amir doesn't have to be an interpreter. He doesn't have to be with journalists. He could still be sitting in a trench. With a gun, having shells fired at him. He could be a soldier like my father.*"

At that point Amir's Serbo-Croat got far too idiomatic for me to follow, but I could make out that he was complaining about Valida's father's appalling tactics and how Valida's father never left the safety of his office.

"*What about your father then?*" Valida asked. "*Or all your friends…*"

I didn't understand what Amir said next, but he was obviously furious.

"Just stop it you lot," said Phil. "I can't understand a word any of you are saying but I tell you, if you don't shut up, I'll make you and Molly get out and walk."

"That would be great story, wouldn't it? Journalist dead. Much better story than one Sarajevan."

"Amir, that's a horrible thing to say!"

"Well it's true. All Sarajevo is just a story for you." I remembered Phil's voice the day I arrived, saying, "The great thing about Sarajevo is you just start talking to anybody and there's your story." He was right. And I wrote about you.

Oh God, please don't ask me, I thought. I could hear Phil saying: "Do you think that guy in the car, *if* he is still alive, which, to be fair to Amir, he probably isn't but we have to check, gives a fuck why we are going to help him. I don't think so. I think he'll say thank you very much."

You said, as if Phil hadn't spoken at all: "When story is over, you leave and go onto another story." You were looking at me. You weren't angry any more. You looked terribly sad. "When war is over, you leave me too?"

I said nothing. The silence was broken only by the rattle of the car. Phil finally said, "I wouldn't worry about that, Amir. You'll have got fed up with Molly long before then."

"Am I just a story for you too?"

"No! No! Amir. No," I said. I grabbed at your hand. You let me take it but you didn't move towards me. You just looked at me, a mixture of suspicion and sorrow.

"You're not just a story. You're not."

Nobody spoke. You didn't move. Then Phil said, "I think we're here."

I dropped your hand and peered past Phil out of the windscreen. The road was deserted, apart from the Golf, maybe fifty yards ahead, dented into the wall where we left it ten minutes ago.

"That's it," I said. It looked empty. "Do you think he's got out?"

"Only one way to find out. The ambulance isn't here."

Phil drove fast, past the lorry and the sandbags hiding the bridge, over which, from the other side, the sniper had fired and hit the man. He parked the Land Rover in the shelter of the wall the Golf had hit.

"Right. Nobody gets out who doesn't want to get out. Nobody moves into the road where they can see you and NOBODY walks towards that bridge." Even Phil didn't say, as he normally did, you'd have to be bloody unlucky to get hit. "Oh, and both of you, get the helmets on. There are a couple of spares in the back."

Phil was already by the Golf by the time we were out of the car. He was staring in through the window looking puzzled. Valida was behind his shoulder.

"How is it?" you said, walking slowly towards the car. You glanced instinctively to the left to check the sniper's view was still blocked.

"I'm not sure," said Phil slowly, then: "Oh my God!"

Phil's lower lip sagged, and his eyes were round-eyed horror. The blue microphone slipped and swung at his side. Valida's eyes rounded too, her throat worked and she turned away from the car and leant against the wall. And Phil said, "Oh God, I think he's still..."

You started to run. You reached the driver's window and yelled: "Molly, don't go round the other side."

So of course I did. "It's fine I said, they can't see me here..." and then I stopped, because the front passenger seat window looked as if it were pressed deep into the bloody contents of a butcher's tray. Bits of meat and chips of bone squelched up against the car window as though it were polythene wrapping, by the weight of the body: except it wasn't a body, in the dead sense of the word. Because, although part of me was saying, he couldn't surely be alive, nothing could work with a hole like that in it, he obviously was, although probably not for long. The flesh glistened and twitched against the glass, the scarlet blood foaming up, dribbling down, collecting in a thin red line where the window slid into the door. And all this, framed by his anorak. Its collar, still intact, cut the neat dark head off from the plate-sized wound. I couldn't see his face. Phil must be staring at that.

I was transfixed. I had no idea what to do. Then, with the next pump of blood, I did what they do in films: I threw up, leaning on the door for support.

"*Don't* touch door," you said. I jumped back. "And *don't* go into road."

Phil stared at me in an amazement I did not understand; maybe Phil had seen this all before in Beirut. Maybe this was what I would have to get used to here.

"Where is ambulance? Phil? You said ambulance come."

"What?" Phil lifted his gaze but the road stretched grey and empty to east and west. "Barry said it would be here..." Phil seemed as confused as me.

"We have not time to wait," you said. You broke into Serbo-Croat, and Valida went running to the Land Rover. She came back with the first aid kit.

"*Hvala.*" You grabbed the first aid kit and opened it up. Inside were a tangle of bottles, syringes in transparent plastic and several thick pink packets, the size of bars of soap; they were field dressings. I had one myself in the front pocket of the flak jacket I was wearing.

"Should we move him? We could put him...we could lie him out in the back of the armoured car..." I'd never heard Phil sound so unsure.

"No. Not move. We must get him to hospital now."

You opened the back door of the car and shoved the first aid box on the seat. Then you leant over to speak to the man. It seemed almost obscene to me, faced as I was, with his raw flesh squelched against the glass. You spoke to him in Serbo-Croat, a soothing voice, and then barked in English: "Molly, are keys still there? Can you get into driver's seat?"

I ran round to the driver's side.

From this side, the man looked almost normal, apart from the fact he was sitting at a strange angle, squashed up against the passenger seat door, with his legs twisted over the gears, and his face looked like death. But other than that, there was nothing to see; white shirt, anorak, even his tie was still intact. He watched me as I opened the door, he watched us all the time, mute, like an animal in a cage; occasionally his head would twitch. I wanted to say something to help, to reassure him, like you were. I didn't understand why he wasn't screaming. Perhaps it was shock. I froze. It was like watching this happen to somebody else.

"Amir," it was Phil. "What do you want us to do?"

"He is nearly dead. I have to stop blood otherwise he die. We have to get him to hospital. We have to drive *this* car to hospital."

We all did what you said. Phil propped the man up from the front, while you handed me one of the pink packets from the first aid kit.

"Open this." Inside was a white oblong, about the size of a bar of soap. Round it went a red tag, like on a cigarette packet.

I pulled the tag. The wrapping split. Out bulged a mass of browny-pink gauze over a thick white pad, with yard-long streamers attached. It looked just like the ancient sanitary towels matron had at school. You ripped off the streamers and shoved the whole thing in the wound.

"Another." I did the next two. Then we'd run out. But you unwound the scarf I'd given you from your neck and stuffed that into the man's back as well. "Take this," I said, and pulled out mine from my pocket.

You told me to reach into your pocket – there was a long, stretchy bandage, wrapped in cellophane. You and Phil wound him round, front and back. Then you said: "Molly, you help hold him. Phil, start the car."

Phil drove us to the hospital at eighty miles an hour. He could. There was nothing else on the road. Valida clanked, miles behind, in Miss Piggy. I didn't even think, at that time, that it was odd the man was in the passenger seat. At one point Phil said, "It would be ironic if *we* were hit." And I remember thinking, but we *can't* be hit. We've just survived. We're helping him. That wouldn't be fair. Not for this man, who thought he had died and has just started to think he might live. There should be a rule; nobody should have to go through this twice.

"We haven't got any more of those field dressings, anyway," said Phil.

You said, after a moment, "I have another in my pocket… right pocket." I was so grateful you'd managed to keep one, when we'd given all of ours away.

The blood jiggled down the window, where the man had been leaning, and collected in the fake pores of the upholstery. We looped past the Presidency and over Marshal Tito then up past the football stadium where all the new graves had been dug since half the cemeteries in town were in the snipers' sights, and the war dead had long overflowed the rest. Phil was giving a running commentary as he drove, using his careful radio voice. His mike was on. For a moment, I was shocked, and then I thought, my brain's on: I'm remembering all of this.

You were the one who was in control that day. When we got to casualty, you told me to run in; you told me what to say in Serbo-Croat. It was pretty easy: "*Snajper*" would have done it.

As I ran in, everyone turned to look; they were waiting on plastic chairs, just as they do in casualty anywhere, surrounded by white walls, notice boards: but it was cold and dark, not hospital bright, and instead of disinfectant, there was the ubiquitous smell of pee. The nurse sitting by a candle at the triage desk snapped upright. I told her what you had told me to say. She ran round a corner, yelled something, and two men appeared. In under a minute they had a trolley and a drip. They ran out to the car, got the man and whisked him away, with Phil, Valida and I tramping in their wake. You didn't want to see the operation, although the surgeons let us watch.

You were sitting in the corridor outside the operating theatre, with a woman by your side, when we came out. She looked pretty, but it was hard to see in the gloom. You stood up as we came out. You gave me an almost frightened look. Then, before we could speak, you turned to the woman.

She had black hair, and in the semi-darkness, the livid bags beneath her eyes seemed to brand her pale skin. Like all women here, she was very slim, and her eyes glinted liquid with shock.

"This is wife," you said, and introduced her as Amra. She grabbed my hand, and started to cry, thanking me.

"*No, No,*" I said, "*Not me, him.*"

I pointed at you, just as Phil grabbed your hand and said, "You saved his life. Amazing."

You looked bewildered from me to Phil.

"Where did you learn to do that?" Phil carried on.

"*Armija,*" you shrugged. "I spent one year on frontline." You looked so worried, as you gazed straight at me. I was about to say something, when the door opened behind us. Our man appeared on the trolley, unconscious, drips in his arms, chest shaved, half naked except for the bandages; behind him, Valida, masked like us, was talking to one of the surgeons.

His wife ran over to where he lay and started to weep. She put her hands out, fingering the air, but no closer – the nurses wouldn't let her touch him. You put your arms round her, and she turned and sobbed into your chest. They wheeled him up the passage, and you followed with her. Phil and I glanced at each other, and then fell in behind.

The nurse in casualty, via Valida, told us you had gone to fetch his wife, in his car, from her apartment in one of the Austrian blocks, tucked away behind the cathedral. You'd got a neighbour to look after the children and brought her to the hospital while we were watching the operation.

We offered to take you back with us to the hotel, but you wanted to stay with her till he woke up.

"She hasn't got anyone else," you said, at her side.

So Phil said, "We'll come back," he didn't say, "after lunch." But that's what he meant. "Is there anything you need?" And she said, nothing, even though the list of what anyone needed in Sarajevo could have started with freedom and ended up with cooking oil. We did bring her some batteries, some chocolate, some cigarettes and some coffee. And we brought you some lunch, cheese rolls. We brought some for her too, which she ate with bewilderment.

Her husband was awake when we returned, his wife at his bedside, holding his hand. Phil and I shuffled, embarrassed, in the far corner of the room, as though we would be more tiring the closer we came. He lay, weighed down by loss of blood and bandages, sprouting tubes. He tried to smile when we were introduced but even that was far too much. His wife picked up a pair of business cards.

"He can't speak," she said, through you. "But he wants to say thank you." Her eyes welled, her voice caught. "I want to say thank you too. He wants to say… he says, if he can help. Ever. If there is anything he can do." And she handed us the cards. One each; half-smeared with blood. But through the brownish stain, I read: *Petrovic Dragan, Detective Inspector.* I looked at it and thought – Dragan – Petrovic – that's a Serb name.

"Amir, you were amazing, you know," Phil said, as we crammed into the front of Miss Piggy.

I squeezed your hand. "You really were," I said.

You still looked worried. "Really," I said. That's when I think you first realised I wasn't angry with you.

You looked into my eyes and said: "You made me go back. That was you."

But I said: "I didn't know what to do. He would have died without you."

You didn't speak. You just looked at me.

"I'm sorry," I said.

"What for?" I didn't know, really – being foreign, for the war. For expecting too much. For the fact that a black-market cabbage cost twenty Deutschmarks and a child could be shot while fetching water from the street.

"I'm sorry too. I am glad you are here," you said.

"Oh…" I gazed at you. Sarajevo whisked past our windscreen but neither of us were looking at the road.

Then Phil's voice broke in: "Amir! I bet you never thought you'd save the life of a Serb policeman."

That night, wrapped up in bed against the cold of my room, I said to you: "In the *Armija*, did you have to do things like that before?"

"A few times." Then you laughed, and shook your head: "Never to a Serb."

"He's a Sarajevo Serb. He stayed here. He's one of you. Wasn't one of your grandmothers a Serb? I thought that was what you were all supposed to be fighting for?"

"That was before." I was horrified by your words. I drew my hands away.

"Don't say that."

"Why not? It's true. Sarajevo is dying in this war."

"It will die if you think like that. That's what makes it die."

"Soon it will be too late," you said. "I think it is too late now." Then you kissed me again, and politics didn't seem important any more.

Later, you leant over me and traced your fingers in my hair. You didn't speak for a moment, and I lay there, dozing into your touch, then you said: "Molly. I want to ask you something."

I turned on my shoulder to look at you, the candlelight flickering on your skin, your dark eyes hooded in the shadows of the night, the scoop of your muscles, that made me want to bite your arm. "Ask me anything," I said.

"Something very important."

I said again: "You can ask me anything." But I felt afraid.

"I love you," you said, but not as if it were the thing in itself; more as if it were the prelude to something else.

"I love you too." I started stroking your cheek, but my stomach had the feeling it had when I was afraid. "What is it?"

You said it in Serbo-Croat first, and I almost didn't understand, and then I thought, you can't have said that, I must have got it wrong. But then you said it again in English, and I knew that I hadn't and my heart sank because I knew what I had to say. I also knew you would never forgive me.

"Will you marry me?" you said.

I said, "I can't."

The Chetniks arrested a group of Muslim women.

"We're going to rape you all," said one of the Chetniks.

"What, even this young girl, she is only 14!" said one of the women.

"I said all of you."

"Even this pregnant woman?"

"All of you."

"Even this old lady, she is over 80?"

Before he could answer, the old woman said: "The man was clear. He said all of us."

February 2000

People keep telling me it wasn't my fault. People have said that to me for years. But I never really believed them. It was the man in the jacuzzi who helped the most. The clinic was wonderful, if rather strange, and I came to love Irene (who turned out to have fled Greece after the Colonels came to power). Sarah, the receptionist, was terribly nice. I wished her the best of luck in her night school course in Psychology. After I left them, after probably the most expensive month of my life (apart from the Gorazde crisis – one of those five-week Serbs-attack-a-Muslim-enclave, the-Great-Powers-align-and-World-War-III-is-about-to-break-out-oh-no-it-isn't frenzies – where my phone bill at the BBC came to $25,000), Irene put me onto someone nearly as nice in London, who I went and whined at twice a week.

They were terribly nice about it all at work, although I did sometimes catch them looking at me a bit strangely, as though they suddenly expected me to knife someone. My boss was very disappointed there hadn't been any celebrities in my bin. She kept asking about the sauna. I think she thought it was Champneys. She also wanted me to be on Prozac, like the poor Princess of Wales, but I said: "What's the point? I'd rather have some real feelings and learn to deal with those."

I was worried about that. Because when they went through the list of the symptoms of what they said I had – the irritability, the mood swings, the obsessive addictions, the inability to make or maintain close relationships – I began to think if they took all those away I'd have no character left at all.

Then they all sat around expecting me to get better. But it takes a long time.

It was six months later I met the man in the jacuzzi. I was on holiday, in the Caribbean, in a sort of spa, with a friend whose boyfriend had chucked her, which was convenient for me because it was becoming increasingly difficult to find people to go on holiday with. It looked just like the posters in the tube in January: azure sea, palm trees, lots of white sand. I kept expecting Sean Connery to come snorkelling out of the shallows, but most guests were obese Americans fleeing their winter.

One afternoon, quite late, I went along to the jacuzzi, which was bubbling under its palm tree, overlooking the beach. A fat Canadian couple, with his-and-hers almost equally plump breasts, were talking with un-jacuzzi animation to a wizened old man. When I got in, all blonde and bikini, the conversation snapped. Then they started again, rather diffidently, and they were talking about Auschwitz, but in a weirdly familiar way, the way I might, say, about Sarajevo. So I started to listen. I could hardly avoid it; we were all simmering away in the same cauldron of tourist soup, and I've always had a bit of a thing about the Holocaust anyway. I remember my mother explaining it to me years ago – she had some cousins who were part Jewish – when I asked her "Who won the war, Mummy?" just as she was trying to help the cook for some embassy cocktail party. "If Hitler had won, all your cousins would have been killed. They would have been sent to the gas oven," she said, opening the oven and popping in a tray of vol-au-vents (it was the seventies after all).

That has always been the image of the Holocaust for me. Trays of human vol-au-vents, popped in the ovens.

The Canadians were listening to this man as though he were the voice of God. They noticed me listening, as you do in a confined space, and the Canadian man turned to me and said, rather apologetically, "We're talking a rather gloomy subject for a holiday."

"Oh, not at all. I'm rather obsessed by the Holocaust."

They looked astounded. The old man said to me, in tones of amazement and a thick Mitteleuropean accent: "But you are not Jewish?"

"No." They looked doubtfully at me – maybe they thought I was German? I was sitting there in my bikini in all my Aryan splendour. The old man said, almost accusingly, "Then why?"

I couldn't explain about the vol-au-vents, not to them, so I said the next thing, which was: "I used to live in a country where there was a genocide."

The Canadian man looked surprised and said, "What, Rwanda?"

"No, Bosnia."

The three of them nodded, considered it, and gave the 200,000 or so dead Muslims the benefit of the doubt. I was allowed to join in. The old man said, proudly, "I was in Auschwitz." And showed me the number on his arm. You could hardly see it now, with the wrinkles and the liver spots. But the Canadians had, because the woman said, rather apologetically, "I noticed it, you see, because my mother has one. That's how we started."

Her husband nodded: "Both our parents are survivors..."

"They never talk about it," said his wife.

The old man started to talk again. I couldn't stop asking him questions. I drew the story out, starting at what I thought would be the end, the day he realised the war was over when he woke up to find the guards had gone. They'd thought it was another trick, then they realised it wasn't. He'd wandered out into the lanes. Some Americans passed him as he stood on the side of the road, and threw him a bag of peanuts, three of which made him too full to eat. I worked him slowly back, back in cinema in his head, back along what he called "the death march", when the Germans forced the prisoners who could move to walk west, away from the Russian advance. Back into Auschwitz, back into the huts, out through the gates and into the train, back to the day he was caught – the last of his family to be arrested, near the end of the war, in Berlin in May 1944. The Canadians sat and listened.

I didn't mean to take over, but it was just like work. Then the old man talked about life after the war: hitching home in the chaos of Germany that summer, staying in a barn for a month with three Polish Jews who wouldn't let him sleep on the bed because he was a *Jacke*, a middle class German Jew; the farmer who let him sleep in the stables but could not look him in the eye; the day he finally came home and found his house in Berlin, a ruin. As he stood in front of the bombed wreck of his childhood, a man in the street said to him: "If you're after the family in that house, they've left a message." Seeing something written in red paint ("that's what people did, they wrote where they had gone in red paint"). It was an address, two underground stops away, and it was signed by his father.

"That meant my father was alive!" he said. He grinned, even now, as he said it. "So I ran across the street to the underground station. And I was so excited I didn't look where I was going. And this German traffic policeman shouted at me – and you must understand, I was very fed up of being shouted at by Germans in uniform by now – he shouted: 'Do you want to get yourself killed?' And in German this is 'Are you tired of life?' So I shouted back, 'No! I will never tire of life!'

"I didn't stop running till I got to the door. *Then* I stopped. I was scared of what I would find. But I knocked, and my sister opened it up. My sister! Alive too. And then, she said to me, 'Shush! Mother is asleep.' I knew then that we had all survived. We were all in different camps but we all survived. We were the only whole family to survive the Holocaust," he said.

People, incidentally, have since told me that's not true, that other whole families did survive, but I will leave him his boast. There can't have been so very many after all.

Then he started to talk about afterwards, he talked about survivor guilt syndrome. I said: "Oh, I think I've got that." He looked at me as if I were completely insane, because he was so far gone inside his past that he had forgotten, I think, that anyone else was here. He said to me, quite rudely, although German accents can make things rude, "Why on earth do *you* have survivor guilt syndrome?" The Canadians both turned to stare.

At this point, the conversation was artificially broken. I think a waiter came up and told us dinner had begun. The Canadians dispersed in a flurry of thanks, and introductions. We all suddenly felt naked, now we knew each other's names.

I heaved myself out of the water too. But the old man said again, in a much more gentle voice: "Why *do* you have survivor guilt syndrome?" But the cinema had stopped. I said, very quickly, "Oh, because I could leave and they couldn't. I could eat and they couldn't." I thanked him and walked back towards the hotel.

He came up to me the next day and said, "I need to ask you a question." But I was in a hurry, so I said, "I can't talk now." He looked at me very carefully and said, "When you have time. You said something yesterday about survivor guilt syndrome, and I asked you why, and you gave me a very glib answer. I want to talk to you."

"I haven't got time now," I said.

He caught up with me at breakfast the following day, his plate piled with food from the veranda buffet. "So," he said, and he stood by my chair, "will you tell me now?"

There was no excuse. I told him about you. The old man looked at me with infinite pity. He waited for maybe ten or twenty seconds before he spoke and then he said: "When I was on the death march from Auschwitz in January 1945, the Germans were shooting the stragglers at the back. I was young. I was only 19. And I'd only been in the camp for six months. I was helping this old, old man to walk. And he was only 35 but he was an old, old man. And we kept getting nearer and nearer to the back. And finally, when we were the last, one of the SS guards, who could see I could still walk, said to me: 'If you don't want to get yourself killed, get your arse up to the front of this line.'"

He waited for another five seconds before he said: "So I left him. And I heard the shot. You have to live with that for the rest of your life. But I did not shoot him and I did not start the war. That is what you have to remember."

He looked out to sea, over his teetering plate.

"I love this place," he said. "I come every year. It's like a camp." He smiled at me, and nodded over at the uniformed Australians whose job was to check we were all having a good enough time. "I call them the guards," he said. "But the food is so good and they give you as much as you want."

WHAT's the difference between Sarajevo and Auschwitz?
In Auschwitz, they had gas.

1994

X

I hadn't wanted to come back this time. I couldn't understand it but I definitely hadn't. Normally my heart leapt at the adventure, at seeing my love, at seeing you. Reassembling the trappings of my life – the short-wave radio, the Swiss Army knife, the thick bunch of fibre-tipped pens now taken by the bushel from the *Herald*'s stationery cupboard rather than bought expensively in WH Smith's at Heathrow. But this time it was different. Even you here, waiting for me, didn't temper that lump of dread.

When I tried to work out what I feared in the exciting new life I had craved so much, it seemed to come down to the people, the Sarajevans – not you of course, never you – but having to talk to the others, which seemed ridiculous, since I loved Sarajevo and its people and to help the people was part of the reason I had gone, that I had stayed. But I'd noticed, frozen as they were into their second winter of war, that they were no longer so keen to talk to me. Even your friends were angrier. As the cold bit deeper, their resentment frothed out, as though the ice was forcing it up, through the veneer of their civilisation they wore to protect them from the shells. They took it out on us: maybe because they were disappointed with the rest of the world but, trapped as they were, we were the only representatives of the rest of the world they could actually vent their frustration on. They no longer seemed to believe that we, the journalists who had chosen to live with them in this siege, had the power to help them back to their lost cosy world.

I was beginning to fear they might be right; that, although

logically I knew I was doing the best I could for Sarajevo by being here, nothing I could do would give them back that cosy ordered world. Even if they won the war, which seemed so unlikely (although the Muslims had, to our amazement, held the Croats in central Bosnia at bay), their pre-war world had gone. Maybe you were just one more person I would disappoint; maybe you would resent me too.

I hadn't wanted to come back but of course I did. It was my job and there was you. Besides, I didn't seem to be able to do anything else any more. Back home, back in England, I still rented a room in my friend Lucy's flat. She said I was the perfect flatmate: paid the bills, was never there. In fact, like Johnny, she used the same phrase: "you left me for a country". Much better than a boyfriend, she said, because countries can't chuck you and send you crawling back to sob your way through all the loo paper. But maybe they can. Perhaps that's what Yugoslavia did to you.

Everything in England just seemed strange. I found myself almost fighting for air. I couldn't bear being inside (which is the best place to be in London in January) and went for endless long walks in the biting rain. I found myself dashing pointlessly over crossroads, having to force myself to walk slow, to make myself remember, at the 7-Eleven corner shop on Westbourne Grove, that there were no men now in the hills with guns trained on me; to make myself walk on the grass, retrain my brain that no-one had ever sown mines in Hyde Park. I couldn't even talk to anyone about it, because they would have thought I was mad, or very pretentious.

I stacked up meetings with friends – lunches, drinks, dinners, even tea if they didn't work. But however much I saw them, I didn't really have anything to say, apart from wowing the girls with Henri's photograph of you. (Although Lucy said, with deep suspicion, "I suppose he's very good-looking". And when I had asked her what she meant, she said: "I don't trust good-looking men. They're never… grateful enough." And I was shot through, because, my poor love, you were definitely grateful.) But my friends all seemed to be obsessed by the most trivial things, and so profoundly ignorant.

It wasn't even cold enough for my hat, the fur hat you bought me. Whenever I wore it, it made my head all sweaty. I wanted to wear it to remind me of you, but in the end it stayed on a shelf in the hall.

You bought it in Merkale, Sarajevo market, on a quiet day the November before. We'd left the car by the side of the road, and headed into the rows of stalls. Of course, there were other market-places during the war; stalls sprang up on any sheltered street on days when the shelling was quiet, but this was the town's main market-place. Women in sagging winter-coats and scuffed leather gloves, with the high cheekbones and red lipstick of Old Sarajevo, stood behind makeshift tables full of china, bits of piping, or single shoes, flogging off the piecemeal of their lives; women with the headscarves, gnarled faces and baggy flower trousers of the Bosnian mountains screamed out, cabbages, only 20DM each, or coffee, 80DM a kilo – rows of tins of UNHCR-issue fish and bottles of UNHCR oil. I'd asked you then, when I saw a sack of peppers for over 200DM, "Where does all the food come from?" I said, "Do they bring it through the tunnel?" Meaning the Bosnian government's worst-kept secret; the city's black-market life-line, a tunnel gouged, once the government had realised that their siege wasn't going to go away, beneath the UN-held airport, linking Sarajevo to the rest of Bosnian government territory, on the far side of the runway. You laughed and said: "What tunnel?" I said. "Come on." But you said, "What tunnel," again and shot me a look.

At the back of the market, two old men, standing behind their stalls of household tat, with the pained dignity of retired schoolmasters, were warming themselves on a pile of burning rubbish, whose acrid smoke drifted over the little square. Most of the men here were past middleage; although I did see a couple of youths in communist-grey fur hats and trainers selling fags. The old men looked askance at you.

"Aren't they all scared to be here?" I asked.

You shrugged. "They have to eat. Snipers can't see. It's quiet today."

We were walking up the stalls, when I saw, on a stall, the kind of hat Anna Karenina might have worn. The man selling it had dark hair, going white. He could have been you, maybe twenty years on, but the war had carved deep lines in his cheeks and his stall, like those of the Sarajevo ladies, was piled with taps, plastic bottles, potatoes and bits of crochet. He looked me up and down when I asked the price. I watched him draw up the courage before he spoke.

"Fifty Deutschmarks," he said, and when I didn't flinch, he suddenly became garrulous. The hat had been his daughter's, he said; I turned for you, but you were chatting to some young guy, smoking by a stall. "*Doesn't she need it?*" I asked, in my limping Serbo-Croat.

"*She's not here.*" He flapped his hand beyond the Serb lines. "*She's out of Sarajevo.*" His eyes suddenly filled with tears. You came back, just as I was asking him what he used to do; a lawyer, and he'd sent his 16-year-old daughter out when the war was beginning, eighteen months ago. You tried to bargain the price down, but I wouldn't let you. It was the *Herald*'s money anyway. Then you paid for it yourself.

I don't know if the old man was there the day the market was shelled. Or perhaps he had already sold everything he owned or perhaps he didn't go every day.

I was still trying to wear your hat, the night I went to a dinner party, in a little mews house in Notting Hill, given by a friend to show off her new boyfriend. Johnny was there, with *his* new girlfriend. He'd wanted me to meet her. She was sweet: pretty, funny, clever, thin. She'd been at Oxford with me, but a couple of years below. She took a fashionable amount of coke – not enough to be a problem, just enough to fit in (they'd all nipped off to the bathroom at various points, in pairs, but I didn't go; that kind of buzz just seemed pointless to me. Adrenalin, I suppose, is free). She ate like that, too: enough to look normal, but not enough, obviously, to put on weight, since her black leather trousers were pretty unforgiving. She had a very smart surname, one of those ones you see on street signs (he must have realised now, poor Johnny, that my father being an ambassador did not make me an ar*is*tocrat, as I noticed he no longer pronounced it). She obviously thought Johnny was wonderful, laughing at all his jokes, which must have been a bit of a relief. I just used to take the piss out of him towards the end. I thought he liked it. Or at least, the fact I thought he liked it was one of the things that made me love him. Perhaps he had hated it all along.

The hostess's new boyfriend, big in Alternative Comedy (which was a big thing to be big in back then) had started sounding off to the table about Bosnia, because in those days Alternative Comedy embraced politics. He had already put everyone's backs up by making it quite clear he thought that we were a bunch of boring Sloanes (his girlfriend was just beginning to shake the dust of the Old Vicarage off her L K Bennett kitten heels and dance off into the Groucho club; this dinner was almost her last backward glance). He started talking your standard ill-informed Balkan rubbish, batting away every interjection with a sneer that made it clear he couldn't believe that anyone who spoke like us could utter anything worth hearing. I could see the others giving me little sideways glances but I didn't speak, because I couldn't face it, but he was talking such crap about Bosnia that finally I felt I *had* to intervene. Slowly, the rest of the table fell silent, until only he and I were left in the ring. They all knew, of course, the others – including his girlfriend, who seemed paralysed at his impending fate. Johnny (who found him particularly irritating, possibly because he had spent a lot of effort becoming a boring Sloane like us and didn't like the idea that maybe his aspirations were being proved anachronistic) actually mouthed across the table to me: "What are you waiting for?" But I didn't want to do it, because it seemed so pointless and unfair.

He walked into it, in the end. "Well, if you know so much about it, when was the last time you were in Sarajevo then?" he said, and I could hear Johnny's intake of breath. There was a pause, and then I replied: "I got back last night."

That was fun. That was worth it. It's a good memory to have. And after the dinner was over, Johnny, slightly drunk, collared me in the corner and said, "You are wonderful. You're wonderful," and ran his fingers down my cheek, then he got into the minicab he had ordered with his nice, pretty, thin, clever, well-connected girlfriend who laughed at his jokes and they went home together, leaving me cross and drunk at the dinner. As for the comedian, to be fair, he completely changed gear. He was quieter and nicer, and not just to me, and asked lots of interesting questions and, once I had started, once I had an audience that seemed interested, and launched into my explanations with a missionary's zeal, he listened long beyond the point at which his girlfriend's eyes began to glaze and small side conversations started up elsewhere round the table. But it was so wonderful to have someone to talk to who seemed to genuinely want to know. It seemed impossible to make people understand, if they hadn't managed to pick it up in two years of front-page news. And even when I had my now traditional lunch with Roger, the foreign editor of the *Herald*, I felt as if he'd hardly read anything I'd written.

Most people asked things like, "Do you actually go anywhere dangerous?" When I tried to explain, they simply looked incredulous, as if no-one could possibly choose to live in a hotel 250 yards from the frontline, where snipers shot outside your window and you were woken up every morning by a bored machine gunner sounding off in the Jewish cemetery up the hill.

As I write those words, I don't blame my friends. Because it seems completely extraordinary to me, now, that that was my life. Like the young do, I took it for granted. But I envied my friends because they still had the cosy, ordered world. I felt like a Victorian match girl watching someone else's Christmas through a snow-flecked window but, unlike the match girl, I had chosen to walk out into the snow. Maybe I had always felt a bit outside-looking-in – if you are brought up in embassies all over the world, you tend to be at home nowhere, or anywhere with high ceilings and people speaking a gaggle of languages you don't really understand. I was too young, as well, to know that most people feel like outsiders too, so I knew that, whatever the dread coagulating in my guts, I had to return to where I belonged.

The dread began to shrink as I started packing. As usual, I had left it to the last half an hour; packing, like writing, expands to fill the time you leave for it, plus 10%, and it wasn't like I didn't know what to pack these days. It was a big case, now, bigger than the one I'd taken last April. It's easy to pack light, when it's just for a few days, but the longer you travel, the more little comforts become indispensable: the portable CD player, with tiny speakers you can set up in your room, the photographs in the little leather frame, the Rose Geranium bath oil to remind you of another life, even if it's only going in a basin of stone-cold water; the piles of books for loneliness and boredom, clothes to look a bit smarter, changes of scruffy clothes, lots of underwear (laundry in a town with no water is a serious problem), make-up, scent; a bottle of whisky to make friends with, chocolate, Marmite; Earl Grey tea bags, most of which I would donate to the BBC and then drink. These are the things which began to weigh me down, let alone the necessities like candles and batteries, deodorant, thermal underwear and pens. I now know why Englishmen would dress for dinner in the bush.

But as I began to gather the necessities of my new life, I felt the start of the old excitement.

I paved the bottom of the case with *Tom Jones* and four of *The Barchester Chronicles* (I'd finished Tolstoy last year), and shoved *The Warden* in my computer bag. The phrase book that never seemed to have the right phrases in it was still in the case, rolling around with all the stuff I had stopped bothering to unpack: the spare batteries and pens, the tampons and the medical kit, the fleecy gloves. I stuffed the helmet with about fifteen pairs of pants and shoved it in one end of the bag (I wouldn't need it until tomorrow when I'd get the plane to Sarajevo). I picked up the shortwave radio, that badge of my profession from by my bed, locked it off and folded it away into the suitcase.

Then I zipped it up, and stood, in my jeans and boots and poloneck and fleece, flak jacket propped against the door, computer in its bag, cushioned in its nest of telephone wires and cables. Notebook in my handbag and two extra pens, along with the great wad of Deutschmarks Roger, my foreign editor, had reluctantly extracted from the *Herald's* managing editor yesterday, and of course my passport (I was picking the ticket up at Heathrow). I found the Swiss Army knife by the wine rack and put it in my handbag too. Now I was armed and ready to commit journalism.

I sat in the minicab heading for Heathrow, being borne off to war, and passed the Lucozade clock, and noticed, as I did every time with unfulfilled curiosity, the red-brick campanile protruding bewildered from the tangle of nameless streets which slipped away beneath the concrete piers my mother had always said were stuffed with the victims of some sixties' gang war. By now, I was smiling, because the adventure had begun.

By the time I had handed over my £17 (special price for Heathrow) and put the receipt, first of many, into the designated receipt pocket of my money belt, checked in with Croatian Airlines (the 12.55, and always slightly late) and was scanning the queue for friends (you nearly always bumped into someone you knew, someone you could share a cab with from the airport, get drunk with on that last night of decent food and wine in Split), London and that life was already far behind. By the time I was stocking up on Silk Cut in the duty free – impossible to get, except in the British officers' mess, miles away in Vitez, deep in Central Bosnia, where the British troops were based, monitoring the Muslim–Croat sideshow civil war. And that wasn't much use anyway, considering journalists were other ranks – it no longer mattered that I had apparently offended someone's mother by drinking and swearing too much at lunch. I was back in Sarajevo long before the RAF Hercules started its long dive into the airport, corkscrewing at an angle to avoid the Serb guns, and hovered on the runway, propellers churning, while we all dashed out, helmeted and jacketed up, towards the safety of the sandbagged terminal. Back with you.

I took the shuttle in from the airport to the PTT and then got a lift with one of the other journalists who was being picked up in a car. It was impossible to know when one would arrive, so I'd given up trying to get you to meet me. But I knew you'd be waiting for me at the hotel, a bit surly, as you always were. You'd be there, when I walked into the BBC office and greeted the incumbent, whoever it was, with "Hi honey, I'm home."

Mujo and Suljo were sprinting in the dark across the airport runway to get out of Sarajevo to find some food. Suddenly Suljo heard a chattering sound coming from Mujo's bag.

Suljo: "What have you got there?"

Mujo: "Fata's false teeth."

Suljo: "Why?"

Mujo: "So that she cannot eat all humanitarian aid while I am gone."

XI

I had just assumed that Bosnia would be more of the same. You and me and Sarajevo and the Holiday Inn. Our same life of cold and no water and no electricity and nobody giving a fuck as the stranglehold increased and the city slowly gave up its dead, the starved, the frozen, the shot, the shelled, as oases of grief in the interminable boredom of the siege. But it wasn't.

The shell that fell on the market changed everything for us. It fell out of a clear blue February sky – another of those perfect Heidi days. It was just like all the other shells that had fallen in the last three months. Only this one didn't just leave a hole in the pavement, or knock through somebody's roof, or maybe kill an old lady dragging her water home, or just blow the legs off a man sprinting back with the sawn-off branches of a tree, or turn to bloody pulp a couple of children playing snowballs. It landed in the middle of Merkale, where you'd bought me my hat.

The market was full of people that day: I saw all their bodies smashed into the crimson snow on television. They probably thought they were safe, although the Serbs did shell the Old Town a lot – most of the inhabitants were Muslims who'd lived there since the days of Ali Pasha.

The market was tucked into one of those deep gullies of Austrian apartment blocks and shops that ran behind the cathedral, where the snipers couldn't see.

It was a beautiful day and the war had been very quiet for a while – "repetitive" had been Roger, my foreign editor's word, when he'd complained again about the cost of the Holiday Inn, and sent me away. Go to Zenica, he'd said, naming a Muslim-held town half-way to Tuzla, across a web of frontlines. I didn't want to go. It was a nightmare to get to and there were no phones in the town so I couldn't talk to you; I couldn't even file to the desk on Saturday; hardly anyone had mobiles then, and the Serbs had long ago shelled the mobile mast anyway. But Roger brushed all this aside: "You haven't been there for ages. They must be up to something there. Forget this week. Nothing's happening. File when you get back." (And I could almost hear him thinking, "and it's so much cheaper".) I didn't ask him how repetitive he thought the war felt for all of you.

The girl in the fur hat at Reception at the hotel in Zenica had a radio to her ear as we came out of lunch: "A shell has fallen on Sarajevo market. Many people are dead." Her dark eyes looked even more pained than they had when I arrived yesterday. I thought, oh my God, how utterly awful – those poor, poor people. And then I thought… Fuck! I'm not there. *And* it's Saturday, and there's no phone! And there's no way I can get back. I'm marooned behind this stupid patchwork of frontlines and I hitched a lift here, so I haven't even got my own car. And all because the *Herald* thought Sarajevo had got too *repetitive*.

Then I thought you might well be in the marketplace that day too. I only just made it to the loo. I sat, my head against the tiles in the pitch-black box, shitting out my fear. It was a while before I could go upstairs for my shortwave. I turned on the radio and heard Phil's voice. I could hear the sirens, the screams, as he described the people who would come here, when the shelling was quiet: black marketeers, ordinary people trying to buy food. He said, nobody could live otherwise in Sarajevo. He said everyone from Sarajevo would have known someone who was here today. He talked about the blood, bits of people everywhere. He didn't say you were dead. But then, how could he? He couldn't say, Molly, if you're listening, I've seen Amir. He's alive.

If I'd been in Sarajevo, you wouldn't have been anywhere near the marketplace that day. It was a Saturday and you'd have been working for me. Not… doing whatever you did in the market when I wasn't there. I never really knew what you did when I wasn't there. I had some sort of idea, but I didn't want to know. It didn't fit in with my idea of you. I was rather squeamish about the black market then; I'd watched too many war films where black marketeers were scum.

You knew I didn't like you selling stuff. When I first found out, last autumn, you'd sold some of the food I gave you, I'd asked you, furious, what prices did you charge? You said to me, "Same as everyone else…"

"But that's extortionate," I'd said. "It's like all those gangsters." I was also hurt. I'd imagined your mother eating the treats I'd bought you. In the real world, it's rude to sell presents.

"Luka, Celo and Cazo," you said, naming the big boys of the Sarajevo underworld, "they were all *heroes* at the beginning of the war. They were the only ones who had guns. They defended the city. I fought *with* the gangsters."

"Well not now. Now they're…" surely everyone knew the gangsters were in the wrong. They were stealing our flak jackets off us, apart from anything else. "Now they're strangling the city…"

You looked at me as if I were a stranger and said: "What do you want me to do? We have to buy food. I am just trying to keep my family alive."

It was one of those moments when I'd glimpse, through a grating, a Hogarthian nether world of a Sarajevo I never normally saw, even with you. I backed down, although I felt a bit more justified when the government rounded up the gangsters a couple of weeks later and shot most of them.

But God, I prayed you weren't in the marketplace that day. The Zenica hotel manager turned the generator on. We all huddled on the sofas in the freezing lobby, the receptionist, the manager, the waiters in their black tie, several aid workers, bundled up, like me, in their boots and hats. There was nothing we could do except watch.

Bosnian TV didn't believe in censoring its pictures, although I later discovered even they had had to cut stuff out. The TV crew had got there within minutes: plastic shopping bags, spilling on the ground, rolling cabbages, tins of fish, the white faces, all amongst the blood and the limbs and loops of gut draped all over the stalls like Christmas decorations in a butcher's shop. And the screams.

I scanned the screen for a glimpse of you. I kept remembering Phil's voice: "You have to be bloody unlucky to be hit by a shell."

I couldn't even run to you, to see if you were alive. I didn't want to be here. It wasn't as if there was anything happening in Zenica anyway.

I'd known Zenica was a bad place to be on a Saturday if you worked for a Sunday paper. I'd said to Roger, what will you do if anything happens on Saturday? He'd said, "Nothing will happen. And don't worry if it does. We'll take it off the wires." Well, he couldn't take this off the wires.

Now I was stuck. I didn't have a car. I'd hitched up here with an aid agency. I couldn't ring you.

I was so stunned by the scenes on the television, it took me ten minutes to remember that upstairs was a bunch of EC monitors, more of the alphabet soup sent to Bosnia by the world; they tended to be male, ex-army, escaping their wives, and banking £90,000 a year in return for driving around frontlines dressed entirely in white, checking who exactly was doing what to whom. But most importantly, they would always have a satellite phone and, although they were not supposed to let me use it, would most likely be susceptible to a blonde in tears.

I ran to the lift. Unfortunately, when I got upstairs, the monitors were out – monitoring something I presumed. Their flint-faced interpreter wouldn't let me use the phone, even though I burst into tears outside her office.

I slid down the wall outside her door and wept for you, for my triple betrayal: you, who could be dead; my poor Sarajevo, the town I'd left, for not being interesting enough; and for my job, for me being in the wrong place at the wrong time.

The interpreter opened the doors in the middle of my hysterics, and let me come in and watch her TV. It was warmer in her office than in the lobby downstairs. We cried together and drank endless cups of instant coffee while I scanned the TV for a sight of you. But she still said she couldn't let me use the phone. When the EC monitors got back, fuzzily pissed from downing slivovic with some local general, they immediately let me ring the desk. Roger was very nice to me, as he should have been, after all it was his stupid fault; but I couldn't ring you. You had no phone I could ring. I tried and tried to ring the BBC, but it was constantly engaged. In the end, the monitors kindly got me drunk and rang round to find me a lift to Sarajevo next day.

I knew you were alive the moment I walked into Phil's room. He leapt up off the sofa, his face greenish-white. Muffy looked concussed.

The blood had been sluiced down in the marketplace; the redundant limbs and loops of intestines gathered and stoked into the hospital incinerator. The Serbs were already blaming the Muslims for doing it to themselves ("The Muslim vice," Phil always said, "shelling themselves...") and the UN ballistics experts were saying they couldn't tell, technically, who had fired the shell: it had crashed through the roof of a stall and exploded when it hit the table below, amongst the flip-flops and cabbages, at stomach height. That's why so many people died, explained the expert the UN dragged into one of our furious press conferences: you are much more likely to die of an abdominal wound, than if you get your leg blown off. It also meant there wasn't a tidy crater the UN could measure for the angle of the trajectory of the shell.

Phil shouted my name when I walked in and Muffy gave me a hug and burst into tears. I was overwhelmed with a surge of relief so strong, my legs buckled and I leant into her arms. You had to be alive. Neither of them looked remotely concerned for me. I let them talk but when I broke in and said: "Where's Amir?" Muffy looked bewildered. She had to concentrate before she said: "He's fine."

The window was open, and through the gap, I could see the pretty white and blue mountains from which the shell must have been fired.

Tears spurted to my eyes and my legs began to wobble. I flumped down on one of the grey draylon chairs.

"You *saw* him *in* the marketplace? After it happened..."

"Yes, yes, he's fine..."

"*Oh God!* I'm sorry," I said. "I shouldn't be crying. I wasn't even here..."

"How did you get in?" asked Phil. "Barry's just rung. The Serbs have cut the place off."

"I hitched..." I said blankly. "Some UN guy... we must have just sneaked through..."

Muffy told me, as we drank cups of coffee: "Phil and I were with one of my families on that street that goes up the hill behind the marketplace, you know, Logavina? We were having coffee. Then we heard the bang... but you hear bangs here all the time...then we heard the screaming. It was like a football match. Then the sirens...one of the neighbours knocked on the door... I got there when I could but..."

"I saw the TV," I said, "I felt so useless."

"I just started crying," said Muffy, and she put up her hands to her eyes, as she spoke. "I just stood there and wept. This photographer came up and slapped me and said, 'Just do your job.'"

"How horrible of him!"

"Not really," she gulped. "I mean, he was right."

"I had to go and file," said Phil; he swallowed too, and walked over to the window. He stared out across the square, where the greying snow lay, untouched, even though it had fallen weeks ago. The ammunition factory stared blankly back. "I couldn't stay and help."

"I heard you on the radio," I said but Muffy carried on talking: "We just loaded people into the back of the car, me and the guy from NBC, and we kept driving up to the hospital, and then back to the market, getting more people. There was blood all the way up the road." She stopped then: it was only later that night, when she was drunk again, that she said: "The car in front had a guy half out of the trunk. His leg fell off, on the way. We nearly hit it."

"I'm so sorry I wasn't there," I said.

Phil looked down at Muffy and moved to her side. He picked up her hand, above the smeared glass coffee table, and started to stroke her fingers. "It was awful. You wouldn't have wanted to be," said Phil. But I did.

They didn't want me to go round to your flat. They said it was too dangerous to go on foot anywhere today.

"Even the Serbs are freaked out by this," said Phil. "They're denying it, of course. They've started saying the Bosnians filled the place with shop-window dummies." He laughed… we all did… what would they think of next? "You were bloody lucky to get back here at all."

We all three listened. Nothing. No cars, no nothing. A machine gun belched, then fell quiet.

"I'll run," I said. "Can I eat some of your cheese? I'm starving and I hate taking their food."

I had a bad feeling in my back when I left the hotel. It was as if the town was holding its breath, like when a child knows it has gone too far and is waiting, frozen, for grown-up retribution. There was no battle, as you'd expect after an attack like yesterday. Just quiet, then a burst of artillery. Then quiet again.

I ran like the clappers out the back of the hotel and zigzagged up between the gym lockers. I ducked under the blankets, grey and old now, like the snow; I ran round the corner, then slowed to a walk past the white blocks of flats. I ran fast across the narrow street which led straight down to the front, and slowed again until I got to the railings, then hell for leather until I reached the other side; then the last slow walk, until I came to the big crossroads, where the snipers had that wide-open horizon, and the broad road flowed emptily by. I stopped, on its shore, but all seemed quiet. Two photographers, the small Spaniard and the tall Dutch, were waiting on the wall by the mosque, where it was safe, by the edge of the row of gym lockers that straddled the road. I waved at them, they waved back at me, and one of them gave me the thumbs up. I ran.

Only you weren't there. Just your mother, sitting alone, drinking coffee. "*Ah, you are safe!*" she embraced me as she opened the door.

"*I'm fine…*" It never occurred to me Maria might think I was hurt.

She looked over my shoulder. I realised later she had been looking for you.

"Come in," she said, but I was already through the door walking past her, into your kitchen. The kitchen was much warmer than the stairs, the stove had nothing on it, but was still belching heat into the white light bouncing in through the window off the snow. There was a glass on the table, and the familiar bottle, an empty coffee cup, but no sign of you.

Maria offered me a glass of slivovic. I took it, of course. It would have been too rude not to; but this time I needed it myself.

"*Ah! it was terrible. So many people. Terrible…*" She poured herself a bit more. "*My neighbour came. She said, something terrible in the marketplace. We didn't know what to do. I didn't know where Amir was. I hoped he was with you, but… but I didn't know. You know, sometimes he goes there… I waited for hours, but then he came. He had been helping, as you know. Then he had to go back. Where is he? Is he coming here too?*"

"*I don't know,*" I said. "*I don't know where he is.*"

"He was with you. I thought he was with you."

"No. no. I wasn't here. I've only just got here. I was in Zenica last night."

"Zenica!"

"Yes."

"But where is he, then?"

She put her glass down on the table and we stared at each other, horrified. *"I'm sure he's fine... He must be fine,"* through my dread. *"It's quiet day today."* I'd know if something had happened. Almost certainly, I'd know...

"He loves you, you know."

I don't know what I was expecting her to say, but it wasn't that. I carried on, as though she hadn't spoken at all...

"Muffy said he'd been helping one of the TV companies."

Did Muffy say that? I hope she had. *"They'd have known, at the* BBC, *if something had happened to him. He probably stayed at the TV station. He probably couldn't get back because of the curfew. He's fine. I'm sure he's fine."*

"He told me he loves you." She leant across the table and took my hand. *"I can see he loves you. I'm glad he found a girl like you."*

"Oh Maria," I said. *"I love him."*

I picked up her other hand, we squeezed each other's fingers for a minute or so, then I said: *"I'd better go back to the hotel. Amir will know where to find me, there."*

"If there was not this war, you are just what I would like as a daughter."

I rang Edin when I got back, but Aida, Valida's sister, answered, and she said she couldn't say where you were.

I sat on Phil's grimy draylon chairs, drinking whisky by candle-light, and listening to the others talk about the shell. I thought you'd come there to find me. But you didn't.

"This woman started screaming at the TV crews 'This is just pornography. What are you doing filming these people?'" said Phil. "One of the Australian cameramen said to her, 'The world has to know this has happened.' But she said, 'Do you think your editors will run this footage? It's too much horror. You are just making money out of these people's suffering.'"

"She was wrong," I said. "I saw the TV in Zenica. It was running on CNN and Sky."

"CNN was completely cut!" said Phil.

"...Phil turned the genny on and we watched it here."

"It was still very strong."

"Not the same," Phil shook his head. "Marina," he said, "thought things had gone quiet. She'd done a trip to Belgrade."

"Poor Marina," I said, for the first time.

I told Phil I'd tried to ring the BBC for hours. He looked embarrassed: he'd taken it off the hook, he said; he'd had people ringing up from all over the world. "They all wanted two-ways..."

"Oh God!" Muffy laughed. "He put it back on, so I could ring my mom, and that second, some radio station rang from LA at 3.00 am." Phil put his head in his hands as Muffy carried on: "They wanted a two-way. He was way too drunk... I said, no! no! but then he started talking about this head..." she stopped.

"What head?" I said.

"Some man's head. I heard him say, on the radio: 'There was blood everywhere. All the blood. And this head, lying on a stall, like it was for sale...'"

"I could just hear Muffy groaning – she was saying, no, no, no..." Phil raised his own head.

"Then he looked at me, like this..." she did a goldfish gawp. "And he said: 'they've hung up.' And I was saying, 'Are you surprised!!!'"

He smiled at her, and she moved closer to him and picked up his hand, staring back in silence. They smiled at each other and I needn't have been there at all. They hardly noticed when I said I thought I'd go to bed.

I thought, on my way upstairs, about Lena, Phil's wife back in Shepherd's Bush, and the baby, that Muffy had told me had been born when Phil was stuck in the Holiday Inn. I'd met her once, when Phil and I had been in London at the same time. She was beautiful, even if she looked rather exhausted. But grumpy. The evening ended with her shouting at Phil in Arabic in the kitchen. She had been his interpreter in Beirut. Like you.

The next morning you were waiting for me, at the briefing, inside the front hall of the PTT.

Even in the filtered gloom, your eyes were so tired you looked like you'd been punched. You hadn't shaved, not for days, your hair looked lank. But you smiled at me, a hesitant smile. I felt my tears rising. I hardly noticed the Legionnaire give me my card back. I came over and you took me in your arms. You didn't speak. I whispered into your neck: "I'm so sorry, so sorry I wasn't here."

You said, "I'm sorry too."

It was that night, in bed, that you told me about the woman.

"She was lying on the ground," you said. You turned away from me and stared up at the ceiling, the candlelight flickering your face in dark shapes across the room.

"She looked a bit funny. She'd obviously been hurt. She said, 'Help me...' I picked up her shoulders, and... and..." then you stopped.

After a few seconds, I said your name. You didn't speak for twenty seconds or so, and then it all suddenly spurted out in a rush.

"...the whole bottom half of her body just fell off. From her waist..." You lay still, staring at the ceiling. I might as well have not been there.

"Then she died. Just then. In my arms. All her blood just flooded out of her body onto the tarmac. I couldn't stop it. She died."

You started to cry. I leant over, and tried to kiss your tears away, but you moved away from me. So I just stroked your hair. Then you curled back towards me like a baby and I crooned over you, as your sobs got deeper and deeper. I was crying too, I was weeping softly for you, but you were giving great grunts of despair. I stroked the back of your head, as your head lay on my breast; soothed you, whispered your name, and slowly the sobs began to die. We lay together, in silence, for a moment, then I felt your head stir between my breasts, then one of your hands moved down and started squeezing my thigh. It hurt. Your fingers were digging into my fat. I moved for you, and let you part my legs. As a reunion, it wasn't much like making love. It felt more as if you were punishing me for not being there before.

The war is over and Mujo and Suljo are deciding what to do.

"I'm going to Zagreb," says Suljo. "All my life is there: my wife, my children. My brother-in-law has a private shop. What about you?"

"I'm off to Belgrade."

"Belgrade! To the Chetniks! They'll kill you! Why are you doing that?"

"All my life is there. My BMW is there, my video recorder, my TV, my fridge...."

XII

You changed after that shell. Sarajevo changed. None of us thought it would make any difference; you were so numbed by the world's indifference by now, you couldn't see that one shell could change things, but it did. Not even the most callous or dithering politician could pretend all those people dead in one afternoon was any kind of acceptable level of violence; odd, really, considering if they'd just been killed in twos and threes over a month, it would have been fine, but there you go. That's the International Community for you: little and often is better than one big splurge.

There was a new general, British. The last UN commander, Belgian, in Bosnia had left with a *cri de cœur*: "*À Sarajevo, j'étais seul,*" he said in his valedictory interview to me, over weak coffee, in his icy office.

"*Je n'avais aucun conseil à mon coté*", he said. Although, sitting in Kiseljak, he wasn't in Sarajevo much at all.

This new general had obviously decided not to take any shit. But then, that was probably what his predecessor had thought as well; the Belgian army are not known for being soft. Him being British was wonderful for us, because it meant that the British public finally had someone they could recognise in the story – not just a bunch of whiny foreigners whose names ended in "itch" – so our desks all perked up.

The new general spent the next few weeks banging heads: naughty Serbs, naughty Muslims… I don't care if you were the ones who were shelled. You must have done something for the Serbs to do that to you. Maybe you even did it yourself. I couldn't see who did it and I'm not going to blame *anyone*. But I'm afraid, if you can't play nicely together, only killing a few people here and there, I'm going to have to take away all your toys.

He announced a twenty kilometre radius exclusion zone for heavy weapons around Sarajevo, backed up by the threat of air strikes, and gave an ultimatum. The UN, he said, would hold the frontlines and all those careful fortifications had to go. Nobody was allowed to shell anyone at all.

Hundreds of journalists turned up to see how it wouldn't work; some so old and famous they had appeared as themselves in *The Deer Hunter*. The Serbs were still not letting anyone in by land or air, so this extra battalion spent days hanging around in the Serb capital Pale or Kiseljak, or for the lucky ones, Split. I think the Serbs let the hacks through in the end out of sheer exasperation: you'd be fed up if you had three hundred frustrated journalists camped in your town.

But it did work – or at least for a bit. But having the defences unwrapped was strangely uncomfortable, like taking off a sticking plaster, or a pedicure.

You didn't want to come back to the Bridge of Brotherhood and Unity, the day the UN were going to take down the barricades. Edin asked you to keep an eye on the CTV office; he said he'd come with Phil and me. We drove back down the great grey road to the blocked-off crossroads, where somewhere to the south, beyond the sandbags and the mines and the ancient Mercedes lorry, according to the maps and you, of course, who remembered full well what your town was like, flowed the river and the bridge – about which I'd heard so much and never actually seen – and the street, leading to a part of Sarajevo that, in a year of living half a mile away, it had been too dangerous for me to see.

The UN sappers slowly unwrapped the crossroads. From out of the tunnel they'd burrowed in the last two years, through the stucco blocks which flanked the bridge, the Bosnian soldiers began to pop their heads up like rabbits; bewildered, blinking at the sudden nakedness of the place they had been guarding for so long, grinning absurdly at this hope of peace. We were just the same; poking our heads round the edge of the holes and the sandbags, watching the fortifications being carefully unpacked: the mines, the sandbags, the weed-woven earth piled up and over the cartoon flat tyres of the lorry parked right across the road to the bridge. One by one, slowly, slowly, we would summon up the courage to creep a bit further, till we were all out on the road to the bridge, sneaking glances straight over the razor wire, at the Serbs, on the other side, who were peering out right back, with equal amazement.

Finally a British squaddie stared at the lorry blocking the road, sucked his teeth, then just got into the cab and started the ignition. That's German engineering: after two years of not moving – let alone being shot at and piled up with earth – the lorry started first time. He drove it off, flat tyres splatting down the street.

It was such an ordinary bridge, now I could see it. Concrete. Two cars wide. And the river, the frontline for so long, was very unimpressive – just a few feet deep and maybe twenty feet across, gurgling through its concrete embankments, goffered with razor-wire. Beyond the river, the sandbags, the razor wire, the staggered chicanes of concrete blocks, stretched a virgin plain of snow-covered grass, up to those white tower blocks, the snipers' eyrie for the last two years. We couldn't see the mines, but we knew they were there.

Then, one by one, again, Bosnians and hacks alike, we'd give in to the tingle of fear, drift back, a little shamefaced, lurk behind the buildings, until curiosity pushed us out again. Considering the hundreds of journalists in the hotel, there weren't that many of us there: Phil and Muffy, and Edin, with some CTV anchorman who'd flown in from America and had cast aspersions, over dinner last night, on the film star who had played him in *The Killing Fields.* As we played grandmother's footsteps on the bridge, he was looking around, taking deep long breaths, as though pulling the war down into his lungs.

At least, that was what we were doing till the general roared up. He must have pissed himself laughing afterwards, at his first line of defence, considering, like most soldiers, he didn't like the press. He set off, behind two rows of French Foreign Legionnaires, onto the bridge, his bodyguards swivelling their eyes and talking into their little black blobs. The Legionnaires were doing that intricate movement you see soldiers do in films which has all the formality of dance at Versailles: four knelt, rifles at the ready, guns trained on the Serb lines in front, while four advanced, guns trained too, avoiding the mines and the scrolls of wire trailing through the railings. After five or six yards, the four in front suddenly dropped to their knees, and the four behind would advance beyond them, and then drop, and the cycle started again. All very neat and orderly, except, of course, for the TV crews… I mean… this is *great* telly. The cameramen ran past the double lines of Foreign Legionnaires and then turned back to film, backing away towards the Serb lines, as the French advanced, in formation. We scampered round the sides, so what the Serbs could see, coming over their bridge, were the backs of half a dozen unarmed foreign journalists.

Edin and I had got the giggles when we reached the other side: Phil couldn't because he was recording, talking in his commentary voice.

"Fuck me. I am in Greater Serbia," said Edin.

Phil said, "Try not to swear," and shoved his mike at him.

"Two years, I have not been on this bridge. Two years, I would be shot if I walk here. Before the war, I used to come every week. My aunt had a flat up there," Edin waved to one of the white blocks where, presumably, we were being watched by, presumably, equally bewildered snipers. "We used to go there for Sunday lunch."

I said: "Visit Serbia, before Serbia visits you."

None of us seemed to know what to do next. I couldn't quite believe the snipers wouldn't change their minds. Greater Serbia was rather anti-climactic and getting cold. After a minute or so, Phil and I shrugged at each other and walked back over the bridge, back home, leaving some of the French Legionnaires behind to start standing guard.

Then we heard a "thwack- phut". Everyone, journalists, soldiers, general, jumped: behind us, a boy was practising tennis strokes against the wall of a block of flats, a grin like a banana splitting his face and all of us, soldiers, general, laughed back in relief. He was ten, he told me, as I scribbled it down; he lived in those shrapnel-scarred, planked-up flats. This was the first time he'd been able to play outside since the war began. If the ultimatum worked, he said, maybe he could go back to practising tennis again. Before the war, his coach had said he was maybe good enough to go to Florida.

The ultimatum did work. Nobody died for weeks, or at least no-one anyone minded about. All the other journalists went home, and I was left with Phil, Muffy and you.

Then Roger told me I had to come home too.

I suppose I shouldn't have been so surprised. I didn't feel I was like the other journalists. You were sitting on Phil's horrible sofa, drinking coffee, beneath a new map, the Demilitarized Zone; teasing Muffy about the French general's bodyguard, who, you said, quite obviously had the hots for her, and Muffy was giggling and flicking glances at Phil. It was early afternoon and the atrium resounded with multilingual curses and thumps, in all the languages of the developed world, as our colleagues dragged their luggage downstairs to check out. You had been there when you heard me say, on the sat phone to the desk: "Come home! But I've hardly been back here at all."

I felt you go still. I turned to look and shook my head: the ceasefire was fragile, I said, to Roger. I thought I was based out here, I said. But all Roger said was: "The Holiday Inn costs a fortune. We want you back..."

The others had gone quiet as well. I met your stare across the room. Dust danced in the light coming in through the window. I fought with Roger; anything might happen, I said... I got him down, in the end, to just a couple of weeks.

You said: "It is always the same, every time."

"It's not me," I said. "I don't want to go."

"You always say that. And you always leave."

"It's not my fault. It's not me..."

You stood up. "That's what you always say..."

I was going to say more, but Phil said: "Hey guys..."

We turned round: "This is my office," said Phil.

You pulled me out onto the gallery. It was dark up here, but down in the depths of the atrium, the light came in off the street. A long queue of little woolly hats snaked away from the reception desk. You pulled me round so that I had to look you in the face.

"It's the ceasefire, isn't it?" you said. "You don't care any more."

"It isn't me. It's the desk."

"So they don't care. They only care when people are dying. And you always do what they say."

"I can't help that. I work for them."

"You will never come back now."

"I will!" I said; even an idiot could see this ceasefire wasn't going to last, but I didn't say that.

"What, because the ceasefire won't last, and more people will die?"

"Because it isn't over," I agreed. "But the *Herald* just won't pay for me to be here now."

You looked away from me, deep down into the atrium, at the light, at the line of anoraks.

"They are all leaving," you said. "It isn't just you."

I didn't say anything.

"If it's the money," you said, "you don't have to stay in the hotel. You could come and stay with us."

"I can't leave the hotel," I said, quickly. "I need the phones."

We didn't speak for a bit. We stared at the heads. The phones were true. And I needed the water, and the intermittent electricity, and the food. But it wasn't just that. I felt mean even thinking it, but it wasn't. If I stayed with your family I could never escape. It would be like your awful Sarajevo parties for ever.

"It's not just the hotel," I said. "It's everything."

You waited for about ten seconds before you said: "You could pay me less."

"Oh Amir!" I turned to face you. "I couldn't do that."

You looked away from me, down at the heads. That would be me tomorrow; waving my bank transfer fax to the woman in her orange knitted hat.

I didn't speak. Then you turned to me and said: "I hate it when you leave. I hate it when you are not here. I *miss* you… I'm lonely when you're not here. And always, I am afraid one day you won't come back."

"I'll never not come back," I said.

You never understood why I wouldn't marry you. You thought I thought you wanted me for the passport. But I didn't think that. At least, most of me didn't think that. When you first met me you didn't even know I could get you cheap chocolate.

It was that night you proposed again, in my icy hotel room, after we'd made love. "You're so beautiful," you said. So I laughed, and said, "You can't see. It's pitch dark."

"I can feel," you said. You ran your hands over my face again, and then down over my breasts onto my belly and I thought, Oh God, why am I leaving. Why are they making me go home? I very nearly said then that I would try and force them to make me stay, when you said: "Why won't you marry me? Please marry me."

"I can't," I said, at once.

"Why not, why can't you?"

I didn't speak, but what I wanted to say was, why did you have to ask me? Why did you have to spoil it? Why can't we just live in the present? Like we always have.

"You say you love me," you said.

"I do love you."

"Then why not?"

I couldn't say it. I couldn't say I don't want to live in a country like this; I don't want my children to be caught up in this mess when it bursts out again a generation away. I don't want to end up like this. I'm not old enough. I haven't thought like that. I don't want to settle down. I don't want to be married to someone who might turn into one of those men on the checkpoints. I don't want to live with your mother or in a horrible flat with an orange Formica kitchen and shrapnel holes in the wall. And think brown smoked glass and heavy carved bits of oak the height of good taste. And eat those horrible minced rat-burger *cevapcici* for ever. And have to look at those mountains every day, knowing the guns are in the trees, and go for a walk and worry about the thick crop of mines under the leaves. If I married you, I could never leave. I could not even go back to the Holiday Inn. But I couldn't say that, so I started to cry; curled up, turned away, with my hands over my face.

"If you married me," I heard you say, as though you were testing ice, "then maybe I could come to England too."

"But I don't *live* in England," I wept, not even lifting my head. And even if I did, what on earth would you do there?

"Then we could live here," you said. "Maybe things will change with this ceasefire."

I said nothing; I didn't have to. Because then I heard you say: "But you don't live here, either, do you? This hotel is not Sarajevo. It's like spaceship, great big yellow spaceship that has landed in the middle of my town. And all you aliens you come in and out. But you always return to the ship."

I lifted my head then: “That’s not fair. I hate it when they make me leave. You know I hate to leave.”

“No you don’t.”

“I *do*!”

“None of you do. Molly, I live in Holiday Inn too, you know. I hear you all, saying: ‘Thank God, getting out, down to the coast, have some sea-food risotto for me. Drink some Posip for me. Fucking locals, what a nightmare.’”

I sat up, and put my hand out towards you. I laid my palm on your chest. “But we always come back. It’s just a rest. I always come back. You know I always want to come back.”

You brushed my hand away. You wouldn’t look at me. You wouldn’t meet my eye. You’d never talked like this before, or not since the day the man was shot.

“You come back. I know. But this is truth. I am here because I have to be and you because you want to be. But what about when the war is over, when I get my home back. Where will you want to be then?”

There was a wave of cold air, and the bed heaved as you got out.

“Where are you going?” I felt a wave of panic as you walked towards the door.

Then you turned: “Nowhere. Where can I? There is nowhere I can go.”

An Englishman, a Frenchman and a Bosnian are stranded on a desert island. They go fishing and catch a golden fish. The fish says, "I am a magic fish, and if you let me go free, I'll give each of you a wish."

The Englishman says, "I wish I were back in London." Pouf! He vanishes.

"I wish I were back in Paris," says the Frenchman. Suddenly, he's gone.

And the Bosnian says: "I wish my friends the Englishman and the Frenchman were back here."

XIII

It was when I was having coffee with Ed that I first realised what was going on. I must have been so stupid not to have known before. Stupid. Or just whizzing down the death slide of the previous four weeks.

Phil had met me at the airport when I came back that time. Nothing strange in that – the airport was no-man's-land. You couldn't have come through the checkpoints anyway.

"Hi, honey, I'm home," I said, when I emerged through the sandbags. He tipped his dark glasses, and replied: "Honey, you won't recognise the place."

We drove back into town, the snow sparkling on the mountains, above the frontline, like Val d'Isère. "*Fuck me!*" I said. "Is that a traffic light?"

"You ain't seen nothin' yet."

"Why are we going this way?"

"Didn't you know there was a one-way system?"

"*Fuck me!*"

"I know. I told you." He went quiet; there were people wandering along the streets, carrying plastic bags, like people you might see anywhere else. Only the burnt-out buildings behind were the same. And the mountains of course.

"I'll take you on a tour."

I said I wanted to get back to see you at the hotel. That's when he told me you weren't there – you were working, he said, for CTV. You'd sent a message, saying you'd see me after work. I didn't even feel angry. I was just glad you had something to do while I'd been away. I was sad, but I never minded spending an afternoon with Phil.

"I'll buy you a coffee."

"*What!!*" I said.

"It only costs a couple of marks. The general's got the Serbs to agree to let people bring food and stuff across the airport. I tell you, Molly, everything's changed."

Phil took me to Ibrahim's: a glass kiosk, on a terrace, in the little park, where you told me all the trees used to be, before everyone cut them down for firewood in the middle of the night. It was owned and manned by a proud and balding man whom I recognised from some politician's bodyguard entourage. Phil sat me outside, wide open, bang in the middle of Sarajevo, and bought me a cup of coffee. It felt all wrong.

Phil sat watching me feeling sick.

"I felt like that the first time too." He twitched. "I still feel like that now." He gave a little twitch, then he said: "I'm thinking of looking for a house."

"*What! Here?*"

"Not for *me*. For the BBC."

"Move out of the *hotel*?"

"Well, yes."

"Phil, *no*!"

He wouldn't look at me as he said: "It's not that bad, surely?"

"You can't leave me. You can't leave me alone in that hotel."

"But you're not alone, Molly. You've got Amir."

He didn't tell me you'd decided to move into a flat with Edin. I think probably he didn't know. He told me there was electricity in the town for a few hours nearly every day. He told me there was water three times a week.

"The hotel has power nearly all the time," he said. "We're priority…whatever that means… You should move out too," I heard him say, and I thought of you. I snapped back: "How would I telephone the desk? Where would I get cups of tea?"

I stared up, over the rooftops, the trees and the snows. Phil said nothing.

I said: "I don't trust this. I don't trust this not to start again."

"I just can't stick that hotel."

"*Can't* you?"

Phil shuddered. "I don't know. I don't know. I've spent too long there."

"It's not so bad."

"You can never get away from anyone."

"Who else is around?" I asked. But Phil said, "Nobody: it's as quiet as the grave."

"Not even Muffy?" I said it, even before I thought about what Muffy had told me three weeks ago, the day we'd left, in Split. Phil played his spoon over the pale brown scum on his coffee, then pulled out a cigarette. He offered me the packet. He lit them both, and slowly inhaled, and then, still staring at the table, he said: "She rang me to say she wasn't coming back. She said she needed a break."

I wasn't surprised. We'd been sitting in Muffy's hotel room, as the sea darkened to violet outside, drinking cappuccinos and eating Croatian ersatz Toblerone. It was like when she cried over John the Spy's wife and kids that last night in our room in Tuzla, a year ago, before she went out to see him and didn't come back. Except of course I knew Muffy much better now. "Phil's such a romantic nit," she'd said. "We never meant to. It just happened. He's got Lena and the baby. Oh God. Fuck the cappuccino, let's open the minibar. Pass me the wine… He's not an arsehole, like Ed. He can't go collecting wives from every war…"

I thought she'd start to cry, but she poured herself a drink and took a large slug: "I've been here way too long. I should go home to Sheridan and have some babies. I'm 37. Be careful you don't stay too long… Miss Molly…"

"But I like being here!" I'd said. That's not the point, she'd said. I said, "I haven't been here as long as you. And I've got Amir…" She gave me a look – and said, "What does *he* have when you're gone? He doesn't turn into a puff of green smoke you know, the moment you check out of the Holiday Inn."

I felt sick. I remember you saying to me, I miss you. I'm lonely…

Phil's voice broke in: "What else did she say?" With pathetic hope.

"Nothing," I said. "Just that she'd been here too long."

"Too long…" he turned his head. Across the park, a woman was walking with her child down the street, and an old lady, with a plastic bag, was panting up the other way. Every now and then they'd glance up to the hills. "I wonder whether that old woman thinks she's been here too long?" he said.

"Well, she's wrong," I said, when he didn't say anything else. I picked up my coffee and looked across at the children playing in the grass, the woman wandering up the street, at Ibrahim, happily busy in his bar, then up at the mountains, above their dark fuzz of trees that presumably still hid the guns, even if they didn't happen to be firing this week. The mountains ignored us, soaring shining to the sun. "She should be here for this."

"Yes," he said. "She should be here for this. Come on, Molly. Time we went back to our ship."

You weren't at the hotel. You rang to say you'd be late. I was getting worried, and Phil was saying, fuck it, let's get him to meet us in Jez. And I was just about to ask, what's Jez?, when there was a knock at the door. There you were, silhouetted against the dim lights from the lobby, your shoulders broad in the doorway, your eyes, those black treacle eyes, hidden in shadow but the swoop of your lashes lay on your cheeks and your smile, your kooky smile, those rambling Bosnian teeth. I leapt up, and ran into your arms. When you kissed me, and I smelt you, and the scent of you hit the back of my nose, I threw my head back, looked up at you, and forgot all about CTV and Edin and whatever else you'd been doing.

In the end, I didn't see so much of you that month. You were working with Edin most of the time. It made more sense that way. You worked for me towards the end of each week but, actually, I didn't need you so much anyway. I spoke the language now, enough to get by; the snipers weren't really shooting, so I could walk around, and if I needed a car, the taxi rank had returned opposite the Presidency.

Besides, the new UN commander had changed things for me too. He moved his headquarters into Sarajevo itself, from that old school in Kiseljak, into what we called, in true colonial style, the Residency. He said he wanted to be closer to the centre, but also, since Sarajevo had long been a French fiefdom, with French troops and a French general as Sector Sarajevo commander, the move had the advantage of putting the French nose out of joint, which seems to be a good part of any British military policy.

As for us, for the British press corps, it meant that our war suddenly changed. Being British, the new general needed or wanted (or thought he did) to use the British press. When his headquarters moved to Sarajevo, his staff obviously came too. Instead of the Frogs having a monopoly on bored soldiers to ply with drink and us Brits having to go all the way to Vitez for that, suddenly we had a whole pool of British officers on site, living at the centre of the storm. It's all terribly tribal, this stuff: the way you get good information is never in interviews or press conferences but slowly, over a few drinks, in a potent fug of empathy and adrenalin. Maybe, if my French had been better, I could have got the French to talk to me, but to be honest, before you build the kind of trust real indiscretion needs, you need a strong common bond: sex is good, and so is sport, but actually race memories of Marmite and *Doctor Who* do pretty well. And, unlike various journalists like loony Pierre-Marie or pouting, eyelash-flapping Chantal, I did not have the French equivalent of that. So I could write what I liked about human misery and do my weekly chats with Ejup Ganic – the government minister who spoke the best English – or even poor old General Divjak, the Sarajevo Serb commander who'd stayed behind to help the siege, but was never quite trusted by his Muslim colleagues so tended to have a lot of time on his hands; you could lay bare for me the soul of Sarajevo, but until this point I never had access to what the western powers were planning next. Of course, I could have had an affair with one of the French and built up trust that way, but I was in love with you. Besides, imagine if I'd picked the wrong one? A Swedish journalist friend did have an affair with one of the Brits the General brought in. She said unfortunately she discovered too late that he was far too thick to be able to tell her anything (you need intelligence for indiscretion: clever people think they can trust their own judgement, and besides, they are vain and they want you to know how clever they are) and he wasn't even gorgeous enough to make up for it, but it would have been very undiplomatic to give him the boot. She was very relieved when his tour of duty came to an end.

So I spent much more time, then, talking to British soldiers. And possibly less time talking to you.

I helped you move house. I wrote a piece about it: life in Sarajevo slowly grinds back to normal – if you could call it normal, still surrounded by men with guns, who were just choosing not to shoot. Edin's flat was halfway up one of the tower blocks, down Sniper Alley, just beyond the Bridge of Brotherhood and Unity. It had an enormous sitting room with vast picture windows, all, of course, boarded up; a fantastic view of the hills, and huge holes where the bullets had come through, and matching holes in the stereo and the bookcases on the other side of the room. The bathroom had taken a rocket through one wall, tiles and bits of concrete still lay in shards in the shower and pale orange dust from the walls over everything like a Kodak light filter. "Good for ventilation," you said.

You told me the flat got water and electricity every other day so we chose one of those days to do the move but I still refused to get in the lift, just in case. We had to send your stuff up in shifts. We felt a bit like a couple in a mortgage ad – wiping cobwebs off each other's chins, or in this case, cement dust – at least I did. Being brought up under communism, you'd never seen a mortgage ad. Then Aida, one of the girls you'd known at CTV, turned up with some coffee and a packet of PX Jaffa Cakes, all lipstick and high heels and a superior pout. Actually, for about the first time, I was quite glad to see Aida. I liked her seeing us together, moving house.

So our days settled into a new kind of routine. I'd be with you from Saturday night, late, after the last edition had gone to press, and stay till Tuesday, because then it didn't matter if I couldn't get to a phone. Obviously, there was no phone in the flat, or rather no line. The phone was still there, Early Learning Centre orange and about as much use as a toy. But on Tuesday, I'd have to go back to my spaceship. And you'd say, oh, Molly's been kidnapped by aliens again. Sometimes I'd come back for the night, but the last two weeks, I hadn't seen you till Thursday.

Phil found a house too, but he hadn't moved in yet. The snowdrops were coming out, and even the icicles were starting to drip.

Then, after three weeks, the *Herald* told me I had to leave. More than that. It was a massive promotion: giving me a staff job, sending me off all over the world. But in London, on the desk, and not based in Sarajevo any more.

It was the week I was doing the psychological legacy of the war. "Where's Amir?" said Phil, who dropped me off at the loony bin.

"Oh, I don't really need him for interviews now," I said.

Phil paused. "Are you still paying him to be your driver?"

I blushed: "It's not very much. He gives most of it to his mother. I haven't had time to change things yet." It seemed rather churlish to stop.

Phil rolled his eyes. "See you at one. We're going to go to the pizza place for lunch. Just make sure they don't keep *you* in there." He waved at the loony bin's gloomy Austro-Gothic façade.

I walked down from the hospital to the pizza parlour. It wasn't just the pizza place that was a sign of change. It was a beautiful day; sunny, and the snow still on the mountains, with a breeze that was fresh enough to whisk the smell of rubbish away although, as I looked around, I noticed even the rubbish wasn't like it used to be. Somebody must have started clearing it up. People were wandering around carrying plastic bags; chatting, being served coffee on Ibrahim's terrace. Tiny green shoots were spouting in the UNPROFOR general's Residency gardens. Soon the white portakabins would be invisible from the road. It was like that bit in *The Lion, the Witch and the Wardrobe*, when the ice starts to thaw, and all the small furry animals go around saying "Aslan is on the move." I told Phil that later at lunch, but he said that line always made him think of the end of constipation.

Some soldiers were lugging away the gym-locker sniper barricades from the big crossroad by the mosque. The street I'd sprinted over, with you, and so many times on my own. I thought of all the people who must have died putting them up, and all the people who'd died on that road since because, although better than nothing, the lockers weren't very effective. I felt tears welling up in my eyes. Maybe I should track one of the families down, I thought. I ran across the street anyway – it would be almost too good a joke not to kill someone the very moment the sniper barricades were being dismantled.

The pizza parlour was safe from any renegade snipers at least,tucked under the crags above the old brewery, across the river. I ran across that bridge as well. The building had wooden walls and those standard un-siege-friendly picture windows, two of which were still UNHCR plastic; the others still had the gleam-and-putty smears of freshly replaced glass. It sat on the edge of one of those little streams tumbling down from high beyond the frontlines, whose water the Sarajevans refused to drink, even in the worst of the war, on the grounds, they said, that the Chetniks were shitting in them upstream.

Through the window I could see Valida and Phil. At their table was Ed, his white hair bobbing up and down, as he gesticulated, pen in hand, a notebook by his fork. Valida smiled when I caught her eye: she'd been staring out of the window looking drawn and fed up. The waitress greeted me with obvious excitement. She only had four other customers and they were foreigners too. The carpet stuck to my feet but there was no discernible smell of pee. But the place was still cold enough for Phil to be in his coat.

Ed gave me a hug. "When did you get here?" I said.

"Molly. Still here… My dear child! Straight off the plane this morning," he said. "Breakfast in Split; lunch in Sarajevo."

"We bumped into him wandering the streets like a tourist," said Phil.

"I was. I was just gawping. What a change. I'm over-dressed. I'm the only hack still wearing a flak jacket."

I said: "You know what they call it here? Half-time…"

"I couldn't believe it when Phil said you were all going out for a pizza. A twenty-dollar pizza! When I think how much a cabbage cost a month ago…"

"Oh, the pizzas used to be good here before the war," said Valida.

"How long are you here for, Ed?" I asked.

"Yeah, and why?" said Phil. "It's so quiet. I'd have figured you'd be in Rwanda…" He stopped. I looked at Valida. We weren't supposed to be talking about Rwanda – it was the rival war.

Henri had rung Valida two days ago, on a satellite phone. He said he was in Gomer, just over the border from Rwanda, in a refugee camp full of mass murderers and he wasn't coming back to Sarajevo. He'd also mentioned that Muffy was in Gomer too. You'd said to Phil: "I thought she wanted a break." Phil didn't say anything. It was Valida who said, "Sarajevo's not fashionable any more…" and then she went out of the room, and I didn't see her for a day. I'd said: "Henri could have let her know before he left," but Phil had made a face and said, "But he didn't know he'd be sent to Rwanda then…"

Ed didn't notice the tricky silence. He never did.

"Christ no. I hate Africa. All those fucking insects. And no-one in America gives a shit."

I thought I heard Phil say, "Except the black people," but maybe I was wrong, and I agreed with Ed about the insects.

"Anyway," he said, "us magazine journalists, we like it when it's quiet. People are so grateful to talk to you. I hate the goat fuck you get on a rolling story," he slugged his beer. "I guess I'll be here a couple of days. Then Pale, I think, and then up to Belgrade." I could almost see the ten thousand words spooling out. "I'd rather shoot myself than be in Rwanda again."

"Have you been to Rwanda?" I asked.

"It wasn't called Rwanda then…it was…" I can't remember what he said, but one of those colonial names that sound like "Bananaland". "They put me in prison for a couple of weeks… Look, here are our pizzas."

By any non-war standard, they were sad bald things, a splat of tomato sauce, a faint smear of cheese, a few sad slices of plastic pink ham, but that didn't stop us four gasping with greed.

"So what's actually going on?" I said.

"Where?" said Ed.

"Rwanda," I said. "I don't understand."

Ed looked past me, out of the window, beyond the hills. "Rwanda. Rwanda," he turned back. "There are two types of people in Rwanda, the short people and the tall people and once every decade or so the short people cut off the legs and other extremities of the tall people. That's it. That's Rwanda."

"That's it?"

"That, believe me, is all you have to know." He ate a piece of his pizza. "This," he said, waving another piece about on his fork, "Is actually quite good."

"How do you explain us?" Valida suddenly said.

Ed wasn't even embarrassed. He carried on stoking pizza: "Now that gets complicated. Because there are three sides, and that's one too many. And the readers can't get their heads round the fact that the Muslims are the goodies. So every time I write about this place, I have to reiterate the fact that nobody expects Valida to walk around in a burqa. And that she drinks alcohol." But actually, I had never seen Valida drink and her pizza didn't have any sad pink slabs of ham.

"How was your shrink?" said Phil, because no-one else spoke.

"Have you been to see a shrink?" said Ed.

"I'm doing something on the after-effects of war… you know… so I thought I could put the mental stuff in with rebuilding everything."

"Did he say anything interesting?" Ed picked up his pen.

I didn't want to talk about it, so I was glad when Valida said: "He let you go? After talking to you? He didn't lock you up?"

"Oh, ha ha ha…"

Ed made some notes in the little book he had on the table.

"It's a good thing Phil didn't go," said Valida. "They'd have locked him up for ever."

"I couldn't have his number now, could I?" said Ed. I was slightly irritated, but I had learnt a lot from Ed. Then he asked to borrow you. I explained you were really working for CTV now; it wasn't up to me, you didn't really work for me so much any more.

Valida said, "My sister, Aida, might be free." But I said, I was sure that you would work for Ed. I knew you loved Ed; he was famous and paid you a fortune.

"You guys not together any more? Sorry to hear that. But I guess it was kind of inevitable. These things never really work."

"Oh, no! We are! He's just not working for me so much."

Ed looked embarrassed. "Oh. Sorry. Well, I said it now."

I stared out of the window at the jumbled streets, a minaret, and the old fort silhouetted on the hill against the mountains, and thought about the man in the loony bin.

"It's such a pretty little town," I said. "Sometimes you forget that."

"It's great," said Ed.

"I preferred it before," said Valida.

"I never saw it before," I said.

"It's a different kind of beauty," said Valida. "It's like seeing a beautiful woman with a scar down her face, and you wonder, that she can still be beautiful with that scar. Because she is, but she also repels you in a way."

"Are we the doctors who are treating her and we fall in love with her because we see the soul behind the scar?" said Phil.

"Maybe you all fall in love with your handiwork. Or her dependence or her gratitude. Or your own heroism."

"Don't say that!" I said.

"She is right," said Ed. I said, No! But he carried on. "The trick is not to care. It took me years to work that out. I mean, what the fuck does it matter to that waitress why I am here. I write her story. The world hears about it, I leave. Why should she mind if I'm motivated by some deep desire to do good or just because I happen to like a bit of an adventure and a break from my wife."

Valida snorted, and I cried: "Don't!" again.

"Are you all right?" said Ed.

"Molly's just had some news," said Phil.

"Sorry. I keep putting my foot in it all over the place today," said Ed. So maybe he did notice things after all. "What's up?"

I told them what the *Herald* had said.

"But this is good news," said Ed. "Let me get this straight. They want you to come back to London, be on the desk. Proper job. Be a fireman. You'll still travel."

"Yes, but anywhere. It won't just be here."

"Does Amir know?" asked Valida. Her face had set.

"Molly, that's fantastic. You deserve it, really, I think you do," then even Ed noticed that nobody else was looking pleased.

I looked at Valida and shook my head.

"Isn't Ed right?" said Valida. "That's what this was about, no? This war, for you. You made it up the next step. Congratulations." But I didn't think it had even been that simple right at the start. "Just make sure you tell Amir first. Don't just leave, and not come back, like Henri did to me."

"Is it Amir?" said Ed. "Is that what it is?"

I started to cry. I think I must have been tired; probably a little hung over. It was all too much. You. The pizza parlour, and the sniper barricades and the waitresses happy in their new jobs, and the sun shining, and coffee on the terrace. You. My new job. And you. I wished you were here. Except if you'd been here, you'd be so angry and sad. I kept saying sorry. Phil put his arm round me and Valida handed me some loo paper.

"Good thing about Sarajevo, always have to have toilet paper in your bag."

I tried to laugh, but I just kept on crying.

"There'll be other boyfriends," said Ed. "I know it doesn't feel like this now, but there will be, believe me. And other stories."

"I don't want another boyfriend. I don't want another story. I want this one. Everything's changing. Today. Everything. It's like Aslan being on the move." That's when Phil made the remark about constipation, which did make me giggle.

"What is Aslan?" said Valida and Ed did one of his lightning political diagnoses on *Narnia*.

"It's a Christian allegory: a land in perpetual winter because of an evil white queen. Aslan is their lion God. When he returns, he dies and is resurrected. He breaks the queen's power; spring comes and everything thaws."

It was after Ed had paid the bill that Phil said to me:

"If you really want to stay here with Amir, you could."

"Yes, you could," said Ed, to my surprise; he was zipping up his money belt, pocketing the receipt, off to the loony bin. "You'd have to set up in a flat in town, but, by the looks of things today, that could be possible."

"We're thinking of moving out of the Holiday Inn," said Phil.

"Shit, are you? That'll make this place a lot less fun... But you see, Molly? It can be done. Hell, I'd hate it, but I'm an old man and I'm not in love. Tell the paper. You have to go back, otherwise they'll just think you've flipped, but when they offer you the job, say: thanks, great, love to be staff, but want to be based in Sarajevo. You can be a fireman from here. The whole region's going to go up in smoke again in six months' time. Any fool can see that." He was utterly oblivious to Valida's reaction to his glib assessment of her little town's peace. "They should go for it, but you have to keep the costs right down. Ask for some fancy title, Chief European Correspondent or something. But if you ask me, it would still be best for your career to go back to the desk."

"What do you want, Molly? What do you actually want?" said Valida.

But I just wanted everything to stay as it was. You never think, when you read *The Lion, the Witch and the Wardrobe*, you'll be rooting for perpetual winter to return.

It was in the car, on the way back to the hotel, after we dropped Ed and Aida off at the loony bin, that Valida asked me, "What did the shrink say?"

I looked out of the window as we drove – past the honey-coloured mosque, over the river, to the minarets crawling up the cliffs. Phil steered Miss Piggy down the road we would never have driven down two months ago, past where the bunch of soldiers were still manhandling the bullet-riddled bodies of the gym-locker barricades into the back of a four-ton truck. "He said you'd all go mad. After the war. And so would we."

I wandered sadly into Phil's office, trying to work out what I could say to you. Valida was playing her eternal Gameboy by the window. Phil made me some tea. "The milk's in the fridge," he said.

It was only after I'd opened the fridge, taken out the milk, between the plastic lumps of cheese, cans of Heineken, and bottles of Posip, and poured it into my tea, that it really hit home: until ten days ago, that fridge was just a table to put the candles on.

"And storage," said Phil. "Don't knock my fridge. We used to keep the spare notebooks in there."

"And now, you can say, quite nonchalantly, the milk's in the fridge. And this morning, Amir had a shower and complained that the water was cold."

Phil paused, before he said, "When Tim first showed me the fridge was working, I was like a child. I kept putting things in it and taking them out. I thought Valida would laugh at me, but she said she'd been just the same. She said, it was like playing dolls' houses. And for the first evening, it was an indescribable pleasure just drinking cold beer. And now it's normal again."

"Yeah," I said sadly. "Everything seems to be working now."

The silence was broken by the local telephone. Phil picked it up and his shoulders went stiff. He said: "Hang on…" and walked with it over to the map on the wall.

"How many?… When did it start?… Valida… *Valida*!"

Valida put her Gameboy down. I put down my tea. Phil's finger was on the bottom of the red circles in the eastern part of the map. Something was happening again. He mimed a pen and paper. Valida brought them to him and he mouthed to her "Ring General Divjak. I want to see him." I pointed at my chest: "Me too."

"What is it, Phil? I have to tell them what it's about!" I didn't know either, but whatever it was, I wanted to be there.

Phil waved her away. He put the phone down, looked at his watch, and dialled again. "What is it?" he just flapped his hand. Valida rolled her eyes at me, and I shrugged back at her.

"Gary?" he'd obviously rung the UNPROFOR spokesman. "Just a quick one: just had a call from Ganic's office… Gorazde… right…" And it was one of those "rights" that go on for some time, a kind of ryyyyyyee-yiiiiiite. "So you do… Thanks Gary… I've got to go now. I've got about ten minutes till we go on air."

I was bolt upright. "Tell me," I said. He shook his head. "No time." He rushed into the other room. Valida shrugged her shoulders and picked up the phone. In the other room we could hear swearings and rustlings and scribbling sounds. "Traffic, traffic. It's Phil Kennedy in Sarajevo here. Can you put me through? I've got a piece for the three… Cheers, thanks a lot… Hi, John? Oh, Brian. Brian; it's Phil in Sarajevo… Great… yes… finally… no… the Serbs are moving again, just as we said… Gorazde… G…O…R…A… Z…D…E… in the east, the southern of the three Muslim enclaves on the right, those blobs, the bottom one… well, it's what we've all been waiting for since the Serbs pulled their kit out of Sarajevo…if they continue, and they will, because they are never going to believe that anyone will stop them, then technically the UN ought to use air strikes… it's a safe haven… no, the new general's much more gung-ho… he's brought the SAS in and everything… No, I can't… because I can't… because it's completely surrounded by Serbs and they won't let me in… yes, I'm sure… OK. I'll go live…"

Oh thank God, I thought, as I heard him read out his story about the shells crashing into the town of Gorazde, the tanks ploughing their way through the outlying villages, torching the houses, the panic-stricken refugees. Thank God. The Serbs are at it again. Now the *Herald* will *have* to let me stay.

I was laughing when Phil came back into the room. "The war is over," I said. "We can all go home…"

"We can't you know. The UN said the Serbs have shut the airport."

"Then I *really* can't leave…" There was a sudden silence in the room as the power cut out.

Valida said: "I'll have to empty the fridge," but she was laughing too.

David Owen, Slobodan Milosevic and Thorwald Staltenberg go to hunt bear. They catch one, but it's alive, and it's too late to take it back to Belgrade. So they chain it to a tree and divide the night into three watches. Staltenberg takes the first, Owen the second and Slobo the third.

At midnight, Staltenberg wakes up Owen and says, "The bear's all yours." The bear growls by its tree. At 4 a.m., Owen wakes up Slobo and says, "Over to you." The bear grunts back.

But at 8 a.m. when the others wake up, there's no bear.

"Where's the bear, Slobo?" they ask.

"What bear?"

"Do you remember we went bear hunting yesterday?" said Owen.

"Yes," says Slobo.

"And do you remember we caught a bear?" says Staltenberg.

"Yes," says Slobo.

"And do you remember we agreed to tie it to a tree and watch over it all night?"

"Yes," says Slobo.

"And it was there, when I woke you up at 4 a.m.," says Owen.

"Oh! Yes," says Slobo.

"So where's the bear?" they both ask.

And Slobo says: "What bear?"

May 2000

I went to Ingrid's book launch last night: *Kosovo: Too Much History*. Her publishers sent it to me at work, with a note from her saying, "Wished you were there. Hope you can review this for me." It was the classic, journalist's it-was-horrible-and-I-was-there account, with a little bit of this-is-why-it-happened. My first thought was, that was quick: she must have written it at about 100 miles an hour. The next was, she's written a book already, and she's been in the Balkans much less time than me – she only took over from *The Times* guy at the end of 1994. Then I remembered that my war was five years old.

I didn't review it, because I don't, and my magazine doesn't care, but I read it at my desk – I'm allowed to read things at work. I got the mag to send a snapper. I said it would be full of famous journalists: Christiane Amanpour, her new man, and Martin Bell.

Phil was there too. I hadn't realised he was over. He's based in Moscow now. It was lovely to see him.

He looked round and said: "This is all right, isn't it?" We were in one of those steak-and-kidney-pudding clubs just off St James's, with heavy panelling, and marble halls, and horribly patterned carpets. I think Ingrid's father was some kind of judge. Then there was a pause. Suddenly he said: "Oh look, there's Jackson, do you know him?" But I wouldn't have known him. I don't know generals any more. Phil introduced me as an old Balkan hand.

"Molly knew Hal in Sarajevo," Phil said to Jackson.

Jackson laughed. "Oh…Hal!" I said. I hadn't thought about Hal for years.

"Hal worked for the general in Kosovo," said Phil.

"We used to take them out to dinner," I said. I could see Jez, the basement restaurant that had opened after the Sarajevo ceasefire, the candlelight, the greasy catch at the back of your nose from the paraffin lamps, the faint, ever-present whiff of pee; it opened after the phoney peace broke out. We went there a lot, before anywhere else opened. Phil liked to say, "I feel like eating subterranean tonight," and flirt with Tanja, the sad-eyed waitress, an Aeroflot blonde, who'd bring steak and chips at 100DM a plate to people like us who could afford the food; black marketeers, the aid workers, and the like. Phil was thrilled to spot that the wine they served was the same as he'd drunk having dinner with the French general.

I looked up to find Jackson cocking an eyebrow at me. I blushed.

"Phil started it," I said.

I'd met Hal before – he'd been one of the clones who'd given Robert and me a lift into Sarajevo. Then he turned up at the briefing one morning, in the very early days of the Gorazde crisis, with a man who sported a drooping moustache that would have been all the rage at a Village People concert. Like the clone in the Land Rover, Moustache was exactly the same shape as Hal, which was a completely different shape to normal people. Phil thought they were SAS – he'd met a few in the Gulf, and the new general had commanded the Iranian embassy siege. He bet me I couldn't find out. I said you're on and walked over with: "Do you remember me?"

"Have you been here since we left you?" he said, when I reminded him. And I said: "God no, I'd go mad." Then I thought about it, and said, "Well, most of the time."

He agreed to a drink that night. You didn't come. You were busy anyway, I think, but, anyway, talking to Hal with you wouldn't work.

I'd arranged to pick him up at the Residency. I'd been there a couple of times before; I'd started to come and talk to the UN head of civil affairs there once a week. It had been Robert's idea. I'd rung him last time I was in London, after I'd been back for a few days; I suppose because I needed to talk to someone with whom I had something in common. He'd asked wistfully about Sarajevo, Valida and Phil. Then he'd asked me if I'd ever spoken to this man in the Residency who had one of those comic names you can't really believe Russians can call their children. Igor, he was called; Igor Ivanov. When I said no, why on earth would he want to talk to me, Robert said, "People are dying to tell you things, if only you ask them."

I was so used to thinking of myself as the new girl, the young one, who could do moving descriptions of human misery, but didn't really have a clue what was going on, I never really believed important people would talk to me.

"But you're not the new girl any more," Robert said.

So I told Robert about the real journalist, the one I always used to think that one day, I would meet: someone who knew exactly what was happening, who had sources of information at his fingertips, which, for some reason, I imagined being spewed out of a printer. Someone who didn't spend his time desperately gathering clues by trailing round the country, talking to the mad or the desperate in unlit offices that smelt faintly of pee and unwashed clothes, sipping tentatively at the glass of slivo thrust into his hand, taking notes on his knee in felt tip pens bought by the bushel at Heathrow, in books from the Croatian equivalent of WH Smith, while specks of dust danced in the faint sunbeams eking through the sandbags. But even as I said it, I could see what had happened. Robert snorted with laughter and said: "You are a real journalist. The nutters, the slivo, that's real journalism."

Then he told me Igor was a colonel in the KGB, "But it's secret," he said. "No-one's supposed to know." So after that I had to meet Igor, just out of curiosity. And once I started going to the Residency, I realised it was full of bored, lonely men dying to talk. And when Igor got drunk he used to say: "One day Russia, the Ukraine and Serbia will be one country stretching to the Mediterranean," which might have been news to the Ukrainians and the Serbs, but gave a pretty good insight into why the Russians kept blocking military intervention in Bosnia in the UN.

It was dark by the time I reached the gates and the frost on the pavement gleamed in the moonlight. The city was dark; the star-spangled velvet you get with no electricity. It was too early for curfew, yet the streets were deserted, even though there was now, with the ceasefire, little risk of being shot. For the first time in Sarajevo, walking on my own, at night, I was afraid of the kind of things that happen in a normal town. I wasn't wearing my flak jacket because the evening felt too safe, and I was very glad I'd made that decision: I might have been mugged for it.

The Residency lights were blazing away – the Residency was

obviously even more "priority" than the hotel. The gate was manned by a group of UN Egyptians. They cat-called me, at first, and I suddenly felt like the blonde in the song, turning up at the barrack gates. The worm of embarrassment turned in my stomach but this was my job, and so I squashed the worm down. Hal told me to ask for the JCOs but when I asked around, no-one else in the hotel seemed to have heard of that particular serving of alphabet soup. It meant something to the Egyptians, though; when they finally rang in my request, it was with very different expressions that they waved me through.

I walked up the drive towards a long low white house, its shrubbery brittle and naked beneath the winter moon. It looked almost English – The Laurels, with fake mullioned windows, sitting behind a hedge on one of the approach roads to Ascot. Through its brightly lit glass, I could see soldiers walking in and out of rooms, holding mugs. The Ascot façade had sprouted a two-storey moustache of portakabins – those white ones that always appear in the wake of the British Army. Sometimes I thought the cavalry must tow them behind their tanks. You can imagine an officer pointing at a map: "We are here. The enemy are there. Have you got your portakabin hitched on to your tow bar?" More portakabins lurked amongst the skeletons of the shrubs.

The hall was large, and comparatively warm. Light bounced off the white walls and parquet floor. Against the walls stood a bench and a round table – that heavy carved fake Ottoman furniture you get all over the Balkans – fake, perhaps, because the real stuff kept getting burnt for firewood in all the wars.

I'd come alone, to look vulnerable and discreet, but Hal had obviously decided he needed protection – but I didn't even know he was called Hal by then. In my mind he was still just one of the Kiseljak clones. He'd brought Moustache from the briefing and another one who, if marginally taller, was also exactly the same shape. They weren't in uniform, just wearing what Englishmen wear when asked to make any kind of non-uniform choice: the nearest they can to the same as everyone else. Moustache and his mate were in fleece and jeans, the twin in Fulham Road cords and a jersey, although he had kept to a kind of desert sand colour; it would have been very good camouflage, if we weren't at the end of a Balkan winter. The collar of a deep blue shirt poked out of the neck: it matched his eyes. I didn't think it was a coincidence.

They were slightly embarrassed too, which made me feel better. The difference is, I suppose, that it was my job to hide mine. We all introduced ourselves – Moustache was Jim, the new man was Ted. "They're just like Australian freelance cameramen," I thought. "They all have really short names you can shout in a hurry, like dogs."

I think Jim was quite surprised to learn I didn't actually know Hal's name. He said: "I thought you knew each other?"

Hal said: "We met last year," just at the same time as I said: "He never told me his name."

Luckily Ted said: "Do you often ask blokes out whose names you don't know?" and we all laughed, in a hurry.

"Round here, all the time," I smiled.

"I've met girls like you before," he said.

"I don't think so," I replied.

Hal said nothing at all but I could feel him standing behind me. Moustaches apart, I also noticed that their faces seemed strangely hairy, almost like a fine layer of fur. As if they just had too much testosterone and it couldn't help sprouting out.

It was Jim who spoke: "So where are we going then?"

"Somewhere called Jez?" They shook their heads. "It's about ten minutes walk away."

It was a crisp night, just a faint tang of rubbish at the back of the throat, and the mountains gleamed in moonlight where the snow shone through the trees. The clouds rolled over the stars like a Victorian poem. As I always did, I glanced up at the crags and wondered whether they were watching me back. I noticed that the others did too. Without discussion, we quickly crossed over to where the buildings blocked the view.

"I still can't get used to *walking* along here," I said to Hal. Ted and Jim had gone ahead; we were side by side but not really looking at each other.

"Do you get leave often? Holiday. Whatever you call it?" Hal asked.

"Quite often..." Then I stopped what I was saying.

"Well, that's good."

"Is it? I don't know if it is. Sometimes it's worse having to readjust."

"I know what you mean," he said. I think he must have done, because he didn't say anything for a while.

After several hundred yards of corners and rubble, and intermittent views of the hills, I could see that Moustache was losing faith. I didn't like the idea of getting lost in front of these men because they would regard getting lost with contempt and I didn't want them to regard me with contempt because nobody tells people stuff if he despises them. Just at the point that I was beginning to get worried, I recognised a corner, an archway, a dank little door. I repeated Phil's joke because I thought they'd appreciate it: "I thought we could eat subterranean tonight." They all laughed.

There was electric light on the stairs as we picked our way down: I wasn't surprised to see that Jez was "priority" too, although it didn't stop the place being perishingly cold. It was hardly packed, and every arrival was an incident. As we came in, the other diners looked up: two tables of fattish men, in shiny purple suits, who looked us over slowly, then returned to their food. Each of the tables was decorated with a pair of skinny, dark-haired girls, wool-wrapped, stolidly forking huge chunks of meat and chips between vermilion lips. In hindsight, Jez was the Rick's Bar of Sarajevo, so the maroon suits probably thought they'd know who we were – and actually, I think they did.

My guests were rather embarrassed when I offered them a drink.

"Are you sure? That's very kind," said Hal.

"I've even seen the prices, so I know how kind it is," I said, and they looked even more embarrassed, but I finished the sentence... "but it's not kind of me, don't worry; it's kind of my paper."

"Well, that's all right then," said Ted. "If you're sure, I'll have a beer."

"Me too," said Moustache.

"What are you having?" said Hal.

"Well, I like drinking wine. And they have proper wine here..." They seemed slightly surprised that I was happy to order a whole bottle for myself, but I explained they didn't sell it any other way: wine by the glass wasn't a convenient smuggling unit. Besides, I could easily finish a bottle of wine by myself by now.

"And the thing is," I said as I took my first sip, "this wine actually tastes nice. The wine in the Holiday Inn is utterly vile."

"They still have wine, do they." said Jim. "I'd have thought you'd have drunk it all by now? They must have bloody big cellars."

Ha ha, how we all laughed. "It's like one of those maths questions," I said. "If 400 journalists each drink one bottle of wine a night for two years, how many cubic metres..."

"Do you think it's smuggled then?" said Ted, and we all laughed again, but then we all looked up as we heard the door.

"And here come the suppliers, I would imagine," I said. My guests shot me a look, so I quickly explained: "Phil drank this same wine when he had dinner with the French general."

Two French soldiers were being shown to a table with the kind of obsequiousness that haunts wannabe Hollywood moguls' dreams. They were in fatigues and the shape of soldiers who actually kill people, rather than mend pipes, or draw graphs, or build roads, or deliver flour, or put up portakabins, or simulate UN extraction plans on the computer or any number of the other tasks it had become apparent to me that soldiers did. As they walked past I saw their badges.

"They're Foreign Legionnaires," I said. They must have heard me, because they turned and one said, "Hello mate," in thick Geordie. He was a good six foot, bull neck, arms bulging with his secret past, his hair that too-short short you see in American films, where every bump on the skull and the scalp shines through. He'd have caused frenzies amongst those Victorian scientists who believed you could trace the mind's construction in the cranium. At some point, someone had broken his nose. They must have been very brave.

"Hi Vince," said Ted; "Molly, this is Vince." We shook hands. "Molly," said Ted, clearly and slowly, "is a journalist."

"Hello," I smiled nicely. Vince nodded back, with those blank eyes I'd often seen on men I'd interviewed out here. When I said, "I think I've seen you before," his eyes got even blanker. Then I remembered, I'd seen him getting in and out of the French general's jeep. "You're Nissent's bodyguard, aren't you?"

Vince thought carefully before he finally spoke: "Aye."

"Would you like a drink?" I said, partly because it seemed rude not to – not that I think Vince was a man much troubled by social nicety – but also it's always useful to know a general's bodyguards. I got a blank-eyed look again. He looked over to Ted, then back to me.

"I'm here with a mate," he waved over to where Tanja, the Aeroflot blonde, was hovering, suddenly smiling, over the table of another Legionnaire.

"He looks bit busy to me…" said Ted.

"Would he like a drink too?"

"I'll go and ask him, like."

Hal gave me a funny look and Ted said: "You're a quick worker!"

I laughed: "Come on, I mean, the *Foreign Legion!* I've seen *Beau Geste*!"

"Do you *know* any of them?" asked Hal.

"No…no, I don't. The French journalists know some of the officers… but, it's different, you know, if you don't speak the same language."

"You speak the same language as Vince," said Ted; then he grinned: "Up to a point."

"I don't think they like journalists very much."

"Most people don't," said Ted.

"That's not fair."

"Well, you always get things wrong," said Ted.

"We try not to. And anyway, there's no way you can feel smug about us getting something wrong if you've purposefully fed us the wrong information."

"You should try harder to get things right, then, shouldn't you…" he was sitting back, squaring up, and I was rather grateful that Vince reappeared at this point, his friend in tow.

"This is Franjo," he said. Like Vince, Franjo had the same thick neck, thick shoulders of his training, and his head, like Vince's, was virtually shaved. Unlike Vince, he was younger, maybe late twenties, and even taller; unlike Vince's Anglo-Saxon pink-faced tow, the stubble on Franjo's skull was dark, and he had the same high cheekbones and deep dark eyes that made you so wonderfully handsome. The name badge on his chest read F. Ivanovic. I thought to myself, my friend, you have come home. I looked into his eyes; like Vince's, like Jim's, they stared back at me without expression.

I said to him, "*Dobra vece, are you from round here?*" His eyes flickered into reaction, before the blinds dropped once more.

He replied, in Vince's English: "What's it to you?" The eyes stared back at me full wattage, and for a moment I actually felt quite scared.

Then the lights went out. There was a second of silence and then I said: "Fuck!" at about the same time as everyone else said it too. I heard two voices apologise for swearing, and I said, "Don't worry about that. I swear like a trooper," before I realised that it was the troopers who were apologising, and we all laughed. While this was going on, there was a chorus of rustling. Ted got there first, flicking his lighter, and lighting the candle on the table, so you could see the rest of us scrabbling for our torches. Across the room, a pool of flickering lights was slowly approaching. Jim's torch swung and the Aeroflot waitress's boots shone in its beam.

"*Izvinite*," she said, as she put the candles down on our table. "*Nema struje*."

"*Don't worry about it, Tanja*," said Franjo; he spoke Serbo-Croat, with the rougher end of Sarajevo accent. "*Can I give you a hand?*" He took the edge of the tray of candles.

"*Why? I'm fine. This is my job.*" But she was fluttering at him, making play with huge dark eyes. "*Sit down, I bring you a drink when I have done this. What you want?*"

"*I'll take the trays round. You bring us two beers.*"

"*Really, no!*" Before she could say anything else, he marched off with the candles. Tanja smiled the way girls do when they have been publicly admired and said in English: "Vince, what you like?"

"Beer please, love. Look at Franjo…" Franjo was putting candles on every table, until the restaurant flickered like a pirates' cave. When he reached the fat maroon men, they grunted, as if not certain how to react. The scrawny bits of arm candy smiled briefly before carrying on with their steaks, as if being waited on by a six foot four Foreign Legionnaire was just another of those random absurdities of war.

"At least when he leaves the Legion he can work as a waiter," said Vince.

"He is very nice man. I get your beer."

"What *do* you do when you leave the Foreign Legion?"

"What's it to do with you?"

"Nothing. I just wanted to know."

"Well it's none of your fucking business."

"Sorry," I said just as Hal said: "Here's your drink." And Ted said to Vince: "So, what did you think about the match?"

We ended up talking in two groups – well, three if you count Franjo and Tanja who had somehow settled at the table next door, with her keeping one eye out for the maroon men and their girls;

me and Hal; Ted, Jim and Vince. Not that Jim did actually talk much. Vince, however, talked quite a lot; about thirty per cent of which consisted of the word fuck. But he did manage to thank me for his drink. And the next one, when it appeared.

Hal and I were doing small talk that was slowly evolving: how long had I been here, did I like it. Ages, and loved it. What about you? Came about three weeks ago. Not sure how long. Probably a few months. It's interesting so far… All that kind of stuff.

It was then that I heard Vince talking about the Legion; they were asking him, the others, some kind of technical stuff, all nodding their heads. I could see that Hal was interested too; we both stopped talking. Into our silence Vince turned on me.

"What are you looking at?" His eyes brimmed blank hostility.

"I'm sorry," I started. "I was just interested in what you were saying."

"Well it's none of your fucking business, is it?"

"She didn't mean any harm," said Ted.

"How do you fucking know?"

"You weren't saying anything secret," I said. "It was just interesting."

"What made it so fucking interesting?"

"I don't know. I mean, it is interesting isn't it. The Foreign Legion's interesting."

"Is it?" Glare.

"Well, yes…" I floundered. "I mean, why do people join it?"

"Why do you journalists write such crap?"

"We *don't* write crap."

"Yeah right."

"I'll rephrase that. *I* don't write crap."

"It's just fucking easy being a journalist isn't it," his voice started to rise. "You come somewhere like this. You write what you like. You don't give a fuck what happens to anyone. Then you can just piss off and leave. Nobody's shooting at you. You're fucking laughing."

If you've never been screamed at by a psychopath, you can't believe how scary it is. His eyes popped, he loomed, his fists balled, his arms bulged as though they would burst from the restraint of not hitting me. Of course what you ought to do in a situation like that is keep quiet, back down, particularly when you are surrounded by people who will make sure it won't happen. That's what you should do. Walk away.

"Actually more journalists have died here than UN troops, thanks very much," I said.

"Only because they are fucking morons."

"I am not a moron."

"You lot make me sick. You're just getting high on somebody else's war." Perhaps what made me angrier was he sounded horribly like you.

"At least I'm trying to do something to help. At least I'm not a mercenary."

"Who are you calling a fucking mercenary?"

"Keep quiet Molly," it was Hal.

"You."

"You what?"

"She didn't say anything," Hal again.

"I bloody did."

"No you didn't. Shut up."

"Vince, mate. I think you've had enough," that was Jim.

"Come on Vince, let's go. Time to go home," said Ted. They stared at each other. For a moment I wasn't sure quite what would happen. Franjo had got up. Tanya was standing warily at one side.

"Vince, *viens,*" he said. Vince looked at him, then glared back at me.

"We'll all go," said Ted. "See you later, Boss."

Vince and I stared at each other. Then I said, because, let's face it, I've got better manners than Vince. "I'm sorry. I didn't mean to upset you."

He shook his head and turned to go. On his way out the door, he said: "Ask these guys about being mercenaries, they're always fighting other people's wars…"

"Vince. Time to go. Bye," said Ted.

"Ask him about Colombia, that la-di-da toff. I don't think the great British public gives a fuck about Colombia."

"Come on, mate," said Jim. "Let's go and see if we can get a beer somewhere else."

Hal and I were left staring at each other by candlelight. He didn't speak, so after a moment I said: "Sorry."

He grunted.

"I didn't mean to… create a row."

"Why did you ask him that then?"

I tried to drink some wine but my glass was empty.

"Would you like some more wine?" He lifted the bottle; there was nothing inside.

"We could get another," I said.

Hal looked at his watch. "Are you sure you want some more?"

I checked mine: 11 p.m. Quite early, really. At the BBC, Phil would just be settling in. The Americans would be filing, if there was anything to file. Muffy would be holding court… no, because she wasn't here. Maybe nothing happened when I wasn't there. Maybe nothing happened at all anywhere… And I didn't have to worry about you, because you were in your flat. "Yah. It's only eleven," I said. He waved at Tanja, now deep in conversation with the scrawny girls, who were being completely ignored by, or completely ignoring, their fat dates.

"I just wanted to know," I said, after a minute. "Why *do* people join the Foreign Legion? I suppose he must have something to hide."

"If he's got something to hide, he's not going to want to tell you."

"He might do," I said. "Nothing ventured, nothing gained. He might be racked by guilt and be dying to talk."

"Piece of advice, don't venture things against Vince, he's bigger than you and I don't think he's the type to be racked by guilt."

"I chose my moment though, didn't I?"

"What do you mean?"

"Well, if he was going to create hell, he couldn't have done it with you lot there."

"He didn't actually tell you, though, did he? And now he doesn't like you."

It's odd that that hurts; I mean, why should I care if a psychotic mercenary dislikes me? But it did.

"Well I don't like him. He tried to thump me."

"He wouldn't have thumped you. We wouldn't have let him."

"He wanted to thump me."

"Now that's different. You were asking him nosy questions."

"Do you thump people who ask you questions?"

"Depends on the questions."

"Is it OK to thump people if they won't answer *your* questions?"

Hal made a face: "In some circles, it is considered perfectly acceptable." And we both started to laugh.

"What time is it?"

"Only midnight," I said.

"Would you like some more… Oh, there isn't any."

"Again."

"Shall we get another…?"

"Fine by me," I said.

"You shouldn't be so mean to Vince," Hal said, as Tanja poured the wine. "You're one of his best customers."

"Ah, so you think he's a black marketeer too!"

"I never said that!"

"But if he were…"

"You'd be one of his best customers!"

"Only because there's nothing else. That's what I don't like. The black market bleeds people dry."

"But you fuel the black market."

"I'm not talking about me."

"How can you talk about the black market and not talk about

you. Everything you eat and drink has been smuggled in. People like you create the market."

"I'm talking about the prices they charged before your general's ceasefire. People were being bled dry."

"As I said, people like you create the market. Supply and demand."

"People like me don't buy coffee and cabbages."

"Your hotel does."

"Stop it. You know I'm right. It's wrong to make money out of other people's misery."

"Stuff has to come in and out. People won't do it unless they're paid. That's reality."

"That's what Amir says."

"Who's Amir?" he asked. I don't know why I didn't tell him then about you, but I didn't. I side-stepped with: "A friend of mine."

"Local?"

I nodded.

"Maybe he's right."

"I don't know. It's just wrong. Look at the shops. They've just started opening up again and the jewellers' are full of engagement rings." He looked puzzled, so I said: "They're having to sell *everything*. An old lady I know," it had been Mrs Selimovic, "tried to sell me her rings the other day. I couldn't buy them, because I couldn't afford them. But I didn't want to beat her down."

"Perhaps she'd have preferred it if you had given her less but she'd got something."

"I couldn't have lived with myself."

"Not much good for her, is it? You not being able to live with yourself. Anyway, aren't you making money out of other people's misery?"

"Working for the *Herald*! No way!"

"Aren't you well paid?"

"God no. The pay's shit. The cameramen get a fortune, but us. No way."

"So why, then… why are you here?"

Well why indeed. I could never answer that question. "I suppose, because it's just so *unfair*!" I almost wailed.

We chatted round and about. He asked me if I'd read journalism at university. "God no!" I replied, and told him I'd done history. He guessed Oxford, and I agreed, then he told me he'd read engineering at Bristol.

There was a silence, where both of us realised that we probably knew at least several people in common, we were the same age, same world… we could have conjured up their ghosts, but I didn't want to. There are times when that's useful, but we were having far too good a time, the two of us. Maybe he felt that too, because he certainly didn't mention any names.

"Still doesn't explain why you ended up here."

I told him then about coming out on my own, the inter-railing and the hitching lifts. I told him about the promotion I'd just got: he was suitably impressed.

"Does that mean you'll leave?" he asked, and I was flattered that he sounded a little disappointed.

"No. God, no!"

He looked surprised at how forceful I sounded. "Why not?"

"Because, because…" but for some reason, again, I didn't mention you. "What's happening here is so *wrong*! And it's the most amazing story. If I have to be a journalist, where else would I be?"

"I don't know. Why do you want to be this kind of journalist?"

"I don't know. I don't know." This was like you saying I was only here for the war. "I don't know," I almost wailed again. "I just do. I don't know why."

"Well you don't have to get upset about it. I was just asking."

"Oh you can ask…" And I laughed to make it light. "As long as you don't thump me if I don't answer. I don't know why."

"I won't thump you. I'm just fascinated why you do your job."

"You're fascinated! I'm fascinated by yours."

"What, the SAS? Oh that's easy. I just wanted to be James Bond."

And we both roared with laughter. "It sounds pathetic," he said, "but it's true."

"I thought it was supposed to be secret."

"What?"

"That you're in the SAS. I thought I wasn't supposed to know."

"Oh shit, yes. I forgot."

We were now laughing so much that our cackles had woken up Tanja, who'd been lying with her head in her hands in corner, where the maroon suits had been.

"OK. I promise I won't tell anyone."

"Cross your heart?"

"Does that work?"

"We use it all the time."

Crossing my heart, I caught sight of my watch.

"Oh shit! It's quarter to two. I'd better get back. My boyfriend will kill me. Oh no, he won't," I'd remembered you were back in your flat.

"Your boyfriend!" said Hal. "You have a boyfriend here?"

Well, you were out now, but it didn't seem to matter so much.

"Where is he?"

"At home. It's fine. I forgot." But Hal didn't seem interested in exactly where you were.

"Doesn't he mind you being out with me?" he said.

"I hope not. I mean, I'm always having to do things for work that he can't do."

"So am I work?"

"No!" I said, thinking, yes, but a very nice part of work. "*Hvala*, Tanja, oh my God! You'd better be work. Look at the size of this!" The bill was 500DM. I was laughing again.

"Fucking hell! Are you sure that's all right."

"Positive. I promise you. But it's just so funny!"

Hal insisted on leaving a tip. He put 50DM on the table.

"That's a lot," I said.

"Ten per cent..."

"We're not in Chelsea now…"

"But we could be, you and I, we could easily just be having dinner in a London restaurant," he said, and helped me into my coat.

We walked up the windy stairs into the night. It was arctic. I shivered into my collar.

Hal seemed impervious. Maybe under his jersey his body, like his face, was covered in fur. We heard a machine gun rattle up on the hill.

"You don't get that in Chelsea," I said, and laughed. Then I shivered again. He put his arm round my shoulder.

"We have to cross here," I said, as we reached Marshal Tito and used the crossing as an excuse to extract myself. "*Idemo*."

"What's that?"

"Let's go… It's pretty basic. Didn't they teach you *anything* before you came out here?"

"Not much. I didn't have much notice. We have interpreters for the tricky stuff."

"Ah. Interpreters… I hope they're pretty."

"Ours is a bloke – a depressed physicist called Bogdan." I'd been going to make a crack about Balkan interpreter syndrome; wherever we went, in Bosnia, we'd see some lonely and lovestruck man, a UN official, an aid worker, or one of those observers – the ex-army EC bunch, or the UN military observers, all still serving soldiers, who got to spend all day in an armoured car driving round a war zone with a girl who spoke with Valida's Bond-girl Slav accent, and who generally had the face to boot, and certainly the figure; as part of the deal of interpreting she got not only hard currency, but also hot showers (when there was water), cigarettes and food. Quite often she got rather more than that, but to be fair, it was very cold – and scary. But I didn't say it. What I actually thought is, no wonder the UN caves in all the time, the general's interpreter's a Serb: Bogdan's a Serb name.

"So who is this boyfriend? Is he another journalist?" said Hal as he loped along.

"Oh God, no," I said quickly. "Journalists make terrible boyfriends. They're always rushing off on a new story and screwing other people."

"Do you do that?"

"What?"

He stopped us in the street, put his hand on my arm and looked down into my eyes. and said: "Rush off and screw other people."

Suddenly, I felt the mood change, as though we had just come round a corner and into the wind. It must have changed before, but I was just oblivious to it. My surprise was almost a physical shock. I was so used to being in love with you; so used to everyone knowing that I was in love. I'd forgotten that getting a contact drunk was also drinking with a man; I was so locked into my love that I had forgotten that drinking with a man in Sarajevo could have any other possible outcome than just a conversation about our loony universe. For a moment I wasn't sure what to say. I didn't want to piss him off; he was a fantastic contact. And anyway, I was actually quite pleased: he seemed terribly nice and was really good-looking.

"I rush off," I said slowly, "But I don't screw other people."

"Really?"

"Really."

"Why not?"

I waited for a moment before I said: "Because I'm rather in love."

"Really?"

I stared back, very levelly, into his handsome furry face and said, "Yeah. Really," and started walking again. To my amazement, I felt a twinge of regret, swiftly followed by a virtuous glow.

Hal caught me up. "What's he like then?" he said.

"Oh," and I could see you suddenly in front of me. "Tall, good-looking, dark, clever, funny. Nice."

"Sounds perfect."

"Maybe he is. Maybe he is. Oh, God." I stopped. Hal stopped too. Then he said, "You don't sound convinced."

"Oh no, I am," I said, and started walking again. I didn't want to rehearse with Hal this endless scene in my head.

Hal said nothing. I repeated: "I am."

"So what's the problem?" He was walking with me again.

"There isn't a problem."

"Well, there must be a problem."

"Why?"

"Well for a start, you're out with me." Of course I couldn't say, "But you're work." So I just said: "I didn't realise that we were going to be so late."

He went on, "And also, you keep saying that there isn't a problem."

"Well, there isn't."

"Yeah, right."

I suppose no woman ever minds a man knowing another one wants to marry her, so I said: "He keeps asking me to marry him."

"And you don't want to?"

"No!"

"Why not?"

"God, you sound like him!"

"How long have you been together?"

"Nearly a year."

"That's not long."

"That's what I think."

"I thought all women wanted to get married and have babies," said Hal. And I couldn't stop myself before it burst out: "But not in *Sarajevo*!"

He laughed: "Fair enough. But maybe he just thought you wanted to get married."

"No, I don't think so."

"How do you know?"

"He's asked me before."

"Ah."

"And I just don't know what to do."

"Can't you just have a good time?"

I thought about that, and then I said rather sadly: "I don't think you can just have a good time if you're in love."

"And you are in love?"

"I am."

We walked a few paces in silence then he said: "You journalists seem to have a good time here."

"Oh," I said. "We do. But you have to, don't you, in a shit-hole like this..." I used to feel a bit guilty about how much fun it was. An old man I interviewed, on my second day, as he queued for water in the shelter of a block of flats behind the hotel, had said to me: "We can hear you, at night, in the Holiday Inn. Laughing and singing." His words flooded me with guilt but after I took up with you, the guilt flowed away. At least you were having a good time too.

"I'm having a good time," he said. Then he paused, and added, a little wistfully, "Although it is terribly quiet."

"I know," I said. "It is terribly quiet. We used to have more fun."

We walked a few paces linked by mutual regret.

"Don't worry, Gorazde is bound to heat things up. It's going to blow," I said.

"Don't say that," he said, but he was grinning.

Then he said: "Tonight was fun."

"Yes," I said and smiled up at him. "Tonight was fun." I walked a few paces further before I said: "We've never really been able to do that before."

"What?"

"Go out like that."

"Why not?"

"Well, there wasn't anywhere until now!"

"So, let's do it again."

I smiled and said, quite truthfully: "That would be fun."

"Yes it would." He waited a moment: "You could bring the boyfriend."

I said: "I don't think I'll do that."

Another pause, and then he said: "Why not?"

I could see the street, with your parents' apartment, on the other side of the park. I couldn't really explain, that there was no way they would tell me *anything* if I had Amir sitting at the table. I mean, even the UN's maps said "not to be shown to any members of the indigenous community," on the corner. "He lives just here," I said.

"Who, the boyfriend?"

"Yes."

"Why?" Hal sounded utterly astonished.

"It's where his parents live. He's always lived here."

"He's a local? Oh my God," and he roared with laughter. "Don't tell me you're shagging your interpreter!"

"It is not like that!"

"Of course it is."

"No, it's not. It really isn't."

"Come off it." He grabbed my arm again.

"I mean it! It was different. He was my boyfriend before he was my interpreter. I mean, he could hardly speak English."

"Oh right, I see. So you couldn't even talk to each other."

"He could speak some English," I said with dignity.

"And now he speaks it better."

"Yes."

"And you speak Serbo-Croat."

"Well, yes..." I started to laugh. "I mean, I know it sounds clichéd. But it's different."

"Yeah, right."

We'd reached the broad end of Marshal Tito, where the bad snipers used to be, and the sniper barricades still blocked off most of the street. I stopped him, while we still stood in the shadow of the mosque.

"Look at that. I love the stars here," I said, to change the subject. "War stars. No light pollution."

"Best stars in the world," and in their light, I could see his grin.

"I guess if the power comes back, they'll be ruined again."

"Who needs electricity anyway?" he said. We stood there, by the little wall where the Sarajevans sat, waiting for the courage to run as the bullets pinged up the street, next to the photographers, waiting to record what happened when they ran. Behind us, the mosque gleamed dully in the moonlight.

"This is where we part, I guess," I said. "You've got to go up there, and I've got to get home."

"How will you get back?"

"I'll walk," I said. "It's only a couple of hundred yards."

"You can't walk that on your own. It's dangerous."

"Don't be ridiculous," I laughed. "It's nowhere near as dangerous as it used to be. Anyway, the back way was always pretty safe." But in the moonlight, the shadows drew demons on the pavements.

"I'll be fine," I said.

"Well, I won't be. I'm not letting you go on your own."

"You'll just have to come back. We've just done the worst bit."

"I'm not talking about that kind of dangerous. It's two o'clock in the morning. You shouldn't walk around on your own. This place is full of nuts."

He was right. I knew he was right. It wasn't just the restaurant scene that had changed with the ceasefire. Maybe the muggers didn't come out when they risked being shot, or maybe, when one was scared of being shot, one didn't worry about being raped.

It took us about another five minutes to make it to the hotel and neither of us spoke very much for a while, until Hal started to ask me about the things that we passed. I gave him a bit of the mini-guided tour: the ruined house, the little street where the snipers could see you to the left, the playground where no children had played for two years, the baseball hoop gnarled in its twist on the tarmac.

"This must have been the road we drove, that first day," he said.

"It was. I remember watching you leave. What were you doing out here anyway?" I didn't say that I'd been really jealous of him and Andy, that they'd been in a pair.

He waited for a moment: "Andy, the other guy, was an UNMO, as you know."

"Yes," I remembered that. "But what were you doing?"

"Me?"

"Yes. You."

Pause. "I was just looking around." It seemed a perfectly valid answer to me. Bosnia was full of people who were looking around. Including me. It would have been lovely if he'd said, "Well, to be perfectly honest, we were planning to assassinate Karadzic, we had a hit squad lined up, but at the last minute – I mean, we were in position – the Queen rang me up on my mobile and vetoed the operation. But it's on again for next Tuesday. Would you like to come and watch?" But he was never going to say that. All journalists fantasise that they'll find someone who says that, but they never do; at least not till years afterwards, when time has dulled people's secrets and they need to take them out, polish them shiny and look into them to see their youth.

We were at the road leading between the chicanes at the back of the hotel. As we strolled round the last row of gym lockers, and the mountains loomed behind the hotel, I said: "I always like to run this bit as well."

"I'll race you."

"Don't be ridiculous. I'll lose."

I did, but not by much, as he was dragging me along by the hand, which I extricated as we got to the hotel.

"Good night," I said, rather brightly, as we stood on the snow-glazed concrete.

"Good night," he said back. "And thank you. That was fun. We should do it again sometime."

"That would be great."

Pause.

He moved closer again, I stepped back.

"I might bring Phil, if you liked." He stopped.

"Who's Phil?"

"He's the BBC correspondent."

"Phil Kennedy? He's good, isn't he?"

"He's great. And really nice, Phil. He's like my best friend here. Apart from Amir, that is. I could bring him, if you'd like to meet him, that is."

"I'd love to," he said, and moved a step back. "It would be really interesting. I've seen him on telly… How do I get in touch?" Then of course we were into Sarajevo communication hell. "The phones don't really work," I said. "But I'm in room 524. I guess the best thing is if I ring you from the BBC. They've got a local landline. I can ring UNPROFOR from there. What's your extension?"

It took about four seconds before he decided to give it to me but in the end, he just said: 2252. I wrote it down, and put SAS Sarajevo beside it. And showed it to him, and laughed. He took my pen, crossed it out, and wrote JCO's. But without the apostrophe.

"Good night," I said, and kissed him on the cheek. "Thank you very much for walking me home."

"It was a pleasure. And thanks for the drinks."

"That's the *Herald*. Be careful going home."

"I'll wait till you're inside."

"Don't worry. I'll be fine. I'll wait till you get to the barricades."

"Just in case I'm shot?"

"Yah. Just in case."

"Will you come and rescue me?"

"I'll probably just panic," I said; I had been useless with the man on Sniper Alley. "You can shout instructions to me as you bleed to death."

"Good night. Good luck," and he kissed me on the cheek again, both cheeks, slightly too long and slightly too close to my mouth. I pulled away and as I did so, I remember thinking, to my amazement, what a shame.

As I watched him sprint behind the first of the gym lockers, I realised I'd never got him to tell me what he was actually doing out here; I'd even forgotten to ask him about Colombia. And when

I got up to my room, I'd completely forgotten you weren't in the hotel...

...Now, at Ingrid's book launch years later, I heard Phil say, "He seemed much less keen on having dinner with me when Molly wasn't there."

Suddenly I wasn't in Sarajevo any more, but back at Ingrid's book launch clutching my glass of cheap white wine, being glared at by rows of dead lawyers.

"Were you in Kosovo?" It was the general.

"I don't really do that kind of thing any more," I shook my head.

He said: "Very wise." I thought he'd move on after that, and talk to someone else, but he stayed to talk to me for a while, which made me feel much better. It made me think, for almost the first time, maybe this isn't the end. Maybe I *could* do that kind of work again.

There was also a stack of other people I hadn't seen for ages; Tim, who I only ever saw on telly these days. Even Ed: he seemed to have travelled with Ingrid during the Kosovo crisis for a while. He asked me if I'd been back to Sarajevo, and I said not, had he? He looked a little shifty and said, "A couple of times."

It was nice seeing Ingrid again. I couldn't stick her in Sarajevo. I tried to be nice to her when she arrived – after the ceasefire, after you had gone. She used to ignore me if I was in the same room as her. Or barge in on a conversation I was having and twist it away. Or try to collect a group to go out to dinner and not include me; all the nasty tricks of the school playground. One night she even started talking about you – Phil said something like, "Molly knows Amir rather better than you." But she just carried on, recycling gossip. I ended up walking out onto the landing.

Then I bumped into her two years ago, at King's Cross, of all places. Her face must have been a mirror of my horrified recognition – oh God, we're going to have to have a conversation; we're both waiting for a train – but after a moment, I suddenly felt pleased. We had a cup of coffee, which then became two. Maybe in Sarajevo we were too similar and it freaked us out, but in the real world, it was rather a relief to find someone vaguely the same. She lives abroad still but we occasionally email each other. I'm glad I went to her book launch. It was like opening up an old… well maybe, I was going to say, a box of old toys. But it wasn't like when I opened the box of books last year. It was wonderful to see everyone again, and they were all pleased to see me. The only thing was that none of them wanted to talk about you.

MUJO AND SULJO were staring at their block of flats with some binoculars. Suddenly, Mujo said:

"Here, look at this Suljo, those EC monitors are fucking our wives."

Suljo: "So, at the moment, we're monitoring them, and they are the ones who are getting fucked."

SARAJEVO 1994

XIV

In the end, I hardly saw you at all that month, even though I didn't leave. It wasn't just that we were all rushed off our feet: you were in the flat – and I couldn't stay, because of the phones, and particularly not, now the electricity had gone. The plan was that you'd spend Thursday to Saturday working for me, and then I'd go over to you on Sunday morning, but it didn't work out. With the airport shut, CTV couldn't get a proper – by which they meant American – crew in, so you and Edin had to do all the work. I'd been pleased for you. It was so good for your career. And you seemed so happy, having your own job to do. You'd been brilliant fixing up people for me to go and see, and had wonderful ideas of how to make things different – the traders who did the walk with supplies in and out of Gorazde, the refugees, the ham radio – but actually, once you'd set things up and rung me about them, I generally went to see these people on my own. I missed you of course, but there was so much to do, and in the evenings I'd hang out with Phil, or we'd go out drinking with Hal and his friends and ask questions.

Gorazde was one of those classic Bosnian crises, like the four weeks of a childhood disease: first spots, quarantine, temperature, a week of high fever, then a tedious week of watching telly wrapped in an eiderdown, half-wishing you could have a relapse to put off going back to school. It was made even better because the Serbs completely sealed Sarajevo; we couldn't leave and no other journalists could get in. I had great satisfaction the next day in telling the *Herald* I was trapped. The *Herald* must have been really strapped for cash, because Roger still said I should leave as soon as I possibly could, when anybody with half a brain could see the way things were going. Luckily, by the following Friday, when Gorazde was constant headline news, he'd taken the other half of his brain out of the account books and had reverted to self-congratulation on having a correspondent in situ, while every other paper was having to file from Split or Kiseljak or Pale or wherever else they'd got as far as before getting stuck.

It was several weeks in, once the fever had broken, and the air strikes we'd all been waiting for the UN and NATO to unleash on the Serbs attacking Gorazde hadn't happened after all, just as we predicted. The Serbs had been slaked and the dead of Gorazde were being buried beneath a mound of reiterated UN resolutions, when I had a cup of coffee with Ed.

Ed had never got to Pale or Belgrade to do his Big Piece. He'd been trapped like us. It was all crap that stuff about hating the goat fuck of the rolling story. His eyes lit up, and he followed us around like a child, asking endless questions about the people we were asking questions of. He was like a mythical creature whose arms ended in a notebook and pen instead of normal hands. To begin with, he didn't have a paper to write for, like the lowliest freelance, since his magazine's deadlines worked three months in advance. Not for him the pathetic run of reverse charge calls I'd had to go through until a year ago. He rang his agent from the BBC sat phone (chalking it all up to his mag, of course); his agent rang the editor of the *New York Times*. In under twenty-four hours, Ed had his string. I don't blame him: it would have been no fun being there without something to do. The *New York Times* regular correspondent was livid, but he was trapped outside Sarajevo, so I guess it was fair game. Even if Ed had not been Ed but the least famous journalist in the world, he was still in the place where the story was – or at least he was as close as it was possible to get. The regular guy told me later that the foreign editor had been livid too. I'm not surprised. It's no fun having to edit someone much more famous and successful than yourself.

Ed had his uses, anyway. Hal loved him, and so did his friend Charlie, who'd suddenly appeared, who was a bit older than Hal, and Hal called him Boss. They were, inevitably, suspicious at first, possibly because he was American, possibly because they were suspicious kind of people, but it turned out that Charlie owned several of Ed's books. Ed lured them in with scraps of Africa, Vietnam, Salvador and Afghanistan. He didn't seem to hate Africa at all when he talked about it with them. He got Charlie to admit how those Afghan hats could be uncomfortably warm, which was interesting, since, back in 1994, the British Army had not been officially deployed in Afghanistan for about 100 years; he even got Hal on to Colombia. He also had an even more lavish expense account than Phil, so the Jez dinners became a regular event – at least, until everything suddenly got very serious, and half of Hal's friends disappeared, and then reappeared, a few weeks later, in Gorazde, with one of them dead.

I bumped into Ed that day on Marshal Tito Street. I was wandering along, looking up the hills, thinking, maybe I could live here; maybe it would be nice. I could live with you and Edin, and then, when I had to travel for work, you wouldn't feel so alone. You'd get your phones fixed up soon. Between the *Herald* and CTV, we must have the clout, when there was Ed, peering around, nostrils twitching in the air.

"Molly! And how are *you*?" The nostrils flared.

I smiled. I'd got fond of Ed. In the last month, he'd become one of us. "Where've you been?"

I said I'd been with Divjak.

"What did he say? Would you like a coffee? Shall we get one here?"

So I said, fine, because it was a lovely spring afternoon.

"Let's go to Café Life," he said. "It's young and hip," he shook his grey locks. "Aida took me there last week."

It was not so far from your street, on the corner of the big road up to the Residency which had been so dangerous until a few weeks ago.

We sat on tinny rickety chairs, ordered two cups of bitter coffee, and stared around and out through the shiny new glass. Around us were the usual crowd: a pair of sad-eyed boys in uniform, who looked vaguely familiar, but then I'd lived here a year, and everyone in Sarajevo looked vaguely familiar now. Two Sarajevo ladies, bags gouged beneath their eyes, gilded clasps on their handbags, and those frosted glasses Edna Everage used to like, faces set in resignation, but with lipstick and their hair in some semblance of a do, one still sporting an engagement ring. A couple of tables of skinny, snake-hipped girls, everyone nursing tiny cups of coffee. Despite the beat of the generator, the pulse of the war, it was gloomy, they weren't wasting electricity on lights and the sunlight fought its way in through the plastic on the windows. As we sat, in our coats, smelling the damp, and the chicory in the coffee, and the faint whiff of pee, Ed tried to warn me. But I wouldn't let him.

He started off with: "So, have you decided what you are going to do about your job?"

So I explained I hadn't had to. They hadn't mentioned it again.

"They will," he said. "They will."

But maybe, I said, and I knew the answer even as I said it, maybe they'll think after this they ought to keep me here.

"Nope," said Ed. "This is going quiet for a while. You know what the locals call it?"

I did. I'd told him a month ago, but I let him go on. "Half-time. It's time for a break. What else can the Serbs do now? They *know* they nearly went too far... They were *that* close," he made the classic thumb and finger gesture, "to having the shit bombed out of them. I had coffee with" (and then he said the name of the American negotiator who the rest of us just saw at press conferences when he flipped in on his plane. I'd forgotten, over the last month of Ed the stringer, quite how distinguished Ed was). "Mladic knows how close it was. He knows he's got to give it a rest. Your general's got them over a barrel...And they," he added happily, "have him over a barrel too. It's a very uncomfortable situation for both of them. Being over a barrel is not nice. Believe me, I've been over several, and it takes quite a while to escape from being over a barrel."

He went on: "You, my dear, are going to have to make up your mind."

"They may not want to keep me in London."

"Well, they may not," said Ed. "But if they have any sense they will. But you've got to decide what you want. Strike while the iron's hot. It's up to you, my dear."

"But I don't want to decide."

"How much have you actually *seen* of Amir, the last few weeks?"

And I said, oh, and explained about CTV and the crew...

"So not much?"

"Well, obviously, we saw each other in the evenings..." I started to say, but actually, when I thought about it, we hadn't seen each other so much. I'd spent a lot of time with Phil and Ed, pouring booze into assorted spooks, Hal and the like, in Jez. You finished work too late to come back to the hotel. And now they were shooting again on Sniper Alley, it was really too dangerous to commute to and fro...and it's not like we could ring each other on our mobiles then. When I thought about it, apart from a quick catch-up at the briefing, I hadn't seen you properly for days.

"Well if you'll forgive an old man for saying this, you should go back to London. Forget Amir. And take the job."

It's not as easy as that, I said. I told him I was in love with you...

"In love," he said. "My dear girl, when you get to my age, you'll know that being in love is wonderful but it does go away. I've been in love with every story I ever did. But love doesn't last. Jobs don't last either, mind. But at least they should, if you do them properly, pave the way for other jobs. Love can have the opposite effect. I think you should take this job."

I told him then I'd almost decided to stay. He asked me if I'd spoken to you.

"No, I haven't had time."

"I'd talk to Amir first."

But I never doubted what you would say. It was only six weeks ago that you had proposed to me. "I will, but I wanted to know what I thought before I did."

"Well maybe you should find out what he thinks too."

"Oh."

"I don't mean it nastily, my dear, but it's a big decision. It will, and I should warn you, screw your career in London. They will think that you've gone native, or whatever. Now that's fine, if you want to spend your life here..."

"My *life*...?" the horror must have shown in my voice.

"Well, yes..."

"But I don't..."

"Then don't do it."

"But last time you told me it was a valid thing to do."

"So I did," he said. For a moment he seemed nonplussed, but then suddenly he got a second wind. "But, that was before all this Gorazde stuff happened," he rattled the words out, almost with relief. "It's going quiet now for ages..." He didn't finish his sentence but stared out across the café.

"Do you see those girls," he said. I turned round; two pretty girls, sunglasses, ski-jackets, long hair, lipstick on their bee-stung lips, were nursing tiny cups of coffee two tables away. They looked familiar, like the two soldiers had done. "I met them with Aida."

I laughed. "I thought you didn't work with female interpreters."

"I couldn't find anyone else," and then he made a funny little face and said: "...and anyway, I was doing news again..." His eyes lit up, staring at some point in the middle distance that was presumably a hotel room in Saigon around 1968. "And I'm an old man now…" He switched his gaze to me and grinned: "Aida took me dancing."

"*Dancing*! In Sarajevo!" I had a vision of ancient Ed scooping Aida up into a foxtrot, but actually he must have been only in his thirties when the Stones became big. "Some place that had just re-opened. It was great. Full of guys straight from the front completely stoned." He smiled: "It reminded me of Vietnam in a way…"

I was suddenly anxious that you'd never taken me dancing. You were always saying you wanted to be normal. Well, that's a normal thing to do. And it's a good story… nightclubs in Sarajevo, and then I thought, perhaps it was because I'd hated those parties so much last year. But it was different now… I knew people… I could understand what they said… at least, I supposed I could. I could understand all the refugees and politicians after all. Maybe you'd been working too hard. Maybe you never went… Maybe I never really gave you a chance this last month. I was too busy trying to extract secrets from my new friends. Then I heard Ed say: "Your Amir was there."

"I suppose it must have been one of the evenings I was working. We're not joined at the hip, you know, Amir and me."

Ed looked at me, I think rather kindly.

"I really love him, you know. I can't imagine not being with him. This is why all these decisions about London are so awful for me. And I feel so guilty," I said, "when I look around now and every-one's happy and drinking coffee and enjoying things being better and I don't want them to be better. I want them to stay the same so I can stay here with him."

"Things never stay the same." Ed put his arm round me.

"I'm sorry," I said. I could feel the tears oozing out. "I'm just so tired."

"You need a break."

"No!" I said. "That's what the paper says… Why can't Amir come on my break with me. It's so unfair. Why can't he?"

Ed didn't say anything; he just gave my shoulders a squeeze.

"I don't envy you. This is a hard decision and it's easy for me to say because I'm much older than you and I can see what I think is right. But maybe I'm wrong. Maybe you and Amir are properly in love."

"We are! We are!"

"In that case, maybe you should stay here with him. But if you do that you must recognise that it could be for ever…"

"*No!*"

"Exactly."

"It's not what you think. It's not like that! I just don't trust this place. I don't trust all this not to happen again."

"So take him out," I heard Ed say. "Take him out to London."

I heard myself say "No!" again: and that No was a much harder one to defend. So I told him, I'd have to marry you to get you out. And Ed said, so if you love him, marry him. And I said, I did love you. But I said I loved you now.

"Well is that love? A lot of people would say it wasn't. I don't know. I've loved a lot of people now."

I tried to explain – I wasn't sure I could be with you forever. But I didn't see how I could find that out here. Then Ed said, "You could always get divorced. There are worse things to do. I should know…"

"You can't go into marriage thinking like that."

"Why not?"

"But…" it was like tripping on a step. Grown-ups weren't supposed to say that. "Marriage isn't *supposed* to be like that," I said.

"I see…" Ed drank some of his coffee.

"Well it isn't," I said, with less certainty now.

"If it's God you're worried about, you couldn't marry him in a church anyway. He's Muslim."

"It's not just God," I said; it was everything. I mean, you're always taught, aren't you, as a girl, never to marry someone if you think it might not work out. Girls think of marriage. We're brought up to think of marriage. Getting married for me is a solemn thing;

vowing eternal love to someone I knew I wanted to be with for ever, or at least I could honestly say at the time, I thought I wanted to be with for ever. Vowing, in a long white dress, before my God, who probably did exist, and several hundred people, who then gorged themselves on smoked salmon and champagne as my father, with a reluctant cheque, finally signed away his largely absentee responsibility. The dress and the God, the smoked salmon and the oaths, until now they had been indivisible to me. I wasn't sure I could sacrifice it all and wed myself to an alien world, thinking in advance maybe it could all go wrong. It wasn't that I minded you being Muslim, but that meant I wouldn't be able to marry you in a church, and somehow, the idea of a civil wedding seemed almost an admission that one thought it might not be permanent, so in that case, why marry at all? The registry office, the hurried pavement farewells. Why do it? Except to get you out of Sarajevo, but *I* didn't want to leave. And always, the tiny, rotting worm of suspicion, that almost I didn't want to name. What did you really want from me? God knows, you knew about the cheap chocolate now.

"And anyway," I said, "what would he do in London?" Sit round the kitchen table in Shepherd's Bush, smoking, with all the other deserters, retiling the odd bathroom, cash in hand.

"He'd find something in the end. He's clever."

"What would we live on?"

Ed looked at me very carefully and said: "You."

"We couldn't live on me," I said. "I can hardly live on me. And anyway, I don't *live* in London. At least, hardly any of the time…"

It was when Ed was off for a pee that I heard the girls. I didn't mean to, but the café had gone quiet and so I couldn't help hearing Aida's name.

"*Poor Aida,*" they were speaking Serbo-Croat of course. "*She's having a nightmare time.*" And a mean part of me thought good; I'd never really forgiven her for not telling me where you were the day after the Sarajevo market massacre.

"*She should just dump him, he's a shit.*"

"She says he's not. She says he's going to leave her just as soon as things calm down." I wasn't really listening. My mind went round and round: did Henri think like this before he left Valida for Rwanda? Did Phil go through this before he married Lena? Is he happy now? Is she happy in the grey of Shepherd's Bush, far from the Chouf and the glinting azure of the Levant?

"He won't."

"How do you know?"

"It's been, what, three months now, and he hasn't left her. Why should he now?"

"Aida says he's fed up because she treats him like shit."

"I'm sure he says all that to Aida."

"She says he's hardly seen her at all for the last few weeks."

"Well that may be but I've seen them at the briefing and believe me, they're all over each other like a rash," and on the word briefing, my attention swung in. *"And Aida's there too. She just watches and does nothing."*

"What's he playing at? Is it the money?"

"I don't know. I mean, I guess he gets a lot out of her. Although what she thinks she's paying him for, God alone knows. But it could just be the kick of having two women at once. You know, your nice Bosnian girl and the other a bit more exotic." I picked up my coffee and thought, no… No, I mean, lots of people go to the briefing.

"Why does she put up with it? Aida is no fool."

"I think he just sprays the charm and fixes her with his lovely dark eyes. You know him…"

"I think she's really in love with him."

"I don't doubt Aida is really in love with him. She's had a crush on him for years. Don't you remember the way she used to follow him around at school? I was in the TV station with her when she thought he'd been in the marketplace. She nearly flipped. What I doubt is that he is really in love with her." And I had another sip of the coffee, as I made myself think… and lots of people were nearly in the marketplace.

Then I heard: *"But do you think he's really in love with that journalist?"* and I thought, no it can't be. This can't be real. I felt sick, and everything, my arm with the cup, the room, the people, the sun, the moon, the earth, the stars, the waitress wending her way through the crowd, seemed to go on hold and the coffee in my cup suddenly seemed disgusting, and my arm flopped it down with a crash onto the saucer as though the muscles in my shoulder had lost the will to live.

I hadn't even noticed Ed come back to the table.

"You feeling better now?" he said.

But I didn't answer Ed because I didn't know what to say. In the background I heard the other girl snort and say: *"Knowing him, I would say he's just in love with himself."*

I wished Phil was here. But he wasn't. Tim had come rushing in the moment the Serbs re-opened the exit routes two weeks ago. I wished Muffy was here, but she was a continent away in another war. Valida was Aida's sister so I could hardly have spoken to her. The hotel was packed with hacks, although they were just beginning to leave, but I didn't really *know* any of them well enough for this. So that left no-one or Ed. And I couldn't face talking to Ed about his. There really wasn't anyone I could talk to here at all.

I left Ed at the hotel and carried on down the street. I told him I was going to see a friend. He wanted to come too: "What kind of friend? What do they do?"

"It's got nothing to do with the war." His interest visibly waned. "It's just… a girl, who had problems with her boyfriend." Ed shrugged and vanished through the door. "Maybe see you for dinner," he said. "Maybe we'll get those boys of yours to come out."

I walked to you. I suppose I could have been shot. They were shooting people every now and again these days. But I didn't really seem to care.

Your lift wasn't working, but I wouldn't have taken it anyway. I walked up the stairs, picking out each chipped concrete lip with my torch. I was thinking too hard to even count them this time.

I could see daylight shining through the tiny shrapnel hole half -way up your door. I rang the bell, but nothing happened. The power was out. I banged on the door. And banged on it again. And for a moment I hoped you wouldn't be there. But you were. And so was she.

You stood in the doorway with your back to what little light was filtering through the planks on the windows facing the front-line. I could hardly see your face, but you didn't look pleased. I looked down; there were two pairs of shoes, on the parquet, just before the horrible orange tufty rug by the door: the Timberlands I had bought you, when you'd given me your size, and a slightly battered-looking pair of black high heels.

You said my name. "How did you get here?" And when I didn't speak, you said: "Are you OK?"

I looked past you into the big sitting room. By a little table with ashtrays and coffee cups, Aida sat, feet tucked up on the huge leather sofa, her black hair fizzing into an aureole in the light through the cracks in the planks. She looked at me probably the same way I was looking at her. Then something flickered over her face, which, had I seen it on anyone else, someone I was interviewing perhaps, would have overwhelmed me with pity. She stood up.

"I was just going. Molly, I'd better go now. Amir and I had some stuff we had to finish, but we can do it another time."

I watched as she tried to find, then close her bag. I hated her, I suppose, but I felt so sorry for her, as she leant over the sofa, fiddling with the clasp, her neat bottom towards me, in its pretty little skirt, and there I was in my filthy old jeans. But I couldn't stop this disgusting corroding feeling in my stomach that had nothing to do with any kind of civilised human behaviour and made me want to run across the room and smash her face into something until her lipstick smeared red all over her foundation.

"You don't have to go. I know all about it."

She stood up. I saw relief – maybe even hope – cross her face.

We both turned to you. You said: "What do you mean?"

I saw her face tighten, then I couldn't bear to look because I suppose she must have been a mirror of me. I turned back to you.

"I know you've been fucking her." You started to speak, and I thought, please don't deny it. Please don't lie to me. Please don't do that, let me keep something of this. Please. And then, just in case you did, because I knew she wouldn't, I said to her: "It's true, Aida, isn't it?"

She said nothing, but just looked at you.

"Amir?" I said.

"Where did you hear this?"

"Does it matter? It's true. It's so obviously true." I looked into your eyes. You stared back with, fear, I think it was fear. I think you were afraid. You said, Molly, again. I could hear Aida moving in the background, but I just stared at you.

"Molly…" you put your hand on my shoulder, and you looked deep inside me. I swallowed. Then I saw Aida move behind your shoulder and I remembered the two girls in the café snorting about your eyes. I pulled away, looked somewhere else, saw her shoes neatly side by side, by my feet. Poor bitch. She couldn't even leave. I was in the doorway.

"Fuck you! You bloody bastard! I would have stayed here with you, you know that? I'd decided to stay."

"Molly, please."

"No!" I wanted to throw something at you. Something you'd given me. But there wasn't anything. I'd never let you give me anything. You'd had too little in the war to give anything away. Except that fur hat, and I wasn't wearing it, now spring had come.

"Goodbye," I said. "And Aida, good luck." I ran down the stairs, as fast as I could in the pitch dark, my torchlight bobbing crazily in front. I heard you clattering after me, but I didn't stop. You caught me up. You grabbed my arm. I could smell you on top of all the other Sarajevo smells of damp and rubbish and urine and rat shit… I swayed. For a moment I thought you'd push me down stairs but you pulled me back.

You said, please. Then you said it again. Please don't – don't go. Please stay with me.

"Let me go," I said. "Let me go." It was too dark on the stairs to see your face.

"Please don't. Don't go. Please stay with me…"

But I pushed you away. Perhaps I hoped you'd follow me after all, come to the hotel, but you didn't that night, and the next day, I flew away, so you couldn't have followed me if you'd wanted to.

MUJO WAS MISSING. Some corpses came in, in a body exchange, from a massacre done by Arkan's Tigers. Fata was asked to come down to the mortuary to identify Mujo, but when she got there, none of the bodies had a head. The mortuary director asked, how will you know your husband? "By his dick," she said. So she started to look. After she lifted the tenth sheet, she said, "Oh, doctor, this one's not from Sarajevo."

XV

I didn't see you again for over six months. You tried to contact me at first. Tim told me you'd come round to the office, the next day; you were waiting when he came back from taking me to the airport. You tried to ring me, on the BBC sat phone, but it was pointless and expensive because I was half a continent away and I didn't want to talk to you anyway. In the end, Tim said, he'd had to stop you because no-one would pay the bill. The *Herald* certainly wouldn't. So then you started to write.

The first letter you sent out with Ed. You said you loved me. You didn't even know my address in London. Ed had to post it to me via the *Herald*. You said you wanted me back. You said you were sorry. You said Aida was a mistake. You said you'd slept with her after the market massacre – which I'd guessed anyway by then… I hadn't been there… But it was just once, you said, until I went away. And you'd been so sad, so fed up, you hadn't meant to, but you'd been working with her… and the last month… You'd been trying to end it, you said, the day I found out. Please, please, you said, give me another chance.

But I wasn't there to give you another chance. I was in London, in my shiny new job, which was exactly what I'd wanted two years ago: London-based fireman, writing across the paper. I got the pension plan and the health insurance, maternity leave, but I didn't think much of maternity leave since, frankly, the thought of touching anyone else after you just made me feel sick.

I did all the things I was supposed to do. Saw my old friends, but none of them understood about you; their lives seemed so alien, it was like watching them on TV.

I didn't write back. But I couldn't stop thinking about you. I hid Henri's photograph but that didn't help. You went everywhere in my head. Whenever Sarajevo was on TV, or in the papers (and although it was quiet, it was still there a lot), I could see you. I read the wires obsessively at work. I missed you so much it actually hurt. You forget, when you're not in love, that it actually hurts. I found myself praying some disaster would happen to Sarajevo so they'd have to send me back. I could give you another chance. Maybe we should get married. I had a flat. I'd just bought one – I'd saved enough for the deposit in those years in Bosnia. It was lovely not to live in a hotel, except for the washing-up. You could always retile *my* bathroom if the worst came to the worst. Every time I thought about doing up the bathroom, I started to cry. Sometimes I even cried reading the wires, but that was at work, so it wasn't wise.

Then your second letter came. Aida was pregnant. You were getting married. I howled like a dog but there was nothing I could do. It was all too late, too far away.

I told Phil. He said all those things that people have to say like: "I'm sorry. It's not your fault. It would never have worked anyway." He also said, these things, they are very difficult to take back home. That at least I felt that he meant. We'd gone out for a drink, it seemed better like that. At least it avoided pissing Lena off. Phil told me he wasn't going to go back to Sarajevo for a while.

I went back to Bosnia a couple of times, that summer, but only for a few days here and there and I didn't see you. Roger hardly let me go to Sarajevo at all: he was so paranoid that I would blow his budget by getting stuck.

There were stories on the home desk I had to write. The trouble was I didn't know anything about home. I think the *Herald* found me very disappointing. I didn't behave like a proper young person – I didn't mind about Blur and Oasis. That's what newspapers employ young people for: they've got fat, middle-aged men with ex-wives to feed to keep abreast of international affairs. But then how many proper young people chose to go and live in a war? It's hard to listen to music when there's no electricity. And we had songs, like teenagers in love, when you imagine the lyrics have some special meaning for you: Dire Straits – whose *Brothers in Arms* I later discovered had become a kind of Sarajevo anthem, although at the time, I thought it was only me. No other young people liked Dire Straits back then.

It was November before I next went to Sarajevo; it was a magazine story – about people coming back. Roger made me promise I'd be in and out in a week. I flew in on a cold crisp day, watching the mountains gathering themselves up far below. There was a dusting of snow on the peaks, denser and denser the closer we got; the real snow hadn't fallen yet, but it was due any day. As the plane rattled and lurched, I twisted my hands deeper into the webbing and the chain-smoking Russian who seemed to be in charge gave the Land Rovers a good kick to check the lashings were safe. The ridges of Mount Bjelasnica sparkled as we sank through the sky, curving over the town, and the sun shone down onto the roofless houses below.

I hitched a lift from the airport with an Italian aid worker who nearly killed me on the way – I wasn't sure whether he drove like that because he was Italian, or whether two and a half years of Sarajevo had given him an abnormally high risk threshold. Or maybe my months in London had made me normal again.

He dropped me off at the Holiday Inn's front door: yes, the front door, looking out onto Sniper Alley, with the fountain chipped by sniper fire, and the fantastic view of the hills. The doors slid open and a uniformed page came out to get my bags. I felt sick as I walked through the sliding glass; the place was still surrounded by guns. It all seemed rather mad, as though the town was completely in denial. Like someone standing in no-man's-land with their hands over their ears going 'LA! LA! LA! Can't hear you!' I later found out the general called it 'hearts and minds'. At least the fountain still didn't work.

The hotel might have its front door working, but inside it had the abandoned air of a resort out of season. There were no groups of hollow-eyed drivers hanging round the bar, touting their work for anyone who'd pay them 150DM a day to risk their cars and their lives. There were no fleece-clad packs of hacks loitering by the desk, or endlessly bashing out the story over tiny cups of coffee on the white plastic mushrooms. I knew that a lot of journalists were staying elsewhere these days, either in flats in town, or in a little *pension* that had opened up the hill, now that the phone lines were connected again; not that there were many hacks around anyway then. The Holiday Inn had doubled its room rate to celebrate peace. If I stayed long, I might move out to the *pension* myself – but to begin with, I thought it would be easier to orientate myself from here. Despite what Phil had said about leaving, the BBC still had its office here. I did hope there would be somebody nice in room 309 but there had been nothing on the news so I didn't know who. In the autumn there had been someone I didn't know. He kept asking me what I wanted when I walked in; Valida had been away. I could hardly say, "I want to feel at home!"

I started lugging my stuff over to the stairs, but the receptionist – who looked unthrilled to have me back – said indignantly: "We have a lift." I still didn't trust lifts in war zones. I put the luggage in and walked up the stairs myself.

My room was an orange one, on the ammunition factory side. Its windows were still glazed only with UNHCR plastic but the heating worked and there was hot water in the taps. I walked along the gallery towards the BBC.

The door was ajar, so I knocked softly but there was no reply. I pushed it open. No Valida to be seen. Peeping over the arm of the sofa was the top of a head, lolling to one side; a pair of jeans-covered legs, ending in Timberland boots, propped up on the far end. On the floor, next to a trailing arm, a book, bent open at the spine: *The Name of the Rose*. Whoever was reading it was a third of the way through.

There was far too much hair for Tim, and it was the wrong colour, and the legs were too thin. It really didn't look like the grumpy man from the autumn. So I said: "Phil?"

The head snapped up, and I said: "Phil?" again, just as he said: "*Molly!*"

I said: "Hi honey, I'm home."

RADOVAN KARADZIC, President of Republika Srpska, is fishing and he catches a golden fish. The fish says, I'm a magic fish, and if you set me free, I will grant you a wish. So Radovan explains – the Contact Group is trying to work out peace in Bosnia; everyone is tired of the war, but no-one seems to be able to come up with a map that all three sides can agree on.

"Bring me the map," says the fish. So Karadzic brings the map down to the river. The fish takes a good long look at it, but in the end, he says, "I'm sorry, I know I am a magic fish, but really, this is beyond me. Haven't you got anything easier?"

Karadzic sighs, then he says, "I have a daughter, Sonja. I'd like you to make her beautiful."

"That's easy," said the fish. "We do that the whole time."

So Karadzic goes up to the house, and brings Sonja down to the river. The fish takes one look at her and says, "Hang on, can I have that map back?"

XVI

I had steeled myself to see you at the briefing. All the way down Sniper Alley I had that stone in my stomach that you get when you think you're going to see someone you love. Phil said, "Are you all right? You're very quiet," but I just said, "Oh, everything's changed so much," without looking at him; I didn't want to stop the cinema running in my head. The women going shopping, the students hanging out, the trams and the cars slipped by, but I was already there, in the room in the PTT, with the sandbags on the windows, and the tanks parked outside, and the big blue UN flag behind the desk, and the maps on the wall covered in plastic sheets, so the UN could wipe out the frontlines they'd drawn in marker pen, and put them back in again, whenever a new village fell; seeing you standing on the other side of those schoolroom chairs.

My stomach was slipping as I walked into the room; it was a small crowd, maybe thirty or so, and some of them were strangers to me. I didn't know what I'd say to you, so I thought I'd wait for you to come up to me. But you didn't. So then I started looking round for you. But I couldn't see you anywhere. Edin was there, he nodded hello, and a couple of other people said, long time no see. Robert was there, talking to someone who looked like an SAS type – because he didn't have any badges on, and anyway, he was exactly the same shape as Hal. I rushed over and kissed Robert: "Robert! Phil reminded me… I'd completely forgotten!" Because of course he was the new UN press spokesman. He laughed and looked a little sheepish and said: "Do you know Andy?" Or maybe he said Chris. Chris shook my hand in a slightly paranoid way.

I was teasing Robert that he'd gone over to the enemy, when Ingrid barged in and said, "More to the point, what are *you* doing here? I thought you'd given up on the place," and then started talking to Chris and Robert about something they'd all done together the week before.

I didn't mention you then. I was too embarrassed, but the next day, when you weren't there again, I said to Edin: "Do you know how Amir is?"

He looked a little uncomfortable, as he replied, "He's fine I think. He doesn't work with me any more."

"What does he do?" I had a vision of you, poor, back in the flat with your mother.

But Edin said, "He's working for one humanitarian aid agency."

"Oh…" So not poor then, and not at the briefing. "Which one?" I asked.

"I don't know, they all sound the same."

"Oh… how's the baby…?" I asked.

Edin shrugged. "The baby's not born yet."

"I should have told you he'd moved jobs," said Phil afterwards. "I didn't think."

But then people never do think about other people's loves. They listen for half an hour or an hour or so; then they like updates, for the soap opera, but when it's just a case of being stuck in front of the same miserable test card for months on end, they just can't get it. They all say things like, "Plenty more fish in the sea", and "You must be over it now". As though they were Mr Spock, saying "But that's illogical, Captain." When of course, love is illogical, isn't it? I mean, that's the point. Why is it that one person, just a look in their eye or the sound of their voice, can make your knees tremble and your heart leap, and the blood quicken in your groin, and the very sound of their name is enough to make you swallow, and you can spend hours staring out of a window smiling at castles in the air, and another, equally handsome or funny, is about as erotic as a Victorian chest of drawers.

I used to make up conversations with you in my head: when you asked me to marry you, I said yes. Back as far as the winter, back before the day that I wasn't there. Sometimes I even re-wrote that day – had myself in town, with you, near the marketplace, so when you needed someone to be with to prove you were alive, it was me, not Aida. It seemed so random that that particular shell had fallen when I was away, when I had been here for so many, with you. But then I suppose it was so random that I met you in the first place. But you always said, it wasn't random, it was fate. *Inshallah.*

I didn't see you until the night before I was due to leave. At that party, in one of the rooms the ground floor of the Holiday Inn. It was a horrible room to have a party in, but at least it meant I could leave whenever I liked, even though I knew I'd probably stay to be tipped out with the ashtrays at the end. I always did.

The downside is I didn't get my Sarajevo night drive in an armoured car, minarets in the moonlight, crags against the stars, the broken silhouettes of roof beams against the sky. But then, the stars weren't as good then anyway, not now there was electricity all over town.

I was smoking, propped up against the table, drinking my wine out of its plastic cup; knackered after all the fragile hopes of the returnees I'd been interviewing for the last week; scanning the room through the thick haze of smoke.

Everyone was there. The whole international world. If I don't see you at something like this, maybe I'll never see you again, I thought. I haven't seen you yet. Roger still wants me to leave tomorrow. This will be my third trip back without seeing you. Will you bring Aida? Or is she too pregnant to move?

I didn't know exactly whose party it was – another spoonful of alphabet soup. I for international and R for relief and then some other initials that stood for no-one quite knew what, and were probably there just to differentiate them from from other IR agencies. There were about 200 of us; the cream of the world of crisis relief. French doctors from MSF chatting up English nurses from the ICRC; Danish paediatricians from the WHO deep in conversation with Australians for whom the UNHCR was better than a two-year travel visa. Men in the UN with MAs from Harvard in international law and uncles who are kings of countries you've nearly never heard of were talking realpolitik with Swedish agronomists with the WFP. A few ECMMs shining through the semi-darkness in their white shirts and trousers, wide-eyed like rabbits at this amount of semi-civilisation, were talking about what they were going to do with their pay. In a corner, the French general's bodyguards, those two Foreign Legionnaires I'd met in Jez, were being chatted up by Ingrid; she was welcome to them.

"Do you think she's ordering supplies?" I asked Andy or Chris.

He laughed and checked the bottle in his hand. "Well, they didn't supply tonight. This one's Italian."

There were firemen, real ones, not paper ones like me; Brits, who had been here throughout the war to help out the Sarajevo fire service. There were hydroelectric engineers who specialised in rebuilding shelled pumping stations, and electrical engineers and telecommunication engineers who were trying to get Sarajevo linked up to the world again. In one corner a Canadian UNMO was being grilled by the man from Reuters, and in another, Phil was trying to get anything other than a sneer out of the latest military press spokesman, a man called Chandler, who hinted at a past more deadly than press information and seemed to regard the Sarajevo press corps as his last combat assignment. He specialised in pooh-poohing any possible deterioration in the wobbly peace the UN had propped up over this war; Phil said he told the most splendid lies.

A Ghanaian UNMO (you see, I did know all their fatigues) was nuzzling the neck of what could only be his interpreter, and her back arched in response, as they shuffled round the dance floor amongst the other couples to *Brothers in Arms*. Then the music changed to something less smoochy but still appropriate – I think it was 'Don't you forget about me' – and suddenly Robert was dancing, surprisingly well, with Valida. I hadn't seen her yet. Phil told me she'd gone to work for the UN. I should have known I'd have seen her tonight.

Andy or Chris and I had been having an easy conversation, the kind that was automatic for me, a sort of flirty slightly confrontational conversation, designed to make him like me and trust me and want to impress. It set me off down some neat little professional railway lines; and it stopped me scouring the room for you. Besides, Chris or Andy was a nice person to have a flirty confrontational conversation with, being good-looking, slightly paranoid, very pleased with himself and obviously starved of female company.

He asked me to dance, and I said no, and then he asked me if I had a boyfriend, and I said, "Not any more…" He'd just said something like: "So tell me, what's a nice girl like you doing in a war like this?" when I felt you. I think you touched me, but I knew it was you even before I turned. I felt you. I felt you from a foot away.

You said: "Molly…" And my heart and my knees and the pit of my stomach did all those things that Mr Spock would think so illogical.

You stood at my shoulder, too close, as you always had. You looked nervous: "*Molly… Hello, how are you?*"

"*Fine. How are you?*"

"Fine. I'm fine. You look amazing." Our mouths were saying any old rubbish to justify our eyes staring. The way you do when you can't say what you want to say without driving off the cliff.

"So do you." You looked different to the Amir I had been carrying around in my head. Less fragile. You looked well; normal. A normal person in a normal town. The Sarajevo pallor had gone from your skin. The bags were still seared beneath your deep dark eyes, but they were less livid, like a wound that had healed. I stared up at you and neither of us spoke.

Then I said: *"I guess it's not being in Sarajevo."* At the same time as you said: *"So how long are you here for?"*

"Tomorrow," I said. At the same time as you said: *"Me too…I've just been out."*

"Out! Oh Amir…" I felt the tears starting to rise. *"Where to?"*

"I went to Italy. For a holiday."

"Oh Amir…" It was a physical effort not to take your hand. *"A holiday…"*

"First time," you said. *"First time in two and a half years."* Your eyes were filling with tears as well. *"Look…"* you pulled your wallet out of your pocket. *"I have a blue card now. I can go on the planes."*

I read aloud in English: Amir Hadzibegovic. Assistant Project Manager IFCR. "This is our party," you said, and made a wry, welcoming face.

"I could never have got you one of those," I said.

"I know."

"If I could have done, I would have done."

You said nothing.

"It's better than mine. You'll be able to bump me off flights."

"I wouldn't do that," he said. We looked at each other, both of us nearly crying, and neither of us spoke for far too long.

I swallowed: *"How's Aida?"* I looked round the room.

He pulled back. *"She's fine,"* he said.

"And the baby?"

"The baby's due any day."

"I thought she would have had it by now," I said. *"I brought it a present."* It was a fluffy sheep. *"I'll leave it with Valida…oh no. Well… Phil…"* Another silence.

"How long are you here for this time?"

"Tomorrow," I said again.

"Tomorrow! But… I… we have to…" He didn't finish the sentence. He just stared at me. I didn't speak either; just stared back, the pair of us, slipping backwards like Doctor Who through the kaleidoscope of this fucking awful party. Then he put out his hand and took hold of mine. "Molly…"

It was just all too much. I pulled back, turned and bumped straight into Chris or Andy or whatever he was called.

"Oh!"

"You OK?"

"I've changed my mind. I would like to dance now after all."

Amir grabbed at my hand again: "No," I said.

"I have to talk to you…There's something I have to say… Please… It's been a terrible mistake… Are you staying here?… I'll ring you tomorrow."

"There is no tomorrow," I said. *"I'm leaving."*

"No!"

I turned to Chris or Andy and said: "Let's go." I put a hand out somewhere in the direction of Chris, who managed to put himself between Amir and me, and shepherd me away. He was very nice, didn't mention anything; I was shaking and feeling slightly sick. I hadn't even noticed the music, but it was slow, which made it all rather odd, as I was dancing with all the erotic languor of a barbed wire fence. And I couldn't stop the fact that I was starting to cry. I trod on his foot and said, sorry Chris, and he said, actually I'm called Andy. I said, I'm sorry. Let's stop. Can we stop? And he took me to the other side of the room, got me another drink. I said something like, sorry about that, and wiped my eyes with my hand. Here, have this he said, and lent me a handkerchief. Then he said, was that the boyfriend? And I said yes, the ex-boyfriend. And he said, well, it's none of my business, but it sounds pretty finally ex to me, if he's having a baby with someone else. I thought, of course, it's final, why the fuck do you think I'm feeling like this. But what I said was: "I'm sorry, I didn't realise you could understand."

"A bit."

"Oh." Then I said, with a kind of reflex suspicion: "I didn't think they bothered to teach you lot. Most British army officers who speak the language come from a long line of pig farmers from Knin."

"Not me. I'm from the Midlands. I just did a course."

"It must be a very broad course if it covered pregnancy."

He looked at me deadpan and said: "They like to prepare us for every eventuality." I did laugh then, even if it was a rather damp laugh.

I kept seeing you, on the other side of the room. I saw you talking to the Foreign Legionnaires, I saw you talking to Robert, I saw you talking to Phil. And while you were talking, every now and then, I'd see you looking at me.

Chris had gone off to get some more wine, when the lights cut out and the music stopped. A general "Ahh!" went up in the dark, and then a sort of studio audience laugh. I said, "Fuck. Fuck. My torch isn't in my bag." I knew where it was, too, in the drawer of the bedside table. I had been duped by all this peace. I wasn't alone. We'd all gone soft. Around me, I could hear people scrabbling in their pockets, but so far, no light had dawned.

Suddenly I felt you again, like a wave of warmth washing over me: "Molly," you said.

I said, because it was all too sad, please go away.

You said: "I have to say this to you. I may not get this chance again. Not ever. Please, let me say..."

I said: "There's no point. You're married. Your wife's about to have a baby." And in the silence, the points of light began to appear. Then you said in Serbo-Croat, very fast, *"I love you. I want to be with you, I love you. It's not too late."*

I said: "*But, Aida, you're having a* baby."

"*Oh God,*" you put your hand on my neck, your fingers under my chin. "*I have tried. I tried to do the right thing. I did try. But it won't work. I think she hates me. Is it right, if all of us are so unhappy? How can it be right…?*" and then you kissed me again; and for a moment I resisted, then my back arched up against you, like the Ghanaian's interpreter, and I felt myself slipping, back in time.

I think it was a relief to hear Phil's voice: "Molly? Where are you? Something's happened…"

I broke away.

"*I don't know,*" I said. "*I can't decide now.*"

"*What shall I do?*"

"*I don't know…*"

"Molly! Are you still there?" Andy's torch was dancing towards me across the room.

"*Are you staying here? Can I see you tomorrow?*"

"*I'm going home tomorrow…*"

"*I've got a blue card. I could leave too…*"

"No!"

"Molly, can you hear me? Where are you? We're going up to 309."

"*I'll ring you tomorrow,*" you said. "*Don't go till the afternoon… please…let me see you tomorrow…*"

I said: "I don't know… you're *married* now…" and I pushed you away.

Mujo and Suljo are sitting in their trench, on the frontline that runs through the old playground. Suddenly, Mujo jumps out of the trench and sits on the swing. "What are you doing?" yells Suljo.

"I'm trying to freak out the Chetnik snipers."

XVII

We passed the corpse the next day on the way to the briefing. Sniper Alley had gone quiet; back to the great grey emptiness of before. The trams, the drift of people plodding into town, had all vanished overnight.

We'd heard about the sniping from the UN that morning. Phil had already filed his piece.

"I guess the news has got round," he said, about the emptiness. "Robert said it happened just down here."

Phil was driving fast; not as fast as he used to drive, and he hadn't reverted to driving on the wrong side of the road, but he still didn't stop at the traffic light on the way out of the hotel. As we came up to the Bridge of Brotherhood and Unity, we saw a UN APC parked in the slip road, both as a threat, I suppose, and to mask the snipers' view. Then, just beyond it, so tidy it looked almost parked, we could see the bonnet of a car, slewed, rather neatly, up against a wall.

"Don't slow down. I don't want to get shot because you've slowed down to look."

"Don't worry," said Phil. "We'll be safe with this lot here."

Whoever it was, he certainly had a good turn-out. I suppose because he was the first to die here for so long. A couple of Brits were clustered round the car; some more, ten yards away, were smoking against the side of a Land Rover.

"Apparently they found him, Robert said," said Phil. I shot them a look but I didn't recognise them. Maybe they were the Royal Engineers who had Sky Sport. Phil said he used to go and watch their telly.

On the other side of the bridge from the car were some Foreign Legionnaires, loitering by one of their tiny white tanks.

"This is their patch. Oh look. Isn't that whatever his name is, the French general's bodyguard?" said Phil. "Ingrid was chatting him up at the party last night. Do you think Nissent's going to be at the briefing? Robert said they were all fucking furious. What's that policeman doing?" They had tape measures out and were taking little notes.

"Making a point," I said. "Amir says the Bosnian Police treat every sniping as a murder."

"Really! I didn't know that…Oh God, they're taking him out."

They were Swedish, I think, the guys with the armoured ambulance. One stood at his head, and another was buried deep inside the passenger door.

"What are they doing?" said Phil. "Christ… His legs are all floppy."

"They must have been breaking the rigor in his knees."

"Yuk."

"Sorry." Apart from the hinge at the knees, the body was stiff with an almost functional rigidity.

"Do you think rigor mortis is nature's way of making corpses easy to carry?" I said into our silence.

"Oh god, Molly…" Phil laughed. "You're sick."

"Come on," I said. "We're going to be late."

Poor man. The awful thing was I wasn't thinking about him. I was thinking about you. About what I should do. Ever since you told me Aida was pregnant, I had just schooled myself to think that there was no hope. And now I didn't know. Maybe, if you were both so unhappy, maybe it wouldn't be so wrong. Maybe I could stay – I couldn't leave now anyway. The lights going out at the party last night, the man who'd been shot on Sniper Alley, they were all part of the same thing. The airport had shut. Half-time was over and the ball was back on the pitch. Roger was going to be furious.

I was surprised not to see you at the briefing; I thought you'd know you could get me here. Maybe you'd realised that all the stuff you said last night was just rubbish, that it couldn't possibly work. But, oh my God, I hoped that it was true. At least I could concentrate on what Robert and Chandler were saying, although frankly we already had learnt most of it last night. Phil had bumped into me in the dark. "Come upstairs. It's Bihac," he said, referring to yet another of those Muslim enclaves surrounded by Serbs; this one was the tip of the arrowhead, pointing into Croatia. "The Bos are trying to break out. They've taken about five miles of land. Robert's coming back when he's taken Valida home."

He turned to Andy and said: "Come up for a drink if you like."

Andy said nothing, just gave off suspicious vibes, then I said: "Bihac. God, I haven't been there for ages."

"You've *been* to Bihac?" both he and Phil said together.

"I thought everyone had been to Bihac," I said.

"The Serbs aren't even letting *us* through now," said Andy.

It was good, because it made me stop thinking about you. We had one of those whisky and candlelight evenings with everyone jabbing fingers at the maps on the wall. The office sounded like a Turkish courtyard, since Phil was filling up both his baths. "I just don't trust this place when the power's out," he said. I agreed: I'd stopped by my room to run mine on the way.

"This map's really out of date," said Andy, who was having a good snoop round.

"It's been up since the war began," said Phil. "Feel free to draw what you like."

"Oh God," said Robert. "I helped you stick the bloody thing up. In 1992..."

"So what's Bihac like?" said Andy.

"Oh, it's Bosnia. It's beautiful and sad. And weird, and cut off, and kind of medieval Shangri-La. Full of refugees, like all the Muslim enclaves. Most of the people fled there in the first summer of the war. All the soldiers are dressed in homemade camouflage…"

"What, vegetable dye?"

Nod: "They look like Robin Hood's merry men…" I could see the mountains, the forests and the ravine, hear the tink tink tink of tiny hammers on metal, and the waters of the Una rushing below the road; feel, with a prickle of fear between my shoulder blades, the long winding gorge between the frontlines. "Are you thinking of going there?"

There was an embarrassed silence.

"Well, don't stay in the Hotel Kladusa. It's the worst hotel in Bosnia."

"Oh."

"And if you do go, you should always order trout."

It was Robert who pointed frontlines and buildings out to him on the map; he'd been there before there ever was a war.

The briefing was thick with the smell of war. But this time, it wasn't pee, it was adrenalin. The room was packed; any UN type who had the slightest excuse was there. Bosnian Army loses was normal. Bosnian Army taking territory, now that was news; and good news to boot, because pretty much everyone there was sympathetic to the Muslims by now – it stands to reason, if one side's shelling you and the other one isn't, which one would you prefer. Even Robert found it hard to hide his pleasure. When Chandler wiped the old frontlines off the map and reworked a finger in blue marker pen pointing the way for Bihac's Refugee Vth Corps to go home, a murmur ran round the room which was nearly a cheer. Even though, as Andy said, we all knew they hadn't a snowball's hope in hell of keeping any of it, the moment Mladic could get his tanks round there, it was nice to think of the Serbs having a bit of a bloody nose. I couldn't understand why you weren't here.

You didn't get in touch with me at all that day. You didn't even try me at the BBC. If you'd really wanted to get in touch with me, that's what you'd have done. Maybe you'd left a message at Reception – the landlines worked now but I didn't trust Reception to pass anything on. Perhaps you thought I wasn't calling you back. You must have known I couldn't have left. But things had gone back to normal, so we were run off our feet: Roger freaking that I had got stuck; me desperately thinking of the best way to do the story for us; ham radio links, possible air strikes, arms smuggling and the secret American training camps instructing the Bosnian Army that I'd heard about from a bored Marine in a bar in Split the week before; listening to Phil file, listening to him explain, as I had to Roger, that although he would obviously *try* to get to Bihac, the chances were about a million to one, since at that point he couldn't even leave Sarajevo.

"It's like talking to a child," I said. "He wanted me to move out of here to somewhere cheaper. I said I didn't think that was a good idea if there was no power and people were being shot in town again. All he said was: "People are always being shot"."

"They haven't been for ages."

"That's what I told him."

I did ring Andy and ask for a lift to Bihac, but all I got was a message back which said: "Nice try." So maybe Reception was taking messages after all.

You still hadn't rung that night, but we had to work anyway. Phil and I took out John, Muffy's old chum from the CIA, and got him drunk. We wanted to get him to spill the beans. At least, I wanted to talk to him about secret American training camps, but he and Phil ended up talking about Muffy; on the subject of Muffy, he was fascinating, but he never said anything about American subversive operations that Phil and I couldn't have speculated to each other. Still, but at least we could quote him as a US Intelligence source. His attitude however, now that was illuminating – he was as thrilled as the Bosnians, as we were, that Bihac's Fifth Corps were doing well.

You still hadn't rung by the time we got back. Over a final glass of whisky in the BBC, I told Phil what you'd tried to say to me yesterday. Phil didn't say anything for a while. He just lit another cigarette. Then he said: "Lots of men get like that just before a baby is born. They panic and they think their wives are neglecting them. It was a party. He was probably drunk."

But actually, you didn't really drink. You were always getting angry with me for getting drunk.

"But even if it's not that, isn't it a bit late…"

"But what if they're both *miserable*? What if they *both* want out?"

"Wouldn't you be better off with some nice boy back home?"

"But I don't seem to fall in love with nice boys back home."

"I'd give it another day," said Phil.

It was the easiest thing to do, besides, what with the war, we were run off our feet.

It was after lunch the next day that I decided to go to the mortuary; a couple more people had been killed overnight. Phil said that he would give me a lift.

"I'll walk," I said; we were at the Pizzeria. It wasn't far.

"But you haven't got your flak jacket."

"Neither have you…"

We looked at each other, then at a woman scurrying down the street.

"It just seemed so rude to put it on," I said.

At the mortuary door, Phil said: "I might as well come in." I was slightly irritated because, although I loved Phil, I thought, if we're like a three-legged race, how the hell am I going to get something different this week? I can't just run the same stuff as the Beeb.

The familiar sweet scent snagged at my throat. Osman, the tallyman, keeper of the dead, normally smiled at me, but this time he just stared. But Osman could be a bit strange; as anyone would be if they spent their life surrounded by stiffs. Besides, I had forgotten he hadn't seen me for months. And anyway, he normally saw me with you.

"*Dober dan Osman,*" I said, in the tone I used for him, which was one of subdued respect, as he was the guardian of the dead. Then I saw Valida, but for a second, that seemed normal too: I was quite used to seeing her at the mortuary with Phil. Then I realised that she was red-eyed, in black. On the sofa sat Valida's mother, her arm round someone else, weeping, fat sobs, into her cupped hands.

I turned to Valida: "I'm so sorry… I didn't know…" But Valida just stared back at me in horror. Then the other woman raised her head, saw me, and sobbed again. For a moment, I did not recognise Maria.

When I did, there was absolutely nothing I could do. I put my hand up, as if to hit it away. I remember feeling sick, and the room started to shake. Somewhere I heard Valida say: "I can't believe you didn't know."

THE LAST Mujo and Suljo joke from the war:
Mujo and Suljo were walking in the wood, when they met Arkan…

XVIII

They buried you that day, at dusk, in the Martyrs' Cemetery, so the snipers couldn't see. Phil drove. As we walked up the hill from where we left the car, a strange ululation drifted up to the frontlines and Phil flicked a switch on his tape recorder. He'd asked me, of course, but I'd said I didn't mind. I hoped you wouldn't have. I don't know. But people in Sarajevo were so used to journalists now.

It was dark, apart from the TV lights, but Phil and I knew that cemetery well by now: the cobbled path, the trickle of water, the fresh-turned earth, the rows of wooden headstones, with names and dates scrawled on in pen.

We weren't the only hacks there. You were news; the first person to die in Sarajevo for months. CNN, ABC, Reuters and AP. Obviously, the Bosnian channels; CTV of course, although I couldn't see Edin, perhaps he couldn't bear to cover your funeral as a story. I was dreading seeing Aida, but of course she wasn't there. I'd forgotten that at Muslim funerals, the women don't come. But Maria was standing on the edge of the graveyard, to see her son buried in his alien faith; and your father, whom I had not seen for six months. He looked older now by far. He stood at one end of a row of men, their white caps gleaming in the moonlight, and the TV lights. One by one, as your body was borne by, they each wiped their cupped hands down their faces, like a chorus line wiping away its tears. Then your body, white shroud almost luminous in the moonlight, was laid into the trench dug in the mud.

I carried on covering your war after you died. Quite apart

from anything else, I was trapped in Sarajevo with you dead for five weeks, so I didn't really have much choice. I wrote about you, for my first story, and after that, it didn't make any sense to stop. I wanted to carry on anyway. I wanted to be there to the end. I wanted to write the day your death would be avenged.

I had to, didn't I? I mean, it was my fault. If I'd listened to you that night at the Holiday Inn, you wouldn't have driven down that road. You wouldn't have left the hotel. You would have been safe upstairs with me in my bed, stroking me, kissing me, fucking me, not driving back to Aida along that road, not lying dead for hours in the night until your lonely little body was wrenched out by a Swedish doctor in camouflage fatigues. Even if I'd just let you talk for a moment longer, maybe someone else would have been driving along that road first; maybe the sniper would have taken aim at another car, then picked up his slivovic, or gone for a piss, or shouldered his rifle, walked down the stairs, or just curled up to rest for a while in the derelict apartment he used as his nest. But I didn't. I let you go. And you died.

But I saw the war through. That next summer, that August, was a joy to cover; at least it was a joy after the terrible sadness of the fall of Srebrenica in June, when the Dutch UN troops surrendered their guns to the Serbs and watched as the Serbs then herded off to their deaths over 7,000 Muslim men. To watch the Serbs finally face defeat; to lose in a few months most of their stupid Greater Serbia they had spent so long stealing off those that they had killed, the Muslims and the Croats finally fighting together, to drive the Serbs out in their turn. And when, at long last, the UN decided to bomb the Serb positions around Sarajevo, we sat up, Tim, Muffy and I, with our glasses of Posip that Tim had brought up from the coast, waiting in the house the BBC had moved into away from the hotel. It was a secret, of course, but Robert had tipped us off that something of some sort was going to happen that night. As the great crumps began, in the depth of the night, wave after wave, we toasted the bombs. And at every house in the street, little candles suddenly flickered at the windows, and the man in the house opposite danced a jig, and suddenly we heard the sound of an accordion, and there, in his porch, was a man serenading the planes. Muffy and Tim and I laughed liked drains and poured out more of our wine. I wished so much that you had been here for that. I wished all the time you were there with me. But you are in Sarajevo, in your little grave, on the hill, with the rest of the dead.

That autumn, 1995, after the Dayton conference, where the peace deal for Bosnia was all stitched up, I left Sarajevo one day. I didn't know it was my last day, you never do. It was just the end of that trip, but that was the last trip of the war. And I never went back to Sarajevo again.

FATA IS WALKING down the street in Sarajevo with a monkey. Mujo comes back from the war: "What are you doing with that?"

Fata: "After UNPROFOR left what could I do?"

Mujo: "You could have had an abortion."

June 2000

I went to a wedding last weekend. Lizzie, a girl from Oxford; she was supposed to be a good friend but actually I probably hadn't seen her alone for years. That's the nice thing I suppose about those Oxford weddings. You all get asked in a group. I didn't know the guy she was marrying at all but he looked very nice. A bit pink and balding, but, let's face it, we're none of us ninteen any more. I hope he's nice. Lizzie deserves someone nice.

I bumped into Johnny outside the church. He looked successful and he had a scrawny blonde on his arm.

"Molly! How are you? I haven't seen you for ages."

"Johnny, hi, I'm fine, how are you?"

"Fine. Fine." He did that azure-eyed staring into my soul thing he always did, then he said: "Oh, do you know Natasha?" I said no.

As he introduced us, he put his arm on her shoulder; she half-shrugged it off, half left it there, and smiled at me. Just like I smiled back. She was as tall as Johnny, and very pretty, if slightly haggard, in that thin posh way. She was wearing one of those flowery-feathery things in her hair that can look a bit like a TV aerial, and the dress was floaty and bias cut, with little spaghetti straps and a triple row of pearls at her throat, with a glittering lump in the middle above the Goya collar bones, and a pashmina draped over one elbow because it was so hot. But then, so was I. In a blank background way I registered that she had one of those surnames you saw a lot in magazines; in my magazine in fact. But actually, Johnny was becoming the sort of person you saw in magazines; six bankers with Goldman Sachs Appeal – or some kind of crap. If you're in one of those pieces, as long as you don't go bankrupt or get sacked, you'll probably feature in them all because, let's face it, that's what newspaper cuttings libraries are about.

He offered me a lift to the reception – I could see him thinking: look at her, on her own again.

"If that's OK, Tash?"

She said: "Fine," in a kind of "why are you bothering to ask me anyway" way.

Johnny's car – sporty and new – was just the right side of vulgarity. Johnny could never have driven a Porsche as a joke. The atmosphere was slightly sticky, until Johnny said: "Have you been back to Sarajevo at all?"

He turned to Tash, who was staring out of the window, and said: "Molly used to be a war correspondent."

I thought about the words: "used to be"; and "war correspondent" which I would never ever have used about myself. I never knew anyone who wasn't a wanker or a fantasist who used it about themselves. But Tash said: "Really?" in tones of genuine interest.

I said: "Yes." Because, I suppose, it was true. "But it was ages ago. I don't do that kind of thing now."

"What do you do now?"

"That's a pile of crap," she said, when I told her I was the features editor on my glossy magazine.

"I know. But at least I get to stay in one place. What about you?"

There was a silence, before she said: "Not really anything at the moment. I spend most of my time getting divorced..."

The house was the standard Old Vicarage, surrounded by gravel and lawn: its honey façade wore an air of being surprised, after two centuries of impoverished clergymen, by the money Lizzie's city-commuting father could afford to spend on gutters and Colefax and Fowler pelmets and, today, on tribal rituals. Suddenly I couldn't think of anything to say; not just to Johnny and Tash, but to anyone, so I wandered out of the back of the house and through the tent, where a man with a tray gave me a glass of champagne. I looked around, at all these people, who were supposed to be my friends. There was a wiggly line building up in one corner of the tent, and behind the backs of hats and the pastel knee-length coats, I could see a black coat, a sweep of cream satin, a spray of flowers, and the occasional flash of jewels in the sun. But I didn't really feel like doing that queue now.

The garden was as English as the view from The Park, but I left The Park nearly a year ago now and Irene says I'm really much better. A lawn vanished into rhododendrons, behind them a high wall. Two bridesmaids were pushing a little boy on the swing. I wasn't sure if I should intervene or not, because he sounded very unhappy. But they weren't mine, and I've noticed with children that if you don't know them, you can just make it worse. Just as I was about to do something anyway, I heard a voice say: "For Christ's sake, Chloe, I've told you. Leave him ALONE!" A woman with thin calves, a tiny bottom and a large pregnant bump, ran past me on the lawn, a pair of shoes in one hand. I thought, lucky her, I'd love to have a baby. She grabbed the weeping boy: "Come on, Alfie, let's find mummy." One of the bridesmaids looked rather shamefaced, but the other giggled. The woman said to her: "Chloe, are you going to behave?" The giggler nodded but stuck out her tongue at the woman's back. Then she turned thoughtfully on her former ally.

I laughed and heard someone else laugh behind me. There, staring at the children, was Hal. Definitely Hal. Older, a bit balder, but him.

"Hal?" He looked blank, and automatically wary.

"It's Molly. Molly Taylor. From Sarajevo."

"Good God...You look completely different." Not surprising, considering I was in lipstick and a large hat. He smiled; the eyes were just as blue, but he didn't seem quite as pleased with himself.

I said quickly: "So what are you doing now? Or am I not allowed to ask?" He sighed: "Christ, you can ask whatever you like. I'm bored stiff at the moment. I'm at the MOD." He stared at me. "You've got a drink? Let's go and sit down. There's a bench over there."

We sat down, and neither of us spoke. Then Hal said: "This is a bit different, isn't it?"

Suddenly I could smell the wood smoke, the cold earth in the air, the faint, ever-present whiff of pee, see the mountains, looming above the town, the pale spikes of minarets, the blackened mortar scars, hear the machine gun spattering from the Jewish cemetery, the ping of a sniper shooting the fountain outside; the evenings in Jez, eating our 100DM steaks, with Phil and Ed telling tales of wars gone by: Russians in Afghanistan, and Yanks in Vietnam, and Hal and his boss slowly telling stories back, of jungles, and mountains, and dead drug lords.

"Have you been back there?" he said.

I swallowed: "No."

"Neither have I."

I remember him saying, one night in Jez: "This is so weird, we could be in a restaurant in Chelsea, but we're here." And I'd made some crack about restaurants in Chelsea being cheaper than this. I remember telling Phil how nice he was, and Phil saying, "As trained killers go." I'd said, "I've got rather used to trained killers out here."

I heard him say: "You had a boyfriend in Sarajevo, didn't you."

"Yes," I said. "But he died." For a moment, you loomed in, as you often did, but somehow the Englishness of it all sent you away.

"God, I'm sorry. I heard about that… That was awful…"

"Yes. But we'd split up by then."

I heard him say: "I was in Kosovo for a bit. I thought you'd be there."

"Oh! No." I wrenched myself back. Then I said, "I don't do that kind of thing any more."

"What do you do?"

"It sounds ghastly," he said, after I'd told him.

"The awful thing is," I said, "that I'm beginning to think you're right."

It was after dinner that I next saw Hal. I'd been sat next to an old friend from Oxford, an ex-boyfriend of the bride, who I knew could have married her and hadn't and seethed with disappointment; he claimed it was because he wasn't successful enough, but I *knew* it was because he'd been fucking someone else and then, when she forgave him for that, turned down her proposal. On the other side was some cousin of Lizzie's who must have been staying in the house, or very near, as he had his three-year-old son on his knee throughout dinner.

"Sorry," he said. "Good thing it's got a pattern," when his son splattered raspberry coulis on my skirt.

"I'm terribly sorry," I stood up. "I think I'd better go and rinse it off while it's still wet."

So I locked myself into the scented womb of a bathroom and sat down on the loo and thought, what on earth am I doing here with all these people? Does everyone walk through life feeling as if it is happening to someone else? I feel like I've been sent down here in a kind of plastic bubble. I can hear them, I can see them, I can even speak. But I just don't get it. And then I thought, how am I ever going to find anyone I can have a real conversation with again? How on earth am I ever going to fall in love again? Because I have to; I knew that anyway, long before I found my diaries hidden in that box; long before Irene had to iron out my brain. It's not that I'm mourning you for ever. I'm not. I just can't find anyone who makes me feel the same.

When dinner was over, the man on my right fled gratefully to his wife, and Adrian, the man on my left, didn't ask me to dance because he was the kind of man who doesn't like asking women to do anything if he feels they are expecting him to. So we sat there, as the table emptied around us, and the dance floor filled up with couples. I felt a tap on my shoulder and I turned and it was Hal. He looked slightly embarrassed.

"I don't suppose you'd like to dance?"

"Are you deserting me?" said Adrian, in tones of genuine grievance.

It was strange dancing with someone with whom I had always had such a very different kind of relationship. For the first time in ages with Hal, I felt rather shy. But then of course, I hadn't seen Hal for ages, but it didn't feel like that. In Sarajevo, after the beginning, I had never felt shy; after all, then I knew exactly what I wanted from him. Also, he didn't actually dance very well. After a couple of dances – maybe he was feeling shy too – he shepherded me off the dance floor. Then the bitter man at dinner reappeared and asked me to dance. He may be bitter, but my goodness he can dance. So I left Hal and went off with Adrian. After a couple of dances the music got slow again, so we left, and Hal was suddenly standing next to me again.

I introduced him to Adrian, who said: "How do you know Lizzie?"

"I was at school with Fred."

"Oh," said Adrian. "How do you two know each other?"

We looked into each others' eyes and smiled and at the same time said, "Sarajevo."

"Oh."

"We haven't seen each other since," I said. "It must be six years now."

"You look exactly the same," said Hal.

"So do you…"

"What were you doing out there? Are you another hack?" said Adrian, in the slightly superior way that people do sometimes talk to journalists. Adrian, inevitably, worked in the City.

Hal and I flicked our eyes at each other, and I raised my eyebrows and he grinned and shrugged and I smiled: "Nope. He was in the SAS."

Adrian's eyes widened, before he got control of himself and said with great suspicion: "I thought you weren't supposed to talk to journalists."

"It depends on the journalist," said Hal. I just smiled.

"I used to try and get Hal drunk so he would tell me secrets."

"And did he?"

"I never knew any."

"You bloody did."

Then Hal turned to me and said: "Would you like a drink now?"

"Yes, thank you." The next thing I knew I was being shepherded away to the bar.

"So," he said, when he'd got a couple of glasses of champagne and we were at the back of the tent: "What's been happening in your life?"

"Well, nothing. I'm just living in London like everyone else."

"But why? I wouldn't have thought you'd be that kind of girl."

"I don't know. I think I wanted to be like everybody else."

"So, you're not married?"

"...No."

"Why not?"

"I don't know really..." I waited for him to say he was, but he didn't. "So what was Kosovo like?" I asked, with a wave of wistfulness.

We were still talking at midnight, when Lizzie and Fred went away. Lizzie had changed into a pistachio green dress and knee-length coat. Fred still looked as if he couldn't believe his luck. The going away car was a racing green Morgan. I was jumping up and down and waving at Lizzie, but not enough to try and catch her attention as she threw the bouquet, because the last thing in the world I wanted was to catch that. Particularly when you're thirty-five and still single; with a man who's single too and who once fancied you.

"Come on," said Hal. "Let's go back and get another drink."

He put his arm round my shoulder and shepherded me in but the party was over; the waiters were clearing our glasses as we got to our table.

The disappointment came out in my: "Oh!"

"How are you getting back?"

"Oh I don't know. I came by train. I just assumed I'd get a lift back to London. I mean, half the people here…" I looked round but the tent was emptying.

There was a pause, as Hal looked into my eyes, then he took my arm and said: "You could always come back with me. I'm in a pub in the village."

"What!" Because I just wasn't expecting it. I mean, in Sarajevo I was on my guard. But here, I wasn't. Suddenly I was terrified, really terrified, terrified like when you're scared of being shot because somebody's shooting at you, rather than just being in the general vicinity of any area the Foreign Office has advised British nationals to leave. Because I would have loved to have gone to bed with Hal, I think. But the old Sarajevo – NO – reaction stepped in. But I thought, with my rational mind, that doesn't matter any more. You are dead. You have been dead for years. I'm not working like this any more. But it was all just too soon, too scary, and far too fast for me. Although I had technically known Hal for years, I hadn't seen him for the vast majority of that time.

So I laughed, and said: "No."

He took my hand: "Why not? It would be fun."

"Absolutely not." I felt more confident now; he's a nice single man and he's based in London. He can bloody well take me out to dinner a few times. That's what happens to everyone else. Then he kissed me. I kissed him back. Then I broke away, giddy with the fear of it; of this monumental abyss that I stood on the edge of; giddy with the thought that suddenly this might be the first time since you died.

There was a tap on my arm: "Molly!" I turned round. It was Adrian.

"Do you want a lift back to London?" He looked at Hal, who had one arm on my shoulder, and then he said to me: "Or are you otherwise engaged?" I said nothing.

Adrian said: "I thought you two hadn't seen each other for years?"

I could feel myself slipping away. I knew I wasn't brave enough to make that decision in front of an audience. It was hard enough trying to make it on my own.

I turned to Hal: "I think I'd better go."

"If you're sure?" He stared into my eyes. Part of me felt like saying – of course I'm not sure. Stop me. Stop me making this ridiculous choice. But I didn't. I just said: "Yuh."

I felt this huge wave of sadness, at the same time as relief; at least the decision was made, and any decision is better than no decision at all. And, with hindsight, perhaps he was relieved too.

"What's your number?" said Hal. I gave him my mobile. "I'll give you a ring."

"That would be lovely. What's yours?"

"What's your email? I'll email it to you."

Adrian just stood there, like a chaperone, as Hal wrote it down. then said: "Are you sure you wouldn't like me to leave you here?" in a rather unpleasant voice.

I could feel myself blushing, but I said: "I'd better go."

Part Two

THE WAR is over and Mujo goes to a fortune teller. "For the first thirty years," she says, "you will be very poor and your life will be hard."

"What happens after that?" he asks.

"You will get used to it."

SARAJEVO 2000

My mobile phone works. I am sitting in a café in Bascarsija, in Sarajevo's old town, looking up at the hills. I nearly jumped out of my skin when it rang. It was my friend Lucy, ringing from London, to see if I was "all right".

I said I was fine, and when she said, was I sure? I sounded strange, I said: "It's because my mobile works."

"Yeah, they work nearly everywhere now. Mine worked in *Fort William* last week!"

Fuck Fort William. In Fort William every house has a phone. I used to hitch-hike across frontlines to get to a phone. There was no point in me being here if I couldn't get to a phone to file once a week. Nothing would have made that girl in the ECMM's office in Zenica let me use the phone the day of the market massacre. The time at the BBC; it was winter, about the end of '93, because Valida still wasn't yet really my friend. I'd run in to file, with my nightie flapping out of the top of my jeans. Valida sat, like Ava Gardner, reading by the window. "I'm sorry, you cannot use the phone," she said. "The *Herald* have not paid."

"But I have to."

"Try Reuters."

"They're out."

She shrugged.

"But I *have* to file."

Shrug. "Sorry, I cannot." She turned back to her book. I fainted to the floor.

I came round because Valida kicked me, then she knelt at my side: "OK. But promise me you will not tell anyone else I let you," she said.

"Where are you now?" said Lucy. I said I was sitting in a café in the main square.

"Is it pretty?"

Pretty. It's wide open to the hills; they can see every move I make. My stomach clenched as I looked up to the trees and the crags. Yet, lots of other people are sitting here, and they don't seem to be afraid. Maybe this was Sarajevo before the first shell fell.

The old town seems to have turned into one big café; table after table, in the view of the hills, basking in the September sun.

Every time I look up, I feel sick. I'm making myself sit here, but I don't feel happy about it. The streets are full of traffic, normal traffic, in traffic jams. I saw a woman run across the street, and my heart jumped – we're in an exposed place – where the trams stop, just at the top of Bascarsija Square, although of course there were no trams for most of the war. The general started them again in the summer of 1994. The snipers used to fire into them but people used them anyway. At least they didn't have to walk.

I don't blame the snipers for shooting at the trams. Maybe it was easier. But did they care by then? Telescopic sights are like a camera – one step away from the target. I'm not saying being a photographer is as bad as being a sniper. Even I don't think that. Nobody could. Not even the Sarajevans. Although they hated us by the end.

There are no snipers any more. They've all gone back to being pig farmers or running a shop or into the police, or training for the Serbian Olympic rifle team or driving taxis in Shepherd's Bush (there is an entire taxi firm there staffed by Serbs from Nis, an über-Serb stronghold near the Bulgarian border. It was a nightmare during the Kosovo war because you'd end up having to defend NATO intervention or, if you were feeling cowardly, agreeing that Albanians really *were* absolutely impossible).

The woman who was running was simply in a hurry. But just seeing her run, across *that* street, her flying silhouette against the chipped stone, with the mountains in the background, my breath drained shallow and I stepped back, looking for cover, for that split second before my rational mind took over. Then I laughed at myself, but I still stared up at the hills.

They look beautiful today. High and green against the blue sky. Like a postcard, another Heidi day. Little red-roofed houses spilling up under the crags, and then, above, stretching up to the sky-line, where the old frontline used to be, the trees, where the Serbs used to sit and pick us off below. Like a video game. And poking out, everywhere, between the houses, the little minarets pricking the sky. I'm sure there are more minarets now than before. But then, I could never have stood here to count them back then.

Lucy asks me if it's pretty. I look around. The paving stones, the roses, the mosque fretted out of chunks of honeycomb, the long low rows of little Turkish shops, wooden shutters pinned back onto their rough stone walls, windows stuffed with those tall thin chased brass coffee grinders, tiny copper jugs, and fake Louis Vuitton bags, and the soldiers everywhere... I don't know who they are any more; I can't seem to recognise their fatigues... maybe there are countries that weren't here before...

I say, in some surprise, down the phone: "Yes, yes it is."

Being here is like living split screen. Everything brings another memory back. Except that everyone seems to be doing the wrong thing. People are ambling along the streets; table after table of girls in dark glasses, with that dyed maroon hair, and blue-chinned men, sitting, sipping coffee. Some soldiers have just walked past, not patrolling, but strolling, to my surprise, hand in hand, carrying plastic bags from which protrude the end of a carved wooden pipe, the tassel of a fez – souvenirs. From their badges I see they are Turks... hence the hand in hand, of course. In many Muslim countries, even the butchest men do that; presumably because they can't hold the hands of girls without being shot by their brothers or forced down the aisle.

The streets are full of expensive German cars that sit in traffic jams on the once-deserted streets. Is this the town Amir tried to tell me about? My poor Amir. Would he recognise this? Would he be bringing up Nermina here? That's what his baby was called. I never saw her. She was born just after he died.

It doesn't even smell the same. It smells of summer dust, and exhaust, and some kind of tree; the sweet scent of rubbish and cordite has long been blown away.

I don't remember the roses.

Maybe they ate the roses during the war. Sarajevo rose consumption, 1992–1995: a report by the World Food Programme.

I wish I wasn't here on my own. I wish I was here with someone who'd find that funny. Who knows how weird it is that my mobile works.

I must know people here. I lived here for years. But suddenly I can't remember anyone at all.

Hal would get that. At least, I suppose he would. Suddenly I missed him so sharply it actually hurt. I remember him saying to me, "Don't you find it strange when you go back to London and all your friends are talking about curtain material?" At the wedding. Or maybe he said that here years ago.

Hal. Fucking Hal. I still feel like such an idiot. Such a silly little girl. A stupid teenage girl with a silly teenage crush.

After that wedding, I built castles in the air. Adrian kept jabbing at me all the way to London, but I wasn't really listening, I kept thinking about Hal. My perfect solution. I'd been waiting for my happy ending and here it was. He'd always liked me. I mean, he'd made a pass at me the first time we'd met – well, not the first time as that was in the UN base, but the first time we'd been on our own. I'd liked him; except of course in those days I had loved Amir so much more.

Amir would have hated Hal. He hated him then.

But Hal was alive and he was in London. But he didn't like London either. He wanted to go back into the SAS. Maybe we could live in a little cottage in Herefordshire with roses round the door (which we would not be reduced to eating because of a siege, and even if we were, Hal could find me better things to eat) and I could write novels and have babies who'd have beautiful blue eyes. Maybe I could write thrillers and he could help me with the research. He could probably do DIY, even balance budgets. Every now and then he'd vanish for a bit, and then come back with exciting stories of what was really going on.

That's what I was thinking, in my pink fuzz, as Adrian drove me back up the M4. Not that he might come back with one leg, or half his face missing, or with mad staring alienated eyes, or not come back at all. Nor that, if he did come back, it wouldn't be like Sarajevo: I wouldn't be the one he'd shared it with.

Adrian tried to kiss me, when we got to London, which he'd never tried before, in fifteen years, even though we'd always known we fancied each other. He was only doing it because of Hal.

Perhaps that was why he was smiling, when I saw him at a party in Shepherd's Bush the following month. He asked me if I had ever heard from "that guy?"

"Which one?"

"The one I had to pull you off at Lizzie's wedding."

I blushed: "A bit." I had heard from him, even though I hadn't seen him. He kept sending me e-mails asking me to do things, and then not being able to make it because he had to rush off and do something else. I was pushier than I would normally be with a man, I suppose, because I was used to needing Hal for work. I cut him some slack because he did have the kind of life where he might rush off at a moment's notice – I chose to ignore that he'd complained his life was rather dull.

"Did you know Fred is the godfather of his new baby?" said Adrian.

"*What!*"

"Yes. He has a boy and a girl. The wife couldn't leave the baby – that's why she wasn't at the wedding…"

"So he's *married*?"

"I thought he was a close friend of yours."

"He was, in Sarajevo…"

I thought I might be sick. I walked straight past Adrian and into the hall. I ignored two people who tried to talk to me. I picked up my coat and walked out into the street. When I couldn't walk any further, I sat down on a doorstep and wept: with rage and humiliation at my own stupidity; at the shattering of my fantasy world; at the lost solution to my horrible life; because now Hal could never even be my friend. I had been perfectly happy, just to have him as a friend, someone I had known in Sarajevo, back as a friend.

He hadn't technically lied to me. But he definitely hadn't told me the truth. I never asked him if he was married, but I had created opportunities for him to tell me he was. I had trusted him. Then I remembered Phil saying all those years ago: "Did he just say; 'Hey babe, I'm in the SAS, how about it?'" Maybe that was it. Maybe he was like Adrian, used to women throwing themselves at him. Maybe I was just like every other stupid girl. With a stupid crush on some cardboard cut-out. It's not surprising he lied. He's been expensively trained to lie with taxpayers' money, along with garrotting people, not washing for weeks, and carrying lumps of concrete. He probably lies as a reflex action to give himself time to think. He's probably a psychopath. How could he lie to me? I knew him in the war. Maybe he thought, stupid woman, knew me in Sarajevo, seems to have weird crush. Not doing anything else tonight. Why not? A quick fuck. How well did I actually know him? I knew him for six weeks, six years ago.

The next time he emailed me, I didn't reply. He sent a couple more. Then they stopped. But I wanted to reply even though I knew he was married. There was this horrid whisper in my head saying, people get divorced all the time. Castles in the air are much harder to knock down – there's nothing to swing the demolition ball at.

It was a few months later that I bumped into him again. It was a book launch at the RGS. *The United Nations: Better than nothing?* by one of those pundits who get flown out to war zones when it's nice and safe. It was full of other pundits, and the top echelons of soldiers and aid workers. Most of my friends were in Sierra Leone.

I was drinking my glass of white wine thinking, when am I ever going to get to write my own book, is this like weddings, when I saw Hal. He had his back to the wall and was talking to someone who was obviously another soldier; their hair was shorter than anyone else's in the room and the other one was wearing a fleece.

They were quite close. I walked over and said: "Hello Hal." His face froze halfway through his welcoming smile, as he took on board that I wasn't being particularly nice.

"How are you?" I didn't smile and I didn't move to kiss him hello.

"I'm fine," he said, but he was wary now.

"Oh good." Then I said nothing.

"Do you know Ben?" he gestured to the other man.

"No." I nodded but didn't smile.

"So have you seen anything of Lizzie lately?"

"Not really."

"Oh..." Then he said: "Have you read this book?"

"No."

"Are you still at that magazine?"

"Yes."

"Oh." There is a limit to how much you can make small talk with someone who won't talk. "Are you all right?"

I said, very slowly: "How's – your – wife?"

"Oh."

"Yes. Oh." Ben, or whatever he was called, glanced at Hal and left, muttering about somebody on the other side of the room.

Hal didn't say anything.

"Is she here?"

He waited for a moment before he said: "No." I thought he was telling the truth because he didn't look round the room first, but who knows? I used to be good at telling if someone was lying.

"I'm surprised she lets you out."

"I'm sorry."

"Good. I'm glad." He stared at me. I said: "Are you so stupid? Did you think I wouldn't find out?"

He shrugged and looked rather tired.

"You lied to me. I hate being lied to. How could you lie like that to me?"

He looked embarrassed but he said: "I didn't lie."

That lit the fuse. "Well, let's face it, you didn't tell the truth."

"Come on, Molly," he put his hand on my arm but I wrenched it away.

"Don't come on Molly me."

Then he said, in a very reasonable voice, as though trying to talk down an enraged Foreign Legionnaire, "I'm really sorry. I'm sorry I didn't tell you and I'm sorry you're so angry."

"Well of course I'm bloody angry!" My voice was getting all high and wobbly. The next thing I knew I was being shepherded out of the room. We ended up in a dark corridor lined with photographs of men with beards, on mountain tops, or beneath man-eating trees. I knew I was just making a fool of myself, but actually, I didn't really care. I mean, he knew. He'd tricked me into being this sad.

"I nearly… I would never… never. If I'd known you had a wife…"

"What can I say," he looked panic-stricken. "I'm sorry. I'm sorry I didn't tell you I was married. I was drunk. It was late. I shouldn't have done it. But I did."

"You weren't drunk when you kept emailing me. Unless you're an alcoholic."

"Oh God. I'm sorry. I'm really sorry you're so upset. I didn't mean to upset you."

"Well you did."

"Please." He swallowed his panic and held out his hand, and smiled his best smile at me. "Can't you just forget that it happened? Or just take it as a compliment?"

"No! It's not a bloody compliment. It's a fucking lie. I mean, you're *married*. You can't go round giving compliments like that. You've got two *children*!"

"For Christ's sake, just stop it. I'm sorry. I've said I was sorry. These things happen. For God's sake."

"Not to me."

"Well maybe it's about time they did."

"Oh *fuck* off!"

I wanted to hit him, but that wouldn't really work. I balled my fists up, like Vince, that psycho, who'd wanted to punch me, back in Jez all those years ago. Then I had to unball them to wipe away my tears. He looked at me in horror, and then suddenly with pity.

"What is this about?" he said. "This can't just be about me?"

I didn't say anything because I couldn't trust myself to speak. I wiped my eyes, but that didn't work, so I put my hands over my face. When I did speak, all I could say was Amir.

"The guy in Sarajevo?… but that was *years* ago…"

I didn't speak, I just leant against the wall.

"Didn't he marry someone else?"

"That wasn't his fault."

"It must have been partly his fault."

"I should have been there."

Hal didn't know what I was talking about. "He treated you like shit," he said. The panic had left his voice; I was back as a problem which needed to be solved.

"I treated him like shit!"

"Molly, he shagged somebody else. Knocked her up and married her. If that isn't treating you like shit, I don't know what is."

"Well, you'd know, wouldn't you?" He had the grace to look ashamed, momentarily.

"Well maybe you both treated each other like shit, but he's dead. He died a long time ago. He'd been married to that other girl for *months* when he died."

"He didn't love her. He told me that the night he died. He wanted to come back to me. He said they were going to get divorced."

That did stop him. "I'm sorry," he said. "I didn't know."

"Why would you know? No-one knew. I wouldn't let him. I sent him away. He went out onto Sniper Alley and he was shot. And, if I hadn't, he'd still have been alive." Those are facts. It doesn't matter how much anyone tells me it isn't my fault. A sniping is so random, such terrible bad luck. Maybe the sniper… One minute later, even one second, he'd still have been alive.

"They would have got him in the end."

"What! Why? Lots of people survived the war. Look at you, look at me. They never got us."

"But that's different."

"Why?"

"Because he…" Hal stopped.

"Because what? The Serbs didn't kill everyone…"

"But Molly, he wasn't *killed* by the Serbs."

"Oh don't give me that UN shit about Muslim snipers killing their own…"

"He wasn't killed by a sniper…" then he stopped.

"Well how did he die then?" It was easier now I was just furious. "He wasn't killed by a shell! I'd have noticed that! They'd have had to hose him off the road. Well, they didn't. I saw his body!"

"It wasn't like that."

"Well, what was it like?"

Hal stopped, and then said something about not remembering exactly.

"I don't want to tell you the wrong thing," he said. "It was a long time ago. I want to get it right…"

"Tell me what?" I said. "You have to tell me…" I was completely at sea – I couldn't understand any of this. It took another minute or so of prevarication, before Hal said: "I can't remember exactly what happened. I don't think I ever knew. I'm sorry. In a way, I don't think it matters too much. But you must understand they'd have got him in the end."

"What do you mean?"

"Just what I said. Somebody wanted to kill him, and... well, they did."

"What?... You mean he was *murdered*?" I winced myself – it's such a melodramatic word, but war is full of melodrama.

"If you want to put it like that..."

"But who? Who would want to do that? Why?"

Hal shrugged: "A lot of funny things happened in that war."

WHAT IS WORSE than a politician who doesn't believe in what he is saying?

One who does.

II

So here I am. Here to find out how Amir died. I have to find out why. But I have no idea how. Do I go to a police station? Won't they just laugh at me? In London this seemed the right thing to do; the only thing to do; like coming out here all those years ago. Now I'm here, I'm not so sure. All I seem to do is stare at those hills. Maybe the murderer had been caught already and I just didn't know. I have been out of Sarajevo a very long time.

This all looks very well, now, very prosperous; the cafés, people sitting in them. That would be wonderful, if Sarajevo were going to be OK.

I've found one of those hardback blue books, like I used during the war. About an hour ago, in the bookshop on Marshal Tito, where I used to buy them in the phoney peace. The covers are shinier now, the paper slightly thinner. I guess they're being made in a different factory, but the Bosnians are still trying to make them as much like the old ones as possible. I'm writing down everything I feel. Irene told me that would be a good thing to do, but anyway, I think I need to keep some notes.

Poor Hal. The party was over by the time we got back; the girls from the publishers were locking up the cash box and folding the posters of the book covers away. Hal and I wandered silently down the stairs, side by side but not together.

Outside the door of the RGS, we stood rather emptily for a moment, saying goodbye. It was a beautiful evening, and only nine o'clock. I didn't have any particular plan for what to do later and I don't think he did either – at a party like that, you're bound to meet someone. Unfortunately, I don't suppose either of us had thought it would be each other.

"I'd better go," I said.

"Yes. Me too."

"Well, goodbye."

"Goodbye," he said, then: "Which direction are you going?"

I pointed up towards the curly black gates of the park.

"Home," I said. "I live up there." He nodded his head.

"Thank you for telling me about Amir."

"I'm sorry if it was a shock."

"It was a shock. But I think it's better to know."

"Much better. Better for you."

"Yes."

"And I'm sorry about…"

"Yes…"

"I didn't mean…"

"It doesn't matter," I lied.

"I am sorry."

"Well, goodbye," I said. "And good luck."

"Thanks. I'll need it." He gave a rueful smile, the first real smile he'd given since he saw me earlier on.

"Oh. I never asked you. How's work?"

"That's the good news," his face lit up. "I'm off back to Happy Valley."

"Are you? Oh, I am pleased." Back to Hereford, back to the SAS. I smiled back, my first smile at him, but I felt a pang of envy; lucky him being called back to do what you enjoy because somebody thought you did it well. "Well done."

"Thanks. I was going a bit crazy…" he looked slightly embarrassed again. "I can't take this desk job stuff."

There was a silence. Perhaps we were both contemplating my role as symptom of desk-induced madness. Then we'd kissed goodbye, with dry, over-exaggerated movements away from each other's lips, and he'd got onto a huge black motorbike and roared away.

Last night I had dinner with Robert and Valida. They still live here – together; they got married at last. Phil gave me Robert's email address. It wasn't a UN one; I'd heard from someone that he'd given up his job.

I was a little nervous about getting in touch. I'd hardly seen Valida since that day at the mortuary. I was worried about seeing Aida again. I was worried about how to tell them what I knew. At least, with Robert, I didn't have the problem I did with Lena: wives don't like the women their husbands get to know during wars. I'd shared far more war with Valida than I had with Robert.

I'd always had this feeling that Valida thought journalists were jackals; but then she went out with Henri and married Robert so maybe I'm being over-sensitive. Poor Henri. She must be glad that didn't work out. It's bad enough being killed in a war, but being kept hostage in Chechnya for three months first…ugh. They found his head in a plastic bag on the Georgian Military Highway.

I've also always thought Robert thought I was a bit silly, but he sounded perfectly friendly when he rang. He didn't seem to think it odd that my mobile worked. He gave me their address, but it meant nothing to me.

"It's in the old town. Just opposite the Martyrs' Cemetery," he said.

I haven't been to that cemetery since the day they buried Amir. I can see Maria, hovering on the edge, by the steep cobbled street; his father, in the double rows of white-capped men, as Amir's body was passed from hand to hand; the yellow forest of pine grave markers, shadows in the dark; too dark to see the names and dates scrawled on in pen, or in those letters you screw into garden gates. 1972–94, 1969–92, 1975–93. At thirty, born 1964, Amir was quite old, compared to some.

"Number Four," said Robert. "You can't miss it. Come at 7.30."

* * *

It was a beautiful evening as I walked up the hill, through tiny streets, beneath the overhanging houses, daub flaking off the wattle, ancient cobblestones bulging through the tarmac. A flight of steps flowed down the opposite side of the gulley, and two old men creaked slowly up. The petrol fumes rose on the evening air; taxis honked and bounced past rows of little shops and women in those tight skirts and white shirts dragged plastic bags past stacks of Sprite, purple bars of Swiss chocolate and crates of dusty peppers spilling out into the street. You could never get chocolate here in the war…

When I got to the corner of the street where Robert lived, the houses fell away to my right to reveal the hills; the grey rocks, the upper slopes furred in dark green, the ragged line of rocks against the blue. I felt as if they were staring back, biding their time; that any minute a bullet might thwack into my chest. I turned away, and found myself staring at the graveyard.

The pine markers of the war had gone. Rows of white turban-topped tombstones gleamed in the evening sun. All weedless and shiny new, in this country where they don't believe in tending their graves and jumbles of turban tops poke out all over the hills. Amir was about two-thirds along; two-thirds the way through the war.

I was about to walk to him when I heard my name. It was Robert, waving out of an upper window. I waved back: "Just coming." I turned my back on Amir's grave; I felt as though I had been caught reading a letter to somebody else.

It was a pebble-dash house, on the other side of the street. He was at his front door by the time I reached the step.

"Come into the courtyard, we're doing a barbecue," he kissed me hello; he looked younger, his face wasn't red and puffy any more. "What do you think of the house?"

I gave a nervous laugh: "This place would have been so dangerous in the war…"

Robert looked surprised.

"…your view…"

Then he smiled: "The previous owner swears it wasn't hit at all."

"You've *bought* it?"

"Why not?"

I couldn't answer. My spine began to itch. I was very glad when he shepherded me inside.

Valida was in the little courtyard at the back, by a barbecue.

"Molly," she gave me a big smile. "How lovely to see you..." I felt stupid to have worried. "You look very well."

"So do you. You both do." She still had the same Ava Gardner bob, the alabaster skin; a little plumper, but then so was I. We weren't running up five flights of stairs God knows how many times a day. She wore less make-up now – maybe now the war was over, she didn't need the protection.

"Would you like a drink?"

"Yes, please." I looked round at their courtyard, its tubs of flowers, the little chairs. "This is so *nice*."

"Thank you. Pour her a drink darling. How's the hotel?" Robert had booked me a room in a *pension*; there are loads, he'd said, central and cheap. You don't have to stay at the Holiday Inn.

"Fine. Lovely."

"It's owned by a cousin of Valida's," said Robert.

Valida snorted: "She is NOT my cousin. She was refugee... from one village, miles beyond Rogatica even!"

She was lucky, the cousin, the refugee. The Serbs put their Muslims through the sawmill in Rogatica, a small town on a main road, deep in the forests; the ones who got away mostly ended up in Srebrenica. It had been rusting and cold when Muffy and I paid a visit, eighteen months into the war. The Serb sawmill director, in his empty office, with his fur-hatted friends, happy for any diversion in the tedium of war, had given us coffee and slivovic, and practised on us, with their guilt-ridden eyes, the version of the slaughter they'd been telling themselves for the last year. I wondered if they could hear the screams of their former colleagues, now the machines were no longer drowning them out.

"OK." Robert rolled his eyes. "She was married to your cousin…"

Valida broke in: "For about five minutes, before he died. I do have a friend who works there. Sabina… you might remember her, she worked for one of the TV companies in the war. But she's just a waitress…" She made a face.

"I've only just checked in."

"Come and see our garden, through there, through the door in the wall," said Robert. "It needs a lot of work. The previous owner hadn't lived here for years. I think he moved to Germany after the war."

"No, Robert. He was in Germany during the war. He came back here for a bit, but he decided to stay in Germany."

The doorway led to a wilderness. I didn't tread on the grass. You have to watch out for a wild garden – they're often mined… "This is all so pretty. You are clever," I said from the doorway. But no-one would have laid any mines here… this was bang in downtown Sarajevo. Still, I backed out.

Then I said again: "And you look so *well*. What I mean is, you always looked lovely, but Robert looks much better than he did before." Maybe he just looked happy.

"It must be being married to me."

"So do you," said Robert. "You look younger than you did five years ago."

"That's what my friends always say." Then there was a silence, because neither of us wanted to start talking about the war.

"The last time I saw you was Dayton." Which at least was the peace.

"Oh! He looked terrible then. No wonder you think he's better now."

"Dayton was a nightmare. I've never worked that hard. Dayton had one good effect, though…"

"What, ending the war?"

"Well, that too, but Valida decided to marry me."

"He looked so dreadful I realised he could never look after himself." They smiled at each other and he picked up her hand. It was several seconds before Valida looked back at me.

"So when did you get here? Robert and I always say it doesn't take long enough to get to Sarajevo these days."

"Oh," I laughed. "It took me long enough."

"Poor Molly came by bus from Split," Robert said.

I'd flown to Split, just like we always used to do, wheeling down between the mountains and the sea. The lemon cyprus scent hit deep into my lungs the moment I stood at the doors of the plane. Then I'd taken the airport bus, which deposited me, just as it always had done, 200 metres from the Hotel Bellevue. Behind the desk was the same surly man I had met on that first trip, just a bit greyer. He didn't recognise me, but when I said I stayed there during the war, he smiled.

I'd rung Robert: "Guess where I am? Split!"

"Why? We've got a proper airport now."

I felt rather stupid but I said: "I wanted to swim in the sea."

His voice changed: "Now that is a good reason. Eat some fish for me… Mind you, there are good fish restaurants here now." I don't trust fish in landlocked countries, I said, but he laughed.

"I might fly in tomorrow. I don't suppose you need a flak jacket to get on a plane these days."

"I don't think they do flights from Split any more."

"*What?*"

It was Robert, like the first time, who suggested I went by bus.

"And which way do they go?" I'd asked.

There was a short silence, before he said: "Up the main road. Following the signs to Sarajevo." I couldn't believe it.

"How long does it take now?"

"About seven hours."

"*What!*"

Just because the war had finished, it didn't stop Sarajevo being very far away.

"It's a good five hours by car," said Valida, when I told her.

There was a short silence, then Valida said: "Robert, show her round the house."

"It was built by the same architect as the old library. This was his restrained period," he said, as we did the tour. I'd passed the ruins of the library this afternoon – the yellow and maroon of its Austro-Islamic fusion still stood gutted, as it had been, by the Serbs at the start of the war.

"Why haven't they rebuilt it?"

"God knows. They seem to be redoing the horrible modern buildings but they haven't done that."

"I saw they'd rebuilt the UNIS towers." I thought it was sad; I loved the way the shattered glass had flamed every evening in the setting sun. "I went past them as I came in. We got stuck in a traffic jam on Sniper Alley. It was really creepy."

Robert paused before he said: "I suppose it must have been. Come and see upstairs."

I took a taxi from the bus station. The traffic had thinned by the time we passed the Holiday Inn, so I wasn't able to look too hard at the hotel. It was just a large yellow blob. The front had been refaced, the glass all put back, and tables and umbrellas dotted the open terrace facing the road. I nearly asked the taxi to stop, but then I thought, for what? What am I going to find there now? A huge ugly room with a lot of small ugly ones off it? The fountain was playing. I used to laugh at its desert basin.

We were on the first floor now. "Come and look at the view." Robert led me to the bay window at the front. The Martyrs' Cemetery below, where he'd seen me earlier, and the mountains and the fir trees, the minarets and the old frontline; beyond the river, more white gravestones, from deaths long ago, pock-marked the hills' lower flanks. The heavy machine gun had been there, just above the cemetery's white cupola. I moved back.

"We'll knock this through," Robert was saying. "And just have one huge room. And we're going to get that lovely old-fashioned

Ottoman furniture, and have that. The bedrooms are upstairs. Come and see the basement."

We went down two flights, beneath the kitchen. It was a good solid space the size of the house, with proper ceilings and several different rooms. One was an old-fashioned Turkish loo – a hole in the ground. There was a thick glass skylight set into the courtyard floor. In a corner was a round wooden circle in the stone.

"What's that?"

"That's the well."

I started to laugh. He stared. "What's up?"

"Apart from the front door, which is a killer, you'll be fine in this house. You've got a bomb-proof room with natural light, its own water supply and loo." I couldn't stop giggling.

"I hadn't thought about that." He looked almost affronted, then he started to laugh too. "Don't worry about the front door. There's a way out the back. I guess we can grow food in the garden."

"So you're fine then."

"Yes," he smiled. "We're fine."

We walked back outside. Robert started doing things with the barbecue, while Valida and I talked. Robert snorted when he heard the name of my magazine.

"It's full of crap," he said, just like Tash.

Valida said: "Fashion is not necessarily crap."

I trotted out my line about wanting to stay in one place.

"A normal thing to want," said Valida.

"Funny place to choose," said Robert. "Don't you get bored of all that garbage?"

"Some of the articles are very good," said Valida.

"So what are you both doing now?" They glanced at each other.

Valida, she said, was a lawyer – nearly a lawyer, finishing the training she'd started before the war. Robert was writing a book – a novel, this time, or maybe a series of short stories, he wasn't sure. I asked him if he'd got bored of the UN, but he smiled at Valida, who took his hand again, and then he said, "I think they got bored of me."

I didn't ask how they could afford it. Valida must have saved a fortune in the war and Robert – I had friends in the UN who made ninety grand a year, tax free. Plus, his book was for ages the only decent book about this place. Everyone who came here had it in their hand. You still see it in shops in the UK.

"Do you see much of Phil or Tim?" Valida asked.

"Not really. Tim's in Africa. I just see him on the telly."

"We're the same," said Valida. "We keep up with our friends from the telly."

"Do you get BBC here?"

"We have satellite," said Valida.

"But Valida doesn't like hearing bad news, so that limits watching the BBC rather dramatically."

"Why hear it?" she said. "You can't do anything. I heard quite enough bad news in the war."

A moment passed before Robert said: "What about Phil? You two were such great friends."

"I know." I minded the way Phil and I had drifted apart. "I couldn't cope with the hangovers." Robert laughed. Then I said: "And I don't think Lena liked me very much."

"Poor Phil. But he's still with her, isn't he?"

"Oh yes. They've had another baby. He's been posted to Jerusalem."

We talked about other people we had known: Jasmina, Valida's successor, had joined the UN, and was now in East Timor.

"Why not?" said Valida. "The UN in Sarajevo was full of Indian and Chinese and God knows what in the war. Why shouldn't Jasmina go to East Timor?"

"No, reason at all," I said.

Edin, she said, was still working for CTV.

"He's based in Chicago," she said. "I think he travels a lot."

"Since when?" I couldn't remember when I'd even last seen Edin around. Valida looked at Robert, who shrugged back.

"Since before Dayton, I think."

"And Lejla?" I asked. Pulling out another name: she had been one of the interpreters for Reuters.

"She's in Washington. She's working for the World Bank." They are all much more successful than me.

We'd done everyone else now. There was only one person left. In the gap where none of us mentioned her, Valida asked me if I'd like another drink and Robert said: "I think the food might be ready. We're having *cevapcici*..." I thought, oh God! Not those rat-burgers we had in the Holiday Inn.

"So why are you here?" asked Valida, as we sat there with our plates. "Are you doing a story?" They stared up at me like little baby birds.

"Oh God no!" I said. "I'm sorry if that sounds rude. But I just couldn't face doing a story from here." I took a bite of *cevapcici*. To my surprise, Robert said: "I understand exactly what you mean."

"Do you?"

"Yes."

"I couldn't bear." I stopped. "I couldn't bear having to..."

"I know."

"To sell it to a desk." What I meant was I just couldn't bear having to convince someone about why this place mattered.

"Why do you think I joined the UN?"

"Oh."

"And why do you think I don't do any journalism now?"

"Oh."

"Here, let me fill up your glass," said Robert. I had stalled on the *cevapcici*. They weren't very nice. I was rather surprised, considering how much the Sarajevans had gone on about them during the war, but maybe Robert wasn't a good cook.

"So, why *are* you here?" said Valida, and I didn't know where to start. It had seemed much more straightforward back in London. But now I was here, I couldn't forget that Aida was Amir's widow, not me. Perhaps, then, I should start with Aida. "How's Aida, by the way?"

They shot glances at each other.

"She's in America too," said Valida.

"America!"

Robert said: "She moved there not long after the war."

"And what about Nermina?" The baby.

"Well, she went too. Obviously," said Robert.

"Oh poor Maria," I said.

Robert and Valida looked at each other. Robert said: "Maria…?"

Valida shrugged; then Robert said, rather carefully: "Yes, I think the whole thing has been very hard on her."

"What's Aida doing there?"

Another silence, then Valida said: "She got married."

"*Married!*"

"Yeah," Robert said – Valida shot him a look. "Some old bloke. They've had another baby."

Before I could ask any more, Valida broke in: "But you still haven't told us why you are here."

"I'm here about Amir," I said. I felt embarrassed now.

Valida stood up, and took some plates into the house.

Robert said: "Poor Amir. That was all so long ago." He looked as if he'd much rather follow Valida.

"Yes, but there's something else…" I stopped. I was hoping for some help, but Robert looked at me warily and didn't ask what.

"I had a strange conversation with someone in England a few weeks ago."

"Oh…" he looked wistfully towards the house, as if he wished he could get up and follow Valida.

"Maybe you know this already, he was married to Aida, but… if you don't know, then maybe… I…"

"Amir caused enough trouble for you, for all of us already." He stood up.

"Yes, but that still doesn't mean that it's right."

"What. What isn't right?" he froze, with a plate in his hand.

"What this guy told me."

"What guy?"

"A Brit."

"Oh."

"Someone who had been in Sarajevo."

"Oh."

"He told me that Amir wasn't killed by a sniper."

"Did he?"

"Yes." Robert didn't move. It was obvious to anyone that Robert already knew.

"You knew."

He nodded, slowly, once.

"When did you know?" He shrugged.

"How did you know?"

He shrugged. "Sarajevo's a small town," he said finally. "Things leak out."

"You could have told me."

He shrugged again.

"I thought he was killed by the Serbs. I thought he was shot by a sniper."

After ten seconds or so Robert said: "I suppose I thought it was better left alone."

"But this guy said he was murdered."

"In a way everyone who died in the war was murdered, weren't they?"

"Oh come off it! He said Amir was killed on purpose. That someone waited for him and killed him on purpose."

"Did he?"

"Yes."

"Oh."

"And is it true?"

Long silence. He held the plate in both hands. "I suppose so."

"But Robert... Robert..." I stopped. I couldn't find the words to say everything I wanted to say: why didn't I know, why didn't you tell me, who did it, why?

But Robert didn't speak. He just looked at me.

"So, do you know who did it? Do you know why? Have I missed something? Was there a trial?"

Long pause: "No. There hasn't been a trial."

He shrugged again.

"Was there any kind of investigation?"

Shrug.

"Don't you want to know? Don't you want to find out?"

"Molly, a lot of horrible things happened here during the war and sometimes it is better not to ask why."

"But that's wrong!"

"Is it? Or is it wrong for us to try and impose our ideas of justice and behaviour on these people…"

"Oh, for God's sake. You sound like the *defence* in a war crimes tribunal."

He flushed. "Maybe they have a point. There's a different culture here."

"And now you sound like some sort of colonial administrator…"

"Maybe that's what I was…" he looked towards the house.

"Robert! Stop talking in generalisations! Amir wasn't just some bloody native… he was…" He was my Amir, my beautiful Amir, with his smile, and his dark eyes, and the ropes of muscles I liked to stroke on his long lean arms, and his way of holding me that made me feel that I was beautiful and fragile and the best thing he had ever had. Suddenly, like a sharp whiff from the grave, I could even smell him, that Sarajevo scent. But maybe it was the wood smoke from the barbecue on the mountain air. My eyes filled with tears and the anger left my voice.

"You could have told me…" I said.

"You weren't here…"

"Oh, *God*!"

"Valida said Aida didn't want anyone to know," he said quickly.

"I'm not just anyone."

There was silence again. I brushed away a tear.

"I suppose you're not," he said in a tired voice. He put down the plate. "I'm sorry. I probably should have told you. I suppose I just thought you knew…" he looked up, as Valida walked out of the kitchen door. "So, how's your hotel?" he said.

Mujo and Suljo wanted to emigrate to Germany. They couldn't get work permits, so they disguised themselves as monkeys. When they got to Germany, they were caught and put in a zoo. After a while, the manager noticed there was something funny about them, so he put them in the same cage as a bear, who was also behaving strangely. Mujo and Suljo were sitting in the corner, waiting for the bear to eat them, when suddenly the bear said: "Hey guys, don't be scared. I'm from Srebrenica."

III

I ate my breakfast and tried to think. There's a lot of thinking going on in this room. It's not a very large room, but then it's not a very large hotel; just two storeys round a courtyard spiral-paved with the Yellow Brick Road. There must be ten tables in this dining room. Behind me is a bar, with mirrors and bottles of strange liqueurs, and more mirrors on one of those disco globes. I'm looking at a courtyard, with a couple of chairs, and net curtains billowing round plate-glass windows in the late summer breeze.

The only noise, apart from the clinks of cutlery, is the occasional slurp. Even the fountain in the courtyard is off. Yet each table, with its blueberries and raspberries in their little glass bowls, the basket of rolls, the pot of yoghurt, the red and white checked cloth, and the coffee, delicious, is a flag for civilisation. At each, one person slowly munches. They're much of a type, my fellow munchers: the men tend to beards; the women to Birkenstocks. They look a bit young to be aid workers but maybe aid workers are getting younger these days.

A waitress is sitting on a stool by the bar, staring at the dead fountain beyond the glass. She's pretty, with long dark hair, long legs and an expression both worried and very far away. She looks rather familiar. But then so do lots of people here. Maybe she's the friend Valida talked about.

"Are you Sabina? I'm a friend of Valida's," I said, as she brought me my coffee.

Her sad face smiled: "I know. She booked you in." But before I could say anything else, she turned back to her stool.

I had thought that Robert and Valida would have helped me find out what happened to Amir. I'd even thought Aida would give me a hand; we could have worked together – not exactly become friends, but at least learnt to see what he'd liked in both of us. I'd imagined playing with Nermina – I've never even seen a picture of her. I could have changed her nappies. But of course, she must be nearly six.

I left my hotel and started walking into town, towards the library, along the bend of the river, and stopped to watch the Coke bottles bob at the bottom of the weir. I'd never walked along the river before, it would have been far too dangerous in the war. I couldn't understand Robert. Surely, like all of us, he'd been drawn here by the injustice of what had happened here. But had he been? Or had he just been repelled? He didn't come for the war, he was here before. When we took that bus, to Kiseljak, in 1993, all he wanted to do was leave. Maybe he didn't care about the injustice after all; everyone said he was hardly in Sarajevo at all. But that can't be right: that first summer of the war, he'd spent months chronicling Arkan and his boys butchering their way through the Drina valley.

The street signs have changed. They're all green now. We used to laugh at the Serbs banging on about green – the colour of Islam, the green road to Istanbul – but given that *was* the paranoia, it seems tactless to put up a load of green signs. The names are very Islamic, very Turkish, too – Ulica Hodza, Hodza Street, Trg Pasha, the Pasha's Square – perhaps they were always called that. I can't remember. Two young girls in scarves walked past; that's new. You never saw the hejab during the war. I couldn't have told what religion Amir's mother was, apart from the fact that her name was Maria.

Maria. I would go and see her. She must know. Or she would help me find out. His father would want to know. He was an academic. He had an enquiring mind. I was planning to see them anyway. I'd bought them a bottle of Scotch in Duty Free. I was very fond of them, although I didn't really see them very much in the last year or so. After Amir married Aida, we were all too embarrassed. I started visiting a bit after Amir died, but every time I thought of going, the well of misery would leech at my soul. I'd pop in once in a while, with some coffee, whisky and the bags of PX mini-Twix; we'd make small talk, about how it had been too long. But, as Robert said, I wasn't there so much then.

Things should be better for them now. Murat would be back at his university. Maria must be working as an architect. God knows, the whole town is being rebuilt. We always joked about how busy she'd be after the war.

I suppose I should have rung to say I was coming, but they never had a number during the war. I was about to go back to the hotel for the whisky, when I saw some, cheaper, in the window of a shop full of yoghurts with German names. I bought coffee, and a big bunch of flowers. Nobody had flowers during the war.

Amir's street still had the same name. The chipped garlands still hung from the stonework but the windows were back. No UNHCR bubble wrap; glass, all the way down the street. The windows looked wrong, then I realised, they were all the same age. They had the blank new uniformity of a Barratt home.

The hole had gone. The huge hole, in the front of his house, which the grand piano hid inside, was now a blurred grey blotch, the size of an armchair, like the blotches all over town.

The stairwell was the same. The fronds of wrought iron were caked in dirt, and the grit still crunched underfoot. It didn't even occur to me to look for the light. The same frosted glass doors, at the top of the stairs, still bearing the same crack in the pane. My stomach churned as I remembered that first day, when Amir had stood in the half-light in front of me, and I had breathed him in.

I knocked. One thing had changed. It smelt musty and damp but it didn't smell of pee.

Nothing happened. I knocked again. I had a flash of hope, like I did in my duty visits after Amir's death, that nobody would be there, but I didn't really want that and I was relieved when I heard the shuffle of feet.

The woman who opened the door gave me so blank a look that for a moment I thought I had the wrong house. And she…then I realised she wasn't gaunt any more.

"*Maria? It's Molly*." I put out my hand.

"*Molly?*" She was shocked blank, then she grabbed me, and smiled an enormous smile. "*You've come back.*"

"*I hope this isn't a really bad time*," was what I tried to say, but my voice had gone all strange and wobbly; besides, I was finding it much harder to speak the language than I thought.

"*No! No! Come in. Please. How could it be a bad time?*" She ushered me in to the hall. "*I nearly didn't hear you, when you knocked. The electric bell works now.*" She pressed it, and I jumped at the *drrring*.

"*I think it would… I forget…*" I pushed the flowers at her – she'd pretended not to notice them until that point.

"*Flowers! How kind…*" I untangled the plastic bag, with the coffee and the whisky. "*This is also for you*."

"*But no, why?*" she smiled, as she unpacked it. "*Coffee*," she giggled. "*I don't need such things now…*"

"*Oh, you know…*" I wanted to say, for old times' sake, but I couldn't remember how. "*Like before*."

"*Oh whisky, thank you. Good Scottish whisky…*"

We stood there, staring at each other, grinning, our eyes filling with tears. She clutched onto my arm, and I swallowed and grabbed her back. I hadn't realised I'd feel like this. When you read about people crying with happiness in books, when you're a child, you don't understand what it means. It's a kind of terrible relief that, in the random shit of life, good things can still happen. She pressed the bell again. And we both laughed.

"*Would you like some coffee?*"

The kitchen looked less cluttered. The UNHCR stove had gone; the one where Amir had showed me how to make airgun pellets that first day. The whole flat was full of Amir for me. Suddenly I wanted to cry again. I looked at his mother, busy over her stove, with her brass long-handled jug. She turned and smiled over her shoulder at me, and I smiled back. When she turned, I wiped my eyes.

I looked round the kitchen again. It wasn't just the stove.

"*It looks… new.*"

"*I'm redecorating. Everything was so dirty after the war.*"

So that was it. Fresh paint. But I still felt I had missed something.

"*Here, coffee, is ready.*"

She brought the jug to the table. She poured the thick black liquid into two tiny white cups and the grounds eddied beneath the steam on the top.

"*Sugar?*"

"*No thank you.*"

"*It is just like old times.*" She smiled at me, then her eyes seemed to fix on something far behind. Suddenly I didn't know what to say: everything we had in common was just so sad.

"*So tell me, are you married now?*"

"*No. No I'm not.*"

"*Are you still war reporter?*"

"*No. No. I don't do that kind of work any more.*"

"*Good,*" she said. "*It is not a good job for a woman.*" She always said that. Eight years ago, I used to argue.

Then she said: "*It is so lovely to see you again.*"

"*Yes.*"

"*I tell you what, let us have a little of your beautiful whisky.*"

"*Oh, no, keep it for yourself.*" It was 11.30 a.m.

"*Yes. We must. You brought it. Just to celebrate.*"

She poured me two inches. She seemed surprised when I asked for water.

"*Like the old days,*" she said. "*You and me, in this kitchen.*" It was almost as though Amir had pulled up a chair. Her voice drifted off and she stared quickly at her whisky. I said: "*So, what are you doing now? Have you got a lot of work to do?*"

"*No. Not really…*" She paused. "*No. I'm not working now.*"

"*But there must be work for architects,*" I said.

"*Maybe… but maybe not for me.*" She took a sip.

"*What about your old firm?*" I said. "*Why you not work for them?*"

"*The head office was in Belgrade. My firm doesn't exist any more.*" She took another sip.

"*How's Murat? I'd love to see him again.*"

Her eyes filled with tears and she took another sip. And another.

"*You do not know?*"

"*Know what?*"

She drank again. "*Murat is dead.*"

Dead! How could I have not known… He must have died right at the end. I saw him in August '95. He must have been one of the last people to have been killed.

"*How did it happen*?" Was he got by a sniper? Or was it a shell? Maybe it was later – after the war – maybe he trod on a mine…

"*He had cancer.*"

"*Cancer!*"

"*Yes. He died last year.*" Last year? So after the war? The tears spilled down her face. She picked up her glass, but it was nearly empty.

"*I'm so sorry. He was such a nice man.*"

She wasn't listening to me, just talking to her glass. "*Everyone here is getting cancer. Maybe stress from the war. Maybe that horrible food. Maybe it was the shells, the depleted uranium shells…*" She took the last gulp. "*The ones NATO fired at the end of the war… Could you pour me a little of that whisky please? Have some too.*"

She topped up my glass and put on a social voice:

"*So, why are you in Sarajevo?*"

"*I'm on holiday.*"

"*Holiday!* Here! *But you could go* anywhere…"

"So could you, now," I said, but as I said it, I realised it wasn't true. She looked old and poor.

"Maybe," she smiled, and for the first time it was like the game we used to play, what she would do after the war.

"I don't want to go anywhere. I wanted to come here."

She smiled, part wistful, part as if she were despising me for being a fool. She picked up her glass and took another drink.

"I wanted to see old friends," I said, but she didn't speak. She didn't seem to want to mention Amir. *"I saw Valida yesterday."* She took another sip.

"She told me that Aida had got married and moved to America."

Sip: *"Best place for them."*

I waited for her to mention Amir or Nermina, but she didn't. There weren't even any photographs of Nermina here. Even strangers show you photographs of their grandchildren. I looked around. Where were the pictures? Any of the pictures?... This flat used always to be cluttered with stuff.

"I've never seen Nermina," I said. *"Does she, does she... look like Amir?"* There, it was out.

She took another sip. *"Oh my poor Amir. He looked just like my Murat. He had just exactly his smile. He looked like Murat when we first met."*

"I thought he looked like you."

She shook her head. *"My poor Amir..."* She took a drink from her glass. I didn't blame her. I drank from mine too.

"Amir is the reason I have come back..."

Your mother glared at me.

"When Amir died..." I floundered for a moment... I used to be good at asking people questions about tragedies but I suppose I'm out of practice now, and besides, this is my tragedy too.

"Did you ever think... did anyone say... was there anything... strange about it?" Her glare concentrated. Sip. Long silence. Snort.

"The whole war was strange..." She took a great long slug of her drink, then looked into my eyes.

"I…"

"It's nothing to do with you."

"Something unusual…"

"Nothing in that time was usual…"

This wasn't working, so I just blurted it out: *"Somebody told me he wasn't shot by the Serbs…"*

"He was killed by the war. That's enough, isn't it?"

"But what happened?"

"He died. That's what happened."

"But how?… I stumbled on… *"I want to know…"* I stopped, and stared at her. She stared implacably back. *"I have to know…"* I started to plead.

"You have to know!…" She snorted, picked up the whisky bottle and poured herself some more. *"You don't have to know anything…"* She laughed. *"It's because of you he's dead!"*

"Maria! No!"

"Yes." She pushed back her chair and stood up.

"No! How? You can't say that. It's not fair!"

"Fair! If you had married him, he would still be alive. My son… Any girl should be pleased to marry him… But he wasn't good enough for you, was he?"

She started to cry, heaving her face in her hands. I stood up and went and crouched by her side. I tried to put my arms round her shoulders but she pushed me away.

"You left Amir and you left Sarajevo. There are things you don't have the right to know. If you had not left him, he would be alive." She looked up, *"Just get out,"* she said. *"Get out of my apartment."*

"Maria…"

"Get out. Now. Please go."

I let myself out and walked down into the street. I didn't want to walk far. I didn't think I could. I went to the little park at the back of the street: the one that Amir had told me had once been full of trees, before they were chopped down for firewood in the dead of night; where Phil and I had drunk coffee, in the little café

Ibrahim had set up during the phoney peace of '94 – it was shelled the first day the peace treaty broke. There were saplings growing in the park. They must have been planted after the war. Ibrahim's café at least was still there, with two women sunning themselves, on the terrace, drinking coffee; two children were running in the grass nearby. How tall will the trees be allowed to grow?

I had just lit my cigarette, when my mobile rang.

"I just wanted to see how you were," it was Robert's voice.

"Thank you so much for dinner last night."

"Not at all, it was lovely to see you… Where are you now?"

"I'm in the little park opposite the Residency."

"Oh, God, my old office, I remember it well. What are you doing there?"

"I've just been to see Maria," I said.

"Oh."

"I didn't know that Murat had died."

"Oh yes, I'm sorry. He had cancer. I didn't know you didn't know."

"How awful, to survive the whole war, and then to die…"

"I know what you mean…" he waited for a few seconds, before he said, "Did you ask Maria about Amir?"

"Yes."

"What did she say?"

I was too shocked to tell anything other than the truth. "It was all rather horrible. She started crying and then she said it was all my fault."

"She said that."

"Yes. She kept saying that."

Long pause. "It wasn't your fault, believe me."

"Well, whose fault was it then?"

"Oh God knows, Molly, but it wasn't yours. I'd just go home if I were you and forget the whole thing."

I watched the women stirring their empty cups, then I heard Robert say, "What are you doing tonight?"

"Oh, I hadn't thought."

There was a pause, before he said, "There's a nice café on Feradiya..."

"Where?"

"Pedestrian zone behind the cathedral..."

I thought he was going to ask me round again but he said, "You could go there for a bit..." Another pause, then he added: "And they have lots of good films on TV... They're in English... not that that matters for you."

"Actually... my Serbo-Croat's nowhere near as good as it was."

"Well, the subtitles will help you improve – sorry... Got to go..."

I smoked another cigarette. I couldn't leave Amir's mother like that. She didn't even know where I was staying. I'll go back after this cigarette. Then I sat a bit longer and had another one.

It was nearly an hour before I left my bench. All I have to do is shove my card at her, and leave. I'd written the hotel's number on the back. I don't think she'll change her mind, but she might.

I waited outside her door for half a minute but I couldn't hear any noise. I rang the bell but no footsteps answered its *drrring*. Maybe she'd gone out in the last hour... I knocked, and this time the door swung open.

I stood in the doorway. "Maria," I said, in a loud voice, and then "Maria," a little louder. But it was not a large flat, so I didn't have to shout.

In the end, I just walked in. The kitchen, where we'd sat an hour ago, was open to my right, but there was no-one there as I hovered by the door. The sitting-room door was ajar. I tapped my fingers on its edge. "Maria?"

I put my head round the door.

I needn't have worried about Maria hearing me. She lay half on her side, mouth open, legs trailing onto the floor. Her grey locks were stirring against the upholstery as her chest rose and fell, a little trail of spit oozing out of her mouth. On the floor, where her hand trailed down, were a glass, the whisky bottle, and a full ashtray. There was no other furniture in the room. No chandelier, no pictures, no table, no chairs, no lace doilies, no crystal vases, no swords above the doors, no rugs; just parquet, white walls, and the grand piano stranded in its corner.

The whisky bottle was empty. Half out of the ashtray, still on its filter, hung two inches of ash, like one of those bodies fleeing Pompeii.

I felt clubbed by pity but I also felt sick. I can't take this. I've got to get out. I can't leave her like this. But there's nothing else I can do for her anyway. The cigarette in the ashtray had long burnt itself out. I checked the stove in the kitchen, but everything was off.

At the door I remembered why I came back. But how could I leave my card? I couldn't leave it by her. She'd know I found her like this. In the end I put it on the kitchen table, where I might have left it earlier. Then I left. I have seldom wanted to leave anywhere so much. It was a race to see if I made it out before I was sick.

TWO PENSIONERS met at Bascarsija main square, where the pigeons flock. The first one said, "Did you bring the bread?" And the second pensioner replied: "No, still I haven't got my pension."

"No problem," said the first pensioner. "Today we will eat the pigeons without bread."

IV

What did you do? Oh my love. Oh Amir, what happened that I don't know?

And your mother… I can't even help her. In the war I could give her food and money; I thought if I wrote about things, then maybe they'd get better. I don't even blame her for the drink.

I made it round the corner before I had to sit down. I breathed in deep, and let the nausea subside. Then I lit myself a cigarette. It was another little park, an older one, opposite the Presidency on Marshal Tito Street; it used to be a graveyard, before the Austrians came. The gravestones, those white marble posts, were dotted about in the grass, some sunk so deep with time that only a lichen-covered blob poked above ground, as though the earth was trying to consume the memory of the dead. Two old men sat, alone, on different benches, under the trees, whose lower trunks were strangely bald; branches had been cut for firewood in the war, of course.

Like always, I found myself glancing up to the hills, no longer now the dress circle of the Serbian dream, the silent trees, the peasants' huts strung along the crag. The mountains met my gaz and from the darkness of the trees, I could hear the whisper; thought we Serbs had lost. Well, maybe we did, but we took down with us.

I sat there for over half an hour. I wish you were h

more than anything that you were here. I need you here. I need to know what on earth went on.

I walked back to my hotel. Even though it was lunchtime, I went to sleep. When I woke up, it was light, but my watch said 4 a.m. I looked at the shortwave, but that said 16.00. Then I remembered your mother, and the whisky, and your father being dead. But I didn't feel sick any more. In fact I felt hungry.

I headed for the mosque and the maze of the old town. I wasn't looking as I stepped out into the road. A car careered round the corner and had to swerve. The driver was young, like you had been, with a beautiful girlfriend at his side. I smiled and said sorry, in Serbo-Croat. But he slewed his car half onto the pavement, and walked towards me, screaming.

"I'm sorry. I didn't realise the light had changed." I was so shocked, I was speaking English.

"Where are you from?" He switched to perfect English.

"London…"

"You come here from London. You think you're God and you cross the road like a primitive." His shaved head was pumping with rage.

"I don't think I'm God…"

"You could have made me crash my car. My car cost 40 000 KM. And you…" he sneered as he looked me up and down. I was an Englishwoman abroad: white T-shirt, flip-flops and a blue denim skirt. I didn't have the henna-ed hair and nailpaint of the girl in the car.

I kept trying to say sorry, but he wouldn't let me; just screamed and shook his fist, while people swerved round his car, and leant on their horns. The girl twisted her pencilled lips into the embarrassed smile that women give each other when their men are being arseholes. Finally, someone else rolled down their window and screamed at the boy; he turned on them, and I ran past him into the square where the cars couldn't go.

I needed to sit down. My knees were shaking. The old man was still on his wooden chair under the tree just as he had been yesterday – was it only yesterday that I arrived?... He was throwing seeds for the pigeons, their little beaks clacking on the paving stones. The old gypsy woman was still begging on the steps of the hexagonal fountain, her back to its fretwork marble walls, where beggars must have sat for hundreds of years, the creamy bulk of the mosque serenely behind. Everything was as it had been this morning. As it probably had been fifty years ago – except the soldiers walking out of the alley would have been German and the gypsy would have been young and beautiful.

I understood why the young man had screamed. He would have been maybe sixteen when the war began; from Tito's wonderland to a frontline, in leaky trainers, on half-rations, waiting to die; nobody had explained to him, that when found he was still alive at the end, he'd be driven into a frenzy of rage by the failure of trivia, after surviving so vast an awfulness. As for the girlfriend, she'd have been about twelve.

I didn't recognise the soldiers' fatigues. As they passed, I automatically checked the badges; the one closest said F. Müller and the flag on his army jacket was the Bundesreich.

I haven't heard a word from your mother since yesterday.

I'm sitting, in that café, in the pedestrian zone beyond the cathedral, with my morning cappuccino. Was it here before the war? It looks like the kind of place that's been here a long time; where the war was just a hiatus, normal service has been resumed. I prefer being here to Bacarsija. I can't really see the hills.

I tried to order a cup of Bosnian coffee, but the waiter sneered at me. "We don't do Bosnian coffee," he said.

Two American girls have just sat down at my table. I heard one say: "I thought they were poor. Why are the cafés always full? These coffees cost 2.5KM each." Konvertible Marks – that's the currency now. It's pegged to the Deutschmark that we used in the war.

"It doesn't cost much to sit in front of a coffee all day," said girl two. "With unemployment at 30 per cent they've got nothing else to do."

I nearly didn't hear the girl ask in Serbo-Croat: "*Do you mind if we sit here?*"

They are in their mid-twenties, all clean and keen American, made-up to look unmade-up, and straight white teeth; one blonde, one dark, as though they came in two colours. I said, "Please do," to them in English, and they were a little upset.

"Oh. You knew," said the blonde; she was the smaller of the two, with blue eyes and that shoulder-length bob that blondes wear when they stop wanting to be Barbie.

"You're English?" I nodded. "We're from the States. But I guess you can tell that," said the other one; her brown hair was in the same post-Rachel cut. "We're not disturbing you?"

"Oh no."

Even if they are not talking to me, it's good to have the company. I feel so alone here, and yet it's full of ghosts.

You seem so much deader here than you were in London. In London you were lost to me anyway. Here, every street, every corner whispers your name. Suddenly for me the road is empty, and I don't even notice I don't know what it's called. The slush is grey on the ground, and you are screeching your car round a corner, to get out of the sights.

I went for a walk last night. I thought I should do something I could never have done before. The people streamed by me on Feradiya – that's this street's name: I saw its name on one of the new green signs. It was the hour of the *passagiata*, the promendade, or whatever it's called in Serbo-Croat. Beautiful girls, with that henna-ed hair, walk past in threes, eyeing up dark-eyed young men. Middle-aged couples arm in arm. One or two of them scowled; I actually had to push my way through. None of them look very happy: mostly they look bewildered. Their faces all seem to say: why me? Why did this happen to my life?

"So I was in Zvornik two days ago..." The dark girl was talking, but suddenly I'm not here any more: the blown mosque, the silent factory, the streets full of mad-eyed men, armed with beards and double-eagle hats and Kalashnikovs; the minutes ticking by while men dreaming the same Serbian dreams scrutinised our passports on both sides of the river; the Drina, fat and turquoise in its gorge, its far bank dotted with the summer houses of the Belgrade elite, round whose jetties eddied the odd rotten corpse, drifting down from where Arkan and his Tigers were wreaking their carnage…

"Urgh. Zvornik. Gross…" so perhaps it hadn't changed that much.

"Then I went to Bijelina, then Prijedor, to see those villages round there." Dried blood dribbled down bullet-riddled walls, and that sweet smell that wouldn't go however much they scrubbed it clean; half-starved skeletons pressing at the wire and women and children lying top to toe in a school gym, the nappies drying on the wallbars, the loos a swamp of shit.

I put down my pen and looked up at the sky. I couldn't see the hills from here.

I order another coffee. "You speak Bosnian," said the blonde.

Bosnian. So that's what they call it now.

"Do you live here?" she asks. She's all polite curiosity.

I would have been pleased to talk half an hour ago, but now I am back with you and don't relish the interruption.

"Not any more."

"But you did?"

"Yes."

"When?" said the blonde.

I paused, looked away: "During the war."

Last night I walked to places we could never have walked in the war. I walked down to the river, facing the hills, then I turned along the embankment and followed it downstream.

I hardly know the town on the far side of the water. In the bad times, the bridges were too exposed to cross. It's where the pizza parlour was, where I had lunch with Ed, the day that I went to visit the shrink. One of Amir's many friends – Jasmina I think she was called, pretty girl, dark hair, lost – her parents had lived there, in a yellow and grey Moominpappa block. They probably still did. We went to see them once – I think her father had a heart condition and I was writing about people being ill during the war. Or maybe we just went for fun. But I didn't think so: this part of town was badly shelled – it wasn't the kind of place you went for fun. I can't remember why it was badly shelled. It's right under the crags, maybe they couldn't resist just chucking stuff down. The brewery – Sarajevkso Pivo – we interviewed the manager once, a Muslim, Fuad, Fikret? I can't remember. But I remember him, in his cold and gloomy office, boasting that Sarajevkso Pivo had never shut, not even in World War II. Now, he said, he was supplying his part of town with water. How many died in the water queue massacre in 1992? Nineteen, twenty-five? I can't remember now.

"You lived here during the war?" said the blonde. Her tone was precise.

"Yes," I said, at least I suppose I had.

"When?"

"Oh, for lots of it really." I felt sick again.

"What, in Bosnia or Sarajevo?" she pronounced it *Sara*-yevo, with a rilled "r", the way the Bosnians do. Not Sara-*ye*vo, the way one does, if one's first acquaintance with the place was Archduke Franz Ferdinand.

"Kind of both. But I suppose I was mainly in Sarajevo."

"*When* were you here?" She wasn't being friendly.

"I first came to Bosnia in July 1992. I got to Sarajevo in April 1993. I did my last trip at the end of 1995."

"Wow," said the brunette.

"Trip? Your last trip? I thought you said you lived here?" said the blonde. I had a flash of irritation and looked across at the brunette; her friendly curiosity calmed me down. "In the beginning, I lived out here. When things got less… less…" what was the word Roger on the desk used to use…"less interesting… I moved back to the UK, and they'd send me out."

"What do you mean, less interesting?"

Oh God, this was like trying to justify myself to you.

"When there was less going on. In '94."

"There was lots going on in '94…"

You dying. That happened in '94. Your broken body being pulled out of your car.

"…*Merkale* happened in '94. What do you mean less was going on?"

That brought me back. "*Mark*…what?" I asked

"*Merkale*… The shell that killed all the people in the market."

"Oh, the market massacre…" You crying in my arms, for the woman who fell apart in yours, weeping for her blood gushing out onto the tarmac; me, sobbing by the TV in the hotel room in Zenica, trying to find a way that I could get back to you. Phil, hung-over, freaked out, the next day, sitting in his office, telling me about the head, on the stall like it was for sale. You and Aida, in the market place together; and afterwards, together, because I wasn't there. Like Phil and Muffy, I suppose, because sex seemed like the only way to wipe it out.

"…Yes, that was early '94."

"So… Lots of things happened in '94."

Suddenly I wanted to scream at her like the boy who'd nearly hit me with his car. Shut the fuck up you silly little girl, with your nit-picking questions, what do you understand? What do you know about the market massacre? You weren't here. I should have been here. I should have been with you, my love. Not away again. And if I'd been with you, you wouldn't have been with Aida, and then maybe, maybe, everything would have changed.

Instead I started to speak as though I were delivering one of the lectures I used to give to schools.

"After the market massacre, in February 1994, the United Nations imposed a twenty-kilometre heavy weapons exclusion zone around

Sarajevo, enforced by the threat of NATO air strikes. That meant that the shelling of the city effectively stopped and it didn't start again until very late the following autumn. Later on that spring, the UN brokered an anti-sniping agreement. People even started being allowed to travel in and out of the city – if they could get the right bits of paper. The water came back on, the electricity sort of worked. Even the gas worked a bit. They got the trams running."

Do you remember the snipers used to shoot into the trams? I was on a tram one day, and a bullet went through three people at once.

"For about nine months, in Sarajevo, there was a quasi-peace, until the Bihac crisis." That was when you'd died. I swallowed and went on: "From a journalistic point of view, it meant that the story got less interesting, so I wasn't here so much then."

"Less interesting because fewer people died?"

"Less interesting because less was going on. On a day to day basis. That's what journalism is about." Otherwise it wouldn't be called journalism, would it?

"Oh. I seeeeeee. So you're a journalist?"

What did she see?

"Did you live in the Holiday Inn?" asked the brunette.

"Yes."

"Reeeally?" said the blonde.

"There really wasn't anywhere else to live," I said.

"I have a friend who was here during the war and he didn't live in the Holiday Inn."

I felt sicker: "Was he a journalist?"

"No."

"Well then. Lots of people who weren't journalists didn't live in the Holiday Inn. Including all the Sarajevans. But if you were a journalist, if you could afford it, it was pretty much the only place to live."

I didn't go to the Holiday Inn last night. I got as far as the open space, beyond the Presidency, by the old mosque, by Skenderija Bridge, the bit I used to run across each day, to come and see you.

Across the river, across where the frontline used to be, were the white towers of Grbavica where the snipers skulked. I stared at them with the fear and hatred I always felt. The snipers must have gone, and the boards had come off most of the windows now. I'd always thought you were shot from there. It was 7 p.m. Time to do something else. In the old days we would have been in my room, using up the last of the light, doing little chores, if it were summer. In winter, we'd have been in bed, bed being the warmest place by far to be. Oh God. I can't think about this any more.

"Reeeeally?" said the blonde.

I nodded. "Really," I said. "And what do you do?"

"I live here," she said. "I'm on a Fulbright." I remember Fulbrights. Clever Americans do them. Clare, who ended up working for an American arts paper in Belgrade, she'd come out on a Fulbright – a PhD in Yugoslav humour, she said. Then she told me all the joke characters had become national politicians, and the jokes went away. They came back, she said, a year into the war. She was so glad that Mujo and Suljo had survived the war.

"I'm studying war crimes, you know; the Tribunal?" said the blonde; she had that polite East Coast rich girl voice, like glass beads dropping on a plate; she handed me a card, with her name on it: Amy something. "Whether post-conflict external justice systems ease re-integration. I get to hang out at mass graves a lot," she gave a little self-deprecating smile. "And Fenella," she waved at the brunette, who smiled prettily, "is doing regional variations in violence."

The brunette was staring at me with the hunger I remembered in myself.

"You were here then? Could I talk to you?"

I found myself nodding, paralysed.

"There are so many questions I want to ask. I mean… why in some villages did they just herd the Muslims onto buses and steal all their stuff, and in others…"

They forced them to bite each other's testicles off at gunpoint?

Why indeed. Weeping women clutching their children and their handbags, their wedding rings gone, as they clambered onto buses under the eyes of the bearded men with guns; the burnt-out mosques; the mad voices saying "the Muslims were building rockets", pointing at the charred rubble of the felled minarets; the rows of zombies in the cattle sheds at the camps at Omarska, ribs showing like ladders through their rags, and the reddened bruises welling on their cheeks. The mayor of the village near Banja Luka whose name I can't recall, showing me the list he'd drawn of things the Muslims couldn't do, like fish, or meet in groups of four, or leave their homes for twenty-two hours a day: "Because we like our Muslims," he'd said, staring with his Steven Berkoff eyes. "It's for their own protection." And his Muslims were the lucky ones.

"Could I? Would you mind?"

I nodded again. I literally couldn't speak.

The blonde looked at her watch, "Oh, we've got to go. We've got a meeting…"

The brunette gave her a nudge.

"Come too if you like; it's the Mothers of Foca…"

Foca: fucking freaky-deaky fucking town in a gorge in the mountains. That mayor, that flat-faced pig, boasting to Muffy and me: "We used to have twenty thousand Muslims in this town and now we have one and he's in prison." The madman in the greengrocer screaming "Genocide, genocide, Tito and Arkan made this genocide!" While everyone else stared at the tomatoes and pretended he didn't exist. The woman who'd followed us in the street to secretly say: "I miss my Muslim friends."

The Mothers, they said, were a refugee pressure group. I shook my head. They've asked me out to dinner as well, but I might do that.

Last night I ended up in a bar on my own, staring wistfully at a group of men in the white trousers and shirts that meant they were EC monitors. They'd all been talking about their day in Tuzla. I can't imagine being able to come back from Tuzla in a day. I wish

I had recognised one of them, then I could have gone over and talked. But they were all strangers to me. You used to tease me about the way I'd pick up strangers in the war; but it was easy, we were all here for the same reason. We'd talk the war, why and where and what would happen next, and order bottle after bottle of wine; then I'd try to remember what they'd said the next day. But it's not like the war. I can't go up and talk to strange men any more. I went back to my hotel. Bosnian TV was playing *Gone with the Wind*. I wept for Scarlett's stupidity and her lost brutal Eden, then I ate some of the chocolate I'd bought at Heathrow and went to sleep.

MUJO WAS ARRESTED and sent to prison. After a while, his wife, Fata, received a letter: "Dear Fata, everything the policeman said is true. I have two crates of ammunition, lots of rifles and grenades buried in the garden." Fata was scared and took the letter to the police. The police came and searched the garden but they found nothing. Soon, a second letter came: "Dear Fata, now where the policemen were digging, plant the potatoes."

V

I went to see you this afternoon. I walked up the hill to the Martyrs' Cemetery. The cobblestones were baking in the late summer sun and beneath my feet, a stream gurgled its way down from the hills, funnelled through some culvert of Austrian water-works. I glanced at Robert's house as I turned into the graveyard, but his windows stayed quiet.

There you were. Two-thirds of the way through the rows of white marble posts: Amir Hadzibegovic, 1964–94.

I'd bought you some flowers but now they seemed silly. I'd never have given you flowers when you were alive. I should have bought you a shirt, or a pair of dark glasses.

I put the flowers on the grass, and sat down by your head. Oh Amir… What happened? Why did you die? What didn't you tell me? What was it? What didn't I let you say? Did I never listen? Did I just make you what I wanted to believe you were? Should I stay, should I try and find out? Do you want me to? Or do you think, like Robert so obviously does, like your poor mother – oh God your mother – that it's none of my business; that I should go home and leave your ghost alone. What would you want? What would you want for your daughter? It's not Aida so much; she's left you now… But Nermina, what do you want her to know?

The boy buried to your right was 1976–94; Haris, on your left, born 1975. At least you had lived longer than them. I gave each of them a flower. Haris had a plastic wreath glued to his stone, its purples and reds rain-washed grey-mauve.

Did you know someone wanted to kill you? What you said, that last night, at the party – when you asked me to run away with you – was it not about me, was it just because you wanted to escape?

I gave the flowers to a dead woman a few graves away and walked back down the hill.

ONE OF SARAJEVO's new businessmen was arrested and put in jail. "How did you end up here?" asked his cell-mate. "My son wrote a school essay on 'my father's profession'," he said.

VI

I took Amy up on her invitation for dinner; I couldn't face another evening like last night. She rattled off the name of some restaurant.

"I don't know where that is."

"You don't?"

"No."

"Ohhhhhhh."

"I don't think it was here when I was last here."

"It's been here a while."

"Well maybe it was shut in those days."

"You think so? We'll be there at eight. It has a great view."

I thought I'd get directions from Sabina so I could walk. But she wasn't drooping silently in Reception. Instead, the TV was shouting German news and even the fountain in the courtyard had splurged into life. There was a woman engrossed in piles of paper, in the office behind the desk. She was shorter than Sabina, by four or five inches, and built from a different stock – thicker arms, thicker legs, broader hips and breasts, all squeezed into her shiny black dress. A child was playing with an Action Man at her feet. I coughed, hello, and when she turned and smiled her teeth were wonky behind the immaculate lips.

"Do you know the Francuski Dom?" I asked – I think that's what Amy had said. "How long would it take to walk?"

"It's miles up there…" The gold chains jangled against her breasts as she waved her arm. "Too far. I'll order a cab. How is your room?" she had a slight American twang.

"It's fine," I said.

"You're a friend of Valida's?"

I nodded.

"She's my cousin. I'm Didi," but Valida had said she wasn't a cousin, what had Valida said?… "This is my hotel. Anything you want, you come to me."

The child had followed her as far as the doorway.

"Is he yours? He's lovely." He looked about four or five, with dark hair and deep Sarajevo eyes.

"My Sulejman," she smiled. "Come and say hello." He came forward and held up a tiny hand. I crouched down and shook it.

"Hello Sulejman. That's a magnificent name. *Dragomir je.*"

Didi smiled. "This lady is a friend of your cousin Valida who married the Englishman." That's right – Valida had said Didi had been *married* to her cousin.

"Hello," he gazed at me with those huge dark eyes, then turned to his mother. She patted him and pushed him back to his toy soldier.

"You speak beautiful English," I said; her smile faded.

"I learnt it in the war," she said.

My taxi wiggled higher and higher to where Sarajevo straggled into villages, up to the pine trees and the old frontline. At a tiny lane, the driver stopped and pointed up. Steps had been carved into the side of the road, and a handrail screwed into the nearest house.

It must be a death trap, in winter, I thought, as I climbed the last twenty yards to a fresh pine door in a fresh cement wall. I rang the bell and turned and saw the view: it must have been a death trap in the war.

The door buzzed open, but I hardly noticed who let me in. Opposite me was a wall of glass, as new as the windows in your mother's street. I moved towards it as if I had no choice. Below was the whole of Sarajevo, deepening into dusk. I could see your flat; the Holiday Inn, laid out like a map; the trams zipping along the embankment; now-you-see-me-now-you-don't cars on Marshal

Tito. Robert's house. This was a sniper's view. I swallowed. This place could *never* have existed in the war.

"Hi! I told you it had a great view," it was Amy. I turned back into a pine-planked room of guns and plastic fruit. The walls were in the fresh pine of a bunk-bed showroom. A pair of swords were crossed over the lintel. Above the fireplace and at other points hung daggers and some, mainly ancient, but probably still deadly guns, all interwoven with the tendrils of plastic vines, or placed on doilies of red-embroidered lace.

She and Fenella were at a window table, with a man with his back to me.

"So, *have* you been here before?" Amy said, as I walked up.

"Oh no," I said. "This place couldn't have existed in the war."

"Reeally?" Amy glanced at the man next to her; he shook his head. She looked surprised, but she didn't question him.

"This is Zach," said Amy. "He was here in the war too." My heart leapt, but as he turned I realised that I didn't know him at all. He had short mousey hair and was about thirty or so. Obviously American, in that indefinably clean way.

Amy and Fenella were looking at us with hungry expectation.

"Hi," I said blankly. He looked blankly back.

Their faces had fallen. Zach and I regarded each other with mutual wariness.

"Fenella was sure you two would be old war buddies..." Amy trailed.

"It was quite a big war," I said, holding out my hand. "Molly Taylor."

"Zach Aldridge." His name meant nothing either.

"Oh well," said Fenella.

"Anyway," said Zach. He nodded me to a chair, but he didn't smile. "Sit down. Would you like a drink?" He had a beer. The girls had water.

"I'd love some wine."

"That's a good idea," said Amy. "Let's get three glasses of wine."

I'd forgotten the fact that Americans don't really drink. Four people; you are going to need a bottle at least. After five minutes of discussion it was decided to order some red. It was I who insisted that we got a bottle. By this time I was actually having difficulty being polite. It's not that I'm an alcoholic. I just like having a glass of wine in my hand if people want to talk to me about the war, and I could see that I was going to have to talk about the war rather a lot this evening.

"I'm drinking far too much in Sarajevo," said Fenella, sipping at her glass.

"Well you won't be alone there," said Zach, and knocked back his beer. "I think I'll have another of those."

Then he turned to me, "So, Amy says you were a journalist?" It was apparent that was little recommendation to him.

"Yes…" I could feel my stomach clenching up. "I still am a journalist." I suppose I am. "What about you?"

He shrugged it off with a: "Oh, I was just an aid worker," with the false modesty of someone who says, "Oh, I just look for the Holy Grail" … "Who do you write for?"

"Well, I don't do that kind of work any more. But during the war, I worked for the *Herald*."

Although, like a good liberal, he gave the *Herald* its due, it failed to stop the inquisition. "Were you in Sarajevo?"

"Most of the time. I suppose. But I also travelled a lot." I could smell the sicky chemical tang of the armoured Land Rover; see the burned beams black against the snow…

"I covered the whole area, really…"

"And when were you here?"

"Well… during the war."

"Were you here all the time?"

"No… No… Not all the time." I mean, I wasn't was I? That was the whole problem.

A shiver of contempt crossed his face: "A lot of journalists came and went."

"I suppose we did a bit."

I looked away, and round the restaurant. It obviously wasn't a place for romance. Each table bore its matching pairs of middle-aged couples; men with plumped, sallow faces, great haunches straining at their maroon suits. Their attendant women, foundation-dead skin and wrought henna-ed hair, were talking amongst themselves. I felt afraid, and I didn't know why.

"Where were you?" I turned back to Zach.

"Oh, nowhere as exciting as you," he said, in a flat voice. "Mainly in Central Bosnia."

"Where?" I asked.

He shrugged and looked out the window: it was a good twenty seconds before he spoke. "A nasty industrial town. It's called Zenica." His face was set and hostile in the night beyond the glass.

Suddenly I was furious. "Did you stay in that ghastly brown hotel by the river with the scary glass lift?" His head snapped round.

"How do *you* know that hotel?"

"I told you: I worked here during the war."

"And you came to *Zenica*?" His hostility was turning to bewilderment.

"I said I covered the whole area."

"I lived in that hotel for months…!" he said.

Our wine arrived. I drank my glass with relief.

"Shall we order?" said Amy.

I looked back at the menu. "I don't know what any of these things are."

"You *don't*?" said Amy.

"No."

"But they have this food everywhere…"

I shrugged. "There wasn't much food here in the war."

Zach said, "The lamb's always good… Did you ever go to that place on the Jablanica road? By the lake?"

"Oh yes…"

Amy broke in: "Oh my God, did you see that thing in *Oslobodjenje* this morning?"

"No," I said just as Zach said: "Yes."

"Don't you read *Oslobodjenje*?" said Amy. "You should...."

Oh God. Like I should know Bosnian food and have spent more time in Zenica and not lived in the Holiday Inn and never left you and read *The Bridge over the Drina* in the original and hung out with Bosnian intellectuals instead of just taking you into my own world, and walked into Gorazde and learned Serbo-Croat – sorry, Bosnian – fluently with all the case endings and the irregular verbs, not just picked up enough to have pidgin conversations. And married you when you wanted me to and not moved back to England and lived here all the time and carried water back to our apartment and not stopped being a foreign correspondent and gone to Kosovo and Sierra Leone, and kept in touch with your parents after I had left and not abandoned your mother yesterday to be sad and drunk and alone. I should have married you and let you escape to London...

"What thing in *Oslobodjenje*?" said Fenella.

"They've found an enormous mass grave. It's the biggest one since the war. About 500 people..."

Mass graves are so sad. And they smell. The side of a skull, a wrist, a bit of tartan shirt sticking out of the orange clay; the forensic scientists, in their expensive anoraks, taking notes in the pit, as the rain drizzles down; the locals, in the blue boiler suits, wielding spades, like the seven dwarves. The six-foot bulges of the white plastic bags, numbered in scrawled black marker pen and heaved into a truck. The man with his gnarled hobbit face, picking something up and carefully wiping off the mud before he gave it to me... an ID card he'd found, Hassan something... born in 1963; he had a short beard, dark eyes, and plump cheeks. The card said he had been an engineer. And it's not just mud. I found a tooth in the sole of my boot.

"...near Tuzla..."

"*Tuzla!* But that's Muslim!" I said.

"It's near Zvornik," said Zach; the scorn in his voice had gone. "They're surprisingly close… just over the old frontline."

"I can't imagine Tuzla being close to anywhere."

Zach was with the UN, Amy said, now, based in Mogadishu.

"He's really important."

He blushed. "Not at the moment. I'm being a bum."

"Not a bum! He's doing a PhD on conflict and post-conflict economics," she said.

I swallowed: that's why I felt afraid. All the men in this restaurant were fat. Only gangsters were fat in the war.

"You could do a lot worse than ask a few people here tonight," I said.

"Why do you think I came back?" he said.

"Do you think there are people who were involved in the black market here tonight?" Amy sounded shocked.

"Yes," said Zach and I together, and then we both laughed.

Dinner turned out quite jolly after that. Zach said he'd take me on a guided tour of what he tactfully described as "Men who'd done *rather* well out of the war…" Black-market war profiteers – "Like the Beverly Hills homes of the stars – the guy who ran the tunnel. He's got some pad. And have you seen…" he named a senior Bosnian politician who we'd got to know quite well… "He lives in a fucking palace."

"Oh dear," I said.

As Amy said, "He's not in politics any more."

"He doesn't *need* to be," said Zach. "He can afford to retire." He smiled at me: "Shall we get another bottle?"

It was at the end of my rendition of General Mladic singing "Twenty-four hours from Tuzla", that Fenella said: "I think you've got a fan."

I turned and the hairs stirred again on my neck. A man by the fireplace was staring at me. He was not fat exactly, but a big man who'd got bigger. There was a brass-blonde beside him, in a black shiny top like Didi's, with gold chains round her neck and deep bags beneath her eyes. He smiled at me, then leant over to the man opposite, who turned round to stare at me as well. I started to look away, but something snagged at my mind. I looked back. I knew him. I didn't know who he was but if I had to place the instinct, I would say I had liked him.

"That's Franjo," said Amy; she sounded impressed.

"Franjo…?" I looked at him again.

"It's his restaurant," she said.

He gave me another slight smile, surprisingly shy for a man of his bulk. The blonde smiled too and gave a tiny lift of her hand. Above their heads were a Kalashnikov crossed with another sort of rifle, and over the fireplace, a large plaque, with some kind of pistol, a regimental badge, and a couple of photos tucked into its edge, of men in uniform grinning and holding guns. On the plaque was written in poker work *Légion Étranger*. Francuski Dom… of course.

I said: "He's a Croat…"

"Franjo's Sarajevan…" said Amy.

"He may be Sarajevan but he's Bosnian Croat. He was in the French Foreign Legion and he was based in Sarajevo during the war."

"How do you know?"

"I recognise him. He was the French general's interpreter. Excuse me."

He stood up as I approached; gave a bashful smile and held out his hand. I remember him, from press conferences, checkpoints, various parties; that night in Jez, when his mate had gone ballistic, he'd been helping the waitresses hand round a tray of candles; the first night I'd been out with Hal… I'd hardly thought of Hal for days.

"*It's Franjo, isn't it? You worked for General Nissent?*"

"*Yes,*" his fingers gripped mine. "*You were journaliste.*"

We smiled at each other. Neither of us spoke. Then we both opened our mouths. I got in first: "So, *how are you?*"

"*Can't complain...*"

"*This is your restaurant? It's great...*"

"*Thanks,*" he gave one of those shrugs of pleased self-deprecation. "*So, are you here for work? Is something happening?*" His gaze was a question of complicit excitement.

"*No...*" I laughed at myself, "*I'm on holiday...*"

He laughed too. "*Looking up your old war buddies?*" He used *drug*, the Serbo-Croat for comrade.

"*The ones that are left... everybody's gone...*"

"*That is the story of Sarajevo,*" the woman gave me a little smile. "*You are well?*" She asked as if she desperately wished me to be...

"*You remember Tanja... my wife?*" She did look familiar...

"*From Jez...*" she said, and smiled at me.

"*Of course!*" The waitress with the tray. "*Hello. How lovely!... How are you?*" I wrung her hand. She clung back. Neither of us spoke. We smiled at each other. It was a relief when Franjo said: "*How long are you here for?*"

I don't know myself. How could I tell him? "*If there is anything I can do.*" He got out a card. It said Franjo Ivanovic, the restaurant, and a mobile. "*I mean it. Really...*"

"*Thanks,*" I said, and got out one of mine. "*How's...*" What was the name of his psycho friend, the other bodyguard... "*Vince, how's Vince?*" I asked.

Franjo gave a grin. "*Vince's fine. You just missed him. He was over here the other day.*"

Well, I'm not sorry I missed Vince. I handed him my card. He read it out: "Molly Taylor," and the name of my magazine. His smile started to ebb. He stared down at the card and then back up at me. I waited for him to speak. When he didn't, I said:

"*I used to work for the* Herald..."

The silence went on. Tanja looked up at him surprised but he just stared at the card. Worry flitted across her face. She turned back to me. I could see whatever we three had been feeling together bleed away.

"*I'd better...*" I looked back at my table; Amy and the others were watching us.

"*Yes. Yes.*" Franjo raised his eyes to mine. The smile returned but now it seemed automatic and his eyes, which had been anxious, now went blank, like eyes I had known in the war.

"*Good luck finding your old friends,*" Tanja fluttered; she cast an anxious glance at her husband.

"*It's not so easy,*" I said. "*Everything's changed.*"

The uncertainty vanished.

"*Oh yes,*" she said emptily, and her hand went to the gold chains at her neck. "*The war changed everything.*"

Mujo was fishing and he caught a golden fish. The fish said to him: "I am a magic fish. Let me go and I will grant you three wishes."

Mujo said, "No way, we are going straight to the goldsmith."

VII

This morning I went for another walk. I walked past the library, past the cathedral, past the bridge where Gavrilo Princip stood to assassinate Archduke Franz Ferdinand. Apparently he was so scared he peed while he was taking aim.

I carried on walking deep into my war. I walked along the river, with the hills rearing to my left, past the Presidency, past the fat cream mosque, over the wide crossroads, where so many people died. I walked down Sniper Alley, where I could never even have driven, except in an armoured car, past the apartment blocks, fresh glass gleaming from their shrapnel-scarred walls. All the time, I kept sneaking looks sideways to where the Serbs had been. Past the grey spiky church – I couldn't remember if it was Catholic or Orthodox, but I do know that a sniper shot someone on its steps. Past the UNIS towers; from this side of the street, the workers bustling through its shiny office doors looked surreal beneath the top ten storeys, still blackened skeletons with their shattered glass.

The Holiday Inn sat over the open patch of grass, as silly as it always looked; the spaceship, you called it. I stopped at the edge of the grass. There was a new glass café bulging out, with tables and chairs dotted outside. Our old door didn't seem to exist any more. They'd be using the front door, by the fountain, round the other side. A waiter walked out with a tray of coffee cups. Why don't I do that? Why don't I just go and have coffee?

I didn't recognise any of the café at all. I wasn't sure if this was because it was a new addition or whether it was a restoration of something so destroyed that it had faded from memory by the time I arrived, but whatever it was, it was rather a relief.

I ordered a cappuccino and stared up at the hills. I felt silly that it was making me feel so dramatic and weird. But it was. I wasn't making it up. I drank my coffee, still not very nice, but nowhere near as vile as it used to be. Then I got up and walked down a marble corridor, past a business centre and some souvenir shops, until the roof soared away and I was in the atrium once more.

It was as gloomy as it had ever been. Even in peacetime, it wasn't properly lit and the dust-draped chandelier was dark at noon. I stood stock still, staring up into the shadows. But the plastic sheeting had gone from the plate-glass wall beyond, and the ice-queen shards no longer trembled in their frames. The fountain chortled away outside.

I was halfway up the first flight of stairs before I realised the lift must work. I climbed. I was knackered; I'm much less fit now than I was in the war; wearing that flak jacket was like living in my own gym.

I came out onto the gallery and walked towards the banisters. I could feel you standing beside me, holding my hand. We hung together staring down into the world beneath our feet, the woolly hats passing by below: the cameramen, the reporters, gathering to leave for the briefing, the odd person trying desperately to check out, Muffy by the bar, surrounded by her lovelorn court of photographers. I wouldn't even have jumped if Phil had thumped up the stairs.

I walked round to room 309. The door was shut. I heard a sound from inside. For a moment I was tempted to knock, to try and explain to whoever answered why I was there; but I didn't. It was probably just the maid, but even if it had been, I don't think I could have explained.

I turned and hung over the rail again, staring down. My head was hurting, like a huge boil on my brain. If I pressed any more, something might spew out… what? Pus? Memories? You? A great terrible craving for a war which had killed hundreds of thousands and ended five years ago?

I swallowed. I understood completely how people can believe in ghosts. I had brought them with me and they were all in my head.

I went downstairs. I walked, of course. I couldn't have taken the lift.

I ordered a cup of coffee at the horseshoe bar. The waiter was tall, and dark, with skin the grey of the atrium's light, and sorrowful eyes: he looked slightly familiar, as everybody did.

"*Did you work here in the war?*" I asked, as he gave me my coffee.

"*Yes.*"

"*I was here too. I was a journalist here.*"

He met my eyes, then shook his head: "*I am sorry I don't remember.*"

I felt as if he'd put up a "Private No Entry" sign.

I took my coffee over to one of the mushroom seats and stared at the ammunition factory across the square. They'd put the roof back on that as well.

"*Excuse me…*" I turned round. "*You were here in the war?*"

It was another waiter; he was tall and dark like the last. He looked at me nervously.

"*Yes,*" I said, equally nervous back.

"*I remember.*" We gazed at each other and gave a shy smile. He did look familiar. I think he really did. There was a pause, then he asked me how I was, so I said fine, and I asked him and he said fine too. Then we smiled rather intensely, for a few seconds, until another customer called him over.

"*Sorry,*" he gave an awkward smile. "*I must go.*" Suddenly I felt bereft. Then I realised it was actually a relief. All my post-war encounters were this banal. We had nothing else to say. I was here in the war. So were you. We probably never even had a conversation before. I was one of the loud journalists who laughed.

I loved his war and he probably hated me and it. But I was just terribly glad he wasn't dead.

When I asked for the bill it was he who hurried back. This time he was smiling as he handed me the slip. "*You are back in Sarajevo?*"

"*Just for a bit.*"

"*For work?*"

"*No. For a holiday.*"

He laughed. "*You are staying here?*"

I laughed back. "*No. I can't afford to if I am paying myself.*"

"*Very expensive now.*"

"*More expensive than in the war.*"

"*Of course. We have water now.*" He giggled at me. I giggled back.

"*Maybe see you again.*"

We both smiled. "*I hope so.*" I held out my hand. He shook it, then walked back to the bar. I realised I did not know his name and he didn't know mine. I might never see him again but it didn't really matter. But I also realised he didn't hate me at all.

I could have gone the back way, the way we always went. But I didn't. I had had enough of the past. I walked across Sniper Alley, narrowly avoiding being run over, and then down towards the river. The tears were filling my eyes again. I couldn't believe the world was all still there. Except the people had gone. It was like visiting an empty stage, or a dream I sometimes have, when I go back to school and everyone's strange. I was so achingly happy there, with you. I brushed a tear away and snapped my dark glasses back down over my face to hide my tears.

What am I going to do? It's been over a day since I saw your mother. What on earth am I going to do? What am I doing here, if I'm not doing that? What was I ever doing here at all? Why did I come?

Muffy had her theory that all foreign correspondents came from broken homes. We'd swapped stories, one long hot car journey, hers of martinis being hurled across Philadelphia swimming pools, and a mother so divorced she could hardly remember her own surname;

Juan, the Reuters photographer, who was actually American, but whose father had fallen in love with Hemingway and left his family to write poetry in Spain; then we'd gone on to continue the conversation at dinner: Valida's poor Henri, from some long-abandoned Francophone colony, who betrayed her for the rotting corpses of Rwanda; the white Kenyan, who got so homesick he had to go back to Mogadishu; the stringer, whose divorced father had made him live out of a car; my dead mother, and my father in embassies all over the world. Was it nothing to do with seeing all those refugees?

But Phil's home wasn't broken; his father had just been poor. And Robert's parents were still together and running the Slavonic Studies department at somewhere like Keele. So that wasn't the reason they ended up here.

Then there was Ray, the mad ex-US marine, who said he was a journalist but never filed a story, and ended up spending his war with your long-haired friend in his trench.

Oh God. Please don't let me end up like Ray.

There's no-one here for me any more. They're all in East Timor – that was on the news today, at least I think it was East Timor, but my German's not very good. And everyone who's not somewhere else is dead.

I turned and started walking back into town. I was on a funny little street; Turkish cottages, tiny garages, and yards full of nettles. I'd never been here before. It must have been the heart of the Bosnian frontline. Maybe the nettles were still mined.

I carried on walking; past the Presidency again, the mosque, down a side street, into a little cement square. There was a bookshop, with English titles in the window, and a café with tables outside, where young men were holding forth earnestly to nodding girls with aubergine-coloured hair.

I walked on. Three streets down, to my left, a ruined building stood. You could tell it had once been a lovely thing, one of those palaces the Austrians built in the centre of town. But its façade was pitted, its windows still boarded up, and nobody had bothered to plug the shell holes with cement. Then I saw the sign, Hotel Europa. The doors were boarded and chained with a double padlock.

It had been bitter cold and still, and the woodsmoke had hung on the air, and the snipers hardly seemed to breathe on the mountains around. Every window of the hotel had been boarded over; out of each frame, between the bubble wrap, poked the silver chimney of a UNHCR stove.

We'd sat in the car in the street outside. "We'd come here every Sunday for cakes and coffee," you'd said. Then you'd taken my hand and led me through the boarded-glass doors, the curved art deco bronze handle twisted by war. "Let's pretend it's like the old days," you'd said.

"We'd take our coats off, and hand them to one girl, behind mahogany counter. And she'd hang them up, on one long metal rack, with lots of other fur coats, and give us brass tag, and my mother would check her reflection, in huge, gold mirror, and we'd walk through into dining room." You pulled me through.

"It smelled of coffee and chocolate cake. They were on trolley over there, just under window, and there were little round tables with white cloths, and chairs were blue velvet. Walls were panelled, with mahogany and blue silk and blue velvet curtains hung at windows. We could see Mount Jahorina covered in snow. And there was string quartet, who played Austrian waltzes, but you could hardly hear them, because of voices. All our friends would be here, and everyone would be talking. All Sarajevo came to Hotel Europa on Sundays."

You had stopped. It wasn't just the cakes and the band and the friends that were no more. The velvet curtains had gone and the blue silk; where the panelling had been, only brick remained. The doors had gone, and so had the mahogany counter, and you could see straight into the lobby through the skeleton of the old wall, and light poked through the beams from the floors above: the plaster, along with all the wood, the cloth, with everything else, had been taken for warmth or food. The room was gutted, Jahorina boarded out of sight and where once the air had been thick with coffee and chocolate, now it was pee and stale sweat and acrid smoke at the throat. In the icy darkness, a floor full of women and children, with the flowered headscarves of the hills, stared up at us from their piles of rags.

What happened to them all? The women and children. They can't have just gone home. They all came from those eastern Bosnian villages long lost now to greater Serb-dom: Rogatica, Foca, Visegrad. Are they still here? The planks were still on the windows but the stove pipes had gone. There's no-one here now; there couldn't be.

I tried to peer in, leant against the boarded windows, straining through the cracks, but I could make nothing out. I put my ear to the plank, but the only rustling I heard was of rats, or cardboard being buffeted by the breeze.

Amir. Oh Amir. Oh God. What am I going to do? Oh God, I wish it was that day again. I wish we could be back in the war. I could be that girl again, the one who fell in love with you, whose life was an adventure full of hope. At least that girl thought that things had to get better.

I tried to pull myself together but I couldn't. So I just gave up. Great snotty blubbery tears coursed down my cheeks. My face convulsed with the kind of sobs that dark glasses can't begin to hide. I walked into a courtyard and sat on a lump of concrete and wailed against the wall, rocking to and fro, my hands covering my face, occasionally wiping snot away; wailing for my past and for a future I can't imagine, for you, and for her, for the girl who'd loved you. I don't know what to do: I don't know how to find out how you died. I don't even know if I should try. What will become of me? Will I be stuck, sad and mad like this, till the day I die?

I felt a tap on my shoulder and I looked up. A woman was holding a glass of water out to me. She had a face like those women I've seen in the street: scarred with misery.

"Are you all right?"

"*Oh, I'm fine. Really, I'm fine.*" But my shoulders were still heaving and I had to wipe my face.

"*Thank you.*" I drank the glass of water, the confines of normality pushing me back into shape.

"*You're foreign.*"

"*Yes. I'm from England.*"

"*I heard you. I live here.*" She pointed to a window on the ground floor.

"*I'm sorry.*"

"*Don't be sorry.*"

There was a pause, and then she said: "*Would you like a cup of coffee?*"

A cup of coffee with a stranger is probably what I need right now. She asks me in. I watch the ritual, the little jug on the stove, the grounds spooned in: "*How come you speak Bosnian?*"

"*I'm a journalist. I was here during the war.*" I pause, then I say: "*This is my first time back.*"

"*The war… Oh,*" she sighs, and passes a hand across her face. "*The war was terrible.*"

"*Yes.*" I could hardly tell her I was crying because I wished I was back there.

Then she told me her story and I was doubly ashamed. She had sent her children out at the start of the war, when she thought it wouldn't last. They'd gone to a cousin in Zagreb. Halfway through the war, the cousin had emigrated to Canada and her children had gone too. Her brother, who had fought in the army, had been killed by a shell, on his day off, in the street. It was fairly normal, as war stories go. Her parents had survived but had never been the same. Her father had a heart attack two years after the war. Her old mother now lived in what was the children's room. Last year her husband died of a heart attack too. Heart attacks and cancer, she said, lighting up a cigarette, were killing everybody now. She'd worked for an insurance company before the war, but she couldn't get work, and her pension was only 170KM a month; the only people with money were criminals or those who'd been refugees in Germany in the war.

"*The war was terrible,*" she said, with a sad smile. "*But in the war, at least we were all the same.*"

I thanked her for the coffee and went out into the street. You spoilt cow, I screamed at myself. How can you weep because this terrible war is over? How can you weep because no-one will help you find out what happened to the man you loved when he has been dead for five years and he left you anyway and what difference will it make to anyone if you never find out. And why are you so vile that all you want to do is leave this woman as soon as possible, before she brings her mother out and you get stuck here all day, having other people's misery being poured like treacle into your brain?

I wandered back to Michele's, the café on Feradiya, for another cup of coffee. I don't drink coffee like this in the UK. I live on herbal tea. Maybe this is partly why I am feeling so strange. I drank my coffee and then I thought of you. Then slowly, I knew what I had to do.

I had to stay. I had to find out. If I run away, I will only have to come back. Maria may not care, but then Maria is definitely not herself at the moment. As for Valida, she did not have your or my best interests at heart. Why should she? Aida's her sister. I have to do this for you. But also for me. For my peace of mind.

But where would I start, if no-one would help me? Where could I go? I still didn't know how you actually died.

Then I remembered Osman. Phil called him the Tallyman. He saw everyone who died and wrote their names down in his Book of the Dead.

TWO PENSIONERS were sitting in the park, watching pretty girls walking past in mini skirts.

"What's going on?" said the first pensioner.

"This is the sexual revolution," said the other.

"Typical. We're always having revolutions in Bosnia and we never have any weapons."

VIII

I walked past the eternal flame, in its concrete doughnut wreath, at the end of Marshal Tito Street. The inscriptions were still to the heroes of Yugoslavia: 1941–45. There wasn't anything about the siege. I walked past the old department store, still sealed off by mine tape, in its weed-strewn piazza where so many people were shot. The same two old men were still sitting on their benches, as yesterday, as I turned to walk up to the hospital. I shot a glance up to where your street was, but carried on up the hill.

I was worried for a moment that I would not recognise the mortuary; I was beginning to learn that what you carry in your memory is not necessarily true. But it was just the same: the white stucco house, below the hospital, built by the Austrians in the shade of a tree; the chipped flowers around the door, the graveyard spilling out through the football stadium below.

I never saw your face that day; Valida said there was no point. Just your grey-green toe poking out of the sheet. Why would I want to see your face, your lovely face, a mess of splintered flesh and bone? I'd seen too many shot faces in the war.

I never saw your face… for a moment my breath caught. Was that what this was about? Maybe you hadn't died at all. But… no… that couldn't be right. Maria was a woman who knew her only son was dead.

There was no answer when I knocked at the mortuary door. I

tried the handle, but the double doors were locked. I waited outside, not knowing quite what to do – Osman had always been in during the war. He even used to sleep here most of the time.

A van pulled up round the side, black with gold writing; it would have been recognisable as an undertaker's van anywhere. Two men got out, with blue overalls and the gnarled faces of the hills, and opened a pair of ecclesiastically vast wooden doors, as though the architects had been all too aware that this was one step on the road to eternity; inside the mortuary was marble, in cool grey light. On the fluted stone table on which I'd last seen you, another body lay humped beneath its sheet.

"*Excuse me.*" The men turned. "*Is Osman Muhovic here?*"

"*No.*" said one. Oh no… Maybe he had gone back to being the driver for the Sarajevo football team; that's what Phil said he'd done before the war. That he'd been a grave-digger on the side, and when the war started the Serb mortuary director fled. Osman, the grave-digger, was forced to step in. Osman said that nobody else wanted the job. Or maybe he'd just gone… whoever was able to seemed to have got out, and he must have made good contacts in the war. Maybe he was living in Canada or Australia now.

"*Does he still work here?*"

"*He's left.*" They glanced at each other and shrugged. Both his sons had both been killed. What would keep him here?

I almost didn't hear the man say: "*He should be back at two.*"

I almost skipped out of the gates and doubled back down along the street. Suddenly I was starving. I looked up at the men, to smile and wave, but one was grinding out his cigarette and the other had started walking back into the mortuary where their next cargo lay.

He was late, of course, because this is the Balkans, but it was a beautiful afternoon. There was a market below the mortuary, beneath the old flyover, above the little park where the trees had come back. It hadn't been there in the war, of course. I bought a grilled chicken breast – they never had those in the war – with onions, in flat

Muslim bread – and sat on the mortuary steps, staring down at the view: an old woman toiling from the market to the tower blocks which crawled up the opposite side of the hill, cars curling round the dual carriageway up from the valley floor, the high walls of the American Embassy, where the British general's Residency used to be, and a young man walking through the football stadium where the war graves lay, its yellow markers now replaced, like yours, with ranks of white stone. The call of the muezzin drifted over the town; I don't remember the muezzin in the war.

A car drew up, and a door banged. I packed up my lunch, and went back to the steps.

The door was open and inside was the same smell. Not the reek of high summer during the war; just that sweet echo of death that lurked in the nostrils, on cold days, when people didn't rot too much.

There was a man at Osman's desk. Perhaps it was him. He looked like the plumper brother of the man I used to know: familiar but different, like a TV celebrity in the flesh. The hair had gone grey, but the cheekbones and the deep-set eyes were still there.

"*Gospodin Muhovic?*" I said.

"*Da.*"

"*Osman Muhovic?*" Just in case it was his brother.

"*Da.*" He turned: it was him. He was just... different. Less miserable, and much less thin. Perhaps he looked normal.

"*It's Molly Taylor.*"

Maybe I looked different. He obviously had to think. But then I'd left, five years ago, with all the other journalists.

"*The English journalist. From the* Herald. *Do you remember me?*"

Then he beamed: "*Of course!*" He pumped my hand, pressing it, and clapped my back. As though he could not grin wide enough to show his pleasure that he and I had survived.

"*Come in, sit down!*"

There was still a folded blanket on his sofa, as there had always been, but I can't imagine he had to sleep here now. The planks had gone from the windows. Suddenly I felt as if you were with me too. I glanced at the sofa as though you might suddenly appear, and the cushion would be all dented and bulging round your ghostly backside.

"I thought you might not be here. I thought perhaps you go back to your old job with the football team…"

"This is my job. It became my job in the war. Now I take my grandchildren to watch football instead."

He offered me coffee, then pulled out his wallet, and extracted two photographs. *"The son of my son,"* he said, and showed me a dark little boy. The other photograph showed a child, nearly the same age, but the print was wrinkled with years of love. *"He was born five months after his father was killed. Look. They are exactly the same."*

I was glad that the coffee arrived just then. I took a sip – it was espresso. Not the gritty little cups he served in the war.

"My other son is married."

But *both* your sons were dead, I thought.

"He has a little boy and a girl." I had got it wrong for all those years but I was glad he still had one son who was alive.

He was talking about his home, a cottage, up on the old frontline. "*We went back to it; in the war we lived here. It was too dangerous to live there… we got a loan to buy sheep. Now we have lots of sheep and cows,*" he was smiling. I never saw him smile, in the war. All those bodies, every day, must have taken their toll. All the grief. How awful to have to wade every day through other people's fresh grief.

"I told my wife, you don't have to do this, run the farm. We don't need the money. But she says she likes to work…" His smile ebbed. *"It stops her thinking about our son."*

Then he asked about me, so I told him a little about my job – a magazine, different kind of work, and he asked if I were married, and I said, *"No,"* and he said, *"Maybe one day."* I said, *"I hope so."*

Then there was a silence, when he waited for me to tell him why I was here. I felt shy for a moment; as if, now that I had finally found someone who could help me, I could not start. I was worried he would react the same way as Maria and Robert.

"*Do you remember my boyfriend – my interpreter – Amir Hadzibegovic?*" I said. "*He died in… in 1994.*"

"*I remember you coming in. I remember everyone. And the ones I don't are written down in my book.*" He leant over to the side of his desk, and pulled it out. The same marbled cover; the same label with the dates. It lay between us but neither of us moved. For a moment Valida was here, and I had just heard Phil walk in, and Maria was sobbing into her hands on the sofa. I wiped a tear away with my hand. I seemed to spend my whole time here in tears.

"*Your book, does it say how people died?*"

Osman shook his head.

"*No, their name, and when, and where.*"

I was so convinced, I remembered, that I almost squawked: "Are you sure?"

"*Oh yes.*"

"*But I remember you once showing me a group, all together. You said they had been killed by the same shell.*" It had been the first time I'd met him, that first day with Phil, an hour or so before I met you… "*You knew it had been a shell…*"

"*That's because they all died at the same time, in the same place. Had to be a shell – besides, I saw their bodies,*" he said. "*I had a group of Chetniks once, brought in here. Dead Chetniks. They'd been killed by a shell. One of them was Mladic's son-in-law. He had a nickname – the Pixie. People came to see them; to see if they were really dead. I was so angry. I said: you never bother to come and see our people.*"

But you are telling me about him, not about your people, I thought, because he was remarkable, and death for your people by then was not. "*Do you remember the date?*" he asked.

I could still smell the heater, feel the scrape of Valida's coat on my cheek: "*October 27th.*"

He opened his book and started flicking through, black loopy writing in neat double columns. I could only see names, but he knew their faces: blank eyes, clammy, blood-drained skin, shards of bone, edged in crimson and yellow fat, the green-grey bruises of violent death.

"Hadzibegovic, Amir, 30, here we are. Sniper Alley. The UN brought him in. But you're wrong. It was October 28th."

"No. It was the 27th. I saw him that night. Just before…"

"28th… my book is never wrong." He peered at the page. I couldn't be bothered to argue. It was the next day that they brought you in, after all.

"Can you remember how he died?" Osman shrugged and stared at the page again. *"From the place I would say he was killed by a sniper."*

I looked at your name in the fading black ink. There was nothing else. The book lay open on the table. Neither of us wanted to close it even though it could give us nothing more. I took a sip of my coffee. "*Osman…*" suddenly with Osman, saying this wasn't hard. Death wasn't embarrassing to him.

"When Amir died, did you ever think there was something… strange?"

"Strange… what do you mean?"

I took a deep breath, because I didn't want to sound like a nut. Then I said: "*I met someone the other day who told me that Amir wasn't shot by a sniper.*" There was no suspicion in his face; he looked unsurprised. *"That someone just shot him…"*

"Maybe. I don't know…" It did not interest him at all.

"But that means he must have been murdered!"

He shrugged: *"In one way everyone who died in the war was murdered."* He looked down at the picture of his son.

"I mean, the people who were killed by snipers, by shells, yes, obviously they too did not die natural deaths, but they were war deaths, weren't they? Deaths that became normal in the war. But Amir, they say he wasn't killed like that. They thought he'd been shot at close range."

"And all the others," said Osman, looking up from his photograph.

"What?" I said.

"The others. They were murdered too."

"What others?"

"It wasn't just the sniping and the grenades that killed people. I had people in here, every day, dead of cold, of hunger, of illnesses that would not have killed them in peace. I had a lot more suicides during the war. In a normal year, I would have, say one thousand people in here. In the first year of the war, I had ten thousand.

"They try in the Hague but only for… extraordinary… crimes. Sniping, shelling, they are supposed to be ordinary in war. My son's death was supposed to be ordinary."

Osman was no longer looking at me. He was staring at the two photographs still on his desk.

I left it for ten seconds or so before I said: *"If there was something odd about his death, wouldn't you have known?"*

"No." He looked up as he spoke, but that was just politeness.

"Surely the police would have asked you questions?"

"No."

"Do you know if there was any kind of investigation? Any trial?"

"No."

So what *did* he know? As if he heard me he went on: *"All I do is get the bodies ready for their families to bury."*

Someone must have known because someone had told Robert and Valida. My fingernails had been digging in my palms. And Maria, she had told me to leave things alone. And Hal. I hadn't made this up.

"So who would know? Who would know how *he died?"* Who else *was* there? Osman was the Lord of the Dead of Sarajevo.

"Dr Radic of course," Osman said in an obvious voice.

"Who?" My hands uncurled.

"Radic."

"Who's he?" I had literally never heard of him.

"He does the autopsies. He did all the autopsies during the war." How on earth could I not have heard of him?

"Would he then, this Dr... Radic... if there had been something... strange, would he have mentioned something to you?"

Osman gave the corpse-joke laugh. *"Oh yes, a normal person would have said something to me. But not Radic..."*

"What?"

"Dr Radic only talks to the dead."

"Eh?" I thought I'd got my Serbo-Croat, sorry Bosnian, in a muddle, when Osman went on:

"At the start of the war we had an argument. Dr Radic did not want journalists to come to the mortuary," he waved a hand round his kingdom; so that's why I never heard of Radic before. *"I told him, I'm boss, I want journalists here. I want them to take pictures. And after that he hardly spoke to me again."*

Well, everyone went a little strange in the war. And Radic – from the sound of his name, I'd say Dr Radic was probably a Serb, and for a Serb to stay in Sarajevo, that was a tough and brave call. I thought I might cut Dr Radic some slack. *"Do you know where he is? Do you think I could see him?"*

"Try. He still works here. He's up at the university at the moment. But we still don't talk to each other."

I thought that Radic wouldn't talk to me but when I rang, and explained what I wanted from him, he said: *"Of course, come now if you like."* He hadn't even asked me my name.

I was halfway up the hill to the university before I understood: I was going to re-introduce him to an old friend from the war.

Mujo was ill and went to the doctor. "You will live for another year," the doctor said.

"But on what, my dear doctor?" Mujo replied.

IX

Radic looked more like Father Christmas than a man who spent his life with the dead. His office was light, and modern, with potted plants and a bank of computers, paper clips and plastic pots full of multi-coloured pens. He welcomed me and offered me coffee. It was three o'clock and my sixth cup of the day.

On one wall were rows of shelves, piled high with multi-coloured marbled files. Another was glass from the waist up – possibly even pre-war glass, since it faced away from the frontline into a garden. Through it, the shins of his students walked by: the Medical Faculty, like so much of Sarajevo, was carved into the side of a hill.

He pulled out a tatty pack of Drina cigarettes and offered me one. I turned it down and pulled out my Silk Cut.

"Silk Cut," he said. "I never seen these."

"*They don't sell them here. They are far too mild.*"

"No, let us speak English. Good practice for me. So how can I help?" There was no embarrassment, no awkward sympathy; we'd never even met before, so there was no tear-swelling, overwhelming surge of relief.

"I have a friend who was killed in the war," I said. "I want to know how he died."

Radic waved a hand like a showman lining up his girls. "I have everyone here. Whoever you want. I am just putting all war onto computer."

He turned to the keyboard.

"Look at this: 2,200 post mortems, 715 exhumations, 183 external examinations…this is just on computer. I have done 18,000 autopsies in my life… So your friend, what was his name? When did he die?"

"Hadzibegovic Amir. He died on 27th October 1994."

Hadzibegovic, Hadzibegovic, ah… No, Hadzibegovic Selma. February 1993. See look, she was killed by a shell." He clicked on her file and a photograph came up. I wish I could say that I looked away in horror, but I couldn't stop staring at the orange bruises on her skin and the pulpy stumps where her legs had been.

"He was called Amir." I sounded faint.

"So not Selma…" Maybe she was a cousin… If she had been a close relative, I am sure you would have said.

"Hadzibegovic… Hadzibegovic… No. No. He is not here."

"But you said you had everybody!"

"Oh, yes, I have. Keep calm. But not everybody on computer." He walked over to the files and trailed his finger along their spines.

"You said 1994?"

"That's right. October. 27th, no, 28th…"

He pulled out a green and black marbled folder, and started flicking through its yellowing pages. His cigarette burnt unnoticed in its ashtray. I remembered the cheap, thin paper from the war. The words were scrawled in faint biro, or typed in faded ribbon, both sides of every sheet of paper, nothing left to waste. In the middle of each page was a little drawing, a head, a leg, a torso; a star mark for the wound, and the whole… limb, body part, whatever… at the centre of a web of lines.

"August, September, October… Here we are." He laid it in front of me and continued to talk but I wasn't listening; I was staring at your head. Back, face on and profile, each in its biro basket, with tiny figures written down the side.

It wasn't as bad as the photographs on the computer. It could have been any young man's head. At the nape of your neck, Radic had drawn a star mark for the wound. Where your hair used to curl. It must have been caught up in the wound.

On profile, a diagonal line ran straight through your brain, from the nape of your neck, to the centre of your forehead; tiny rows of numbers flanked your skull.

Across your face, horizontal and vertical lines intersected just above your brows, and more tiny figures were written by the side of your ear.

There was a click. I looked up to see Radic opening the locks on an old leather bag. Inside, silver prods and spikes, and filigree saws were laid out in rows on purple velvet trays. He pulled out a right-angled ruler. One end was chipped, and heavily stained. He poked the end of it into your brain.

"The bullet went in at base of skull and travelled up through brain, to here…" jab into your forehead, "where bullet ended its journey."

"It stopped in his head?"

"Yes."

"So his face would have looked OK?" It was all I could think of to say.

"Why not? You must understand, with this kind of bullet…" He pointed to a steamed pudding-shaped bullet drawn on a graph. "I don't how you call in your language. We say… *zatupljeno.*" It meant nothing to me. Dr Radic was looking at me hopefully but I don't know what steamed pudding-shaped bullets are called in my language either. He sighed, "Makes very big hole in brain. Look," the ruler plonked again on the broad front. "It goes flat," he put his fingers in the shape of a ten pence piece. "All way through. So, it stops soon. If had been normal bullet," he drew a pointy bullet shape on a yellow post-it note, "then hole is much smaller. And bullet comes out other side." He put the biro where the two lines crossed just above your eyebrows.

I was feeling a little sick. "I thought rifle bullets went through anything…" Walls, I'd been told. For hundreds of yards. You thought you were safe inside but you weren't.

"Rifle? This was not rifle! How is possible? Look at where is entry wound!" the ruler pushed into the nape of your neck. "To be shot here, like this, with rifle, man must be lying face down on the ground. This man was found sitting in car. Look, here, bullet fired at… *apsolutno blizu*… I don't know how you say…" He put two fingers up to his skull.

"Point blank?" That I could guess.

"Yes! Is .22 bullet fired at point blank. The powder disperses, further gun is from wound."

"So what was it then?"

"Pistol, of course! I tell you as I told police." Police? "He was in his car. Somebody in back seat put gun against his head and pulled the trigger. This is like execution… Very professionally done."

"So, he wasn't killed by the Serbs?" Was all I could say. Even though of course I thought Radic was Serb.

"No! I don't think. Not unless they sneak across the Miljacka…" He wriggled a sneaky little mime.

"Were there lots of… executions like this in Sarajevo then?"

"No… no, very, very rare. I only remember one other, in Sarajevo that was like some kind of criminal type." A criminal type. I sat there so long Radic turned back to his computer.

"Did you talk to the police?" He nearly jumped when I spoke.

"Of course! I had to talk to the police."

"Why?"

"They come all times when someone is shot."

"What, *every* time anyone was shot? In the war?" And as I said that I remembered you telling me that the police treated every death in the war as murder.

"Peace, war. Is same. Judge, police inspector, you know, from criminal police. And technical man to take the photographs."

I waited for nearly twenty seconds before I said: "So, did they catch the killer?"

"What?" He was back on his computer, and he turned and looked blank.

"Was there a trial?"

He shrugged, "No, I think no."

"Don't you *know*?"

He checked his notes. "No. I think no. I never had to give evidence."

"Did they *try* to catch someone?"

"How do I know?" He shrugged again. "It's not my job to know about investigations."

"Well, didn't they come and ask you more questions?"

He looked down at his notes once more, and said, "No. I don't think so."

I thanked him for his time, and he smiled again.

"My pleasure. I always love to talk about these things."

It was then that I thought of something else.

"Is it true," I asked, "that if you have the bullet you can identify which gun it was fired from?"

"Of course!" he said, half amazed that anyone needed to ask. From the bullet, and from the cartridge, he said.

"No cartridge, whoever killed him must have picked it up. It falls to ground when bullet is fired. I gave the bullet to the police when I extracted it from brain."

"Would they still have it?"

"I think so. Is evidence in murder case." But there must have been a million guns in Sarajevo then.

When I got to the door, I turned. Radic was deep inside some wound on his screen. I had to speak twice before he heard what I said.

"Isn't it terribly dangerous to shoot someone in the head while they are driving? Dr Radic?" He jumped, but after he smiled up at me, he leant over and re-checked his notes.

"Not driving. He was in passenger seat." You never let anyone drive your car.

"I tell you one thing though in which he was lucky," he said, as an afterthought, as I turned back to the door.

"Lucky!" You were dead...

"His last meal was steak, red wine and potatoes," said Radic, as though I had not spoken.

Steak! "Are you *sure*?" There'd been no steak at that party. "When did he *die* then?"

"Between 1 and 4 a.m. Maybe."

It was about 10.30 when the lights had cut, and maybe 10.35 when I pushed you away. At least two and a half hours for you to go and eat steak.

"Not once in all war for four years," I heard Radic say, "did I eat meat."

I knew, now, I absolutely knew, that you hadn't stormed out to your car, after I'd sent you away, and driven down Sniper Alley straight into the sights of your killer. You had gone off and eaten steak with somebody else. And then you had been taken out and shot with a pistol in the back of the head.

It's hard to rearrange your mind, when you've spent so long thinking something wrong. It's like having your back realigned by a chiropractor. You get so used to being wonky that being straight feels strange.

I walked as far as Marshal Tito Street and sat down in the little park looking at the hills. The two old men were on their separate benches again. At my feet, a white turban-top tombstone poked out just above the ground. Maybe the earth would continue to swallow it – in another hundred years, there would be nothing left of it except a slight hardness, like a pimple, beneath the grass, or maybe all the tarmac and drains and officious guardianship of the modern world would freeze its slow descent.

Straight in front of me, as always, were the hills. This was what they had known, Maria and Robert and Valida and the hills; how you had died. It's just that I went away and no-one told me. It hadn't been the Serbs on the hills at all. Whatever I'd thought, whatever Maria said, it couldn't have been my fault either.

It was possible that Dr Radic had lied. But I didn't think so.

He wouldn't see the point. You have to be interested in repercussions to lie and Dr Radic only cared about how the living met their deaths. He didn't care about why, or what came next. But then he hadn't loved you. I had.

How did the golden fish die?

Mujo went fishing and he caught a golden fish. The fish said: "Let me go. I am a magic fish and I will give you three wishes." Mujo said: "C'mon, stop shittin' me." And the fish died from blocked gut.

X

Robert rang me at about four o'clock: was I still around? Phil was in town; could I meet them for dinner?

I saw them in the dusk as I crossed over the river, sitting on the terrace of a wonky little house. Phil, Robert and Valida, and a guy, with meaty shoulders. Phil was pouring himself some more wine as I arrived.

"Have a drink," he said, when he'd finished hugging me; he looked less haggard than in London and the awkwardness of our last few meetings melted away. "Do you know Wayne?" Wayne, who looked, of course, vaguely familiar, was an Australian cameraman. "Robert's just been telling me the story of this restaurant..."

I gazed around. It was one of those old Bosnian houses, drooping wattle and daub, with fretted wood at its eaves, and much fretted wood inside.

"Start again for Molly," Valida smiled as she sipped her glass of water. Robert beamed, got up, and kissed me hello. There was no shadow of the grief of our last conversation.

"When the Austrians were building the library they bought up all the houses that were in the way. This house was over there then," Robert pointed to the ruined crenellations over the water. "All the owners agreed, except the guy who owned this house. However much they offered him, he refused. In the end, he insisted the Austrians move his house on rollers. He rebuilt the entire thing, bang across the river, so he could stare at the library. It's called *Inat Kuca*. It means 'the spite house'."

"Typical Bosnia," said Valida, with pride.

Phil pulled a face when I asked him why he was here; it was the mass grave, the one near Zvornik. He took another drink.

"They pulled the spine of a child out while I was there today," he said.

Valida looked away and Robert picked up her hand.

"Poor little thing," I said.

"So why are *you* here?" Phil asked. "Are you going to do anything on the grave?"

"Definitely not." I looked across at Robert; he met my glance but he didn't speak.

"I'm sort of on holiday," I said. I didn't want to say anything to him now.

Phil opened his mouth but Robert beat him to it. "What shall we eat?" he handed over the menu.

"I think we should get another bottle," said Phil.

"We can't stay late," said Robert. "Valida has college tomorrow."

The dusk sank into night as we ate strange gristly stews, drank rough wine, and called up the ghost; the divorces, the successes, the suicides, the do-you-remembers; slightly constrained by Wayne who didn't, as he'd spent his war in Vitez, in Central Bosnia instead. He needed Zach. They'd have had a good time.

At the end of dinner, we'd moved on to the future. Robert asked Phil about Jerusalem. After five minutes of burble about Palestinians and peace processes, Phil replied with: "And what about here?" grimacing, as though he couldn't bear the answer he was about to hear. Robert looked across at Valida, before he replied: "I think they're fine… People seem to be OK."

I thought of your mother, drunk, her furniture gone; the boys and girls in Michele's, stirring their lives in empty coffee cups; that woman who'd brought me coffee this morning by the empty Europa Hotel; almost everyone I knew had left.

"Lots of people don't seem to have jobs," I said. "And Amir's mother…"

"I think we ought to go," said Robert, shooting a glance at Valida; "Valida's got an essay crisis. Let's get the bill," he stood up.

"Forget the bill," said Phil. "This is on the Beeb."

We watched them walk over the bridge, in the moonlight, hand in hand. "That's a happy Sarajevo story," said Phil… there was an embarrassed pause, before he said: "It's very early. What do you think?"

"I think we should go and get another drink."

He relaxed. "Where's good?"

"God knows. I've only been back a few days."

We walked fifty paces or so in silence, before he said: "Let's go to Jez. Let's eat subterranean tonight – well, drink, anyway." He squeezed my arm and smiled.

We got rid of Wayne at the cathedral and picked our way through our memories to Jez. We found the doorway, by the back of the Orthodox Church. The steps were no longer bathed in candlelight, and the smell of pee had gone. We walked down, between walls strewn with weapons and poster-sized prints of a man in fatigues, holding a rocket-propelled grenade launcher, with a huge grin on his face.

"Do you think that's the owner?" said Phil.

"The happiest days of his life."

"Oh dear. I know one shouldn't say that, but they were fun… let's sit there! Look, the corner…where we always used to sit!" He moved to the table by the fireplace, but we could have sat anywhere. The restaurant was empty save for ghosts.

"Shall we get another bottle? Do you think the menu's changed? I should think the last time I was here was with you. Have you been back here yet?"

"No. I was waiting for the right moment."

"Do you remember those Sass blokes we used to take out here? What happened to them?"

Hal – I'd completely forgotten about him. I shrugged. "I don't know," I said.

I had been worried Phil might not need to talk to me as much as I needed to talk to him; he'd had Sierra Leone; he'd had Kosovo. Perhaps he didn't still feel the way I felt. But I couldn't have been more wrong. We sat and soaked ourselves in our war... we did the reminiscences, the analyses, and where it all went wrong. We wrung it out, and then we lay on our backs and licked the drops.

"Do you ever feel guilty about it being so much fun?" I said.

"I didn't come to have fun. That was a side effect, because the people were so nice."

"The Sarajevans?"

"Well, yes, the Sarajevans, but also the other hacks."

We both drank a bit more.

"I wish I'd had more Sarajevan friends," I said.

"But you had Amir!"

"But I made him hang out with us. It's partly why we broke up I think. I couldn't bear it with his friends... I couldn't relax."

I had a drink. "I couldn't bear talking to *any* Sarajevans in the end. They were all too sad."

Drink. "When I first went to Beirut, the other correspondents asked me to have dinner with them," said Phil. "I was shocked. I wanted to meet Lebanese students and find out what people were *really* thinking. I think I was even like that at the beginning of Sarajevo. But by 1994, the last fucking thing I wanted to do in the evening was have dinner with Sarajevans. I couldn't switch off."

"That's the same for me. That was what seeing Amir's friends was like. It was always work."

We had another drink.

"But Robert had friends here."

"Robert knew them before the war."

We had another drink.

"I don't know how many friends Robert has here now. He wrote a book. If you write a book about here, everybody hates you. I should know."

We had another drink.

"I seem to have an infinite capacity to feel guilt about this place," I said.

"But we shouldn't."

We had another drink.

"I know. I think they hated us at the end," I said.

"Yes, I think they did."

We had another drink.

"They didn't hate us. They hated the world. We were the only foreigners they could take it out on," said Phil.

We had another drink.

"They never forgave us for leaving them for Chechnya. In 1994," he said. "Until then, they thought we felt like they did about Sarajevo. Then they realised that for us, they were just another war."

We had another drink.

"I don't blame them for hating the world. The world doesn't care."

"They don't care, do they? I had enough trouble getting the desk to send me to the biggest mass grave in Europe since World War II. Why is that?"

"It's the same reason men demonise their ex-wives. The West treated this place like shit, so they have to convince themselves they all deserved it."

We had another drink.

"It's more than that," said Phil. "They don't fucking understand. And that freaked them out."

"But it's not that hard!"

"I'm not talking about morality. I'm talking office politics. The big boys all trained on Russia and the Middle East. Suddenly this huge story comes along – first war in Europe for forty-five years… blah blah… they couldn't cope with their knowledge being worth next to nothing…"

"I thought you *were* one of the big boys. I thought *you* were a star..."

"You are kind... I can tell you... I really wasn't then..."

We had another drink.

"The Middle East *does* involve oil," I said. "Which everyone puts in their cars."

"The former Yugoslavia place haemorrhages people. You can't walk through Shepherd's Bush without seeing how all these wars, Kosovo, Bosnia, Croatia, have affected life in Britain. It's not just Café Rouge the Albanians run these days. Half the organised crime in Europe comes through here."

We had another drink.

"Oil is easy," I said, "everyone knows we want it to be cheap."

We had another drink.

"Bosnia's unlucky," I said. "People are always horrid to unlucky people. They have to convince themselves unlucky people deserved it. Otherwise there's no reason it needn't happen to them."

We had another drink.

"The trouble is," said Phil, "Tito's Yugoslavia was such a lovely place to live."

It was time for another bottle.

"What's it like being back?" He grimaced again, as if he wasn't sure he wanted to know.

"Not much fun. Rather lonely. I don't know anyone any more."

"So why are you here? Why don't you just leave?"

He was wary at first when I mentioned your name. He'd had a lot of conversations with me about you in the past. He tried to stop me with "Molly..." But when I talked through him, he was gripped.

"Who told you?" he said. So I explained about Hal – at least not all about Hal, but that bit anyway.

Phil nodded, but the next thing he said was: "How on earth did you get to see Radic? He never spoke to *anybody*."

"I think he's lonelier now."

"Does Robert know Amir was…?" even he couldn't say the word murdered.

"Oh yes. Everybody knew. Everybody except me."

He had a drink.

"Well at least you can't think it's your fault now."

It was after the next drink that he said: "So what are you going to do?"

"I want to find out why. But it's very hard. Like Robert said, it's not my war. But I can't just leave. Maybe it's better not to know why. Everyone says he must have done something… The way they're all behaving… he *must* have done something… Maybe it's better for Maria… for Nermina, to have a dead hero for a father than a dead criminal."

"For *Nermina*?" Phil had another drink. "Have you *seen* Nermina?"

"No. I've never seen her. She and Aida are in Washington."

"What, with Ed?"

"*Ed?*"

Phil looked shifty.

"What, famous, old Ed?"

He nodded.

"No. Why? *Phil*… Why on earth should Aida be with Ed?"

Phil had another drink.

"I thought you knew."

"Knew what?"

He had another drink.

"Phil? What else don't I know?"

Long drink. Then Phil said, very slowly, "I don't think that Nermina is Amir's child."

"*What!*" I felt sick; the tingles went up and down my limbs. "So whose child is she?"

Nothing. Phil just stared at me.

"Oh God, oh God, don't tell me. Not… not… not… Ed?"

He nodded.

"Jesus Christ. Jesus Christ. That horrible old man. How could he? How could she? He was so bald and old and wrinkly! How *could* she! And how could Ed let her marry my Amir like that? Fuck him. How *could* he? How *could* he ruin my life?"

"To be fair to Ed, I don't think he knew."

"He fucking knows now, doesn't he? The bastard."

Phil nodded. And had another drink.

"No wonder Maria had no photographs in the house. There were none, you know. When I mentioned Aida being in America, she said, 'Best place for her.' So she must know."

"Well… everybody knows," said Phil.

"I bloody didn't."

Phil took another drink.

"Did Aida know when she married Amir?"

"I don't know."

"Oh God. No wonder the baby was so late. I thought it was late. Do you remember, when I came back, I thought it should have been born? Do you think Amir knew when he said all that to me at the party?"

"I don't know."

"Oh God. Oh God."

"I don't think he can have," Phil said quickly.

"Why not? Everyone else seems to have known."

"Because if he had known, he would have told you. From what you've always said, he was trying to get you back."

"He was…" Your desperate whispers on my cheek, your hand entwined at the nape of my neck. You had used everything you had that night. "No, he didn't know. But everybody else has known for years, everything, except for me."

Phil handed me a napkin as I started to cry; I seemed to have spent most of today in tears.

"I'm so sorry. I just assumed you knew," he said as I wiped my eyes.

"How was I supposed to bloody know? I can't believe I didn't know. I don't think I know anything any more. I thought I knew Amir, and then I discover this… that he… I don't know what he did… I thought I knew Sarajevo, and I come back here, I don't know what any of the streets are called. I don't even know what Sniper Alley's called."

Phil had a drink, before he said: "Neither do I."

It was then I heard a voice chirrup: "Hi Molly."

I ground my tears out and turned in my chair.

"Oh hi!" Amy was standing there with Zach.

"Phil, this is…" but Phil and Zach were staring at each other.

"Matt… Bart…" Phil was floundering slightly, but goal in sight, nonetheless. "Weren't you on the Convoy of Hope?" he said.

"Oh my God, *Phil*. Phil from the… BBC? It's Zach!"

Phil leapt up. They did that half handshake, half hug thing that men do.

"How are you, man?"

"I'm really well. How are you?"

"Great. Things are great."

"It's been… it's been… what, five years?"

"Six, over six."

"Fuck. Well, it's great. You look great."

"So do you." They stared at each other, and then Phil said, "So… what are you doing now?"

"What, right now, or with my life?"

"Well, that too, but right now…"

"Well, we were just leaving."

"Stay, stay and have another drink."

Amy coughed and said: "I think Alma would like us to leave."

"But it's only quarter past eleven," said Phil.

"Don't worry, man. There are loads of other places now. Amy, this is Phil Kennedy…"

"Oh… wow, I have your book."

We walked down the street under the stars, Phil and Zach side by side, and slightly ahead, and occasional phrases floated back.

"...the bearded ladies..."

"...Christ, just thinking about it..."

"...pitch forks..."

"*Errgh*... Still, you're here now."

"*We're* here now."

"Are you *still* here?"

"Nah, just back for a bit..."

"Me too..."

"What's this... *thing*... they're talking about?" Amy said to me. It was a convoy, I heard myself say; a Muslim charity, bringing food into Central Bosnia, in '93. It was ambushed by the Croats and the Muslim drivers were stabbed to death by old women with pitchforks.

Amy looked sick.

We turned into one of those deep Austrian streets, with café tables right down to the river. Phil stood stock still, between the banks of buildings.

"The bread queue massacre happened just here. Oh God. People *sit* out here."

Zach's bar was called Nostalgia. There was a man with a fez on the wall outside. Inside were black and white photographs of old Sarajevo and along one wall ran a panorama of Istanbul. Dire Straits was playing on the sound system. Under the window sat a man drinking a glass of wine and doing his accounts. He had the heavy gaze and heavy bulk of someone who had learnt to do things in the war you hoped he would never do anywhere near you; unless, of course, you were a psychotic cameraman. But he smiled when he saw Zach, and stood up and moved to the bar: "Welcome back," he said.

"Hi Bogdan," said Zach; above the bar, on the wall, was a picture of a younger, thinner Bogdan, with the fleur de lys on his arm, grinning against one of those gym-locker barricades, with the burn-smeared façades of Sarajevo at his back. As I walked back to find the loo, I heard Amy say: "*Bogdan*! That's Serb name... strange..."

"There are lots of Serbs in Sarajevo… at least there were," said Phil. "Shall we get a bottle?"

I took a long time in the loo but I wanted to be alone. I wanted to talk to you about Nermina in my head. And I was tired, so tired. It felt like I'd been back two weeks, when in fact only three days ago, I was still in Split. When I returned, Zach and Phil were well entrenched, and Amy was sitting, slightly piqued, alone to one side. "Are you OK?" Phil said, as I sat down.

His hair had gone all wispy, and he was waving his arms. I said I was fine. "You don't look very fine," said Amy, staring at my reddened eyes.

I said, "Well, I am," at the same time as Phil said, "Molly has a dilemma on her hands."

"I like dilemmas," said Amy. I said nothing. I wasn't sure I wanted her to know, but then I wasn't doing very well on my own.

"It's complicated," said Phil, when I didn't speak.

"Amy has a law degree from Harvard. She does complicated dilemmas," said Zach.

So of course I told them about you. I'm a journalist. I don't do suffering in silence. I'm too used to being paid by the word.

I didn't tell them about the baby not being yours, or Aida, or the smell of burnt rubbish on the winter's air, or you being in love with me, or me being in love with you and never forgiving myself for letting you go. I didn't tell them I'd left you all alone. That didn't matter to them. I just told them that I'd found out you'd been murdered and your family wanted me to let things lie.

Zach said, "Tricky," at almost exactly the same time as Amy said: "So where's the dilemma?"

We all gawped.

"Somebody killed him, right?" she went on.

"Well, yes."

"And they've never been caught, right?"

"No."

"No dilemma."

"Why?" In the midst of my irritation, I felt a pang of wistfulness for her magnificent simplicity.

"Killing people is wrong."

"What?" said Phil.

"Killing people is wrong. You shouldn't do it. And if you do it, you ought to pay."

The silence stretched through several bars of *Brothers in Arms*. Then Phil said: "She's absolutely right, you know. Killing people is wrong."

"Well, it is," she was blushing. "And what's more, but this is another point, if you kill people and get away with it, then you'll probably kill more people."

"It's just wrong to kill people," said Phil. "Can you pass that bottle. Killing people is wrong. And if more people realised that, then none of this would ever have happened."

"So what do I do now?"

"Go… to… the… police," she said, as though she was spelling it out for the mentally retarded. Zach and Phil both laughed.

"It's not funny," I snapped. She seemed to have no understanding of how difficult this was. She didn't seem to understand this country at all. "The police *know*. It was the police who didn't investigate."

"So report *that* to the police."

"I just don't *trust* the police here," I said.

"They can't all be corrupt," said Amy. "Well, they can't be. They found the guys who burgled my flat in three days."

"I think we saw too many policemen in the war," said Phil.

It was 2 a.m. before Bogdan kicked us out and the streets outside were like the old days, just us and the stars. Amy had been half asleep for an hour. She and Zach peeled off at the cathedral.

"I'll walk you back to your hotel," said Phil.

"You don't have to."

"I want to," he said. "Where are you staying? Not at the Holiday Inn?"

"Oh, God no!"

We walked a bit before he said: "Have you been back?"

Was it only this morning? "Yes."

"To room 309?"

"I went and stood outside it," I said.

"What was it like?"

I was staring down with the dark atrium sucking at my brain. "Horrid," I said. "Empty. Weird."

"Same staff?"

"Some. One of the waiters knew me."

Phil didn't speak for another twenty yards. Then he said: "I just don't think I could face going back."

"I know what you mean."

We walked on. "Was it worth it?"

Worth it? In what way? Had it helped? Helped what? God knows. I guess it was just another chapter in my war. "I suppose so," I said. "But it's not the same."

"No?"

"It's nowhere near as nice without you."

We walked past the fountain in the square and the old mosque.

"It's down here," I said. "Robert booked it for me."

"Didi's place? I've stayed there before. Bugger. It was full this time. How's Didi? God, what do you think of her story?"

"I don't know her story."

"Well, you should try and ask."

We'd reached the corner of the street and my hotel. Far above, on its cliff, the old fort was silhouetted against the stars.

"This is it," I said.

He smiled down at me in the moonlight. "So goodnight," he said. But he didn't move. Then he said: "She's right, you know, that girl. About your Amir. Don't worry about what Robert or Valida think. You were in love with him, remember that. And even if you hadn't been, it would still be the right thing to do."

"I wish you were staying," I said.

He made a face: "So do I."

"I'm not sure I can do this on my own."

"Of course you can. Just keep asking questions."

"I'm not used to asking questions any more."

"It's like riding a bike. You never forget." He patted the top of my arm and left his hand there too long.

"Chuck in that stupid job."

I nodded: I knew by now it had to go. "God knows what I'll do instead."

"Amir's death had nothing to do with you. It had nothing to do with journalism. You know, you mustn't let what these people thought at the end of the war put you off. You were a good journalist. And that isn't a bad thing to be. Somebody has to be a foreign correspondent, and it's better that it was someone like you."

We sat down on a wall and looked up at the broken bulge of the old library, the glint of granite in the moonlight, the shadow of the fir trees on the old frontline.

"God, it's beautiful. I'd forgotten how beautiful it was."

"It's not forgetting. We'd never have looked like this then."

We must have stared at the stars and the mountains under the moon for over a minute before he said: "Would you change it? Would you swap back? If you could, would you change what you chose then?"

Take away my war, take away you, take away Phil, the best years of my life…

"No, no, I wouldn't."

"Well, that's good. Because you can't."

"I'd like to feel about somewhere again the way I felt about here."

"You won't. This was our Spanish Civil War. You don't fall in love like that twice."

"Did you fall in love with Beirut?"

He paused before he said: "No."

"Why not? You were young and impressionable…"

"I was, but the war was old."

I didn't reply.

"Do you ever see Tim?" he said.

"Not any more," I said.

"He sees ghosts from here."

He must have felt my shudder because he gave my arm a squeeze.

"Come to Jerusalem with me. You can stay in the flat. There's loads of space. It's a great story. The Middle East is never going way. And lots of interesting single men."

"What, Arabs?"

"Not just Arabs. Israelis too, you might have noticed. Lots of NGOs and diplomats, you know, the usual suspects..."

"I don't fancy being married to an Arab. Or an Israeli. Or an NGO."

"You don't have to marry them. Just have a fling." I thought about telling him about Hal. Poor Hal. He seemed almost irrelevant now. What a burden, to bear the weight of all my expectations. I know he's trained to carry blocks of concrete, but my expectations were heavier than that... I wanted the film. I wanted the romantic ending. But to Hal, of course, I suddenly realised, it hadn't been my film at all. It was his film. The film in which he saves the world. And in that film, there's always a girl, and he gets to shag her, and she's never in the sequel. But where did that leave Amir and me?

"Don't fall in love?" I asked.

"It makes life so much easier..." said Phil.

"Like you would know." And I smiled up at him.

He didn't speak for a moment, just stared down at me, and I saw, in the street light, the little wrinkles gathering at the corner of his eyes with his smile, and his hair, still enough of it to flop down to one side.

"Oh Phil, oh dear, it was so lovely to see you again."

"It was."

"Goodnight."

He kissed me, on both cheeks, and hugged me, and then kissed me again a third time, and then held my shoulders and looked into my eyes, and I stared back up into his. It was about two or three seconds before I put my hands on his arms and said: "Send my love to Lena and the children."

He smiled, maybe with relief. He took his hands down and said: "Thanks. I'll tell her. And good luck."

I left him in the street. The trouble is, in a way, I do love Phil. And Phil loves me. So it could never have been a fling. It would just have been a disaster.

MUJO WAS LIVING in Germany and he married a German girl. One summer they decided to drive on a visit to Bosnia.

"How will I know when we are in Bosnia?" said the girl.

"You will know," he said. "Everybody is stupid there."

After two days in the car, they passed an imam, in his white hat, hobbling along.

"Ah, we're in Bosnia," said the girl.

"How do you know?"

"You said they were stupid. That man's got a sore leg, but he's put the bandage on his head."

XI

I watched the white light dancing on the ceiling. For a moment, I thought I'd escaped, and then the hangover crawled over my brain like a wave on a beach next to an industrial effluent pipe. My eyeballs felt as though they were being poached in vinegar and as the vinegar vaporised, the fumes were rising, expanding in my skull and compressing my brain. I wallowed on the pillows. It was rather nostalgic to feel like this. There weren't that many people I could drink like that with any more and I'd had much worse hangovers drinking in the war with Phil.

My dilemma hit me at the same time as the headache kicked in. If I walked into a police station here – a foreign woman, on holiday – saying "I want to report a murder that happened in the war..." Whatever Amy said about the police being marvellous, even without the hangover, the thought made me quail. The shrugs, the sexist remarks, the sleazy inefficiency. The feet-dragging once they realised I'd be gone in ten days – less now, only just over a week. Maybe I'm wrong. But I just don't think the police force in the Balkans attracts the nicest people. Besides, the police had known all along. Someone who knew someone in the police would help.

That's how it works in this place. You don't come in off the street.

Didi was in the dining room. It was 9.55 and I was the only person left. All the other guests had gone to their various offices to continue busily re-constructing the Balkans. "Do you know any policemen?" I said, as she brought me my coffee. "I need to find a policeman."

She shuddered. "Policemen… I hate policemen."

The German news on the TV was rat-a-tat into my brain. "The only policeman you can trust here is someone you already know," she said. "And even then…" She shuddered and turned away.

Know. I must have known some policemen – the bearded lady at the Serb checkpoint Sierra One? I don't think so… She'd hardly be in Sarajevo anyway… I must have written an article about a policeman. A nice one…

"You should ask Valida…" Didi's voice broke in, a little keen. I could hardly explain Valida was the last person who'd give me any help. So I said: "I saw her last night, she says hello." Didi looked pleased. "And Phil," I added, "from the BBC, he says hello."

"Oh Phil, he is a nice man."

"Very…" I took a deep breath. "He says you are from Rogatica."

She didn't speak for a moment, then she said.

"Not from Rogatica. One small village, near it, high, in the hills."

"What's it called?"

"You will not know it. It is far from here."

"Try me." I could see it, one of those white strings of houses, dotted in pasture land, on the mountain's flank; red roofs, green fields, blue sky, mosque at one end, church at the other, with each religion hugger-mugger with their own.

"There's no point," her voice broke in.

"I travelled a lot."

She shrugged and said a name; Zhiv something. She was right, I didn't know it.

"I know Rogatica, though. I went there in the war."

"I will never go back to Rogatica again." She put down my coffee and moved over to the bar. But she came back a minute or so later and stood by my table. She didn't go, but she didn't want to start talking. I said to her, "Could I have another coffee? Why don't you have a coffee with me?"

The fountain splattered in the breeze as I waited for her return. She came back with two cups of Bosnian coffee. "Please sit down."

We both stirred the grains with our spoon. Neither of us seemed to want to start again.

"Are you enjoying being back in Sarajevo?" she said, after a bit.

"I don't know. It's different."

"It's hard to go back somewhere." She was still gripping her coffee spoon.

"Yes."

Neither of us spoke. She tapped the spoon into the saucer.

"When did you come to Sarajevo? Was it after the war?" I asked.

"Ha! No. I would be dead if it was after the war. No. I came here in 1992." She took a sip of the coffee.

"What, before the siege began?"

"No. Much later. Like refugee."

"But… but… Sarajevo was being shelled…"

"Believe me, lady, Sarajevo was better than Rogatica…" She looked out of the window, then she turned back to me, "…and Rogatica was better than my old village."

I waited. She was back in her head. Suddenly I wanted to get into her head too; it was like the old days, the curiosity to know, to let someone tell their story to me. I waited, silent, for her to come to me, but she pushed back her chair, picked up her cup, and said, "I must get on." Then walked off before I could say anything else. I stared after her, feeling as if I'd just realised I'd left a book I'd been reading on the train.

Mujo rang his wife Fata from Germany.
"Hello my love. Is that you?" he said.
"Yes, my only one. And who are you?"

XII

It didn't take me long to find Dragan on the internet. He'd come back into my head as Didi was talking… the mess, the blood, pooling in the pores in the upholstery on the car door, his dank eyes staring at me. Your voice: I never thought I'd save the life of a Serb policeman.

I wandered down to the old mosque. A girl with maroon hair sold me a cappuccino in an internet cafe. I drank it while I googled away; luckily, this war was still very well documented by various nutters and pressure groups. It didn't take long until I found him in my piece on an anti-war website. Dragan Petrovic.

He had been an inspector, back in 1993.

The main police station would be the best place to start. They'd have records. If he was still here, if he was alive, if he hadn't given up and gone to Germany or Chicago like everyone else, he would help. He owed you that. You had saved his life. I asked the maroon girl where the main police station was. I couldn't miss it, she said; just behind the Presidency, covered in lots of big flags. It looked just like a police station, she said.

She was right. It was down a side street, between the Presidency and the river, flying the flags of the EU, the UN and the yellow triangle on blue of the new Bosnian Federation. I walked through the double doors in its imperial façade. Three men were manhandling a youth in reception. The boy looked scared and the policemen angry. One of the policemen stood back and smoked, while two others were pushing the boy into a chair. None of them looked familiar. The boy struggled briefly, but he was handcuffed and they were three.

There was a cough to my right. Another maroon-haired girl was sitting behind a sheet of glass.

"*I am trying to find Dragan Petrovic please?*" I said. I was expecting her to say who? Or, this is not the right place. Or, he has moved to Australia. But she just picked up the phone.

"*What is your name?*"

"*Molly Taylor.*" She repeated it into the phone. I started to say: "*I am an English journalist and an old friend from the war.*" But she cut me off.

"*He is coming. Wait here.*"

He was older, when he walked through the door, with white streaks in his hair, but the grey skin of the war was now tanned. We spoke each other's names at the same time and with the same tremor of uncertainty.

"*Dragan?*"

"*Molly?*"

He rushed forward and started pumping my hand. "*Is you. It is really you.*" He had tears in his eyes as he turned to the girl: "*This woman, she saved my life in war.*"

"*It wasn't me, really, it was my boyfriend,*" I smiled abashed, but the girl didn't look that impressed.

"*All of you. You save my life. Come upstairs.*"

He saw me glance at the youth cowering in his chair.

"*They caught him stealing purses on the tram,*" he said.

We walked through double doors and up two flights of stairs, all lino, police posters and limp rubber plants.

"*Here is my office,*" he said. The room was as grey as the stairs: grey carpet and grey walls and chairs upholstered in greying fake black leather.

"*Coffee, tea, juice?*"

"*Coffee.*" He picked up the phone.

"*So. So. You. How are you?*"

"Fine." I smiled. I couldn't think of anything else to say. *"Really well,"* and smiled again. The last time I had seen him, he'd been in hospital. He'd been as grey as this room with shock, full of tubes, but happy. His wife had been massaging his hand, grabbing at his fingers, as though she were desperate to reassure herself his flesh was still warm. He'd been medivac-ed to Germany and we'd lost touch.

We sat grinning at each other, with nothing to say.

"How's your wife?" I said.

"Fine. She is fine."

"And the children?"

His face lit up. *"Very well…"*

"Both?"

"Both! We have three now. We had another after the war. Maybe like new life… And you?"

"No. I don't have any children. And I'm not married."

He looked a bit doubtful: *"There is still time."* The door opened and a minion came in with coffee. He handed me a cup. *"For you and me, it is just enough to be alive. In my job, you see lots of bad marriages anyway."*

"And in mine." We both laughed. Then there was a silence.

"Sarajevo is so different now."

"Very different! No more bang bang…" he mimed putting a rifle to his shoulder. *"Is this your first time back?"*

"Yes. Since the end of the war."

He sighed. *"Very different."* This time he didn't laugh.

"Yes."

I offered him a cigarette. He shook his head.

"I don't smoke," he said.

"You must be the only person in Sarajevo who doesn't."

"With one lung, you don't smoke. Not if you want to live." I put my cigarette out.

I'd forgotten he'd lost a lung when he'd been shot. This man smiling at me, the dark grey eyes under the head of greying hair, the heavy face, handing me a cup of coffee, sitting at his desk, would be dead now, if it hadn't been for us driving by. His wife would be a widow. Their third child would not have been conceived. Someone else would be doing this job. What are they doing instead? But if he'd driven a couple of miles an hour faster or slower, or left the house a few minutes earlier or later, he wouldn't have been hit at all.

We sipped our coffee and, first sip done, it was as though the starting whistle had blown; he put down his cup and said: *"Your first time back. Why now? And why have you come to see me?"*

I took a deep breath. He must have seen something in my face because he picked up a pen.

"Is this an official visit?"

"Yes, it's official."

Dragan kept me in the police station for over three hours; in his office, at first, but it didn't take long to discover there had never been an investigation, so then we moved to an interview room downstairs. The thief from the tram was in the room next door. They wanted to know what Amir had said to me that night; who else I'd seen him talking to. I said it was a party, everyone was there. They wanted to know as many names as I could possibly remember. It's four years ago, I said, and anyway, they've all gone. No-one's here any more. They're all in Kosovo or New York or Jakarta or Washington. He's looking for the policeman who was at the autopsy. Poor man. I hope it's not… I don't know what I hope. Maybe I have to hope that policeman was just a bad man.

I had to tell them you'd told me you'd said you wanted to leave Aida for me. Then they wanted to know what I was doing when you were killed. I had to give them Phil's name and number as my alibi. They asked if I remembered anyone else who'd been with me that night. I told them about Robert. Then I remembered Andy, so I gave them his name; I was about to say I didn't know where he was, when Dragan said, I know him, he works with me. For IPTF, whatever that is, doing organised crime.

"I hope he didn't know they were going to kill him," I said.

"It was a quick death," said Dragan, and gave me another Kleenex.

"It wasn't quick," I said, after I'd blown my nose. *"He was in the passenger seat. He never let anyone else drive that car."*

"It wasn't a long drive. And there were no other marks on him."

Dragan's henchmen took it all down, clicking on their keyboards: it had been manual typewriters during the war. Dragan told me I'd got to stay in Sarajevo for the next few days. I hadn't thought about that. I hope I can leave before my holiday runs out. But I can see their point. Technically, I could have killed you myself.

"What should I do?"

"What you like." He laughed. *"Be a tourist here. Just don't ask questions any more. Don't tell anyone you came to see me. Be careful. Your boyfriend was killed by a professional hit."*

"Why would a professional want to kill him?" I'd never even thought I might be in danger myself.

Balkan shrug. *"That is what I hope we will find out."*

A man rushed in from downstairs with a small plastic bag. It was covered in that thick chalky dust from the war, like builder's dust, the kind you get from demolition. Dragan wiped it as clean as he could and crooned at what he could see inside. It was a metal blob, smeared in browny-black. He brought it over to show the label to me.

"It's the bullet," he said. *"It was in the evidence room. Look, here it is."* Amir's name and the date were on the label, with some kind of reference number, and another name. *"Now all we have to do is find this man."* He pointed to the second name.

I couldn't read it. Elvir Something-ovic. *"The policeman,"* said Dragan.

"But why did he keep it? Why didn't he throw it away?" I hoped Elvir wasn't happily married with five children, this was the one bad thing he'd done, and I was going to ruin his life.

"If he kept it, he always had a hold on the killer."

"I nearly didn't come," I said, as Dragan walked with me to the door. *"Nobody wanted me to... so many people died in the war..."*

"None of them should have died," said Dragan. *"But he was not killed like the others."*

"Robert told me a lot of deaths happened like this in the war."

"That isn't true. This was like execution. In Sarajevo, that was very rare."

We were standing in the lobby, where I'd seen the policemen grapple with the thief from the tram, this morning, or whatever time zone it had been that I had come in here.

"But if he was... executed..." I didn't want to think this of you, but the way Maria and Robert were behaving, this had to be the case... *"Maybe he had done something to deserve it... Maybe he deserved to die... Maybe it's better not to dig it up..."*

Dragan suddenly grabbed me and yanked me out into the street.

"See those hills?" His voice had switched to fury, as quick as the young man who'd nearly run me over a few days ago, and his fingers were digging into the flesh of my arm. With his other hand he pointed up the cliff, to where the old frontline used to be, where the road cut deep through the trees. Where the Serbs sat – used to sit – in their shacks, by the side of the road, drinking coffee, huddled under their fur hats, and point out Sarajevo to us, directly below, through the gun ports burrowed through barricades they'd built from the fir trees around them; the four C's in a cross of Greater Serbia sprayed on the wooden walls; the man who'd come back to fight, from his job in a bubble-gum factory in Germany, who laughed at himself as he said, "What could I do, I'm a Serb...? I had to protect my family, my home... my little pig!"

"The men up there in those hills thought they had some ancient right on their side. Well, they were wrong. You cannot take justice into your own hands. Because then it is not justice, but revenge. And revenge breeds revenge. I am a Serb. I could have left Sarajevo in 1992. I chose to stay. And then I get shot." He prodded at his chest.

"I could have stayed in Germany, where they medivac-ed me... I was offered a good job there. But I chose to come back. This is my town and I believe that my town needs men who believe in the law. If those – those – his face seethed, like a pot of boiling porridge, "*those* criminals", he spat out, which was obviously the worst word he could think of, "*in Pale had obeyed the law, this stupid war would never have happened and my country would still be one country. And believe me, my country was a very nice place to live.*"

"I'm sorry..."

"*Look at the cars...*" They were parked everywhere, jumbled up on the pavements, fat and shiny Mercedes, Audis, great Cherokee jeeps, growling past. The street reeked of money and exhaust. "*It is almost impossible to make enough money legally in this town to buy that kind of car... unless you work for an international organisation, of course... There is 30 per cent unemployment in Bosnia at the moment. People cannot live on the pensions they have...*

"People who make a success at crime don't stop. They carry on until they are caught. That's what I hope to catch with what you have brought me. What gave that man who shot your boyfriend the right to choose who he can shoot and who he can't? I do not care what he thought your boyfriend might or might not have done. We all do things in war that perhaps we'd rather not do."

I said: "*But you were very brave in the war. You chose to stay.*"

"My wife is Muslim. It is easier to be brave when you have no choice."

"*It's easy to be brave if you don't understand the consequences,*" I said.

Mujo went to Germany and found a strange fruit machine. He put a coin in, pressed the button, and out came a cup of coffee. He put another coin in, pressed the button, and this time he got a Coca Cola. After an hour there was a huge queue behind him. One man said, "Please, can you let someone else use the machine?"

"No way," said Mujo, "I'm still winning."

XIII

I walked up along Feradiya towards Michele's and sat down again, under the awning, two chintz chairs away from where I had been yesterday. It was packed. I'm sure I recognised some of the same people I'd walked past on my way to the police station three hours ago. But they probably recognised me by now as well.

What am I going to do about Robert? I've been told not to tell anyone but I ought to tell him. I ordered a cup of coffee. I couldn't face Robert's barrage of smugness unarmed. I rang Phil. I told him everything Dragan had said.

"You're doing the right thing. Don't worry about Robert. Even in the old days, he was a bit of a killjoy."

"Where are you? Are you back in London?" I could hear a tannoy pontificating through his phone.

"No. I'm stuck at the airport. My flight's delayed. It's quite like old times."

"Telling me. The police won't *let* me leave Sarajevo."

"Good God! I hadn't thought of that."

Neither had I. "What's the airport like now?" There had been no tannoy on my last flight out, just a soldier with a parade ground voice, and a departure lounge built from sandbags and huge concrete blocks. They'd fought hard for the airport, in the early days of the war, and somewhere, apparently, the wrecked remains of the airport buildings had stood but it had always been too dangerous, and pointless, to poke a head round the concrete and take a look.

"Could be Luton," he said. "Got to go. See you soon. I meant it about Jerusalem."

I didn't want him to ring off. He was my last friend here. I said: "Phil, oh Phil, Didi sends her regards… "

"Poor her. Poor guy. What a tragedy. Survive the whole war and you think you're OK, and then to die like that, right at the end."

"But she's alive…?"

"Not her, of course. Her husband! He was shot right at the end."

"Was he? She didn't tell me about him," I said.

"What did she tell you? Did she tell you her own story?"

"I didn't ask her," I said.

"Oh," he sounded disappointed, but then he said, "Well, frankly, you'd have heard it a hundred times before."

My phone rang. There were only three people in Sarajevo who had my number, and one of them was Robert. But it was Amy, wanting to know if I needed any help going to the police.

"I've done it."

"My, what did they say?"

"They're looking into it."

"Great."

"Yes. Great. Thanks."

"Are you OK?"

"I'm fine."

"Do you want to have coffee?"

"No," I said, "I've got someone I have to ring."

"Dinner? What about dinner? I'm meeting up with Zach and some friends of his later. Come. It will be fun."

"I'd like that," I said.

I lit a cigarette and put off ringing Robert and Valida a bit more and thought about the conversation I'd had yesterday. Yesterday, was it only yesterday, when I still had nothing to do but wander round Sarajevo floundering in the peace. Valida's friend, the waitress, had recommended some cousin of hers who ran a beauty parlour behind the brewery. Briefly surfacing from her semi-trance, she'd made an appointment for me and I'd kept it anyway, after I'd seen Radic. It was nice to have an ordinary appointment to keep.

The salon was up one of those dark valleys across the river, scored deep in the mountains' northern flank. The street was alive with running water from the captured streams beneath the road and it told of all of Bosnia's past. There was a mosque, with a little fountain and a tumbled, weedy graveyard, a brand-new minaret and a woman, wiping her hands past her face in prayer, standing at a grille in its wall. Beyond were a row of Austro-Hungarian houses, rising above their daubs of brand-new cement and shiny glass, with the Teutonic self-delusion of the bourgeoisie. The salon was the next block up. From its size and position, commanding the slopes, it must once, in some Pasha-led past, have been the house of a great official, or great in the terms of Bosnia, for even the greatest of the Turkish lords here did not live as grandly a Victorian vicar. Veiled women would have bustled between its courtyards, soothing the brow of the merchant or administrator, who sat on the cushions of his divan, probably just as despairing of the twistiness of his compatriots, as his counterparts in the UN had been during my time. Even now, the house wasn't small, but the twentieth century had swallowed its courtyards up, and gouged windows into its outside walls, and then, right at the very end, knocked it down and rebuilt it all again.

The girl, the cousin I suppose, gave me a facial, a wax and a pedicure, for the cost of a few cappuccinos in London.

"Are you working for one of the Internationals?" she asked, with the practised air of one who knows the reply.

"No," I said. "I'm on holiday." The scalpel halted for a second.

"Oh! Is it your first time here?"

"No. I used to live here... I'm a journalist." The scalpel moved on.

"In the war?"

"Yes."

"Is it your first time back?"

"Yes."

She concentrated very hard on my toe, as she asked: "What do you think?"

I laughed. "Most of my friends have gone."

"People who can go have gone."

"You are from here?" I assumed she was, as she was Sabina's cousin, and Sabina had Sarajevo written all over her.

"Yes. But my brother is in Chicago."

"Why didn't you go?"

"Well, we have thought about it," she looked up from my foot. "In many ways it is a dream to go to America. To bring my children up there. Now I can't even get a visa to go on holiday. But we have a good business here." She moved on to another toe. She didn't speak again, until I said: "It's very different to the war."

"The war," she laughed, but it wasn't a happy sound. "In the war, of course it was terrible, but in many ways, we were all equal. You faced things together. Now, there are a lot of problems with people who spent the war in Germany and came back with money and people who lived through the war here, who have nothing. And people from the villages, who have come into Sarajevo. There are more people from Foca or Gorazde here now, than old Sarajevo. People say Feradiya is like the main street in Gorazde. All my friends, they have all gone. Just like you have found. Everyone left is so poor. And they complain about it. But they don't understand that you have to work. Our parents' generation, they don't understand that. They think it will go back to being like the old days, like Yugoslavia. But it won't."

"Are they really so poor?" I said. "All the cafés seem full."

"Cafés! It is not hard to buy one cup of coffee and sit there for three hours. They say, there are no jobs, what can they do? Unemployment is, like, what, maybe 30 per cent. But people aren't prepared to change. They aren't prepared to do what work there is. We do well here because I work. This was our house. I turn it into salon. My husband, he used to be… like social scientist, a professor. And then in the war, he had to learn about cars. So now he does that. We have a garage here, out the back." I could hear a clanking sound coming through the windows.

"There are a lot of new cars in Sarajevo now."

"A lot," she gave that laugh again, and rubbed her fingers in the classic sign for corruption. "So we have money now. But we work hard for it. And we changed." She was holding my foot close up to her face, carving bits out from under my yellowing toenails. "But it is hard work. And it is hard to change. Look at Sabina."

"Sabina who works at my hotel?"

"Before the war, she worked for the Tourist Board. During the war, she worked as interpreter for some American TV station. Not CNN. Not so large. Well, the TV people went one day, after the war, and left her with almost nothing. She had worked for them for all the war. Four years. They gave her some money but it doesn't last. Then she got job two years ago as interpreter for OSCE but now all the internationals are moving to Kosovo. So she works like waitress. She went to Didi and Didi gave her a job."

"That's kind of Didi."

"Didi is good like that. But don't get me wrong, it's good for Didi to have waitress who speaks English and German. She has lots of internationals staying in her hotel. Sabina will get something else one day, I am sure. But at the moment, she has to work like waitress in our family's old house."

"Your family?"

"Didi married my cousin, but he died…" she paused… "in the war. The house had been hit anyway. Like ours. She had it completely rebuilt. It was old. Now it is new hotel. Look at Didi – she changed! She learnt how to change." The girl's laugh was still harsh, but full of respect. "Before war, she was just one village girl from the mountains. Now she has smart new hotel and she is Sarajevo lady. But she works. She worked for it all. She met my cousin in army."

"Army?"

"Yes. She didn't have to go and fight."

"What were you before, before the war?" I asked.

"I was training to be a lawyer." She didn't look at me then, but carefully marshalled the bottles of coloured varnish.

"Like Valida? Do you know her?"

"Valida! You know Valida! Of course. You would. You're a journalist. All journalists know Valida. Huh. I have nothing against Valida," she concentrated on unscrewing the nail varnish. "I know she had a terrible time in the war. I mean, we all had terrible times and she was working for BBC and had money and food and water and lived in hotel, but she had to *see* everything, *all* the bad things. We didn't have to see. But then Valida made a lot of money out of the war. The BBC treated her better than Sabina's TV company. And she married an International. And now she does nothing."

"But she's training to be a lawyer."

"She is not! She says she is training to be lawyer, but every time she had to take her exams, she gets sick."

Robert's voice was all jolly when he answered the phone.

"You must be feeling rough. I expect you and Phil had a late one. I don't know how you two do it."

"We don't really any more."

"When are you off?" I looked round Michele's; there they were, the sad-eyed boys – men really, in their tatty jeans; the ladies, forty-something, henna-ed hair carefully sprayed, white shirts pressed, the two men dressed for the office, suits, ties neatly tied, who obviously have no office to go to at all, all talking to each other over their empty cups. "Maybe we could have a drink tonight, although, actually I think..."

"I think I'll be around for a bit," I said.

"Oh..." The jolliness seeped from his voice.

"I rang to tell you that I reported Amir's death to the police this afternoon."

"You did what!" He didn't sound surprised, just utterly fed up but I repeated it anyway.

"I reported Amir's death to the police."

"Oh Molly. Can't you leave anything alone?"

"Robert. I don't think this should be left alone. I just thought you should know."

"I should know. What do you mean I should know? You know I know already."

"You know what I mean. I thought you should know about the police. I think they are going to want to ask questions and things."

"You told them about us?" His voice rose with rage.

"I had to. They wanted to know. They needed to know all about his family here. They needed to know who I was with that night."

"For Christ's sake. Why couldn't you just leave this alone?"

"Because I don't think it should be."

"You always have to charge into things. Couldn't you just think, couldn't you think for a moment what this would do?"

"I have thought. What do you think I've been doing here for the last week?"

"Well maybe you should have thought about this like a bloody grown-up and not like a quixotic teenager. It was years ago, Molly! The war's over. You can't go around digging things up."

"I think there are some things that have to be dug up."

"You don't live here. You don't understand the place. Believe me, you are completely wrong. You don't want to start digging around into what happened then. Just let sleeping dogs lie. That's the only way this place works."

"I don't think so, Robert. Sleeping dogs wake up."

"This isn't a story. You can't file this and move on. It's not some temporary adrenalin trip. This is real."

"What are you talking about?"

"It's not a game, Molly. It's not like journalism."

"Journalism isn't a bloody game, Robert. It's real too."

"Journalism," he snorted, "is an excuse to feel part of something important and then walk away. It's the perfect excuse never to be involved. Zooming self-importantly from war to war."

"Is that what you think of Phil? I thought you were his friend."

"I am his friend. But that doesn't stop me knowing that what Phil does is just an excuse to escape from his life."

"And what you're doing here is so real? Holding Valida's hand while she pretends she's going to finish her degree?"

He didn't answer that. "I know about her degree. She gets ill before she has to take any of her exams."

"Leave Valida out of this."

"I can't leave Valida out of this." I was furious now, goaded by his patronizing self-delusion. "You're protecting Valida. That's what this is about. It's not about Amir or me or journalism or anything like that. You just don't want anything to… upset her… well, that's fine. I understand that. You love her. But you can't change the world to protect Valida."

"For Christ's sake…"

"Robert, shut the fuck up. Will you? Just listen. I know this is real." I sounded even angrier than I meant to, because some of the anger was directed at the doubts I'd had myself. "I know you live here. And I know Valida is Aida's sister. But Amir was real too. And now he's really dead. And he didn't deserve that."

"How do you know?"

"You didn't know him. I did. Besides, nobody deserves to die like that," which was actually untrue – I'd met a lot of men out here who had deserved to die like that, but Amir hadn't been one of them. But then perhaps those men deserved more than being dead; to be cornered, in their hometowns, on a summer's day, in front of the neighbours they have known all their lives, and understand, the moment they saw the first foreign soldier storming into their house, or bursting out of the helicopter on the shores of the lake, or kicking down the door of their hospital office, that this was the last Clint Eastwood moment of their petty epic; that judgement day had finally come. That they'd be taken to the Hague, to be forced to admit, shuffling, in their cheap maroon suits, under the eyes of their fellow human beings, to those crimes they once boasted about, as every bloody act of their small-town inhumanity, the butchery in the heat of war, in the heat of the day, amongst the shades of their ancestors and to seeming applause, was dissected, for months on end, under the cold neon light of international law; to serve out their sentence in a foreign land, far from the forests and gorges their blood-lust had scoured, and to know, in the depths of their hearts, that perhaps their old neighbours, their fellow Serbs, in whose name of Greater Serbdom those heroic deeds were done, might actually be relieved, because now the festering glory of the war had been lanced, and they were free to make a living in the present once more.

"Well all I can say," Robert's voice ranted on, "is you may not like what you're about to find out."

"Well, maybe I won't," I said, coming back to today. "But at least he did the right thing by that bloody bitch Aida, which is more than you can say for her… But I am really not sure I can actually talk about this now…"

"So you know about that." The rage had bled out of his voice.

"Yes."

"I'm sorry."

"It's a bit late now."

"Valida didn't know at the time."

"I'm glad to hear it."

There was another long pause.

"What makes you think the police will do anything anyway?" he said. "They've known all along. It was the police who told me."

"This policeman didn't know. There never was an investigation."

"And why should this policeman care, when nobody else has cared?"

I didn't want to tell him about you saving Dragan's life. I didn't want him to think you were getting special service.

I said: "Because this policeman believes that killing people is wrong."

MUJO WENT to see Suljo in Germany, where he had emigrated as a refugee in the war. Suljo met him at the bus station.

"I'll show you my house, but first let's drive round the part of the city where I live – it's the most expensive bit."

"Look, look at these houses, my friend," said Mujo. "You really succeeded."

Suljo took him up a hill: "There, you can look down on my villa."

"Is that where you live? It's incredible."

"See that blonde by the pool? That's my wife."

"I can't believe my eyes!" said Mujo.

"And see this young, handsome man that is going towards my wife? That is me."

XIV

I propped myself up in bed and let my hangover settle. My brain felt as if it had been bashed and spread out in the sun, like an octopus on a Croatian quay, and then run over repeatedly by a child on a tricycle.

Didi was checking tablecloths, when I came into breakfast. I ordered my coffee and sat in the window. The fountain swaggered in the courtyard outside.

"Did you find your policeman?" she asked, as she brought my cup.

"Yes thank you," I said.

She made a face. "How was it?"

"It was good. They were very helpful."

"That I cannot believe."

"No, they were."

I drank some more and she drifted off from my table.

Last night I'd gone out with Zach and Amy.

"We're off to Pale," Zach had said. "Been back there yet?" As they picked me up in a white Toyota Land Cruiser with some initials down the side, driven by a friend of Zach's.

"Nope. How does one get to Pale these days?" I said.

"You just go straight ahead, up the Pale road," said Zach. "We're going to the Trout Farm. Know that?"

"No. What's the Trout Farm?" I'd asked.

"You don't know the *Trout Farm*?" said Amy.

Of course I didn't. I knew the Press Centre, in the Hotel Olympic, the old ski chalet, where the bill always came to 52DM for a room and dinner, no matter what you ate or drank. Run by the miserable couple, who took pride in never having anything that one asked for: Gospodin Nema and his wife, Gospodza Nista. I knew the Hotel Panorama, where Karadzic used to live, a wooden lodge overlooking his sleepy ski resort; where he'd read me his poetry and showed me his plans for "Sarajevo: twin cities". I knew the tractor factory where he'd held his stupid parliaments and priests with beards and black stove-pipe hats would come down from their mountain churches and pass laws on the freedom of goats to roam the streets and the need to carry the bones of your ancestors around in sacks.

"When did you last go to Pale?" said Zach's friend; he was English, pale and gangly, in his late thirties, little round glasses set on the road.

"Not since… not since the war."

"I think you'll find it's changed," he laughed.

"Were you here in the war?"

"No. Just at the end."

"I know Tom from your embassy in Mogadishu," said Zach.

When we got to Pale, I hardly recognised the place. The tiny ski resort had sprouted office blocks, and house after house, Holland Park-size mansions, in hideous brick.

"Where the fuck," I said, "does the money come from?"

"People make money in wars," said Zach.

"I didn't make any bloody money. Did you make any money?"

"Bad people make money in wars," said Amy.

"Unfortunately half the bad people are still running the place," Zach turned to me, "They've had over six billion dollars in aid, and most of it's been siphoned into off-shore accounts and German cars. And that, Miss Sarajevo press corps journalist, goes for both sides."

"I know," I said sadly. "You gave me the black-marketeer's tour."

"Are you a journalist?" asked Tom, his eyes momentarily sliding off the road.

"Yes. But don't worry, I'm on holiday."

"Well, I wouldn't read too much into these palaces," said Tom. "Unemployment's even worse in RS than in the Federation."

Good, I thought, serve them bloody well right.

Halfway up the mountain, beyond Pale, the stream tumbling down beside the road swirled out of a series of cement pools, leading upwards, in ever more improbable shapes, with black swarms of trout at each waterfall's lip. At the head of the concrete cascade, on an island inside a concrete moat, a pine cabin stood, with a yellow sign of fish and a knife and fork.

"This was the restaurant of choice of the Serb high command," said Tom, as he parked the car beside rows of Mercedes and black SUVs.

"Was he bad, the Trout Farm man?" I didn't unbuckle my seat belt. I wasn't sure I wanted to go to a restaurant owned by a bad Serb.

"Not bad, just bored," said Zach. "He was a builder in Sarajevo before the war. This was his weekend house. When the war happened, he came to live here. He had nothing to do. So he started building. Then he opened a restaurant, and it made money, so he just carried on building. And the war went on and on."

The men in the restaurant had the bulk of Franjo's clientele – fat, powerful men who'd done well out of the war. Zach glanced around the room and then at Tom.

"Not one of mine," said Tom.

"What's yours?"

"Tom is paid to look for brothels," said Zach, when Tom just blushed.

"I thought he said you were a diplomat."

"I'm on secondment."

"What to?"

"The IPTF."

"What's that?" Even all the initials had changed.

"International Police Task Force." I was about to say it sounded like *Thunderbirds*, when I thought of a better thing to say instead.

"Are there a lot of brothels here?"

Tom blushed again.

"Does it matter so much?" I said.

Amy made an outraged noise but I said: "It's not like there's anything else for them to do."

"They're not there because they want to be," said Tom.

"Bosnia's the women-trafficking centre of Europe," said Zach.

My ears pricked.

Tom's reticence vanished as he started to speak: "They're mainly from poor countries like Moldova or the Ukraine. A woman in their home town offers them a job in Paris or Milan. Sometimes they think they're going to be cocktail waitresses; sometimes they know it's prostitution. A lot of them have children of their own but there are no jobs for them back home. Their passports are taken from them, and then they're sold on. They're told they have to sleep with clients, but they won't get a penny of the money. If they refuse, they're raped and beaten until they give in. Sometimes they're sold to brothels in the West, sometimes they're just kept here. We rescued a girl a few weeks ago like that. She had a four-year-old daughter, in some village in the middle of nowhere at the back of the Ukraine. She'd thought she'd be able to send money back and give her baby a better life. She had no idea what would happen to her. She was brought to Serbia by the woman who recruited her, and then she was sold. They took her passport, she didn't speak the language. She was kept in a room above a bar in a town near Tuzla. It was called the Hotel Florida – they always have fake American names like that. She was told if she ran away, she'd be hunted down and killed. One of the other girls told her about being taken to see some graves in the woods. She was told she couldn't go to the police, because she was here illegally, so she'd be put in jail… often the local police are in on the whole thing. We have to be careful how much we let *them* in on what we're doing. When we raided that bar, the local police chief was drinking downstairs."

"Has it got much worse since the war?" I asked.

"It didn't happen before the war," said Zach.

Amy had said to me, "You should write something on that."

I'd said, "I know."

"Do you need anything else?" It was Didi again.

"Oh, no, thanks, I'm fine." Except I really wasn't. We'd drunk a reassuringly non-American amount of wine. It was like the old days. Then I remembered Phil.

"Oh, Phil, from the BBC, he says he was so sorry he could not find the time to come. He's had to go."

"Oh, I am sad not to see him. He did a story on me once," she gave a little proud smile. "He wanted to know about being woman in army on first frontline."

"You were on first frontline?"

"Only as nurse…"

"Still…" I hated going right to the front. I remember meeting some of those nurses. I kept thinking, how do they go to the loo? All those pumped-up men… the cold. And the shells of course, too… "So dangerous…"

"Believe me," I heard her say, "it was better on frontline than freezing to death in Hotel Europa with my mother… and Nenad, and other refugees, all complaining and sleeping with UNPROFOR soldiers for money."

For a moment those women, in their rags, in the frozen darkness of the Europa's Viennese café, scuttled out of the crannies of my brain, but Didi carried on and her voiced called me back. "I would never have met my husband if I had not gone to frontline."

She stared out of the window at the fountain in the yard.

"I would never have met him if had not been war. It's always strange he is not here. This was his house. We plan hotel together. He was so handsome, such a charming man. He was older than me, maybe ten years, and sophisticated, self-confident. He had car. Of course, he could not use car in war, no petrol. But we knew he had it, safe in garage. I had never met a man like that. He came from family with money. He wore real gold round his neck," she pointed to the chain at the V of her dress. "This was his."

"Was it love at first sight?"

She blushed: "For me, maybe, but not for him. He was like hero… he had girlfriend in town, one Sarajevan girl, same age as him – I was young then, you know, maybe sixteen, seventeen. And I was… different, I suppose. I was just one girl from one village. It was all very new. The town was new. The war was new. Men like Selim, *they* were new. Then there was shell… He gets medivac-ed to Germany. He spent time in Germany when he was little boy, his uncle was *Gastarbeiter*, like builder. He has family there. And they cut off his leg. Just here," she points to just below her knee. "He played football. He used to play for club before war. I never saw him play. Except once, in courtyard, near one block of flats in war.

"But shell saved him. He was away, when government tried that stupid thing of making us break out of Sarajevo." June 1995. Muffy and I had stood by the radio mast and watched the toy soldiers swarming up the opposite hill, and then car after car driving up into Casualty, with the broken soldiers piled in the back. It was a total failure and hundreds died.

"I will never forget," she said. "I'd moved to hospital by then. They all came in, so many, all the boys I had known."

"After war, Selim comes back. He said to me, he couldn't bear to live in Germany. He said he could not settle. He thought only of coming back. Of Sarajevo. Nobody could understand him. His family in Germany, they could not understand. His uncle, they all say, stay here, nobody is shooting at you. Germany is safe. But he said, he just wanted to be in Sarajevo. Come home. Be with his friends."

"So he comes back, just before Dayton. But there is nobody left from our unit. They are all dead. Then he meets me at hospital. He is there for his leg. So… anyway… we get married. And we start rebuilding this house. It was his. It was hit badly by shells in start of the war. His parents were killed then.

"I said, why not rebuild as hotel – there are so many Internationals here. They need somewhere to stay. I speak English. I made myself learn it in war. And is so central. And is something for Selim to do. You don't need two legs to run hotel. And Selim knows how to build. He learnt from his uncle. Then, one day, he went off to… do some business, and he didn't come back.

"I was going to ring police, but policeman came to see me first. He said Selim had been attacked by robbers and killed. They said the robbers must have stolen his money – his wallet had gone – and gone back to Republika Srpska. It was very bad time. March 1996. Were you here?"

"No. I'd gone."

"Yes. All journalists had gone. The war was over but Chetniks were still on the hills. A lot of things happening. A lot of bad men coming in from RS and doing robberies… He never even knew I was having baby. I found out after he was dead."

"I'm so sorry," I said.

She went to the office, and came back with a photograph. "This is Selim," she said. He was laughing, in fatigues, and he had a gun in his hand, and his arm was around a girl, also in uniform, who must have been Didi but was almost unrecognisable today, so thin and young and unpolished was she. "American took it. He sent it to me after Selim died." She was gazing up at Selim in adoration, and he was gazing at the camera in camaraderie. He had a gold chain round his neck, the one she wore now, and his long dark hair was held off his eyes by a red bandana.

"I still don't believe it was just robbery. They did not take the car," but I wasn't really listening to her; I was back at the first party you took me to. Back in the room with all the smoke, and the desperate dancing, and the sad-eyed crippled DJ; and you sitting next to Selim, where he held court on the sofa, with his whisky, and his charm, and the beautiful, scrawny girls; when I couldn't understand the language, and all I could do was hand out cigarettes and try and make the man with the beard realise I didn't want to have sex, but I was so in love with you that I didn't care. Then I was on the frontline, that night in Selim's trench, when I'd gone with Phil, and we'd run into that mad American ex-marine, who Selim called "our journalist" except that Phil told me he had never filed once and the *Anchorage Bugle* had refused to pay his phonebill; I suppose I recognised Didi now, as the girl, the nurse, who had been with them. Except she had changed so much.

I hardly heard her as she said: "The policeman said maybe thieves panicked, but I don't think so. They shot him like that," she mimed a gun at the nape of her neck. "Point blank. Now to me, that is not panic, that's how professional kills."

"What?" I was back in the present now.

"Well, that's what I think, but policeman told me just to be glad I still had car. He said lot of people were killed like that."

Robert rang as I finished my coffee.

"I need to see you, now." He sounded furious.

"What's this about?"

"You know what it's about. You're the one who dragged it all up."

He had a cappuccino in front of him, by the time I reached Michele's, and was sitting amidst the sad-eyed boys and girls with purple hair, with their half-drunk coffee cups. He didn't kiss me hello. He didn't even stand up.

"What would you like?"

"Oh, same as you. Thanks very much." He tried to call the waiter over, but it didn't work. Neither of us spoke. Every second the waiter didn't come stretched out the unsaid business between us. Finally he got up and walked into the café.

"Right," he said, when he sat back down. He didn't look at me, just stirred the froth. Then he said: "We had the police round. Asking Valida questions."

"I told you I'd told the police."

He still wouldn't look at me, just bit his lip, tapping his saucer with his coffee spoon. "Maybe this is my fault. Maybe I should have told you before."

"Maybe you should. Amongst the other things it would have been kind to tell me. Like that fact that Nermina wasn't Amir's baby."

He looked momentarily put out, before he said: "I didn't come here to talk about that."

"So what did you come to talk about?" I asked.

"I came to tell you that Amir was a black marketeer."

Once I suppose I might have been shocked. Now I said: "So? Didn't everyone do that?"

My coffee had arrived and I took a sip.

"I'm not talking the odd cabbage and a bit of chocolate."

"So what are you talking about?"

"He smuggled people out of Sarajevo."

"Did he! Bloody hell! He could have told me!" It would have made the most wonderful piece. "I didn't think Amir was that kind of person."

"What kind of person?" Robert was nonplussed.

"I didn't think he was that brave."

"I think they paid him very well for it," Robert said dryly. "And I think working for an NGO eliminated most of the risks."

"Why are you telling me now?"

Robert stirred his coffee, then he said, "Because he killed someone."

"What!"

"You heard me."

"He *killed* someone… Amir." You hated fighting. You weren't good at it.

"He was taking someone out of Sarajevo who was carrying a lot of money. He killed them and stole the money."

I felt sick. My cup fell down on the table.

"Did he really?"

"Yes, he really did."

"So who killed him?"

Robert shrugged. "This is the Balkans. Everyone's related to someone. I guess someone decided tit for tat. That's what the police told Aida, at the time."

"Why didn't you tell me before?" I'd never have gone to the police if I'd known this.

"I guess I just thought you'd… go away." He couldn't meet my eye. "You hadn't bothered to come here for the last five years…"

"It seems so unlike him." I swallowed. I felt numb.

"People do strange things in wars," said Robert. He put some money on the table and got up to go. "That's why I don't like wars. Unlike you, I don't like what wars do to people."

"Oh, and by the way," he said, as he turned. "There's a one-way system on Feradiya. Hadn't you noticed that yet?"

"What are you talking about? There's no traffic now."

"I'm talking about the pedestrians." The maroon-haired girls and the boys in trainers and the Sarajevo ladies in their laundered shirts were wandering past in two opposite flows. "When you walked here, you were just barging into everyone. Or didn't you notice?"

"No…" I said.

"Looks like you didn't know very much," he said, and walked away down Feradiya, in line with the crowd.

* * *

The Amir that I loved, who I thought loved me, surely he wasn't like that. Surely he couldn't have done something like that. Had I known you at all? Or had I dressed you up, like a doll, a Sarajevan Ken? Squelched you into a mould of what I wanted to believe. No wonder Maria drank as she did. What does she have left? Each memory, each smile, each touch, is tainted by this. There's no excuse, as Robert said; you didn't need the money. I'd known you were weak, but I hadn't thought of this.

I left my cup of coffee and walked down to the river. I kept trying to talk to you in my head, but you wouldn't answer. This is the third time I've lost you; once to Aida and once to death. But this is the worst. This time it's as if I never knew you at all.

I didn't see you the last six months. Not at all, not since I found out about Aida. Did you change that much in that time? That night at the party, it was already too late. You must have done it by then, because that's when they killed you, wasn't it? Just after that, after you laid your life at my feet. How could you have lied to me like that, lied to me about what you were like, lied to me to let me love you, because I could never have fallen in love if I'd known you were like that.

Did you panic, was that it? I could see you panicking, if you were caught, if someone started shooting, I could see you running away and leaving him for dead. But to murder someone... Were you trying to get enough for all of you to get out? But then why would you say all that to me? Or maybe you just wanted me to help you escape.

The library's crenellations were gap-toothed against the hills and through the broken window boards, the used condoms flapped in the rubble. A sleek, rich German car drove by. You fools, I wanted to scream at the loitering crowds, if you can buy cars like that, why can't you mend your lovely library, or do you prefer having this large sore in the centre of your town? So that everyone is reminded of how much you suffered in the war? It's not an excuse – I shouted in my head – it's not an excuse for ever. Sometimes you have to take responsibility for the things you do.

I rang Dragan from the edge of the river, and told him what Robert had said to me.

"Looks like we need to talk to the widow," he said. *"You can go now. We don't need to keep you in Sarajevo any more. As long as we know how to get hold of you in England."*

I told him about Selim. He said, thank you very much.

"Maybe it was the same policeman," I said.

"That's not possible. That policeman is dead..."

"Was he...?"

"No," Dragan cut in. *"He really was killed by a sniper; putting the anti-sniping barricades back up in June 1995."*

Thank God I can leave.

Didi wasn't in her office when I got back to the hotel. There was a young man playing on the computer at Reception, lanky and in his early twenties, with dark eyes, and a long scar on his forehead half hidden by his fringe. Behind the desk, a little boy, about seven or eight, was tunnelling with Sulejman, through an assault course, built from box-files, chairs and the waste-paper basket, in the office at the back. I hadn't seen either of them before.

I asked the young man in Bosnian about bus times to Dubrovnik. And he answered, in English, I'll just look it up. It never occurred to me they had the internet here. Why on earth had I gone to the café in town?

"7 a.m.," he said. "One a day. From the main bus station."

I'll get that. Tomorrow. I'll leave this place behind.

Then Didi bustled in, black and shiny, with a lot of gold chains, in some wrap-around dress with a jungle print, as if she were in the throes of metamorphosing into a shrubbery.

"Ah, Molly! It is you! I must talk," she said. Her eyes were wide and her breath came fast and she grabbed my arm and pulled me to one side. "The police came today. They were asking me questions."

"Oh, God," I glanced at the boy, but he was deep in some corner of the World Wide Web. "I'm so sorry. It was..." I was about to go off into some long explanation of… what… justice… retribution… that maybe I was wrong.

"Mind! No! Why would I mind? It's wonderful." Didi swallowed and her dark irises glistened. She pulled me to her and gave me a hug. When she released me, her hands moved in jerks, as if she was changing her mind about any gesture she made, since none could ever be large enough. Then she put up her hand to the photograph hanging behind the till and said: "I never thought Selim's death would matter to anyone except me. Do you have time? Have a coffee with me…"

She talked about Selim, again; her time in the trench. She talked to me about the Europa Hotel, with a sad smile of complicity – our Sarajevo, old days in the war.

"Sarajevo," she said. "When I was a teenager, Sarajevo was like a fantasy for us. I used to dream of coming to live here…"

I waited, because I knew now it might come, and her face turned slightly away from mine. I heard my voice prompting her, "How did you get here?" Almost as though I had been someone else. Her eyes no longer looked at me, but back into her past.

"We knew things were getting bad, but we never thought it could happen to us," she said. "We'd never had problems with our Serbs in our village. We were high, really high up in the mountains, where you almost feel you can smell the sky. We were a good village. We stuck together. But…" And I found myself thinking, don't stop. Don't stop this now. But I didn't have to nudge her, she just went on:

"My father had a friend, Jovan, a policeman; he was a Serb. He said to my father, be careful, could we go and stay with friends far away? But we didn't have any friends like that.

"A girl came to us, one day. She was crying. She had walked from the other side of the mountain. She said her father and mother had been shot. She said her baby brother had been killed; she said she had been raped but she managed to get away. Someone in the village took her in. My mother gave her clothes and food. My father and the other men went down to the café and spent all night talking. But someone said she was crazy. Who would kill a baby? Someone else said her father had been a bad man. We got on well with our Serbs. We drank coffee together every day."

Suddenly she switched into Serbo-Croat:

> "It was the next day the men came to our village. Most were strangers. Some wore black and had beards and hats with double eagles on them. Some wore uniform. Like police, or our army. The JNA. But they said they were the Serb army now. They drove into our village and stopped by the mosque. It was a warm spring day but there was still snow on the tops of the mountains. They shouted for everyone to come out. We didn't know what to do. We hid in the house. They had some of our people with them, in the back of one of those open trucks my dad used for the harvest. I couldn't see their hands. Then I realised their hands were tied. Fuad, the plumber, and Ahmet who farmed across the valley, and Ali, who everyone knew was always drunk. Ali had blood coming from his nose. Some of our Serbs were standing by the truck. Jovan, the policeman, my father's friend: he looked like he didn't know what to do; Milan, who had the garage at the end of the village: he used to mend my bike. Radislav, he was a farmer like my father. Svetko, the fat man. He owed my father money; he was puffing on a cigarette. Milorad, the policeman from the next-door village. They all had guns. Nobody was talking. Our men in the truck looked very afraid. There were about five or six women, in another truck. They were sitting in the back. Fuad's wife, Sabehida, same name like me, she was crying and Ahmet's sister was giving her a hug.
>
> "Then Izmet came out of his house; he was one of our people, and a policeman too. He said, "What are you doing? Jovan, what's going on?" Jovan looked very embarrassed.

"He said, 'We're here to protect you. We need to take you away.'

'Why?'

'You'll be safer.'

"Izmet said, it doesn't look very safe to me. Jovan said, believe me, it's better, Izmet, this way. There are some bad things happening. Izmet said, this looks pretty bad now. They stood there for five minutes or so, shouting to each other across the street. Then another man drove up in a huge black car. He was in uniform, but he had a skull tied to its bonnet; not a man, some big animal. Maybe a cow. He got out and said, 'What's going on?' Nobody spoke. Both Jovan and Izmet stared at him. One of the strangers said, this man won't let us come through. The new man said, he's not so big… He just lifted up his gun and shot Izmet. Like that… dadadadadada… Just like you see on the television. I had only seen it on television then. Izmet fell on his knees and then he just crumpled. It couldn't be our village. It was like a film. The street was silent. Then all the women in the truck started to wail.

"My father said, we stay in the house. We don't move. But the man in the black car told one of the soldiers to get going. One of them threw a grenade in the window of a house four down the street. It was where Samra, my schoolteacher lived. There was an explosion. Then they kicked the door down. We heard shooting and screams. The screams went on and on and then they stopped. When they stopped, that was worse than the screams. We didn't know what to do at all. They did the same with the house next door, where my best friend, Amira lived. I heard her scream, No! We heard them shoot. Then that was that. I never saw Amira again.

"Then my mother said, maybe we should all go out into the square. We didn't have guns. We couldn't fight. But my father told us to stay there, and be very quiet. He took a white shirt, and went to the door. My mother said, No, no... but he shushed her away. 'It's best,' he said. He waved it, and went out. Jovan shouted, come over here, Emir; you'll be safe here. He said, Jovan, what's happening? and one of the strangers yelled to him to shut up and walk over to the others. 'Where's your family?' said Jovan. 'Bring them out too. They'll be safe here.' But he said, 'They've gone. I sent them away.' That's when I understood he wanted us to escape. But Jovan knew we hadn't gone. Tata walked over to where the others were. I could see him out of the window. They grabbed him and one of the men in black hit his face. 'Where are they?' screamed one of the men. 'I've told. They've gone to Rogatica...' And they all laughed. 'We'll see them soon, then, won't we,' said the man who'd shot Izmet. And they all laughed again. But Jovan didn't laugh. He stared at our house. But he didn't say anything. Then the man in black said, 'We'll soon see if they've gone...' He took a grenade off his belt. I saw my father looking back at us through the window. Suddenly he punched the man standing next to him. The guy hit him back, and he fell to the ground. They started kicking him. I never saw my *Tata* again.

"I said to my mother, we've got to get out. She said, I can't leave him, but I said, Mamma. We've got to go. She said, we haven't got any clothes. I said, GET OUT! Our house had windows onto the woods. We climbed out of the window, my mother and me, and my little brother, Ado. He was only twelve. My mother carried Nenad, the baby; he was not even one. We ran and ran into the woods. Our father had meant we should go to Rogatica. He had had a cousin there. Mehmet. He had a good job, at the sawmill. There were lots of Muslims in Rogatica. It would be safe. We ran into the woods, as fast as we could, and high. We climbed and ran until we couldn't run any more. Then walked all night. My mother kept crying and crying. Ado and I took turns carrying Nenad; he was heavy. I made her keep walking. Afterwards they said the Serbs had mined the woods, but we were lucky. We never hit any mines. It was morning before we got to Rogatica. I really thought it would be safer there. It was the 18th May when we arrived.

"Mehmet said of course we could stay with him. We thought we'd be able to go back home soon. Mamma, Nenad and Ado and I slept in the room of my little cousin. He had to go and share with his sister, and he was very cross, but his mother told him to keep quiet; it wouldn't be for long. We weren't sure what to do. Most of the Serbs had left the town. We didn't know if we should go but we wanted to hear about my father. Besides, we didn't have anywhere to go.

"On the 22nd May the Serbs started shelling Rogatica. The Muslim parts. They shelled us for weeks. At the time I didn't see how anyone could survive. Now I know what people can go through and live. My cousin had food and we hid in his basement. They would shout to us with loudspeakers, the Serbs, to surrender, to lay down our guns, to go to the Veljko Vlahovic School. But we didn't have any guns. Then the Serb soldiers started moving in, like they had in my village. Street by street. It took a long time; days and days. Sometimes nothing would happen for hours and then the shooting and the explosions would start again. They threw grenades into the houses, and then they shot people who ran away. They burned the houses afterwards. We could hear the screams. We could smell the smoke. They got to our street. They had grenades and flame throwers. Machine guns, shooting. At the last minute, we managed to escape. That was July. 19th July. The shelling had gone on for two months. My cousin got us out; he said, run to the main square. There are some big new buildings there, solidly built. We ran and ran. Nenad cried all the time. He was so heavy and he wriggled and you can't explain things to a baby. We could hear guns all the time. Rat-rat-rat-rat and explosions. And the crackle of the houses they were burning down. There was smoke everywhere, that black smoke, the smell of burning plastic and stuff like that. My cousin thought that 300 people had died just in his street and the two streets either side just that day. They were all streets lived in by Muslim people. Some of them, the Serbs took away. We didn't know where.

"Conditions in the square were bad. There must have been about two or three thousand people, who had all taken refuge in a big building there. We were in the basements. It was awful. It stank. The toilets were terrible. There was shit everywhere. Everyone was sleeping crowded up. It was dark inside, all the power had gone. Children were crying. My mother was crying. Luckily this time we'd been able to bring some stuff with us, blankets, tins of food. Clothes. We'd had little bags packed ready to run this time. Although we'd eaten most of the food in the last two months and there wasn't much left. The Serbs kept shouting through loud-speakers; telling us to surrender, to come to the secondary school. But there were too many of us to do that. There was a man called Rajko Kusic who said he was the Serb Commander. I'd never heard of him before. But later, in the camp he said we had to call him Vojvoda – the Duke.

"One time a man came up in a tank. Zivojin Novakovic; Mehmet recognised him. He read out orders through a loudspeaker. Mehmet took a white flag and went to talk to him. Mehmet explained that there were too many of us here to go to the school. We won't fit in. He said, why don't you bring the Serb flag here. Fly it here. If we recognise the Serb republic and the flag, will you stop the shelling? Novakovic said he'd do his best. He drove away, but he came back and said, it was no good. 'You all have to go to the secondary school centre, to the school building in order to avoid the cleansing' – that's what they called it. They said, it was just for two or three days. Bring any food if you have it; but we had hardly anything left. We thought it safer to go, for all of us. We came out, and they made us walk in rows. I carried Nenad. My mother held Ado's hand. They said we would only have to stay in the school for a couple of days. But we were there for three months.

"For the first few days things weren't so bad, although we weren't allowed to leave the building; they said that was for our own safety. But on the third day, people I didn't know came; they had different kind of uniforms, with guns. Mehmet didn't know them and he knew everyone in Rogatica. They looked like the men who had come to our village. In the camp they said one of them was Arkan, and do you know Seselj? Him and his White Eagles. We knew their names from the terrible things they did already in the war in Croatia in 1991.

"They started to… do… things… bad things… to people in the camp. They took all our jewellery. My mother's wedding ring. She didn't have much. But Mehmet's wife had more. She packed all her jewellery for our run to the school. They took my earrings. I saw them rip them out of one girl's ears, so I took mine off and gave them to the man myself. They took Ado's watch. It was just a stupid watch, with Mickey Mouse. But he loved it. They screamed at us, that we were Turkish scum, fundamentalists…We couldn't escape. By the entrance to the school grounds, on the right, there was a building, with a machine-gun nest on a roof, with soldiers in it, all the time. The entrance to the school was fastened with a thick chain. We were told that the whole area round the school had been mined and if anyone tried to run away or jump out of the window, they would be blown up. And there were guards on duty all the time. You couldn't leave, and you didn't dare leave.

"There was nothing to eat. We finished the food we brought very quickly. Then nobody had any food left. The place was packed. There were forty-seven people sleeping in our room. I counted them. Day after day. It was an old class-room. We moved most of the desks to the side of the room, some we broke up and burnt, to cook our food. It was August; we didn't need fires to keep warm. If anything, we were far too hot. Others we used to make walls, between our little groups, to try and get a little privacy.

"It still had maps on the walls, of Yugoslavia, as it used to be, when I was growing up, Croatia and Slovenia and Serbia and Bosnia-Hercegovina, Macedonia and Montenegro, and Kosovo and Vojvodina. Once Ado and I found a photograph of Tito in the stationery cupboard; there were two families living in the stationery cupboard. We were very jealous because, although their window was tiny, they were private and could sleep on the shelves. Then I found a book, an English book. I started to teach myself English; I learnt lots of words. I never thought I didn't know how they were supposed to sound. There was a map of the world. I used to lie there, on Mehmet's blanket, on the wooden floor, wondering what other countries were like. I had never even been to Serbia before. Now I have so many foreigners here. I used to draw Nenad pictures with the coloured chalk, but that was at the start. The chalk soon ran out.

"Nenad wasn't the only baby. There were lots and they cried all the time. There were over a thousand people in the camp. It was a camp. It felt like a camp. We were all Muslims, except for two Serb ladies, who were married to Muslims. There were fifteen thousand Muslims in Rogatica before the war. God knows where they are now. Mehmet knew a soldier who said that some had gone to the school, and some to a factory, and some to some old barns down by a farm. Some went to the sawmill where Mehmet used to work.

"One day Jovan came to the camp to look for us. He said he was sorry about my father. He said he was glad we had survived. He said he'd been looking in all the camps for us. He told us our village had been burnt. He said he didn't know what had happened to Ali and Fuad, Sabehida and the others, but he wouldn't look me in the eye when he said that. He gave us cigarettes. He went away, and then he came back with food for us and baby food and nappies for Nenad and some soap. My mother started to cry and Jovan looked as if he might cry too. He looked different. I think he looked older. He said he'd come back soon, but we didn't see him again. Nenad soon ate up the food. He got all thin, like a baby in Africa on the TV. He used to be so fat and round. But he'd crawl into everything; it's hard to keep control of a baby, when there are so many of you. He learnt to walk in the camp. He was a good baby but he had a naughty smile. He used to play with the other babies. There were quite a few in our camp. Forty or fifty. We'd put them in a corner and they'd wave at each other, and crawl around. I think they quite liked all their friends. Three women had babies while we were all there. That was awful. One of them, we thought she'd die. I wasn't much use, but the older women knew more what to do. We'd all take turns to try and help each other with the children. Nenad didn't cry much. Some babies were much worse. But you can't really blame them when they did.

"Sometimes we'd have nothing to eat for days; sometimes Serb soldiers would turn up with sacks of potatoes, or some cooking oil or pasta. A little flour. We'd all queue up. One day my family got three potatoes, and a few bits of pasta, but they had run out of cooking oil by the time I got to the top of the line. They only brought the food once a week or so. Sometimes they let people who lived nearby go back home for supplies. The women came back crying. They said everything was burnt and broken. Everything had been stolen. The televisions, fridges, everything gone. Cars. Everything. Often they'd bring in a large group of women and children. A bit later, they'd bring some food, but it wasn't enough even to feed the women they had just brought in. They never brought any more men. Nobody knew where the men had gone.

"There was hardly any water either in the school. Some soldiers in a tank had fallen through the ground and broken the water pipes. Even with Jovan's soap, I only managed to wash myself a few times in the three months I was there. None of us could wash.

"Mehmet saw a Serb soldier he knew, Tomo Batinic. Tomo told us that it was too late, that all the Muslims would disappear. That everyone in the school would disappear. People disappeared from the school every day. We'd see them be taken out the back, then we'd hear gunshots, and then we'd never see them again. Or they'd be taken to a lorry, and we'd never see them again. One day they took cousin Mehmet. He never came back. They took Ado, my little brother, after that. My mother was screaming, No! She gave me Nenad and grabbed at his arm. She was saying, he's only a little boy, but Mehmet's friend, the Serb soldier he knew, said not to worry. It was only to work. It was such a relief. Ado came back every few days. He'd have bruises. Sometimes he'd have a black eye. He said they made him dig trenches, carry ammunition. He had to build machine-gun nests from sandbags. They made him bury the bodies in the town. He said it was fine, but someone else said they used to beat him. If he didn't work hard enough. Then he told me that: they'd hit him, swear at him, threaten to kill

> him. But for us it was enough that he was alive. He was only thirteen. He'd had his birthday when we were in Mehmet's house. I'm glad he had his birthday there.
>
> "We were lucky. One of the guards had known Mehmet at the sawmill. He tried to make sure that things weren't too bad. He'd bring us food a bit. I heard another guard gave some people Serb travel documents so they could escape. One of the guards let a woman sleep at a different apartment so she wouldn't be raped."

She stopped there and took a sip of her coffee; I can't ask her any more. This isn't my business. I'm not working now. But she started again.

> "They used to come and take us away at night. They'd take us to a church. A group of us. Girls. Some were very young. As young as Ado. It was full of soldiers and they'd all be drunk. They'd… well… they'd do what they wanted and then they'd take us back to the school in the morning. Once they'd had you, they'd wait a while, till the next time. There were a lot of different girls in the school.
>
> "I don't know why they let us go in the end. One day, when we had been in the camp for two months, they told some of us we had to leave. They made us get into buses. My mother didn't want to go, because Ado wasn't with us. She was screaming his name, but they said, do you think we'll let him go to kill us all again. We were all terrified. The camp was awful, but at least we were alive. Nobody who left was ever heard of again. I don't know what happened to the people who didn't come. Maybe they died. Maybe they went to Germany. It took ages, to get the buses moving. Hours. We went to sleep by the side of the road. We spent a day and a night in the bus, with hardly any food or water. We all took turns with Nenad. Then they told us that we

were at Sarajevo. Sarajevo used to be just an hour and a half from Rogatica. They said this was the frontline. They said it was a five-kilometre walk. We could see the road was mined. They hadn't told the Muslims we were coming. 'They can feed you now', they said. 'They can pay for you. If they don't shoot you by mistake.'

"We walked along the road. I kept thinking they would change their minds and shoot us in the back. But they didn't. All around the road were burnt-out cars, and rubbish, and just nothing. It's so strange to be on a big main road where there is nothing. It should be full of cars. And it's a long way to walk carrying a baby. We were scared our own soldiers would shoot us. Every time we came to a corner in the road, we'd shout 'don't shoot! We are Muslim! We are from Rogatica!'

"I can't tell you how amazing it was to get to Sarajevo. Just to be here. To see our soldiers. To know we were safe. Even though I lost the baby after that walk."

"What! Not Nenad!" I said.

"No," she flushed and smiled. "Not him. You couldn't lose him." The smile leaked away. "No. My baby but, really, it was for the best… I am not sure if I… but the worst thing was leaving Ado behind."

"When did you see him again?"

"Not till after the war. Not till he was seventeen."

There was the purr of an engine, as a car drew up outside. She blushed, checked herself in the mirror by her dead husband's photograph, the mascara that had smeared a little beneath her eyes.

"Sorry, I must go. Tomorrow," she said, and stood up quickly. "We'll talk properly tomorrow."

I didn't have time to tell her I wanted to leave. I didn't have time to say I was on the next bus out.

But I don't have to go. I could stay and talk to her more. I've got another few days' holiday. Or I could work. God knows, there's enough going on.

I thought again about what Tom had said about his girls last night.

"Why has it got worse since the war?" I'd asked him, when Tom had conjured the smokey despair of his brothels. "Is it just demand and supply, with all the foreign soldiers?" I'd asked.

He'd shaken his head. "In a war like this, you get a criminal class who smuggle guns, people, food, drugs. After the war, the criminals just change the commodity they move. Since Kosovo, things have got worse. The PKK, the Albanian separatist army, is really just a criminal organisation. They run most of the drugs and the illegal immigration networks into Europe. Bosnia is paradise for them. There are no rules. You smuggle anything you like into Croatia from here, and from Croatia you've got the coast, and from there it's Schengen Europe. There are no barriers at all.

"I know you're officially on holiday, but if you want to do something, if I can be of any help," he'd said, and given me his card. "Let's have a drink."

I could stay.

I could stay and talk to Tom. My magazine may be crap, but it is for women. And I'm an editor; I can commission myself. I was about to say I'd stay, when Didi whirled away, in and out of her study, in a flurry of strokes and kisses. The two little boys watched her leave; as the younger one's lip began to wobble, the elder, grabbed at his hand and said, "Hey, Sulejman, bet you can't catch me!" And ran round behind the waste-paper basket, with Sulejman in fat pursuit.

"He's sweet. Is he yours?" I asked the young man at the computer doubtfully; he was not much more than a teenager himself.

"Nenad! Na! He's my little brother," said the boy. "I'm babysitting for my sister tonight."

Epilogue

Kabul, November 2001

I was watching a burqa sway through the lobby of the Kabul Intercontinental, when I heard a voice say, "Now that's what I call a nice Muslim girl". I laughed. What with the snow on the mountains and the minarets and the sunlight streaming in through the bullet-broken glass, and having to wear a hat indoors because the heating didn't work, the candlelight and the occasional crack of a bullet across the square, it took me a moment to clock he was speaking Serbo-Croat.

It was Edin. A bit fatter, a bit balder, but then, the hotel was full of people who were fatter and balder than they had been six years ago. "*Kako ste?*" I said. He did a double take. He was still wearing a flak jacket that said CTV.

We didn't talk about Amir then. We just said hello, hugged each other, congratulated each other on being alive – on the seeming *success* we'd made of still being alive – "If you can call still being shot at for a living making a success," Edin laughed. Then he said, I was sorry to hear about Phil, the Israelis were bastards; and I said, yes, that had been terribly sad, unlucky too. I didn't want to think about it – I still can't bear to think about Phil. I miss him much more here than I did back in London, but I suppose this is where he ought to be. He always said you had to be terribly unlucky to be hit by a shell.

I heard Edin say, did I know that Muffy was around, and I laughed and said we'd been sharing a tent in the Panshir valley – she'd gone to a press conference. That's where I'm going, he said… sorry, got to rush, aren't you going? He looked surprised, and a little superior, as I shook my head, and said I had interviews to do. See you later, he said, and I was left alone in the lobby, waiting for my interpreter;

that's the one thing I miss about not doing news, the self-important urgency of it all. I had weeks to find my Taliban-era undercover schoolmistresses, my female doctors, would-be members of parliament and burgeoning TV anchorwomen for American *Vogue*.

It was later that evening in the bar that we started to talk. We didn't talk about Sarajevo for a bit: Edin was keen to tell me about Sierra Leone, and East Timor; places I hadn't been, that CTV had sent him; keen to show he wasn't any longer just a local hire. But then slowly, one of us, I think it was Muffy, said something like, "Do you ever get back there?" and Edin made a face, and said, "Not so much." I could feel the dread in my stomach; I couldn't have stopped her – perhaps I didn't want to – but she had had a bit to drink; she said to Edin, you knew Amir, what was your take on that? Did you go back for the trial?

"Oh God, no," I said.

But Muffy said: "Shh."

I knew, of course, that Amir's killer had been caught. They found Selim's bullet in the evidence room and matched it to the same gun. The policeman who'd witnessed that autopsy was still alive, so they pulled him in for what Tom referred to as "interview without coffee." It didn't take very long. He said it had been Franjo, the Foreign Legionnaire; he still had the gun on the wall of his restaurant, mounted on a plaque above the fireplace. It was Franjo's cousin that Amir had killed.

I'd noticed the gun, that night we'd been there, it was a funny shape, and had *Legio Patria Nostra and Honneur et Fidélité* written on it in poker work, and a photograph stuck into the top, of him and Vince, that English thug who nearly punched me when I was in Jez with Hal; they were by a UN APC on Sniper Alley, with the same gun. Underneath, in the same letters, it said, "Sarajevo 1992–95". It turned out to be a present from Vince. Vince had had it mounted by a man who stuffed fish in Newcastle. Tom told me that they found four Moldovan girls locked up on the upper floors of the restaurant. Franjo and Vince had been trafficking them through Bosnia all the way to the north of England. It all came out at the trial: Franjo realised, during the investigation, that Vince had been tricking him with other scams, so he spilled the beans. Selim, it turned out, had been killed by Vince because Vince had nicked the money Selim had paid for black market cement – there'd been a booming business in all the building materials sent to Sarajevo by aid agencies just after the war.

I didn't go back for the trial. I was in America, doing a piece for the *Telegraph* magazine about a Hispanic cricket team in a ghetto in LA. I'd resigned from my magazine the day Milosevic fell, which happened to be the first week I got back from Sarajevo. I wrote the women-trafficking piece for *Marie Claire* – Sabina found me a photographer she knew from the war and my magazine was too crap to care – and then followed it up with one on love-struck Muslim couples holed-up in bed-sits in Bradford fleeing arranged marriages. The work took off: a Weight Watchers' convention weekend in Disneyland for the *Independent Magazine*, that sort of thing. I was even sent to test out a five-star hotel in Venice.

Then all this war started and I wanted to write about something that mattered again… except arranged marriages in Bradford do matter as well, so I don't know… I wanted to… Oh God… smell cordite on the air… drive through a checkpoint on a mountain road… Maybe I wanted to fall in love. But as Phil said, you don't fall in love like that twice.

Edin went quiet and when he started to speak, it was to me, as if Muffy didn't exist.

"It wasn't like that," he said, then he broke into Serbo-Croat: "*It wasn't how they said in the trial.*" Muffy looked annoyed, she couldn't understand what he said, but Edin didn't notice. He and Amir, for a year or so, he said, had been smuggling food and stuff into Sarajevo. We all knew that by now. It had started with Selim, buying stuff from the Serbs across the frontline. He had friends in the special forces who'd bring things in through the tunnel, under the airport. Amir and Edin, with their cars, and their petrol and their UN IDs, would help sell the stuff on. Then Amir got his blue card, in the summer of '94, and they began bringing booze and cigarettes in on UNHCR flights. His voice sang on and on, the story of his war, and neither Muffy nor I needed to have been there at all. He was the voiceover to the cinema in his head.

"Then we started taking people. It was my idea. We put them in Amir's car. It was an aid agency car; nobody could check that. He didn't want to at first – but I said it was easy money. We'd drive them across the line, to Kasandolska; out by the airport, after Dobrinje, in no-man's-land. We'd give the guys at the last checkpoint their cut. It was scary, of course, but you know how it was… there were so many ways to die in Sarajevo then.

"We never drove as far as the Serbs. We stopped in Kasandolska, and the Serb we used to buy food from would come and meet us there.

"After about three months, one of those Foreign Legionnaires said they wanted to meet us for a beer. Vince, he was called. The English one. I thought they'd be pissed off that we were moving in on their patch. The French had been doing stuff for years – you know. But they were all right. We met in Jez, like to show it was their place. Vince did the talking. He said he thought we could help. He said they'd seen what we'd been doing. He said they had more work than they could handle; maybe we could do things with them; for a cut of course. He kept playing with his gun, all the time. He was very proud of it. He said it had been used by SOE in the Second World War, and he'd bought it from an old man in Sarajevo. 'It's the most silent weapon in the world. It's still used by the SAS. For assassinations…' It was the one they said he'd used at the trial."

I could suddenly see it stuck on Franjo's wall, and feel its muzzle at the nape of my neck. Your neck, and you were next to me, in the guttering candlelight, on the international hotel beige banquettes.

> "We didn't hear anything for a week or so. We talked about it, tried to work out what was the catch. But there didn't seem to be one. Then Vince rang us, and said there was a guy who needed to get out. It had to be done that night, he said. Franjo was away, and he, Vince, had to be on the Serb side that afternoon; he'd meet us halfway, but not to let on. The money he was offering, we'd have been mad to turn it down."

Edin swallowed, then carried on; Muffy was staring at the pair of us, transfixed; she might not speak the language properly, but even she knew something extraordinary was going on.

> "He gave us an address and a time to pick the man up. It was one of those Austrian flats, not far from where Amir's parents lived.
>
> "The man was in the flat. He was on his own. He was in his early forties, I suppose, although the war made it difficult to tell, and besides, it was getting dark. Josip Markovic. A Sarajevo Croat. thirty-eight. They said at the trial, but we didn't know his full name. It was cold outside. He was in a thick anorak. He had a hat, but he wasn't wearing it, because his hair was damp. He'd washed for the trip. He was nervous. But Amir said, don't worry, we've done this a lot before. It's always fine. He had a suitcase, in one hand, and in the other he had a briefcase. He'd been a lawyer before the war. You know these refugees. It was like it was his identity."

Edin didn't even glance at the camera he seemed to have on him, all the time.

"He showed us pictures of his family in the car. He was going to see them. He'd sent them to Zagreb at the start of the war. He hadn't seen them since. 'My wife, Katerina,' he said, 'my two little girls.' It was a photograph of them by the sea. 'That's new,' he said. 'A journalist brought them to me last year. They are so big now. I haven't seen them grow this big. I can't believe I am going to see them again.'

"I left him and Amir at the TV station. Vince had said it was better not to have too many, better if Amir or I came alone. We didn't want to argue – the money was so much. I said to Josip: say hello to the coast, eat some fish for me. He shook my hand; he said he couldn't thank me enough… He even waved to me, from the back of the car."

Edin stopped. I didn't speak. He started again but he wasn't looking at me.

"It was two hours later when I saw Amir again. He rang the bell at my flat. I said how did it go, but then I looked at him: his face was completely grey, no colour at all, and sweating, drops on his nose. What happened, I said. How's Josip? Then I saw he had Josip's briefcase in his hand. He sat down on the sofa and put his head in his hands. I started asking questions, what's wrong? Why've you got that? How's Josip? But Amir said, shut up. Just shut up. He didn't move his hands, not even when he said, Josip's dead. I poured him some whisky and he drank half the glass. I didn't know what to do. I said, what do you mean? He took another gulp. Who killed him? I said. Amir looked up at me, and said: 'I did.'

"I said, 'What!' And he said, I didn't mean to. He took another gulp. Amir never drank like that. I said, what went wrong? And Amir said, I don't know… and then he said, 'I don't think anything went wrong. I think it was meant to happen that way."

Edin drank his drink.

> "Amir said he'd got to the place where Vince said we should meet; it was one of those ruined houses in Kasandolska."

Those ghostly houses, I could see them, with their broken beams, and the mine-filled gardens thick with winter weeds.

> "Amir said, 'Vince was waiting there, with his UN Land Rover. Josip wasn't surprised to see the UN car. Amir got out, and went over to Vince. Vince asked, is it all clear, and Amir said, clear as day. Then Vince said, right, let's get him out of the car.
>
> "Josip smiled when he saw Vince. Amir said he obviously knew him from before. Vince said to him, have you got a weapon? and Josip looked a little embarrassed. He had an old revolver. Vince said, 'Better give it to me, just to be safe.' Vince emptied the bullets out and put it in his pocket. Or at least Amir thought he'd emptied the bullets out. Then he asked Amir, but Amir said, no. Vince didn't believe him; Vince obviously couldn't believe anyone could go around Sarajevo without a gun. Amir hated guns. But I made him keep one in the glove compartment. He told Vince about that one, and Vince seemed to think that was OK. Vince still had his rifle slung on his shoulder, but Amir didn't think anything of it. Everyone was armed in Sarajevo then.
>
> "Vince told them to go inside the house. 'It's safer in there. Don't worry. I know it's not mined.'
>
> "The next thing he knew, there was that clunk-click, and Vince was pointing the rifle and saying to Josip, 'Get down on your knees.' Josip didn't even speak. He gaped like a fish. Amir said, 'What the fuck's going on?' But Vince turned the gun on him and said, 'Shut up, you. And you,

kneel down.' Josip knelt. He still had his briefcase at his chest, like a baby, Amir said.

"Vince said to Amir, 'Right you, come here.' Amir said Vince walked him round behind Josip. Josip said, 'Oh God'. He started to pray. Amir said he was praying. Clutching his bag and praying. Vince pointed at Josip and said, 'Right, You do him. Don't even think about doing anything funny. The moment you do, I'll kill you both.' Amir said Vince gave him Josip's gun and moved away, covering him with his rifle. Amir said: 'But you've taken the bullets out.' But Vince said, 'No mate, I've left enough.' Vince just stood there. Amir said, he couldn't believe what Vince wanted him to do. I couldn't do it, he kept repeating, I couldn't do it. But Vince said: 'Do it, or I'll just kill you both.' He fired a burst of rounds round Amir's feet. He didn't even think of firing at Vince. There was no point – Vince said: "Don't even think about it. You'll be dead before the muzzle's pointed at me." And there was Josip, praying, at Amir's feet. Amir said to me, he didn't even know the gun. Then Vince said: "Do it, put it up against his head." Amir said he put it against Josip's head because he thought Vince might stop. He didn't think he'd actually pull the trigger. He said, he didn't think he actually could. But when he put the gun there, Vince said, pull the trigger. He said, no. But Vince said, fucking do it! And he shot a burst of rounds, again. On the ground by Amir's feet. Amir said he pissed himself then. He could feel it trickling down his leg, he was glad it was too dark for Vince to see. He heard Josip say, 'Oh God, please no. My little girls.' Amir said his finger just clenched on the trigger. It was like it wasn't him. There was a bang, and half Josip's head was blown away and he fell forward onto his briefcase in the mud. Amir said he thought Vince was going to kill him then, but he didn't. Vince said: 'drop the gun – that's the last bullet anyway'. Amir said he'd never been happier to drop a gun. He just wanted to do what he had been told. Then Vince told him to pull out Josip's briefcase. He had to prise it out of Josip's fingers. Vince told him to open it. Inside was a thick brown envelope. It was stuffed with 1000DM notes. Vince said, show me. So Amir took one out. Vince said, 'Right, take out three more and throw the rest to me.' Amir thought Vince was going to shoot him then, but he didn't. Vince picked up the envelope. Amir was just standing there, holding 4000DM. Vince said: 'That's your cut. This didn't happen, right? If you breathe a fucking word, I'll kill you. And I'll kill your fucking family. Josip was happy as a lamb when he got in the car with me. And I'm going to drop him off in Kiseljak. Right, now get back to your crappy little siege. And if you do see me, act normal.'

"Amir said he couldn't believe that he was still alive."

A couple of other hacks had wandered by and gave us a funny look as they clocked the language being spoken, but Edin carried on as though none of us were here… as for me, I wasn't here either; I was twenty-eight years old, a continent, another war away, in an icy, gun-ringed town, stranded in the Balkans, now the tides of empire had ebbed. I was with you. The you I had loved. You were dead of course, but I could deal with that; for I knew that the boy I had loved had been real after all. You weren't a murderer, you weren't a thief. You were just a boy, an ordinary young man, swamped then tossed by the waves of war, swept away by something far more terrible, far greater than you.

I hardly heard Edin as he carried on:

"Amir said he'd ran to the car. He couldn't remember when he'd last been so scared. He didn't even notice he still had the briefcase. He kept thinking Vince was going to kill him as he drove away. He came straight to me. He couldn't sleep that night – we stayed up till three or four, talking, trying to work out what on earth was going on. But of course, we thought Franjo was in on it too.

"I've had a lot of time to think about it now."

He was still staring out into the centre of the bar, not noticing anyone passing, anything said.

"I think Vince was counting on things taking a long time. Josip's body could have lain there for months. His wife wouldn't have known for days that he hadn't turned up. Anything could have happened in the badlands between Sarajevo and the coast. I think Amir was just plan B for Vince. So if things came back to roost, he had someone to blame. But Josip came back a few days later, on a body exchange. I suppose that was really bad luck. Bad luck for Amir too. Because that was when Vince had to use plan B.

"I'd told Amir, anyway, he should get out of town. He had his blue card. He'd been in Italy a few weeks before. But there was Aida, and the baby was due, and his mother. He didn't know what to do. But he said, "It should be OK. If he'd wanted to kill me, believe me, I'd be dead." But I thought he was wrong. I said, a dead husband's no use to Aida at all.

"That last night, Amir told me Vince wanted to have a word. I said be careful, but he said, it's all right. He's in it too, he said. He'd even been paid for it after all, although he didn't mention that. He'd left the money in my flat. And the briefcase too. He'd put them both on the table in front of him. He took the money out of his pocket and put it on the table too. It was like he couldn't face seeing either of them again.

"That last night, I saw him leave the party with Vince and Franjo, when the power went. I didn't know, then, that Josip was Franjo's cousin… I didn't know that Franjo had no idea.

I think Vince just wanted to nick all that cash. It was Franjo's life savings. Amir said there was a fortune in there.

"I left the next day, the moment I heard Amir was killed. Of course, I didn't have Amir's car any more. I went through the tunnel the way we always did. I took the money Amir had left behind. It cost me 10,000DM but..."

Edin drained his glass and slammed it down on the table, then, for the first time in five minutes, he turned and looked me in the eye, screening finally over, credits rolling, lights turning up. "*Fuck it, I'm still here,*" he said.

During the four-year siege of Sarajevo, over 10,000 people were killed by artillery or gunfire, and 60,000 injured, from a population of 350,000 – which meant a one-in-five chance of being hit.

Reportage Press Charity

Part of the profits of this book will go to the Sarajevo schools' charity Education Builds Bosnia, founded by General Jovan Divjak and the Frontline Club's Fixers' Fund, which helps interpreters and local journalists in conflict zones.